the
BARON BOLD
and the
BEAUTEOUS
MAID

a compact history
of Canadian theatre

The
Baron Bold
and the
Beauteous Maid
a compact history of Canadian theatre

Brian Kennedy

Playwrights Canada Press
Toronto • Canada

The Baron Bold and the Beauteous Maid: A Compact History of Canadian Theatre ©
Copyright 2004 Brian Kennedy
The authors assert moral rights.

Playwrights Canada Press
The Canadian Drama Publisher
215 Spadina Avenue, Suite 230, Toronto, Ontario CANADA M5T 2C7
416-703-0013   fax 416-408-3402
orders@playwrightscanada.com • www.playwrightscanada.com

This book would be twice its cover price were it not for the support of Canadian taxpayers through the
Government of Canada Book Publishing Industry Development Programme, Canada Council for the Arts,
Ontario Arts Council, and the Ontario Media Development Corporation.

Cover image: Ida Van Cortland. Taverner Collection, Performing Arts Centre,
Toronto Public Library
Production Editor/Cover Design: JLArt

Library and Archives Canada Cataloguing in Publication

Kennedy, Brian, 1951-
   The baron bold and the beauteous maid : a compact history of
Canadian theatre / Brian Kennedy.

Includes bibliographical references.
ISBN 978-0-88754-692-1

   1. Theater--Canada--History. 2. Canadian drama--History and criticism.

I. Title.

PN2301.K45 2005   792'.0971   C2005-900238-7

First edition: August 2005. Second printing: December 2007.
Printed and bound by AGMV Marquis at Quebec, Canada.

Publisher's Acknowledgments

House of Anansi for
Leaving Home, David French

NeWest Press for
Blood Relations, Sharon Pollock

Talonbooks for
Les Belles-soeurs, Michel Tremblay
The Coronation Voyage, Michel Marc Bouchard
The Ecstasy of Rita Joe, George Ryga

Jennnifer Surridge for
At My Heart's Core, Robertson Davies

Anton Wagner for
Teach Me How to Cry, Patricia Joudry
Hill-Land, Herman Voaden

and playwrights
h. jay bunyan, *Prodigals in a Promised Land*
Marcel Dubé, *Zone*
Gratien Gélinas, *Tit-Coq*
Tomson Highway, *Aria, A One-Woman Play in One Act*
Paul Thompson, *The Farm Show*

"Shall I tell you a story of the jealous Moor
or of the old king and his three daughters?
No. I shall tell you a story of myself when
fifteen years ago I was sixteen."

—James Reaney, Prologue to *The Sun and the Moon*

Acknowledgements

I gratefully acknowledge the assistance of the Archives at the Performing Arts Centre of Toronto Reference Library, and the Carleton University Library, Queen's University's Stauffer Library, the Ottawa Public Library and the National Library of Canada. I would like to thank Dene Barnett for invaluable and scholarly research on Restoration acting techniques.

I am indebted as well to Linda Reinke for her masterly editing skills. I would like to thank Tom Nowak for his timely help with the text of *Camille*; Susan and Del Campbell, George and Rosemary Kaufman, and Bill and Wendy Hyndman for their hospitality and support. The editing skill and diligence of Jodi Armstrong of JLArt and the encouragement and patience of Angela Rebeiro of Playwrights Canada Press made this anthology possible.

Finally, I wish to thank my wife, Maureen, and my son, Liam, who are my best advisers.

For
Liam

CONTENTS

PROLOGUE

Too often in Canadian literature or drama courses, when teachers want to view plays as a part of an evolving tradition rather than as single texts, they must spend hours searching through a variety of resources in order to assemble one simple chronology. Primary materials, the plays themselves, are published in a bewildering array – as single texts, as periodical articles, or as collected works. Many plays written before 1900 can be discovered only in weekly journals long out of print, or in the repositories of rare book rooms. Moreover, critical sources for a particular play text, or a historical period—the required reading teachers need for senior students—are strewn just as far and wide, among a variety of scholarly publications and critical introductions. Broader cultural histories of Canada in the 1800s have simply not yet been written. The cost alone (aside from the research time) to present students with some taste of the richness of Canadian theatre history leaves even the most eager educator disheartened.

This book attempts to present the teacher of English or Drama with a simple introduction to Canadian theatre history. There is no attempt to present a Canadian canon; what follows is a very modest anthology of scenes selected not only for their widely acknowledged significance within the Canadian tradition, but also for their appeal to students. Readers are first introduced to some of the historical and cultural context in each of six historical eras, then, specifically to the four or five selected playwrights and their contribution to each period. Finally, each scene is introduced with a summary of the context of the scene within the larger drama, and offers some notes on performance. As scenes are read aloud or performed, I hope it will become obvious to your students (as it has been to mine) that Canadian theatre has a long and fascinating story, that it has evolved as logically as any other nation's drama, that it is consistent, as one might expect, with the social and economic eras of Canadian history, and, finally, that it is as unique as the nation itself.

Acknowledging that much of Canada's past is a reflection of British and U.S. culture is the key to interpreting Canadian dramatic tastes, especially in the hundred years previous to World War I. When the educated officers of the British army, circa 1800, stage a dramatic "entertainment" at the Halifax or Kingston garrison, they naturally choose Sheridan or Shakespeare not only because it is what they know best, but also because it promotes British culture in the colony. It is good propaganda. (For the same reasons, architects of the Roman Empire inset a huge statue of Caesar to dominate the upstage wall of their amphitheatres in Gaul.) "This programme brought to you by…" is a message not lost on developing Canada, and one that naturally evolves into a taste for all things British by those who attend the high Victorian "opera houses" of the 1880s. It is not surprising then, when Ottawa civil servant Henry Fuller sits down to write a satire of Sir John A. Macdonald and his party's National Policy, that he chooses to parody the most popular entertainment of the time, and the *H.M.S. Parliament* is born. Or that, in 1887, when Sarah Anne Curzon writes her heroic play about Laura Secord, she produces a drama that "worked within and promoted British cultural values." [1] One can either dismiss all Canadian plays of the 1800s as derivative (and many commentators have done so) [2] or view them as a rare opportunity to look realistically at Canada's cultural contexts. By choosing the latter, students can begin to understand the complex relationship between culture and politics, history and art. If, on the other hand, dramatic texts of the 19th century are taught as "second-rate literature" an instructor simply continues to promote the propaganda begun by the good officers of the garrison.

For present purposes, Canada's theatrical past is divided into six, roughly chronological, eras – reflected in the chapter headings (in bold) that follow. Chapter One, **The Velvet Gloves of the Garrison,** describes theatrical entertainments of the military – from Canada's first indigenous drama, written by Marc Lescarbot in 1606, to the more pervasive amusements staged by British officers during the military period following the siege of Quebec in 1759. The commercial boom period of the 1830s creates a plentiful array of weekly journals – with a need to fill the pages between the ads for new goods arriving in the thriving colony. Canadian playwrights oblige, writing numerous short, satirical dramas, which entertain their readers and frequently offer barbed comments on life in the new nation. *The Baron Bold and the Beauteous Maid* is a satire of this type and era, and it and other forms of indigenous dramas are described in Chapter Two, **The Baron Bold.** By the 1880s a few writers, such as the remarkable Sara Anne Curzon, begin to write full length plays designed for audiences of the new Confederation. Curzon struggles against the vastly more popular theatre of the day: stock melodramas produced by foreign touring companies. These early "star" vehicles, geared for broad appeal, travel "circuits" created by the new railways, inspire an infrastructure of new "opera houses" in practically every town and city from Halifax to Winnipeg. In general, touring companies define the High Victorian era; they also, in one form or another, make the production of original Canadian dramas almost impossible well into the next century. A Canadian touring company, managed by Albert Taverner and starring his wife, Ida Van Cortland, is profiled to represent this era. Van Cortland's personal account of her life as a Victorian actress offers compelling insight into the theatre of that time.

Following the hiatus of World War I, the great touring companies themselves succumb, as their grand theatres become the projection houses for the new conqueror, Hollywood. Yet, just as the touring companies provide the first theatrical training for many Canadians, this new, national cultural vacuum creates its own opportunities as well. Amateur clubs, such as the University of Toronto's Hart House Theatre and Worker's Theatre, soon invigorate both the Canadian stage and amateur playwrighting in the 1920s and 1930s. These unlikely companions pick up the threads of the previous century; the first by furthering the efforts for a "national drama" and the second by transforming political satire into its bolder form, "agitation-propaganda" or *agit-prop*. Both styles are promoted at one time or another by the long-lived and celebrated umbrella of Canadian amateur theatre, the Dominion Drama Festival; thus, this era is described in Chapter Three, **The Dominion Years**.

After World War II, Canadian government funding of the arts, in the form of the Canada Council, creates the first era of Canadian professional theatre. Two significant events chart this new direction for culture. Sir John Aird in his *Report* of 1929 is the first politician to establish the policy of federal intervention in the cultural life of the country. Aird's Report leads to the creation of the CBC, creating a significant talent pool for radio and, later, television drama in both French and English. This principle is reiterated by the Massey Commission *Report* of 1951, which generates unprecedented federal support for the arts through the Canada Council. Federal tax dollars then build both a national theatre (Ottawa's National Arts Centre) and create a more or less continuous funding of numerous regional and "alternative" theatres – from Halifax's Neptune Theatre, to the Stratford Festival, to Vancouver's East Cultural Centre (born, like many alternative stages in the early 1970s with the aid of a Local Initiatives Program grant from the Federal government). Many of these financial seeds begin to blossom just as Canada celebrates its centennial year; original Canadian dramatists flourish as never before.

In Quebec, support for artists such as Gratien Gélinas and Michel Tremblay create venues for their important works that inspire **A Revolution in Quebec**, Chapter Four. In English Canada a range of theatrical styles exists, including the drama of successive waves of 20th century immigration. This era is defined by an unprecedented outpouring of original drama dominated by one unique form, the Collective, with connections to early satire, although excerpts from many styles compose **A Revolution in English Canada**, Chapter Five. In a final chapter, **Web and Circle**, the plays of Canada's First Nations are explored. Beginning some 2500 years ago on the shores of the Pacific, the powerful native mythology rises again seven lifetimes after Columbus, within the plays of Highway and George Ryga.[3]

As timelines overlap and co-exist, so do styles. Anton Wagner concludes that Victorian publications "suggest a distinct genre of political satire."[4] The Canadian talent and taste for political satire appears through several chapters, as do themes such as the colonial struggle to survive against well-financed, foreign competition, or in Quebec, the struggle to overcome censorship by Church and state. These broad chapter categories are the clearest historical divisions of act and scene, given the limitations of this anthology. Natalie Rewa concludes that garrison theatre ceased to exist after Confederation simply because the British soldiers left. Yet the style and structure of the military legacy can be found in the Dumbbells of WWI and perhaps even in revues such as the annual *Spring Thaw* (not to mention "SCTV," "The Royal Canadian Air Farce" and "This Hour Has 22 Minutes") a century later. The grand touring companies from Britain and the U.S. that fill the grand theatres of the Victorian era by staging popular melodramas re-emerge as Andrew Lloyd Webber "mega-musicals," ironically staged in many of the same

Toronto theatres, restored to their former glory for the tourists of the 1980s. Michel Tremblay creates a revolution in Quebec theatre in the 1960s, facing down this time the same combined forces of Church and State that prohibited a performance of Molière in Quebec two hundred years before. The Canadian nationalism that in 1921 inspires Roy Mitchell and Merrill Denison at Hart House to write *Brothers In Arms*, the first consciously Canadian play, drives the writing and production of more than fifty original Canadian dramas between 1970 and 1973 in Toronto "alternate" theatres. Similarly in Quebec, by 1974 "more than 1500 actors/writers and more than one hundred groups were presenting collective creations across the province."[5] And finally and fittingly, the Trickster encircles all by disappearing into the primeval forests of Haida British Columbia some 2500 years ago only to reappear, as full of mischief, in the plays of Tomson Highway in the 1990s.

Producing this anthology has been made much easier by the many recent scholarly publications in Canadian theatre history. Among the most relied upon works for this are: Anton Wagner and Richard Plant's multi-volume collection, *Canada's Lost Plays*, an invaluable reprinting of scripts from the 1800s, and Prof. Wagner's companion text, The *Brock Bibliography of Canadian Plays in English 1766–1978*; Anne Saddlemyer's impressive investigation of 19th century Ontario theatre, *Early Stages* and its companion volume, *Later Stages*; Elaine Nardocchio's *Theatre and Politics in Modern Quebec*; Renate Usmiani's documentation of the alternate theatre of the 1960s, *Second Stage*; Djanet Sears' remarkable anthologies of Black theatre history, *Testifyin' I & II*. Finally, much of this research has been summarized in the invaluable reference text, *The Oxford Companion to Canadian Theatre*, edited by Eugene Benson and L.W. Conolly. Thus, very few of these ideas are mine. References to these sources and others have been noted at the end of each chapter, with a bibliography at the end of the anthology.

In light of all this excellent research, what follows can only hope to present a concise, popular introduction to some major themes and eras, and provide some representative and appealing scripts, small appetizers to a much greater banquet.

ENDNOTES to Prologue

[1] Celeste Derkson, "Out of the Closet: Dramatic Works by Sarah Anne Curzon" *Theatre Research in Canada / Recherches Theatrales au Canada* 15:2 (Spring 1994), 9.

[2] Ibid., 4.

[3] Nancy Wigston, "Nanabush In The City," *Books in Canada* (March, 1989), 9.

[4] Anton Wagner, "Introduction" *The Brock Bibliography of Published Canadian Plays in English* 1766–1978, ed. Anton Wagner (Toronto: Playwrights Canada Press, 1980), iii.

[5] Elaine F. Nardocchio, *Theatre and Politics in Modern Quebec* (Edmonton: U of Alberta Press, 1986) 82.

The Velvet Gloves

of the Garrison

In the 18ᵗʰ century, capturing a new country required merely a few quick and glorious battles; occupation was a considerably longer and more monotonous task. After the cannon smoke cleared from Britain's Seven Years' War with France, this was the position in which new rulers of the Canadian colonies found themselves in 1760.

In only a few years, the British Navy had blown up the fortress of Louisbourg on Ile Royale (Cape Breton), had cruelly scattered the French in Acadia far to the south, and after a summer-long siege in 1759, had defeated Montcalm at Quebec. These actions effectively ended more than 150 years of French dominion in Canada.

Ruling this new possession, populated overwhelmingly by French settlers, and keeping it away from the Americans (who threatened after their 1776 rebellion to invade this nearby British colony), required a prolonged and varied military strategy. Enter, stage left, a British officer dressed as Sheridan's "Lady Teazle." Amateur theatre at the garrison, as it turned out, fit the bill in a number of ways.

British garrisons in Halifax, Montreal, and the newer towns of Upper Canada became far outposts of the London stage for more than a hundred years. First, theatre kept the men entertained, and popular British plays reminded them of all the good things about home during the long Canadian winter. Secondly, to the post commander's great relief, theatre, together with horse races and hunting, kept his men away from the demon rum. From the fall of Quebec until Confederation in 1867, garrison theatricals amused British officers of the day, who were "generally well-educated career soldiers from military families… urbane, sophisticated, and desperate for entertainment [to satisfy their] high cultural expectations." [1] Thus, they filled their leisure time with amateur productions of Shakespeare, recent hits of the London Restoration stage (such as Sheridan's *School for Scandal*), and popular farces and melodramas of the time.

Garrison commanders realized as well that theatre not only kept the men happy during the long winter, but also performed a more enduring "parapolitical" role. "British colonial officials apparently encouraged public theatricals as a means of creating civil stability and asserting—albeit unobtrusively—British cultural and political supremacy." Indeed, this "velvet-glove method of cultural assertion" flourished best at the garrison,

> …in periods of political or cultural crisis: in Quebec City during the late eighteenth and early nineteenth centuries, probably in response to the Napoleonic threat overseas, in London and Quebec City following the 1837 Rebellions; in Montreal and Kingston when U.S. threats challenged British sovereignty; and in the 1860s when Britain was withdrawing military support of British North America. [2]

This latter effect outlived the occupation. Officers of the regiment were naturally viewed as a social elite by the largely Loyalist towns of Upper Canada and as a result, possessed considerable social stature and cultural influence. A "taste" for British theatre then left an enduring impression on the young colony. According to Leslie O'Dell, garrison farces and revues broadly influenced Ontario theatre tradition right down to the present day:

> The tradition of military theatricals was passed on to the Canadian army, which absorbed British regimental traditions whole-heartedly, and it helped lay the foundation of amateur theatrical activity which continues as a vital form of entertainment in Ontario to the present day. [3]

In addition, Anton Wagner has noted of all pre-Confederation drama, "...many ...publications suggest a distinct genre of political satire scrutinizing society in colonial Canada and the post-Confederation new Dominion." [4] Is the preference for farce among the colonists also an effect of garrison theatricals? Could this preference be the genesis of what appears to be a particularly Canadian taste—and skill—for comedy and political satire? *My Fur Lady*, the many touring *Army Shows* and later *Spring Thaws* of Canada's mid-century, contemporary TV shows such as the "Royal Canadian Air Farce" and "This Hour Has 22 Minutes," and the plentiful Canadian comic talent south of the border all seem to suggest a cultural tradition of satire rooted in the military outposts of 18th century Canada.

It is certain that amateur theatre was the perfect peacetime plan. Burgeoning towns such as Kingston, flush with successive waves of first Loyalists (in the 1780s), then British settlers (after the end of the Napoleonic Wars in 1816), welcomed both the economic impact of a local garrison and the cultural one, placing "officers of the British regiment... automatically at the highest level, ...an exciting addition to the existing social life of the community." Yet, although the soldiers wisely donated any theatre door receipts to charity and encouraged local actors to participate, especially actresses (no doubt for social as well as casting reasons), the colonials themselves were still, and inevitably, merely colonials. O'Dell also notes that commanding Colonel Garnet Wolseley dryly recorded at the time:

> Altogether, it was an elysium of bliss for young officers, the only trouble being to keep single. Several impressionable young captains and subalterns had to be sent home hurriedly to save them from imprudent marriages. Although these Canadian ladies were very charming, they were not richly endowed with worldly goods. [5]

Nevertheless, by the time the British officers turned over their velvet gloves to Canadian soldiers at Confederation, a little more than a hundred years after the fall of Quebec, British theatrical tastes had a firm hold on Canadian audiences. Indeed, for whatever aging British star might wish to "tread the boards of the colonies," Canada proved a very receptive, and lucrative, market for many years to come.

SCENE ONE

Le Théâtre de Neptune, Marc Lescarbot

The one exception to the parapolitical culture of the British garrison—but well within the definition of this style of theatre—occurred more than 150 years *before* the fall of Quebec. This play has been traditionally termed Canada's first theatrical production. Marc Lescarbot's *Le Théâtre de Neptune en La Nouvelle France.*

Lescarbot was a French advocate who had been convinced in 1606 to spend a year in the New World at Port Royal on the Bay of Fundy, the first French settlement in Canada. Later that same year, Lescarbot's friend and patron, the Sieur, left him in charge of the tiny settlement of natives, trappers and sailors to allow de Poutrincourt and his partner, Samuel de Champlain, time to explore the coastline of Maine. From Lescarbot's introduction to *Le Theatre de Neptune*, published in France some years later, the poet was very anxious over his temporary post command and looked forward to welcoming his patron back for several reasons. In Lescarbot's own words:

> About the time we were expecting his return, whereof we had great desire, the more so that if evil had come upon him *we had been in danger of a mutiny*, I bethought me to go out to meet him with some jovial spectacle, and so we did.[6]

Theatre to the rescue again: Lescarbot hastily wrote several rhymed speeches, costumed his sailors and trappers as Neptune and his six attendants, or Tritons, and placed them with several paddlers on open boats to brave the cold November day waters of Annapolis Basin. In doing so, he staged the first European dramatic production in North America. It was a resounding success. As a result of Lescarbot's poetic talents, he became that winter the first *animateur* of Champlain's famous Port Royal company, the Order of Good Cheer. In the autumn of the next year, however, the lawyer-poet gave up the insecurities of the New World to return to France. There he resumed his practice, married a noblewoman, and successfully published the *Histoire de la Nouvelle France*, the first history book of Canada.

— • —

LE THÉÂTRE DE NEPTUNE

NEPTUNE
Halt, mighty Sagamo, no further fare
Look on a god who holds thee in his care,
Thou know'st me not? I am of Saturn's line,
Brother to Pluto dark and Jove divine.

We three of old the universe divided;
Heav'n was to Jove, to Pluto Hell confided,
While I, a bolder spirit, proudly reign
O'er all the Seven Seas, my moist domain.
Neptune, my name, I, Neptune rule the salt
Sea waves, most potent under heaven's vault.
If man would taste the spice of fortune's savour
He needs must seek the aid of Neptune's favour
For stay-at-homes who doze on kitchen settles
Earn no more glory than their pots and kettles.

Thyself indeed despite thy deeds of daring
Hads't never sighted land, my sea-lanes faring,
Nor won the joy of landing on this coast
–Thou whose exploits thy fellows proudly boast.
Mine, mine the back that bore thy vessels' weight
When thou didst choose to visit me in state.
And yet again a hundred times I've shielded
Their ships and men from fate, and constant wielded
The sea-god's power to guard thee in thy ways.
Thus I will keep thee safe through all thy days.

Hold then thy course and fortune go with thee
Where fate decides; for destiny I see
Prepares for France a rich and vast empire
In this New World, whence fame's immortal lyre
Shall to the Old World evermore proclaim
Thine own, de Monts' and puissant Henry's* name.

> *NEPTUNE ceasing, a trumpet begins to blow a loud call and encourages the Tritons to do likewise. Meanwhile, Sieur de Poutrincourt keeps his sword in hand and does not sheathe it until the TRITONS have spoken as follows:*

FIRST TRITON
(apparently a pompous fellow)
Thou mayst, great Sagamo, right thankful be
Because a god vouchsafes thee his assistance
In this bold enterprise which hardily
Thou lead'st in spite of Aeolus' resistance.
Now friend, now foe, the god of winds is jealous
And treacherous plots, his fickle breath inspire,
But sceptred Neptune, now thy champion zealous,
Will dissipate like morning smoke his ire.

---

* de Monts was Poutrincourt's friend and chief patron; Henry II of Navarre was King of France.

SECOND TRITON

We're his Tritons and we pine
To see thy labours ended;
So shall Neptune's glory shine
By thy renown attended.

THIRD TRITON

The fair fame of France
Her children enhance,
Whose courage is bolder
Than hearts that are older.
Not once in past ages
Related by sages
Were Frenchmen more eager
To seize and beleaguer
The fortress of glory
And blazon the story
That stirs and amazes
In chanting her praises.

FOURTH TRITON

The man who never risks a fall
Proves he has no heart at all,
But he who firm of will and brave
Fronts the fury of the wave,
Shows himself to be a lad
With valour armed and virtue clad.
Such a one will never let
History his name forget.

FIFTH TRITON

(speaks in Gascon)
I go tell you what I tink.
Old man Neptune naughty fellow,
Dress himself in blue and yellow,
Look himself in glass and wink.

Went and kissed a pretty maid,
Never asked the lassie's father.
Did she like it? – She – well, rather
Not – I tell you what she said–

I don't trust a sailor man,
Specially when he's old and dripping.
Neptune dear you'd best be flipping
Out of here so quick you can.

SIXTH TRITON
Long life to Henry sovran King of France
Who justly rules in stable governance
The wandering peoples of his proud new realm.
Neptune, we hope, with Henry at the helm,
Will here be reverenced as he was of yore
By faithful subjects on the Gallic shore,
Or whereso'er their grandsires' ships have fared
And Gallic hearts the risks of ocean dared.

> *NEPTUNE's chariot now gives place to a canoe manned by four Indians,*
> *bringing each a present to the said Sieur de Poutrincourt.*

INDIAN
(*offering a quarter of moose*)
Great chief, before thee here we bow
Humble knees and offer now
Homage to the lily-flower,
Symbol of the royal power.
Loyalty we swear to thee
Legate of his Majesty.

> *Poutrincourt makes a speech of thanks to NEPTUNE and to the INDIANS,*
> *the composition of which the author naturally leaves to the chief. Everyone*
> *is invited to visit Fort Royal and break bread. At this point the TRITONS*
> *sing in harmony, apparently forgetting their role and becoming sailors*
> *once more:*

TRITONS
Great god Neptune, send our fleet
In safety o'er the waters,
And bring us homeward all to meet
Our loving wives and daughters.

> *More trumpets, general movement, gunfire and long-rolling echoes. The*
> *company moves up to the fort, and as Poutrincourt approaches the gate,*
> *a merry FELLOW who had been standing waiting for him speaks thus:*

FELLOW
Long have we watched, great chieftain to behold
Thy safe return. At last our hopes grown cold
Were warmed to joy and heaven's boundless grace
Vouchsafed the vision of thy conquering face.

> *He pauses for a moment, and turning gaily to a group within the gate:*

Up, then, stewards, scullions, batmen!
Hurry, lean, and scurry, fat men!
Clatter out your pots and dishes,

Roast your haunches, fry your fishes,
Pour your flagons, fill our glasses,
Drinks for everyone that passes.
Let them swill all they can swallow,
Throats are dry and bellies hollow.

Stir your stumps you turnspit loon,
We must have our dinner soon.
Are those ducklings duly basted?
Not a moment must be wasted!
Chop the heads off forty chickens,
Heat the soup until it thickens,
Beat the batter soft and yellow,
Stuff to fill a hungry fellow.

Come my lads from field and stable,
Set your knees beneath the table.
Come my lords and noble red men,
Here is wine to turn your head, men!
But before you start your capers,
Sneeze aloud to clear the vapours,
This play's ended, that is certain,
Naught remains but draw the curtain.

— • —

Director's Notes: *Le Theatre de Neptune*

An amateur production of *Le Theatre de Neptune* involves a little costuming, some sense of the rhythmic "swing" of the poetry (perhaps justified as much by the "sway" of the open boats as the rhythm of the poetry), some suitable extemporizing by the actors playing Poutrincourt and Champlain, a comic characterization or two, and a couple of sets or acting areas. The entire playlet is not much longer than that which precedes, which is edited to give the gist of the original presentation. Lescarbot provides students with good practice in speaking a variety of rhythms and rhyme schemes – from Neptune's formal couplets of iambic pentameter, to the more forced couplets of the first Triton, to the informal, rocking verse of the Fifth Triton. Each speech has its unique challenges in rhythm and articulation.

The first monologue belongs to Neptune, standing tall in his boat, regally costumed in "blue and yellow." (According to the comic portrait given by the Fifth Triton, the god is also "old and dripping" – certainly *that* actor's best line.) Each succeeding Triton should of course be distinctive by dialect or direction, and generally provide slightly comic foils for the god-like, but pedantic, Neptune. One "Indian" speech here represents four in the original, avoiding the noble (and not so noble) portrait of the Micmac sketched by Lescarbot, typical of his day. Following the Indian's gift, Poutrincourt should improvise a short speech of appropriate surprise and pleasure at the spectacle, perhaps followed by a few similar lines from Champlain, who is standing by his side.

The dramatic action then moves to land, with lines sung, sea-shanty style, by the Tritons. This is followed by a welcoming monologue from the "merry fellow at the gate." He can be the last speaker before "curtain," or, for a more rousing finale, follow his eight-line verse with a closing chorus from the entire *troupe de Neptune* (all actors involved in the drama) sharing the last two octets.

Two more notes about the text. The term "Sagamos" (in the first line) was later footnoted by Lescarbot: "*C'est un mot de Sauvage, qui signifie Captaine*," clearing that mystery. More fun however is Neptune's reference to "stay-at-homes." This is probably a private joke, with an ironic twist. According to W. L. Grant,

> While in Acadia, ...[Lescarbot] seems to have quarrelled with Champlain, who speaks of him as a stay-at-home. In one respect the lawyer was wiser than the explorer, or indeed than his time; for almost alone of his contemporaries he had grasped the truth that a colony must be rooted in the soil. The history of the New World might have been altered, if Spain and France had taken to heart the words of Marc Lescarbot. [7]

The student actor's tone should try to convey this "joke" between the poet and the explorer, if only for the reason that this subtext has survived four hundred years!

Unfortunately, this short piece remains one of the only dramatic performances of the French colonial era in Canada. In 1694, Bishop Saint-Vallier of Quebec banned garrison theatricals by French officers because of a planned production of *Tartuffe*. The good bishop perhaps saved the souls of the colony from the presumed blasphemies of Molière, but in doing so, missed a grand opportunity for fifty-odd years of good, colonial propaganda from the homeland. This fact was not lost on the British, though, whose officers would later stage their *own* versions of Molière, in French, after 1759 *pour les citoyens de les villes occupé de Montréal et Québec*. Ah, *c'est la guerre moderne*!

— • —

SCENE TWO

The Halifax Prologues

Regardless of place or purpose, however, the first words spoken on a real stage in Canada were no doubt part of a dramatic *prologue*. As Patrick O'Neill explains:

> Prologues and epilogues were a bit of extra nonsense, but they were a necessary piece of nonsense at all evenings in the theatre in Canada and elsewhere. From the time of the reopening of the theatres in the Restoration until the second decade of the nineteenth century every new full-length comedy and tragedy in England was customarily introduced by a prologue and concluded by an epilogue. [8]

Professor O'Neill dates the first prologue from the winter of 1734 in Annapolis Royal and notes that Canadian prologues "stand favourably in company with those written by authors from any other country," although Canadian prologues served distinctly different purposes than those written in England and Europe. [9]

Garrison actors used these short pieces to *persuade* an audience with oratory, rather than *entertain* them with poetry. (See *The Drury Lane Prologue* by Samuel Johnson, performed by David Garrick in 1747 as an excellent example of the European style). [10] In Canada, prologues often functioned: (a) to remind audiences to be indulgent – that the performance was less to create high art than it was to fund a local charity; (b) to counter any public criticism that officers should not be entertaining, but only defending the townsfolk; (c) to justify theatre morally – as local newspapers would frequently condemn any theatrical performance as immoral, and encourage citizens to stay away: "the purpose of the prologue was to cajole the audience into a pleasant frame of mind so that they would be in [a] friendly mood when the curtain was drawn up." [11]

These considerations made Canadian prologues unique, and offered a revealing portrait of the audiences of two hundred years ago. Also, adds O'Neill, the most frequent difference between prologues of Canada and those of England was the speaker. In half the British prologues, women spoke the lines; in Canada, this was rare because there were few, if any, Canadian professional actresses before the prologue went out of style, around 1840.

— • —

THE HALIFAX PROLOGUE OF 26 AUGUST 1768

To warm the Passions by the nicer Rules,
Is the first Lesson in Theatric Schools,
To wake each tender feeling of the Mind,
Reform our Manners and be more refin'd,

Teach us what 'tis to Sympathy we owe,
To joy at other's Good, to melt at other's Woe.
To form the Husband, make the Father, Friend,
Is all the Stage wou'd wish to recommend.
Not that we boast, but with our Art had Pow'r
To please this Circle for a leisure Hour.
Then if reciting other Works we gain
One Mind from Error, we the end obtain:
One Eye to weep at Shore's unhappy Woe,
And the soft Tear of Charity bestow;
One Heart so swell with Zanga's honest hate,
One female Breast to mourn a Juliet's Fate,
'Tis all we aim at, all we hope to gain,
Completing this, no Labour is a Pain.
The Comic Muse your Favour too shou'd win,
And lash each Folly with her archer Grin.
And if your kind Indulgence we shou'd ask,
For Preparation is the doubled Task;
Or beg one moment's Patience for delay,
We'll strive to mend it in the Part we play:
Or shou'd our Ladies, as they will appear,
(For the best Wives some Times the Breeches wear)
A little diff'rent from the Sex they claim,
You'll on our scanty Numbers lay the blame.
But shou'd we raise Recruits, we'll change the Page,
And Shakespeare's Elves shall gambol o'er the Stage;
Here dart his Lightnings, there his Thunders roll,
Here the drawn Dagger, there the poison Bowl:
Then Richard strains with those that manly Force,
A Horse, A House, my Kingdom for a Horse!
The Air-drawn Dagger here shall lead Macbeth,
While Hecate charms, and Witches dance the Heath:
Then strive to touch the heart-struck Woe of Lear,
—Here Nature, thou dear Goddess hear!
Then Ranger climb for Love, or Mischief's sake,
Up I go, Neck, or nothing, shou'd the Ladder break.
Nay, for Relief, we'll leave black Verse and Rhyme,
And run the Gauntlet in a Pantomime.
A thinner White, than me must fill the motley Scene,
I'll make a better Falstaff than a Harlequin.
But passing an attempt at Wit away,
Our serious Sentence give me leave to say;
Our scanty Numbers will I'm taught to fear,
Make one in various Characters appear,
If you'll excuse that Fault, we'll prove it true,

We'll place each Character in better View;
To your Protection, to your Aid we sue.
Nor can we fail when patronized by you:
Nor heed th'Advice which Anti Thespis gave,
For sure we know how Britons will behave,
Since none were ever cruel than were brave.

— • —

THE HALIFAX PROLOGUE IN THE YEAR 1773

THE summer's suns, no more our spirits cheer
And dreary winter desolates the year;
The pleasing prospect of the verdant field,
To trackless snow too soon must nature yield:
Inclement skies prevent our sports by day,
And tedious nights are spent in cards and tea.
Since such the case, with ardour we engage
To furnish entertainment from the Stage.
Our slipper'd heroes we once more enrol,
To combat all the passions of the soul,
Where gloomy thoughts deject, or eating care
Distracts the mind and drives us to despair.
Happy the Poet and the Player's art,
Who jointly guide th'emotions of the heart,
And real ills by fancied scenes beguile,
Changing our deepest sorrow to a smile.
But foes like these must all our pow'r withstand,
Unless you grant the success we demand.
Join then your aid, and where the actor fails
Give just applause, if sense, or wit prevails.
Laugh where you can, with spirits duly rais'd,
And shew a disposition to be pleased.
Such favour now the stage may justly claim,
Depriv'd of actors of its greatest fame.
No WATSON here with mimic art displays,
With action just and unaffected ease,
The Female characters. —No MARSH we find
Who various talents for amusement join'd;
Who equal pleasure to his hearers gave
In rattling Fuddle, or in Fulmer grave;
Or when he self important Pamphlet play'd,
Or humble Jerry, or his wife afraid.
GRATTAN, with Paddy's blunders, now no more
In bursts of laughter makes the audience roar.

Nor TIFFIN, bless'd with humour and with ease,
Who play'd his part, just as he spent his days,
With much applause and universal praise.
Some new recruits indeed our stage may boast,
Yet still we must lament the vet'rans lost.
But tho' unskilled in acting we appear,
We dread not satire nor the critic's sneer;

For, unambitious of an actors fame,
To please the audience is our only aim.
Judg'd by this circle, amiable as fair,
Good nature yet cou'd never be severe,
We hope indulgence, when our faults are known,
May, as on like occasions, now be shewn.

— • —

Director's Notes: *The Halifax Prologues of 1768 and 1773*

It is difficult for us to imagine anything in our past being better than what we have today. In this regard, the theatres of Halifax and St. John of two hundred years ago challenge our notions of progress. It is best to see these stages as places of imagination and amusement that are as entertaining and, as the century progresses, as familiar to audiences of the day as movie theatres are today. With his usual insight, Robertson Davies reminds us, "it would be a misunderstanding to suppose that our theatre before that time was meagre or backward... our 19th century forebears were by no means theatrically naïve or ill-served." [12] The following excerpt from *The New Brunswick Courier*, Saint John, on 7 August 1830 conveys, albeit in a tragic way, some of the broad dimensions of production at the time, as well as the enthusiasm shared by actors and audiences alike for theatre:

Death on the Saint John Stage, 1830
Melancholy accident, attended *with loss of Life.*

Last night, while the Theatricals were amusing their audience with a representation of the memorable battle of Waterloo, a number of the Soldiers from the Barracks were engaged to personify what a considerable number of them had actually experienced *propria persona*, little thinking of the real scene they were about to display. When the engagement became general, and the field covered with the wounded and the dying; we are truly sorry to state this part of the play was but too real, for two of the men were severely wounded: one in the face by the wadding, the other was found lying insensible, with a ram-rod driven firm into the brain above the left eye. Medical assistance was instantly upon the spot, and every thing done that science or humanity could afford, but all proved abortive. He remained in the same state of insensibility until this morning, when death terminated the unfortunate man's earthly career – thus evincing the uncertainty of life. We are happy to say, that in the hands of the scientific Dr. HADAWAY, of the Army, little danger is to be expected to the other more fortunate sufferer. We cannot but censure the spirit the men betrayed during the sham fight, they seemed inspired with all the feeling of reality, as almost every man pointed his musket as directly for his opponent as he would have done in the real field of Waterloo. It is fortunate more did not suffer, as another ram-rod was discharged, which rebounded against the opposite side of the house.

The distance between the early 19th century stage and the globally produced mega-musicals of today—or even the latest Jackie Chan thriller—may be shorter than Jackie's next line.

Thus the preceding prologues were no doubt intended as introductions to an evening of ambitious entertainment at the Halifax garrison. These prologues were solo pieces; however, there is no reason that each could not be approached also as a choral presentation. (Indeed, both pieces use the first person *plural*.) As well, students should be aware, like most if not all prologues of that time, these are written in *heroic couplets* (with the occasional *triplet*) with an *iambic pentameter rhythm*. What this means is that the poet gives the actor not just a line, but a clear direction on the important words – the five syllables that receive the stress in the unstressed, stressed pattern of the iamb. The actor should be sensitive to this rhythm, but not so emphatic that the rendition begins to sound like lines from a primary school Christmas pageant. In other words, "the actor must avoid getting trapped in the vocal patterns of both rhythm and rhyme"[15] Avoid emphasizing the last word in each line especially because it not only rhymes strongly—heroically—with the previous, but at the same time, receives a stress from the rhythm.

There are two skills actors use to avoid "getting trapped" in this way: *pausing* and proper *emphasis*. As with blank verse, pausing is done at punctuation, not at the end of lines. Thus, in the following, a short breath is taken at the comma, not after "Pow'r." The actor should wait until the *end of the couplet* before taking another breath.

> Not that we boast, but with our Art had Pow'r
> To please this Circle for a leisure Hour.

The second technique to avoid sounding repetitive is for the actor to realize, that in any line written in iambic pentameter, there are five syllables that are stressed, amounting to five artistic choices for the actor. One actor's choice of emphasis may slightly alter the *meaning* of the line from the next actor's interpretation. Additionally, one or two of these emphasized syllables usually belong to what actors call "pointing words": words that carry the most of the meaning of each line to the audience. Most Restoration poets who capitalize the most important words in each line make discovering the pointing words among these stressed syllables rather easy.

In the following couplet, for example, the five stressed syllables ("beg" "mo-" "Pat-" "for" "lay") are the choices for emphasis. If the actors are skillful and well-rehearsed, their rendition will vary the emphasis over the whole line rather than produce an unrehearsed, all-in-one emphasis on the final rhyme word. Note as well, that articles, prepositions and pronouns are probably the least important words in a line in terms of choices for emphasis, and thus, a deliberate stress on "for" would not be a best choice for an actor, unless he or she had a definite interpretation in mind. Finally, this rhythm will demand that at times a three-syllable word such as "Patience" be pronounced as a two syllable word in order to maintain the iambic pentameter (For all the above see Ron Cameron, *Acting Skills For Life*, 312–16 – a marvelous source for student acting techniques.) [13]

> Or beg one moment's Patience for delay,
> We'll strive to mend it in the Part we play:

By rehearsing these techniques in a performance of these two prologues, students get excellent practice for reading and performing Shakespeare. As a matter of fact, Shakespeare's blank verse may seem easier to make sound "real" to you after pronouncing one hundred or so lines of *rhyming* couplets in an original way. And remember, of course, the most memorable lines in the world of theatre are in fact from a prologue:

> Two households, both alike in dignity,
> In fair Verona, where we lay our scene.

— • —

SCENE THREE

The School For Scandal

What is playing at the garrison? Commentator Natalie Rewa strongly suggests the popularity of "English comedies and farces" [14] with military audiences of the early 19th century. And, Canada's master of Victoriana, Robertson Davies, expands this notion beyond the garrison:

> The yearning towards the eighteenth century was part of the yearning for England—England as Home, as the Great Good place—which was a part of the psychology of many Ontarians during the whole of their lives. Old Comedy presented an England that probably never was, but that was none the less real to the imagination.
>
> The repertoire of Old Comedy was not large. Sheridan's two comedies, *The Rivals* (1774) and *The School For Scandal* (1777) headed the list of favourites… [15]

Richard Brinsley Sheridan was an Irish-born, English-educated playwright and Member of Parliament, who, with his friend, the famous actor David Garrick, owned the Theatre Royal in Drury Lane, London. In the 1780s, Sheridan staged triple successes at Drury Lane, *A Trip To Scarborough*, *The School For Scandal* and *The Rivals*, and amply demonstrated his "acute verbal wit." [16] For modern audiences, this theatrical hat trick has come to define the essential qualities of the Restoration stage.

These qualities—the witty dialogue, the comic entrances and exits, the mistaken identities, the lack of sentimentality—found in abundance in the melodramas of the time, and the underlying social commentary on the lives, manners, and morality of the aristocracy, are perhaps best exemplified by the climax to *The School For Scandal* – the famous "screen scene." It is an absolutely brilliant accumulation of comic moments. When you laugh at an episode of "Frasier," you're laughing at techniques used by Sheridan more than two hundred years before television's Crane brothers.

— • —

Notes on the 18th Century Art of Gesture

Although there are many good sources of Restoration drama, there are very few available which describe the vocabulary of basic gestures which were well known to actors of the 18th and 19th centuries. Teaching theatre students "less to seek the inner causes, than to observe what the outer display is" [17] has not been a popular approach to understanding character "motivation" for a hundred years or more. "Mere imitation," as a colleague of mine once exclaimed, "flies in the face of everything I've ever taught my drama students." It is true: asking post-Stanislavsky actors, universally exposed and schooled in American "method acting," to forget the discovery of inner motivation in favour of the study of a set of outward character gestures, is a daunting task. Yet, it is these almost photographic gestures or poses, showing a character's embarrassment, surprise or jealousy, which make a scene from Sheridan come alive.

The art of stage gesture is derived from the ancient art of oratory. And, as scholar Dene Barnett notes: "Throughout the 17th and 18th centuries, oratory and eloquence were a part of educated life… taught intensively… in schools and universities."[18] As part of a humanist education, Jesuit institutions in particular encouraged the writing of plays and teaching of the vocabulary of gesture to its students – the future audience members of Sheridan and Racine (a young Marc Lescarbot was likely one of these Jesuit school students). So strong were these rhetorical traditions, descending from the Romans, that acting itself was to a certain extent "regarded as a genre of oratory,"[19] and it is this connection that quite naturally gave rise to the prologue.

In both the prologue and the play, the actor's hands and eyes are the principal instruments of gesture. Literally, actors are trained, as Hamlet instructs, to suit the action to the word. Individual words in a line of text, often the *pointing* words, are matched with a movement of the hand, arm or facial expression to emphasize or to bring to life "events past, things distant, imaginary or abstract"[20]

All stage gestures are made with the right hand; the left functions merely as an accompaniment. Restoration instructors classify gestures as either *indicative*, *imitative* or *expressive*. *Indicative gestures* are mainly pointing movements made with the hand. Each *indicated* whether the script refers to the speaker himself, or to another character on stage. *Imitative gestures* are used to recreate, using the arms mainly, "the size or speed of an object, person or event by imitating that feature."[21] Finally—and here the vocabulary extends to the full range of human emotions—*expressive gestures* are used to accompany the emotions of the character, such as surprise, aversion or jealousy. Rather than using the hands and arms, this vocabulary relies primarily on the face and the eyes of the educated actor. There are additional gestures used to commence, to emphasize, or to conclude an important point of dialogue.

In a sense, Restoration actors memorize two scripts—the dialogue and the appropriate accompanying gestures—in much the same way as musical performers sing and dance at once.

The best actors of the Restoration stage could create these complex movements "distinct and discrete, but elegantly linked together."[22] Their gestures would accompany the words in as subtle a manner as music underscores emotions in a modern film.

Action in general, such as one should understand it here, is the Art of depicting ideas and feeling with gestures, by the whole deportment of the body, and especially by the appearance of the face... [an actor's] gestures must sometimes be fearsome, other times they must allow themselves only pleasing ones, they must now make haughty graces stand out, now artless graces, now solemn graces, now playful graces, now lively, piquant graces, and now careless, tender graces.[23]

The *transition* from one gesture into the next needs to be as pleasing, as natural, and as convincing to the audience's trained eye as the gesture itself.

The opening exchange, for example, between Sir Peter and Joseph, could be acted in the following way, according to the art of gesture. The actor should first underline what he or she believes to be the most *important* words in each line – the *pointing* words. With this information, each line is then accompanied by a gesture rehearsed separately (perhaps in a preliminary pantomime of the dialogue under study).

Even if an actor could find them, it is not necessary to pore endlessly over 18th century hand and face diagrams to arrive at each appropriate gesture; imaginative actors can easily make up their own vocabularies of gesture. As Barnett reminds us: "...each of the basic gestures in the actor's vocabulary is to be found in everyday life, for we point, we frown in anger and emphasize important words with hand movements."[24] Indeed, a creative drama instructor can have a good deal of fun with such vocabulary-building exercises. Once given the encouragement to be physical in this way, most students soon lose their natural self-conscious "small-ness" on stage, and begin to exclaim and declaim with alarming exaggeration.

Sir Peter's first speech in the selection has many good choices for pointing words, but at its heart, it is a *plea,* which leads to a *shared secret,* and finally a *trap* (in the speaker's mind at least). In other words, it is a conspiracy to which the audience willingly eavesdrops and is thus cleverly drawn in as a co-conspirator. To promote these notions in the mind of the listener then, the following words could be selected for emphasis:

SIR PETER TEAZLE
Now, my **good** friend, oblige me, I **entreat** you. Before Charles comes, let me **conceal** myself somewhere. Then do you tax him on the point **we** have been talking on, and his **answers** may satisfy me at once.

The first two pointing words indicate the *plea*; the next two, the *shared secret* and the last word, the *trap*. A hand, arm, body or facial gesture accompanies each noted word. Look over some following examples (taken from a unique history of the art of gesture by Dene Barnett) to understand how students in 1800 might have studied the role of Sir Peter.

Notes on the Art of Gesture: 1. The Hands

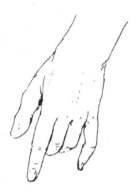

a. Hand Posture 1

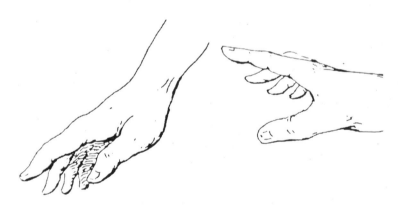

b. Hand Posture 2

"There were two normal hand postures. The actor and singer used one or other of these most of the time he was on stage." [25]

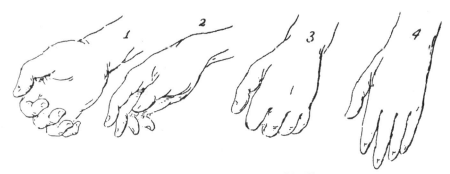

c. Hand Postures "to be avoided":

"These three hands [i.e. nos. 1, 2, and 3] look more like claws than hands… what a wretched habit! I hope, that this example will be enough, to draw your attention to it, so that you will always avoid it. – Yet don't think, Dear Students! That the hand hanging down with straight fingers can wholly redress this, no, although better than with crooked fingers, N. 4 is the hand of a soldier, who with arms and fingers stretched out, learns to hold the hand by the side, for marching." [26]

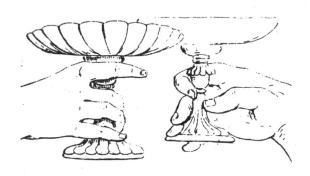

d. Hand Postures when holding objects [27]

Notes on the Art of Gesture: 2. The Arms

"Colloquial gesture, which is at the opposite extreme from epic, differs from it essentially in the manner of the action of the arm. Instead of unfolding the whole oratorical weapon, as in tragedy… the upper arm in colloquial gesture is barely detached from the side; and the elbow, instead of the shoulder, becomes the principal centre of motion." [28]

BELOW: Some more exaggerated, "systematic" arm gestures. [29]

Notes on the Art of Gesture: 3. The Body

a. Astonishment (mixed with terror):
"But when… surprise reaches the superlative degree, which I take to be astonishment, the whole body is actuated; it is thrown back, with one leg set before the other, both hands elevated, the eyes larger than usual, the brows drawn up, and the mouth not quite shut." [30]

b. Welcome:
"Surprise causes the body and lower limbs to retire, and affection stimulates the person to advance…" [31]

Notes on the Art of Gesture: 4. The Face and Eyes

Jealousy: Expressive gestures such as this one are used to convey "a passion of the character being portrayed." [32]

Old Sir Peter's *plea,* for example, is an attempt to draw Joseph into his scheme, so perhaps a less exaggerated version of the "Welcome" is appropriate. Although this gesture is intended for a character entrance, it would give the audience this sense of intimacy as well. The right arm extended, and the hand open with the fore finger beckoning, appropriately accompanies Peter's shared secret. Finally, the word "answer" could be paired with a decisive downward movement of the right arm, or the light slapping of the back of the right hand into the palm of the left.

Joseph's reply: "O fie, Sir Peter! Would you have me join in so mean a trick?" is at once an honest attempt (as honest as the character of Joseph can be) to avoid cornering his brother (who knows too much, as we later see) and to impress Sir Peter with his innocent nature. It is made ironic by the concealment of Sir Peter's young wife behind the screen nearby. Sir Peter's reaction is astonishment – not quite so exaggerated to imply "terror" (as in 3a above: as Hamlet might show terror on seeing the ghost) – but certainly enough to illustrate comic fear, which implies Joseph's growing anxiety and lack of control. It's Sir Peter's turn to show "surprise" on the next line, as he almost runs into his wife behind the screen. When Lady Teazle is revealed at the end of the selection, Sir Peter might try the "jealousy" pose above (4).

Of course, there is a danger of going overboard when using gesture for the first time. The famous British actor of the early 1800s, Henry Siddons (sketched in 3b above) reminds his students—not so gently—in this fashion:

> For as the actor ought to employ the aid of emphasis for *principal* words alone, without accenting them *all* with the same precision, which would render them confused, pompous, and ridiculous... A perpetual see-saw of the arms, such as we observe in schoolboys, when repeating their set speeches, fatigues the eye, by its insipidity, as much as in indiscriminate emphasis [sic] on every word, in a long sentence, fatigues and disgusts a well-governed ear by its tiresomeness and monotony. "Any thing so overdone is from the purpose of playing." Shakespeare. [33]

Lastly, here is "A Practical Guide To Dialogue Acting" offered by Barnett that may prove useful to any aspiring Restoration actor.

a. face, chest and voice to be directed towards the spectators; the eyes and hands towards the interlocutor
b. the listener may turn away a little from the spectators and towards the speaker
c. the listener to be downstage a step or two so that the speaker can see him without turning his face away from the spectators
d. the foot nearer one's interlocutor to be set forward
e. the weight may be on the foot further from one's interlocutor so that the torso inclines elegantly towards him
f. the change from speaker's position to listener's position should be practised to attain grace [34]

The result of all this "extra" rehearsing is acting that is well paced and clearly expressed – attributes that are appreciated by any audience regardless of century.

— • —

THE "SCREEN SCENE" FROM SHERIDAN'S *THE SCHOOL FOR SCANDAL*

SIR PETER TEAZLE Now, my good friend, oblige me, I entreat you. Before Charles comes, let me conceal myself somewhere. Then do you tax him on the point we have been talking on, and his answers may satisfy me at once.

JOSEPH SURFACE O fie, Sir Peter! Would you have me join in so mean a trick? To trepan my brother to–

SIR PETER TEAZLE Nay, you tell me you are *sure* he is innocent. If so, you do him the greatest service in giving him an opportunity to clear himself; and you will set my heart at rest. Come, you shall not refuse me. Here, behind this screen will be–

SIR PETER TEAZLE goes to the screen.

Hey, what the devil! There seems to be one listener here already. I'll swear I saw a petticoat.

JOSEPH SURFACE Ha, ha, ha! Well, this is ridiculous enough. I'll tell you, Sir Peter. Though I hold a man of intrigue to be a most despicable character, yet you know it doesn't follow that one is to be an absolute Joseph either. Harkee. 'Tis a little French milliner, a silly rogue that plagues me; and, having some character, on your coming she ran behind the screen.

SIR PETER TEAZLE Ah, you rogue! But, egad, she has overheard all I have been saying of my wife.

JOSEPH SURFACE O, 'twill never go any further; you may depend on't.

SIR PETER TEAZLE No! Then, i'faith, let her hear it out. Here's a closet will do as well.

JOSEPH SURFACE Well, go in then.

SIR PETER TEAZLE Sly rogue, sly rogue!

SIR PETER TEAZLE goes into the closet.

JOSEPH SURFACE A very narrow escape indeed! And a curious situation I'm in! To part man and wife in this manner!

LADY TEAZLE *(peeping from the screen)* Couldn't I steal off?

JOSEPH SURFACE Keep close, my angel.

SIR PETER TEAZLE *(peeping out)* Joseph, tax him home.

JOSEPH SURFACE Back, my dear friend!

LADY TEAZLE *(peeping)* Couldn't you lock Sir Peter in?

JOSEPH SURFACE Be still, my life.

SIR PETER TEAZLE *(peeping)* You're sure the milliner won't blab?

JOSEPH SURFACE In, in, my good Sir Peter! *(aside)* 'Fore Gad, I wish I had a key to the door.

Enter CHARLES SURFACE.

CHARLES SURFACE Hollo! Brother, what has been the matter? Your fellow wouldn't let me up at first. What, have you had a Jew or a wench with you?

JOSEPH SURFACE Neither, brother, I assure you.

CHARLES SURFACE But what has made Sir Peter steal off? I thought he had been with you.

JOSEPH SURFACE He *was*, brother; but, hearing you were coming, he did not choose to stay.

CHARLES SURFACE What, was the old gentleman afraid I wanted to borrow money of him?

JOSEPH SURFACE No, sir; but I am sorry to find, Charles, that you have lately given that worthy man grounds for great uneasiness.

CHARLES SURFACE Yes, they tell me I do that to a great many worthy men. But how so, pray?

JOSEPH SURFACE To be plain with you, brother, he thinks you are endeavouring to gain Lady Teazle's affections from him.

CHARLES SURFACE Who, I? O lud, not I, upon my word. Ha, ha, ha! So the old fellow has found out that he has got a young wife, has he? Or, what's worse, has her ladyship discovered that she has an old husband?

JOSEPH SURFACE This is no subject to jest on, brother. He who can laugh–

CHARLES SURFACE True, brother, as you were going to say. Then, seriously, I never had the least idea of what you charge me with, upon my honour.

JOSEPH SURFACE *(aloud)* Well, it will give Sir Peter great satisfaction to hear this.

CHARLES SURFACE To be sure, I once thought the lady seemed to have taken a fancy to me; but, upon my soul, I never gave her the least encouragement. Besides, you know my attachment to Maria.

JOSEPH SURFACE But, sure, brother, even if Lady Teazle had betrayed the fondest partiality for you–

CHARLES SURFACE Why, lookee, Joseph. I hope I shall never deliberately do a dishonourable action; but, if a pretty woman were purposely to throw herself in my way, and that pretty woman married to a man old enough to be her father–

JOSEPH SURFACE Well!

CHARLES SURFACE Why, I believe I should be obliged to borrow a little of your mortality; that's all. But, brother, do you know now that you surprise me exceedingly by naming *me* with Lady Teazle, for, faith, I always understood *you* were her favourite?

JOSEPH SURFACE O, for shame, Charles; this retort is foolish.

CHARLES SURFACE Nay, I swear I have seen you exchange such significant glances.

JOSEPH SURFACE Nay, nay, sir, this is no jest.

CHARLES SURFACE Egad, I'm serious. Don't you remember? One day when I called here–

JOSEPH SURFACE Nay, prithee, Charles–

CHARLES SURFACE And found you together.

JOSEPH SURFACE Zounds, sir, I insist–

CHARLES SURFACE And another time when your servant–

JOSEPH SURFACE Brother, brother, a word with you. *(aside)* Gad, I must stop him.

CHARLES SURFACE Informed me, I say, that–

JOSEPH SURFACE Hush! I beg your pardon, but Sir Peter has overheard all we have been saying. I knew you would clear yourself, or I should not have consented.

CHARLES SURFACE How, Sir Peter! Where is he?

JOSEPH SURFACE *(softly)* There.

JOSEPH SURFACE points to the closet.

CHARLES SURFACE O, 'fore heaven, I'll have him out. – Sir Peter, come forth.

JOSEPH SURFACE No, no!

CHARLES SURFACE I say, Sir Peter, come into court.

CHARLES SURFACE pulls in SIR PETER TEAZLE.

What, my old guardian, what, turn inquisitor and take evidence, incog.?

SIR PETER TEAZLE Give me your hand, Charles; I believe I have suspected you wrongfully. But you mustn't be angry with Joseph; 'twas my plan.

CHARLES SURFACE Indeed!

SIR PETER TEAZLE But I acquit you. I promise you I don't think near so ill of you as I did; what I have heard has given me great satisfaction.

CHARLES SURFACE Egad, then 'twas lucky you didn't hear any more– *(half aside)* wasn't it, Joseph?

SIR PETER TEAZLE Ah, you would have retorted on him.

CHARLES SURFACE Ay, ay; that was a joke.

SIR PETER TEAZLE Yes, yes; I know his honour too well.

CHARLES SURFACE But you might as well have suspected him as me in this matter for all that– *(half aside)* mightn't he, Joseph?

SIR PETER TEAZLE Well, well, I believe you.

JOSEPH SURFACE *(aside)* Would they were both well out of the room.

Enter Servant, who whispers to JOSEPH SURFACE.

SIR PETER TEAZLE And in future, perhaps, we may not be such strangers.

JOSEPH SURFACE *(aside, to Servant)* Lady Sneerwell! Stop her by all means.

Exit Servant.

Gentlemen, I beg pardon; I must wait on you down stairs. Here is a person come on particular business.

CHARLES SURFACE Well, you can see him in another room. Sir Peter and I haven't met in a long time and I have something to say to him.

JOSEPH SURFACE *(aside)* They must not be left together. I'll contrive to send Lady Sneerwell away, and return directly. *(aside to SIR PETER)* Sir Peter, not a word of the French milliner.

SIR PETER TEAZLE O not for the world!

Exit JOSEPH SURFACE.

Ah, Charles, if you associated more with your brother, one might indeed hope for your reformation. He is a man of sentiment. Well, there is nothing in the world so noble as a man of sentiment!

CHARLES SURFACE Pshaw! He is too moral by half, and so apprehensive of his good name, as he calls it, that I suppose he would as soon let a priest into his house as a girl.

SIR PETER TEAZLE No, no, come, come, you wrong him. No, no, Joseph is no rake, but he is not such a saint in that respect either. *(aside)* I have a great mind to tell him; we should have a laugh.

CHARLES SURFACE O hang him! He's a very anchorite, a young hermit.

SIR PETER TEAZLE Harkee; you must not abuse him. He may chance to hear of it again, I promise you.

CHARLES SURFACE Why, you won't tell him?

SIR PETER TEAZLE No, but – this way– *(aside)* Egad, I'll tell him! – Harkee. Have you a mind to have a good laugh at Joseph?

CHARLES SURFACE I should like it of all things.

SIR PETER TEAZLE Then, i'faith, we will. *(aside)* I'll be quit with him for discovering me. *(whispering)* He had a girl with him when I called.

CHARLES SURFACE What, Joseph! You jest.

SIR PETER TEAZLE Hush! *(whispers)* A little French milliner. And the best of the jest is she's in the room now.

CHARLES SURFACE The devil she is.

SIR PETER TEAZLE Hush. I tell you. *(points)*

CHARLES SURFACE Behind the screen! 'Slife, let us unveil her.

SIR PETER TEAZLE No, no! He's coming. You shan't indeed.

CHARLES SURFACE O, egad, we'll have a peep at the little milliner.

SIR PETER TEAZLE Not for the world. Joseph will never forgive me.

CHARLES SURFACE I'll stand by you.

SIR PETER TEAZLE *(struggling with CHARLES)* Od's, here he is.

> *JOSEPH SURFACE enters just as CHARLES SURFACE throws down the screen.*

CHARLES SURFACE Lady Teazle! – by all that's wonderful!

SIR PETER TEAZLE Lady Teazle! – by all that's horrible!

— • —

Director's Notes: The "Screen Scene" from *The School For Scandal*

To try to summarize to a friend the complex antics of Frasier and Niles Crane from an episode of "Frasier" is as difficult a job as trying to describe the intricate plot details of the screen scene – so, hang on. The two central characters of *The School For Scandal* are Sir Peter Teazle, an aged aristocrat, and his new, resourceful and much younger bride, Lady Teazle. In this scene they each pay coincidental visits to Joseph Surface, the supposedly studious and moral elder brother of Charles. While Charles is described by Lady Sneerwell (the name says it all) in the very first scene of the play as a "libertine... bankrupt in fortune and reputation," his pious brother, Joseph, is beyond reproach. It is not Charles, however, who lusts after Lady Teazle, but Joseph. Indeed, Joseph is in the process of seducing Lady T. when her jealous husband drops by for a chat. Because of this unexpected arrival of Sir Peter, Lady Teazle is persuaded to conceal herself behind a screen. Just as Joseph is successfully extricating himself from this delicate situation, his brother Charles is announced, forcing Sir Peter himself to hide (at his suggestion) to overhear whatever confession Joseph can wring from Charles, who Sir Peter is convinced is his wife's lover. As the old man hurriedly crosses the stage to hide himself behind the same screen which conceals his wife, he is hastily steered toward a closet by a frantic Joseph, but not before Sir Peter catches a glimpse of "petticoat" behind the screen. Much to Sir Peter's amusement, Joseph cleverly contrives that this is merely a "little French milliner" he himself had been seducing at the time of Sir Peter's entrance.

With both jealous husband and philandering wife concealed in different parts of the room, Joseph nervously draws his brother to confess quickly that he does not love Lady Teazle. A lesser playwright would end the scene there; however, Sheridan then adds a delicious icing to the cake. Before Joseph can divert his brother, Charles blurts that he suspects it is Joseph who *really* desires Lady T. To quash this truth before it completely destroys him, Joseph is forced to reveal Sir Peter. Believing his wife is safe at least from the philandering Charles, a relieved and relaxed Sir Peter is now delighted to show his new friend, Charles, that his brother is not so pious after all, and suggests that he reveal the "French milliner" to the astounded Charles. With the removal of the screen, of course, not only is Lady Teazle revealed, but also what Joseph has been dreading, and the audience anticipating, all along – the comic humiliation of Joseph and Lady Teazle.

The most obvious acting skills required here are comic timing and reaction. The scene provides much potential for practice in these essential stage skills. It is fun, historically instructive, and technically challenging. The actor must step back from the modern stage momentarily and try to re-create some acting techniques of the Restoration. (The result can be no worse than those wintry performances by the officers of the Canadian garrison, and perhaps, with practice, up to the standards of Drury Lane). Regardless of the stage, actors of the Restoration era (and long after) would have known and practiced the 18th century vocabulary of the stage. Today this is scholarly history, and known as *the art of gesture.*

— • —

SCENE FOUR

Leo, The Royal Cadet

On the evening of July 11, 1889, ten days after Canada celebrated its twenty-second anniversary as a nation, officers and men from Kingston's Royal Military College premiered a new musical titled appropriately, *Leo, The Royal Cadet*. This light, military opera had been penned some years earlier by George F. Cameron, himself a graduate of Queen's University in Kingston, who unfortunately never lived to see his creation take shape. Cameron died in 1885 at the tender age of thirty-one. And so, this bright, lively musical event of the year—*Leo*'s opening night—was, as well, homage to its imaginative author. The occasion also marked a significant moment in the tradition of garrison theatricals in Canada.

In the first place, *Leo* was a musical performed by Canadian soldiers, not British ones. The British army had effectively left the country following Confederation, their cultural legacy intact. *Leo* was in many respects a typical garrison theatrical. Billed as "A Spirited Military Opera," it offered simply drawn character types, a little like Lescarbot's "Tritons," permitted movement and dialogue, and possessed a singular intention to entertain, as the speaker of *The Halifax Prologues* had promised the audience of his day.

In addition, *Leo* featured romance (including the final, dramatic return of our hero, Leo, thought dead by his true love, Nellie) and many handsome, young officers valiantly defending the far reaches of the British Empire. *Leo* was melodrama, choruses, and cultural propaganda all set to a stalwart marching tune. It was also war propaganda: patriotic songs, especially lyrics such as those sung by Bloodswigger in "Glory and Victory," reflect popular sentiments of the era in Canada, and go a long way to prove that theatre was indeed the effective propaganda tool British garrison commanders had hoped. (One measure of this effect may well have been the massive enlistment of Canadians in 1914). Certainly the enthusiasm of loyal colonials for the motherland gave *Leo* its unstoppable momentum. The velvet glove proved a mighty sword.

The musical began when Oscar Telgmann, a Kingston music shop owner, scored Cameron's play from the libretto by George's brother, Charles. From opening night in Kingston, *Leo* went on to a "national tour" which included Ottawa (on New Year's Night, 1889), Guelph, Toronto, Woodstock, and even an international venture to Utica, NY. Judging by the newspaper reviews of these performances, *Leo* was a hit in every venue:

> *Leo* has an abundance of tuneful music. Its Military Character gives it brightness. It is not marred by parts that "drag." Its thorough Canadian Character strikes a responsive chord in all Canadians. [35]

...The Royal Cadet reflects credit upon its authors. There is such a variety of characters that great scope is given for the display of every talent. There are soldiers and a fort, a man of the world and naughty dudes, pretty girls, countrymen, Zulus and civilians; and all of all nationalities. The Zulus were the fiercest things seen here in years. [36]

It is easy to see why. The characters are strong; a good chorus is only interrupted for necessary action; and the audience is treated to settings both familiar (Kingston) and exotic (South Africa); the climax offers a compelling stage battle. Although neither the clever repartee nor the characterization is up to the standards of Sheridan, *Leo* is a bold and creative demonstration of garrison theatre at its best.

— • —

LEO, THE ROYAL CADET

from Act One, Scene One

Picnic ground at Kingston Mills.

GASPARD Yes, landlord, it's a fact. Every time I empty a bottle of Burgundie, I feel a thrill pass around my collar and shoot clear through to the heels of my boots.

QUIP You must have felt many a thrill in your collar, then.

GASPARD Several, landlord, several – but we won't pursue the theme any further.

QUIP I'm agreeable – on the principle that if you want a hen to lay, you mustn't go too near her nest.

GASPARD Yes; that for one thing.

QUIP And for another?

GASPARD That I would rather think of the goblets I am yet to empty than of the ones I've emptied already.

QUIP So it's "coming events" that catch you, eh?

GASPARD If it's a dozen of Burgundy that's coming – yes!

QUIP You're a queer sort of fish, Gaspard. A strange fellow!

GASPARD Right, my ancient fossil! For strange times it takes strange fellows. But *(looks out)* here's a stranger coming.

QUIP *(starting up)* A stranger!

GASPARD I mean a stranger fellow than I am.

QUIP Bah! I thought you meant a traveller.

GASPARD A traveller, oh no! It's only sweet Wind, the poet.

LEO He looks as if he were composing a sonnet on his lady-love's locks.

BLOODSWIGGER Or apostrophizing starlight on a drum stick.

QUIP You're both wrong. Wind is getting up a new opera of some sort, and he's roaming around like the roaring lion of which you've *not* all heard, seeking what ideas he may devour.

GASPARD Oh, he's looking up material, is he? He's going the other way. I'll hail him.

QUIP *(and all)* No, no; don't!

GASPARD No? Why?

QUIP Because we're going to have another song.

GASPARD What of that? Wind can sing too. *(calling off right)* Hello! Wind, old chap! Change cars and blow yourself this way. There; he heard me; he's coming. Slow though – like the end of the world.

BLOODSWIGGER Oh, he's a nuisance!

GASPARD Like the end of the world again. But what have all you chaps got against me?

SEVERAL Nothing – nothing.

LEO Not much, I haven't.

QUIP I have.

GASPARD What?

QUIP Fifty, and fifty, and fifty, – a dollar and a half. *(ALL: Ha, ha, ha.)*

GASPARD Oh, confound you and your dollar and a half! You and Shylock should have been partners. But here's our gentle breeze. Come on, old man.

> *Enter WIND.*

WIND *(chord in C)* "God rest you, merry gentlemen,
May nothing you dismay–"

LEO Hold on, there. This ain't Christmas! And we don't want any carolling. Give us something about the Queen's birthday.

ANDY The Queen, be blessed! Are you going to let the Queen spoil a good song?

BLOODSWIGGER Come, come, now – drop that! No man shall say a word against her Majesty while I've an arm to strike for her. Take that back, or *(drawing sword)* I'll split you like an eel.

ANDY Split me, will you? Well, try it on! *(with a club in hand)*

QUIP No, no, gentlemen! *(stepping between)* No quarrel!

BLOODSWIGGER Well, let him take it back. No man shall speak slightly of the Queen while Wellington Bloodswigger wears her livery.

GASPARD Certainly not. But are you going to let the Queen spoil a good song?

BLOODSWIGGER A song?

QUIP Yes, a song. What say you, boys?

ALL The song! The song!

ANDY All right, lads! The song you shall have: but, first, to soothe the Captain's feelings, a bumper to the Queen.

ALL *(clinking glasses)* The Queen!

BLOODSWIGGER *(shaking hands with ANDY)* All right, old boy. Duty's due. I can't go back on my colours. *(pointing to jacket)* And now that I've done my duty, do you do yours? The song!

ANDY But, the chorus?

ALL We'll attend to that.

ANDY So be it. Well, here's to Liberty!

> *Song: "Crook The Elbow." ANDY solo.*

Crook the elbow – lift the chorus!
What care we for crown or pall
All is ours that lies before us
Liberty for one and all!

Have these houses? They must lose them
When we've taught the nabobs how

CHORUS
Crook the elbow – lift the chorus!
What care we for crown or pall
All is ours that lies before us
Liberty for one and all!

WIND Aw, bai Jove! Did you heah that? What blooming fine sentiments those are – hey? And poetwy, too. I'll just wite that down befoah I fohget it. Aw – just how does that go now?

Crook the chorus – lift the glasses!
What care we for pall or crown?
All who do not drink are asses,
Take your swig *(lifting glasses)*

QUIP And pay cash down!

ALL Hahaha!

GASPARD He had you there, Wind, old fell. The publican is one too many for the poet.

WIND Bai Jove! *(gasping)* He's dwiven all the west of the song out of my mind! Aw, Gaspard, how did that song go?

GASPARD The way of all flesh, my chicken!

LEO But, Gaspard, you're a traveller, aren't you?

GASPARD Some, my infant, – just a few.

LEO Well, tell us some of the sights you have seen,–

BLOODSWIGGER Or the deeds you have done,–

QUIP Or the places you have been.

GASPARD Come, come – draw it mild: I'm no talker, I'm not.

BLOODSWIGGER But, you're a singer, which is better.

GASPARD Oh, if it's a song you want–

WIND *(aside)* that's just what I do want – for my new Faewy Opewa.

ALL Dry up, Wind. Silence for Gaspard's song!

GASPARD All right gentlemen, here you are:–

> *Song: "The Bohemian." GASPARD solo.*

I've written some Psalms and some songs,
I've dabbled in most of the arts:
Quixote-like, righted some wrongs–
In fact, I have played many parts.

I have seen both the bright and the dark
Of the world and the things that are its,
Like the dove that flew forth from the ark:
In a word, I am given to flits.

CHORUS
For the life of a rover is mine,
A rover by land and by sea:
With a lady to love and a flagon of wine,
Oh, the World is the Village for me!

GASPARD
Today, as you see, I am here,
Enjoying my pipe and my bowl:
Tomorrow, and I may appear

Inscribing my name on the Pole.
The next day may see me once more,
Content as a hog upon ice,
Far down on the Florida shore,
Existing on bacon and rice.

Repeat Chorus.

QUIP   That's what you may call a song, Captain. In the words of my late lamented
grandfather, "That's a song as is a song." The World is the Village for me.

WIND   *(hums)* Oh, the life of a poet is mine,
And my opewa soon you will see:
For the lady I love is flagon of wine
And that is the spooning of me!

Aw, bai Jove, don't you know! I'll just wite that down befoah I fohget it.

LEO   I wish I had travelled as you have and seen as much of the world as you,
Gaspard.

BLOODSWIGGER   You're better as you are, my lad. Gaspard's travelling has not
improved his morals much.

GASPARD   As much as your soldiering has done yours! But, then, a soldier has no
morals.

BLOODSWIGGER   No morals! Don't listen to him, boy! If the sacred
performance of duty in the teeth of danger, and oftentimes of death, be not
morality, where will you find it? Strike from the pages of your history the
deeds of heroism and self-sacrifice done by the soldier at home and abroad,
and the ethics of humanity could be written in a small compass.

GASPARD   Bah! A soldier is only a machine – a marionette pulled by his
commanding officer. There is no morality in *Necessity.*

BLOODSWIGGER   Tush, tush, Gaspard! You are out of your head. While you are
squandering your life and means in pursuit of pleasure, the soldier is using his,
in protecting the life and prosperity of this fellow and in upholding the honour
of his country. Never heed him, boy! The song you have just heard is that of
a man with little Past, less Present, and no Future. *(takes LEO to front of stage)*
But now listen to me while I tell you what your own afterlife will be as
a British Soldier.

ALL   *(standing and drinking)* The army! The army!

Song: "Glory and Victory."

BLOODSWIGGER   *(solo)*
I cannot sing of ladies fair,
Or damosels of high degree;

For themes like these let others care,
Such things are bubbles all to me.
More manly thoughts usurp my breast
Than love's delights or love's alarms:
Fill up! My toast is of the best–
The good old *first* profession – Arms!

Glory and Victory!– These are the themes I sing,
And these I follow around the world as the swallow follows the spring:
Glory and Victory! This is the soldier's aim
With sword and shield, in an open field,
To win a wreath of Fame.

CHORUS
Glory and Victory!– These are the themes I sing,
And these I follow around the world as the swallow follows the spring:
Glory and Victory! This is the soldier's aim
With sword and shield, in an open field,
To win a wreath of Fame.

BLOODSWIGGER *(solo)*
The dance, the song – be these for you;
The stirrup-cup for me, who go
To war it with the tried and true
Against the fierce and faithless foe.

For stately courts that some hold dear
I have no love – or lordly halls:
I breathe the purest atmosphere
Upon the field where duty calls.

Repeat Chorus.

LEO That settles it, Captain! I'll be a soldier – Hurrah for the army!

BLOODSWIGGER Spoken like a man! You'll never regret it!

All repeat the Chorus.

— • —

LEO, THE ROYAL CADET

from Act Four, Scene One

The Village Green. Home on the St. Lawrence River. NELLIE discovered sitting on a mound, mourning for LEO's death.

NELLIE Oh, I could bear it better had we parted in kindness. My poor, dear boy –
dead! And I told him to go and to come back with a cross upon his breast, or
not at all. Shall I ever forget the look which he gave me when I said this! How
cold he must have thought me!

> *Song: "He Sleeps The Sleep." NELLIE solo.*

He sleeps the sleep that knows no waking
Upon a far and distant shore,
Not knowing that my heart is breaking,–
Unheeding of the love I bore.

He thought me cold and cruel-hearted,
Who loved him best beneath the sky;
And then we kissed – one kiss – and parted,
Myself to live – and he to die!

> *At close of song NELLIE breaks down, and as she seats herself on the
> grass, enter CAROLINE and MAIDENS.*

CAROLINE *(going over to NELLIE)* Nellie, dear, you mustn't give way like this.
If Leo is gone, he died like a soldier, doing his duty and loving you to the last.
And though his body may be dead, his spirit is not. And that spirit will love
you forever. Love, dear, after all, is the best thing, for it is imperishable. Listen!

> *Song: "True Love Can Never Alter." CAROLINE solo.*

True love can never alter,
True love can never die;
False love alone can falter,
False love alone can fly.

Love, darling, needs to borrow
No beauty fro the morn;
Through day to the to-morrow
It smiles with scorn on scorn.

On hate – but devils only
Can hate – it ever glows;
True love leaves no heart lonely,
It glads where'er it goes.

Even through the dust and ashes
Of hope, wet by sad tears,
It flings a flame which flashes
Athwart the coming years.

Aye, as the wild years, flying,
For swiftness lose their breath,

It goes with them: in dying,
It takes the hand of death.

Enter WIND, in full uniform, bronzed, etc.

CAROLINE AND MAIDENS Mr. Wind! *(crowding around him)*

MAIDENS And you're alive – you're not dead – you weren't killed after all!

WIND Aw, no – I mean, yes – I *am* alive – I'm not dead – I wasn't killed – as, no bai Jove! Pwetty neah it, though – aw, yes!

CAROLINE *(shaking her)* Nellie, here is Mr. Wind.

NELLIE *(starting violently)* Mr. Wind!

WIND *(coming over)* Aw, yes, Nellie – poor old Wind is back again.

NELLIE *(taking both hands)* How can I thank you for your noble conduct! You saved poor Leo's body for us, if you couldn't save his life. What a noble fellow you are!

WIND Aw, don't, now! You'll make me bweak down if you don't stop – *(in great confusion)*

NELLIE And you brought back his body.

WIND Aw–

NELLIE You did not bury him there? You didn't? You didn't?

WIND Aw, no! Of course not, my dear! *(aside)* Aw, dem it! This is worse than the – aw – Zulus.

NELLIE Oh, thank you! Thank you! And when will it be here?

WIND It? Aw–

CAROLINE Yes, it – the body – Leo's body!

WIND Leo's body? Why – here it comes!

Soldier's tramp is heard, and the chorus "Glory and Victory."

NELLIE *(starting back)* I do not understand!

Chorus louder and louder, and enter the Soldiers, CAPT. WELLINGTON, the COMMANDANT, LEO, with broken arm and Victoria Cross, also with a star.

NELLIE *(with a shriek)* LEO! *(rushes towards him)*

WIND That's the way I bwought him home to you.

LEO Nellie! *(embracing her)*

WIND Aw, bai Jove! No one – aw – hugs me, don't you know!

> *CAROLINE and MAIDENS throw their arms about him and half choke him.*

Aw, help! *(as they release him)* Bai Jove! I'll just wite that down befoah I fohget it.

CAROLINE, NELLIE AND MAIDENS
True love can never alter,
True love can never die;
False love alone can falter,
False love alone can fly.

ALL
True love can never alter,
True love can never die;
False love alone can falter,
False love alone can fly.

Glory and Victory! – These are the themes I sing,
And these I follow around the world as the swallow follows the spring:
Glory and Victory! This is the soldier's aim
With sword and shield, in an open field,
To win a wreath of Fame.

— • —

Director's Notes: *Leo, The Royal Cadet*

The plot is simple: Leo is a young man looking for a purpose in life. The curtain rises on a "Picnic ground at Kingston Mills" when Leo and his male companions have been temporarily abandoned by the "ladies" who are "away gathering flowers." Leo discovers his friends have plenty of musical advice for him on his future.

Gaspard, the "man of the world" referred to in the review, opens the musical with a song celebrating the pleasures of a good "burgundie" wine and the freedom of the wanderer's life with the drinking song, "Fill Up The Bowl, Boys." This quick and cheerful drinking song in 6/8 time sets the military tone of *Leo*. It is followed by several beats of similarly-paced dialogue that, after Quip the Landlord's suggestive pun, introduces the remaining male leads. Wind, the poet, is the comic relief of the piece. He joins the military with Leo and ventures to South Africa to fight the Zulus with our hero. It is also Wind who brings the news, in typically comic fashion, to Nellie that Leo is still alive and thus cues their romantic reunion and final duet and chorus in Act Four. Wind's character is played with an obvious lisp and all the affected, "nerd-like" airs the actor can muster. Wellington Bloodswigger, as his name unmistakably implies, is a career soldier brimming with patriotism. He and

"Andy" cross over respect for the Queen. (In the premiere version of the script, Andy was a character named "Schouvaloff" – pronounced "shovel-off" surely – and sang a tune titled "Socialism." Interestingly, because his character or his politics weren't portrayed foolishly enough perhaps for *Leo's* conservative audience, this character's lyrics were reduced, with lines implying class revolt removed for the tour of *Leo*.)

To draw Scene One to a close, and to return to the theme of Leo's dilemma over his future direction, Gaspard and Bloodswigger battle it out musically for the heart of our hero. Gaspard sings "The Bohemian," extolling the "life of the rover," but is no match for the compelling and patriotic march led by Bloodswigger, "Glory and Victory," the signature piece of *Leo*, that gives the scene a rousing and decisive finish when Leo declares: "That settles it, Captain! I'll be a soldier – Hurrah for the army!"

Act Two is devoted to the romance of Leo and Nellie, as both Leo and Wind train at the Royal Military College. Act Three opens with news of commissions in the army for both men, and finishes with what must have been a remarkable battle scene. The soldiers are sent to South Africa to quell a Zulu uprising in "Isandula," giving the Victorian audience the mix of patriotism and exoticisms they had come to expect from melodrama of the time. The Zulus may have been "the fiercest things" seen in little Woodstock, Ontario, for a long time, but Cameron, to his credit, gives them a notable song and chorus before the battle that shows insight perhaps beyond many in his audience. Cetcho, the Zulu chief, sings "The Stars As They Look" which boldly curses "the Northerner" and asks:

> But the justice we asked – our possession from birth –
> We shall take with the brand and the shield
> And the whites who would trample our dear native earth
> Shall yet learn how the Zulus yield!

Act Four begins with solo lament sung by Nellie titled "He Sleeps The Sleep," mourning the loss of Leo. Then, Caroline, her best friend, consoles her with her solo, "True Love Can Never Alter." If the audience isn't set by now for a dramatic reversal and a rousing finale, they never will be, and the musical ends with the return of Wind, then Leo, and the reunion of the lovers.

The excerpts are taken from the opening and closing acts. They should provide enough for a simple reading with the songs spoken or chanted, giving a reasonable taste for both the tone of the piece and character of *Leo*. And, for those with a little talent on the piano and some courageous singers and chorus, the fun is trebled by playing the score provided in an appendix to this book (pages 262–73). As in any musical, the dialogue is secondary means of communicating both story and character. These pieces, once heard, also set an unmistakable and enjoyable Victorian "air" for *Leo*. The four solos chosen provide enough opportunity for individual performers of both genders to shine.

The selections begin just *after* the opening song with the dialogue that introduces the male leads, Gaspard, Quip, Leo, Bloodswigger, Wind and Andy, together with the male chorus – a drinking scene filled with loud voices and lusty song. I've included just the chorus of "Crook the Elbow" to set the tone. It is followed with some character dialogue for Wind, and then Gaspard's solo, "The Life Of A Rover Is Mine," extending the cheery allegretto mood of the first two songs, and leading to the introduction of the tune the audience leaves humming, "Glory and Victory." Begun by Bloodswigger, the signature piece is then sung by all present as loudly and as gloriously as possible. The next song is from the closing act, Nellie's "He Sleeps The Sleep," followed by Caroline's attempt to cheer her, "True Love Can Never Alter." Subsequent to the final lines, the piece can be effectively ended with another chorus of "Glory and Victory," sung by all.

— • —

ENDNOTES to Chapter One: *The Velvet Gloves of the Garrison*

1   Leslie O'Dell, "Amateurs of the Regiment" in Anne Saddlemyer, ed. *Early Stages: Theatre in Ontario 1800–1914* (Toronto: Ontario Historical Studies Series, 1990) 54.
2   Natalie Rewa, "Garrison Theatre" in Eugene Benson and L.W. Conolly, eds. *The Oxford Companion to Canadian Theatre* (Toronto: Oxford University Press, 1989), 224–26.
3   O'Dell, "Amateurs of the Regiment" 52.
4   Anton Wagner, ed. *The Brock Bibliography of Published Canadian Plays in English 1766–1978* (Toronto: Playwrights Canada Press, 1980), iii.
5   This quotation and above in O'Dell, "Amateurs of the Regiment," 54.
6   Marc Lescarbot quoted by W.L. Grant in his Introduction to "Le Theatre de Neptune" in *Queen's Quarterly*, Vol. 34 No. 2 (October, 1926), 216 (italics added).
7   Ibid., 216.
8   Patrick O'Neill, "Prologues and Epilogues as Performed on English Canadian Stages" in *Scripts and Documents in Electronic Form* at the ACTS (Atlantic Canada Theatre Scripts) site of *The Electronic Text Centre of the University of New Brunswick Libraries*, http://www.lib.unb.ca/Texts/Theatre/
9   Ibid., 1.
10   *The Drury Lane Prologue by Samuel Johnson and The Epilogue by David Garrick, 1747* Humphrey Milford, ed. *(London: Oxford University Press, 1924)*
11   O'Neill, "Prologues…," 1.
12   Robertson Davies "The Nineteenth Century Repertoire" in Anne Saddlemyer, ed. *Early Stages*, 90.
13   For this quotation and much of what follows, Ron Cameron, *Acting Skills For Life* (Toronto: Simon and Pierre, 1991), 314.
14   Rewa, "Garrison Theatre," 224.
15   Davies, "The Nineteenth Century Repertoire," 103.
16   Ibid., 104.
17   Quoting Johannes Jelgerhuis, a Dutch teacher and actor in the early 19th century, in Dene Barnett, *The Art of Gesture: The Practices and Principles of 18th Century Acting* (Heidelberg: C. Winter, 1987), 7.
18   Barnett, 11.
19   Ibid., 14.
20   Ibid., 10.
21   Ibid., 33.
22   Ibid., 18.
23   Ibid., 18.
24   Ibid., 89.
25   Ibid., 95–96.
26   Ibid., quoting Johannes Jelgerhuis, 98.
27   Ibid., 10.

28 Ibid., quoting Gilbert Austin, 333.
29 Ibid., 446.
30 Ibid., quoting Wilkes, 47.
31 Ibid., quoting Austin, 68.
32 Ibid., 36.
33 Ibid., quoting Henry Siddons, 77.
34 Ibid., 440.
35 Quoted in a review (undated) from the *Guelph Mercury* in the introductory pages in George Frederic Cameron and Oscar F. Telgmann, *Leo, The Royal Cadet* (Kingston: Henderson and Co., 1889).
36 Ibid., from the *Woodstock Sentinel Review*, also undated.

chapter
2

The Baron Bold

An evening at the theatre in Victorian Canada was as common as a night out at the movies a century later. Touring theatre companies, performing everything from melodrama and farce to the classics, trod the boards in opulent (if fire-prone) venues called "opera houses," which were the centrepieces of every city and town from Halifax to Winnipeg, from Niagara to Rat Portage, where the imposing, four-storey Hilliard's Opera House dominated the site of the future city of Kenora.

In these generally prosperous years surrounding Confederation, towns and cities boomed—Ontario alone shot up from 952,000 citizens in 1851 to 2.7 million by 1914—and for the first time, urban outpaced rural growth.[1] With the addition of the Grand Trunk Railway (1856), and later the nation-building Pacific Railway (1885), travelling actors met welcoming audiences in virtually every whistle stop in the new country.

Plentiful patrons, accessible railways and reliable ocean crossings from Great Britain and Europe bore touring companies and their pantheon of aging, foreign stars into the lives of most Canadians of the 1800s. Legends, such as Sir Henry Irving, the Polish star Helena Modjeska, and the great Sarah Bernhardt (who toured Canada no less than nine times from 1880 to 1917), played their favourite Shakespearean roles or indulged in the parts that had made them famous. Local, "stock" (repertory) actors played the supporting roles.

This professional arrangement became a cultural metaphor as well. While detrimental to the development of Canadian theatre, the tours and their stars made theatres profitable enough to flourish, supporting a wide spectrum of secondary theatre work. By the close of the century, entrepreneurs had replaced even the local actors with entire touring casts and, to increase revenues further, had bought theatre chains, controlling the distribution of product as well. Gilbert and Sullivan's remarkably successful *H.M.S. Pinafore* toured this way – which, though ensuring a consistent profit, pushed locals to the back of the stage – or off it entirely.

The curtain fell unexpectedly on all this enterprise. Its bustle was replaced by the grim sound and fury of the First World War. Not long after came commercial radio, and then the Hollywood film. The overwhelming popularity of these modern media announced the beginning of a new age that struck from the theatres of Canada forever the grand gestures of Victorian stage.

Within these years, though, a Canadian theatre tradition was confirmed. Actors had emerged from the garrison to play the centre of town. Inspired by the surge of theatrical activity (even though much of it appeared, ironically, designed to keep local talent from their own stages), Canadian actors, managers and playwrights found the Victorian age to be fertile ground for the culture of theatre. Admittedly, very few performances at this time were plays written by Canadians. Yet, there were notable exceptions. These reflect both the culture of the times and the emergence of Canadian taste for political satire – perhaps itself a legacy of the light-hearted revues at the garrison.

From the 1830s on, local newspapers, or weeklies, such as Toronto's *Grip* and *The Canadian Illustrated News,* were replete with the satirical scenes and sketches of local writers. Richard Plant, in his retrospective introduction to *Canada's Lost Plays, Vol.1*, draws the vital connection between these "Punch-like" Victorian journals and their predilection for politics, and Canadian theatre tradition:

> The influence of journalistic polemical writing with its direct address to the public is evident in many nineteenth century plays.... One of the origins of contemporary Canadian theatre and drama can in fact be attributed to the conjunction of live theatre and the Canadian focus of the local press in the Canada of the eighteen hundreds. [2]

As the literary journals of the time, such as Montreal's *Literary Garland*, provided an outlet for longer, generally unstageable "poetic dramas" (the most famous of which was Charles Heavysege's *Saul* – "a sententious, prolix, and moralizing blank verse drama... now considered unreadable"), [3] such publications were invariably upstaged in importance by the satirical weeklies and their often anonymously written stabs at society.

Society Idyls was such a work. Short, set in Canada, and published under a pseudonym, it gently satirized young love. In fact, it contained a surprisingly feminist ending, appearing in the pages of *Grip* (July, 1882), a weekly journal specializing in politics and satire. The longer playlet, *The Baron Bold and the Beauteous Maid,* was also anonymous, and delightfully satirized the theatrical excesses of the most popular theatrical form of the era, the melodrama. But by far the most significant of these three indigenous dramas that appeared in weeklies was Sarah Anne Curzon's *The Sweet Girl Graduate.* This three-act play pointed the finger at a serious shortcoming in society at the time – the inadmissibility of female students to the University of Toronto. Curzon's heroine, Kate, successfully completes her degree—dressed as a man—her true identity revealed only at the graduation ceremony. The play's publication resulted, two years later, in Provincial Legislation that changed the admission requirements at the university by 1884 to include female applicants. [4]

Public performance of such playlets was limited in an age when the touring companies monopolized the stages of Canada. In spite of the predominance of largely U.S. touring companies of the *Pinafore* variety, there were successful Canadian acting companies as well. The Marks Brothers (not Marx), "the Canadian Kings of Repertoire," toured from the 1870s to the 1920s. With Christie Lake, Ontario (near Perth) as the family's permanent home, the seven brothers and their wives filled the void left by New York theatrical monopolies by touring smaller towns and villages the large U.S. companies chose to ignore. Their repertoire was the conservative, standard fare well known to audiences of the time (melodramatic classics such as *Uncle Tom's Cabin* and *East Lynne.*) [5]

The most documented Canadian touring company of the time is the Tavernier Company. Ida Van Cortland, its star, left a compelling account of her life in the theatre in a speech she gave to the Women's Club of Ottawa in 1918, some sixteen years after she left the "road."[6] Van Cortland was a rarity: a professional Canadian actor who came up through the ranks from the lowest actor of the ballet, or extra, in a Toronto stock theatre, to star by 1894 in her own company, in a theatre in Guelph, Ontario, managed by her husband, Albert Taverner.[7] The tours of Canada's first theatrical couple, Tavernier (who changed the last three letters of his name to make it sound more exotic) and Van Cortland, spanned much of the Victorian era. Her unique career offered a portrait of a life in the theatre of the time.

One of Van Cortland's most popular roles was Marguerite Gautier, the tragic heroine of Alexandre Dumas' *Lady of the Camelias*. It was a role she had learned, in her words, "at the feet of Modjeska," by playing Nanine, the servant, to the great actress's portrayal of Marguerite while on tour at Mrs. Morrison's. Because *Lady of the Camelias* was arguably the most popular play of the 1800s (later becoming the basis for Verdi's *La Traviata*), and because Ida Van Cortland uniquely represents the Canadian version of the touring company, the climactic scene of this play (taken from a prompt book script probably used by Van Cortland)[8] has been included here.

The most successful Canadian play of the 1880s, however, was also clearly a development in the tradition of "journalistic polemical writing": William Henry Fuller's comic opera, *H.M.S. Parliament; or, The Lady who Loved a Government Clerk.*[9] Fuller (himself a retired government clerk) satirized then Prime Minister John A. Macdonald's protectionist National Policy and other political leaders of the post-Confederation era. As Richard Plant notes, Fuller took polemical writing out of the weekly journal and onto the public stage. Performed first in 1880 to Fuller's home audience in Ottawa, *Parliament* was so successful that the show was then toured from Winnipeg to Halifax. It was a Canadian play, about Canada, written by a Canadian, which made Fuller "the most persistent and successful of the 19th century Canadian satirists."[10]

Theatre in Victorian Canada, then, was much more than foreign tours of British melodrama. Historian J.M.S. Careless sees a "garrison tradition" linking the performances of Sheridan in the early part of the century to satires such as Fuller's *Parliament* in the latter half. Careless notes, "In the new federal capital of Ottawa, from 1867, an increasing civil garrison of administrative and political functionaries [such as Fuller] provided a further base"[11] for garrison theatre.

The 19th century was progress. It was the building of a theatre infrastructure – from the construction of opera houses and the building of railways, to the formation of stock repertoire companies, and the development of an audience for satirical sketches in the local press. Similar to the early years of the next century, when the Amateur Theatre movement initiated a momentum for a national dramatic literature, the latter half of the 19th century furnished the stage for what was to come by furthering the traditions of the garrison. Moreover, as scholars Richard Plant and Anton Wagner suggest: "...[19th century] Canadian musical comedies, operettas, revues and melodramas… suggest the basis of a Canadian popular theatre and drama with considerable literary, social and cultural dimensions with which a comparison with 20ᵗʰ century English Canadian theatre and drama can be made." [12]

SCENE FIVE

Society Idyls

This short sketch, written in 1881 by "C.P.M.," a frequent contributor of such satirical pieces to the weekly newspaper *Grip*, offers an unexpected reversal of the innocent maiden role. [13] Miss Alice agrees to cruise up the Niagara River at midnight with her new lover (identified only as "He") and the audience expects a romantic scene of elopement. Instead, Miss Alice proves herself not like "those other maidens whose boots parade the dusty streets of Toronto," but rather a "prudent maid, a clever girl of Toronto" who deftly escapes her pursuer after roundly chastizing him for so underestimating her character.

For its time, such a delightful dialogue offers a surprisingly feminist Alice. Details such as this unusual reversal, and the surprisingly unromantic setting—on the Niagara River between the two principal forts, Fort George (Upper Canada) and Fort Niagara (U.S.), the site of major battles of the War of 1812—suggest there may be more here than a tale of romantic rejection. The readership of the satirical journal *Grip*, in July 1881, was no doubt well versed in the controversies of the day: the years of acrimonious debate surrounding Prime Minister John A. Macdonald's nationalist dream of a Pacific Railway (finally signed into law February 1, 1881), and Macdonald's Tories' protectionist National Policy of 1879. The Opposition Grits argued instead for a railway through the U.S. to the Pacific and for trade reciprocity, without tariffs, with the U.S. Both arguments were set against the background of a new cultural nationalism in Canada, known as the Canada First Movement, paralleling Macdonald's economic policies, and Ontario's strong Loyalist tradition. [14]

It would not be difficult to read this little satire as a clever allusion: the concerns of imperial nationhood versus the evils of U.S. republicanism. The "prudent maid of Toronto" refuses to marry her nameless Niagara suitor, the "kind dispenser of 'taffy'" who tries to steer our heroine away from Canada toward the U.S. at Lewistown, NY, where she must leave forever her "mamma" and "her cousins, sisters and aunts" (i.e., Great Britain and the Empire) behind. *Society Idyls* may be a measure of political allegory as well as social satire.

— • —

SOCIETY IDYLS

Scene: Boat on the river near old Niagara town. Time: Midnight.

HE Awfully glad you have come! Step on to the stern sheets, steady!
Wrap yourself well in your shawl – now steer for the Lewistown landing.
See how the lamps are gone out in the old Niagara main street–

Cold, grey court house and sombre church, like ghosts in the moonlight,
Frown over Fort St. George with its gunless, gaunt embrasures.
Starboard a point or so! Let us keep to the midst of the channel.

SHE What shall I do if mamma should wake and find I am missing?
Yet the night was so fine I could not resist the temptation,
So when mamma had gone in, and cousins, sisters, and aunts were
Safe in bed, and you asked me to go for a pull in the river,
Quite "too too" it seemed to me such a novel excitement
After that stupid dance, those dreary, conventional people!

HE Do you remember last June, when I first met you, Miss Alice?

SHE Call me "Alice," and *miss* the "Miss."

HE As I entered the garden,
There in the porch you sat, a spray of clambering roses
Bent caressing above the flower-like grace of your figure?

SHE Yes, I remember. I wore a *princesse* of wine-coloured satin
Trimmed with the real maltese, and a skirt of loveliest velvet.

HE We have met often since then, at dances, parties, and pic-nics,
Yet could I never speak as now I speak to you, Alice!
'Mid that frivolous crowd, that life insane and untruthful,
Could not profane the name of love – for Alice, I love you!

SHE Since that day at the Falls I always thought that you liked me.

HE Liked you? I *loved* you, thought of you always, lived for you only.

SHE *Apres?*

HE Be my wife. I have sufficient to live on,
Am not afraid to work, and yet will win a position!

SHE See how the dark green tide beneath us gliding unbroken,
Ever flows on the same, yet not the same for a moment!
Such am I. I like you, and yet know well that I can not
Like you long, fond youth, and kind dispenser of "taffy."
Know, had your unwise words been haply spoken to other
Maidens whose boots parade the dusty streets of Toronto
Straight had it there been run into the matrimonial prison!
I, more merciful, spare; but when the years shall have taught thee
Sense, and the ways of the world, and the noble science of flirting,
Say, "These things I have learned. I once had the greenest of chickens,
Taught by a prudent maid, a clever girl of Toronto:
So if hearts I have mashed while my pulsations were normal,
If I have played with love unsinged by the fire that is sacred,

"I was the pupil, the teacher she, to her be the glory."
Here is the wharf – good night. Forget my words – or remember!

— • —

Director's Notes: *Society Idyls*

In the classroom, most students need some help with the vocabulary of this playlet before beginning. Terms such as "sheets," which in the plural means a space at the bow or stern of an open boat (not a main sail rope), and "embrasures" which are the bevelled walls at the sides of cannon emplacements in a fort, need to be clearly understood and pronounced. Actors can have some fun with the flowery language of "He": a line such as, "There in the porch you sat, a spray of clambering roses/Bent caressing above the flower-like grace of your figure?" begs for a little excess of execution to equal the language.

Some knowledge of the geography of the setting may be useful as well. If the journey begins at Fort Niagara, then the couple travels *upstream* on the Niagara River to land at Lewistown, some 15 km south. (The unlikelihood of such a journey below the Falls, especially at midnight in an open boat, tries the imagination and lends further credibility to the allegorical interpretation.) Whether the Loyalist nature of the piece is emphasized (and getting your audience to understand that message would be a true dramatic challenge), the actors should realize that for most of the time it is midnight and they are on a rather shaky, wooden boat in the middle of a fairly substantial river. These details may provide some opportunity for a little comic exaggeration by actors.

— • —

SCENE SIX

The Baron Bold and the Beauteous Maid

Anne Saddlemyer claims, "The authors of playlets printed in the satirical newspaper *Grip*... saw their works reach the Ottawa stage..."[15] Surely the following parody of melodrama itself, by the author with the comic pseudonym, "Titus A. Drum,"[16] would have made a perfect piece for an *entr'acte* in the new capital's famous Russell Theatre or even at the home of the Governor-General, Rideau Hall. Whatever the production history, *The Baron Bold and the Beauteous Maid*, subtitled, "An Old Time Melodrama," shows that Victorian audiences grew as weary of theatre without wit or content as viewers of popular film or television fare today.

The Baron Bold is a short, three-act parody that was published in July 1884. Not unlike the previous playlet, it too has a comic twist at close when the villain's true evil nature is attributed to his authorship of editorials for *The Globe* and even worse, *The New York Police News*. Toronto's *The Globe and Mail* newspaper was published by George Brown, a father of Confederation and a leading opposition voice of his day. Ottawa's (and Ontario's) mainly Tory audience at that time would no doubt have enjoyed the jab.

— • —

THE BARON BOLD AND THE BEAUTEOUS MAID
AN OLD TIME MELODRAMA

Characters: Baron Berasco;
                 Father Twoots;
                 Maurice, The Lover;
                 Blanche, The Maid.

ACT ONE

Scene: A woodland dell. Cottage left. Enter BARON, enwrapped in black mantle.

BARON I love her. She shall be mine, beautiful Blanche, poor but proud. Why does she scorn me? 'Tis the varlet Maurice that lies in my path. Curse him! He shall be dispatched. *(draws a tremendous horse-pistol)* No, I will not soil my hands in his gore. My trusty retainers shall end his life this day.

Enter Father TWOOTS.

TWOOTS Good morrow, Baron, how goes it'with you?

BARON But ill, Father Twoots. Thou know'st I love thy daughter, but she scorns my simple love.

TWOOTS Has she dared do that, Baron? May the curses of an only father–

BARON Nay, Twoots, no sentiment. If she be not mine ere another day, thou shalt pay the forfcit. Do'st understand?

TWOOTS I doth. I will call her. *([He] goes to the cottage and calls. Enter BLANCHE.)* What is this I hear of thee? Thou scornest the Baron's suit.

BLANCHE Father, I love him not! My heart pants for another.

BARON *(aside)* She she-all be mee-ine.

BLANCHE Would'st thou have me enter a madhouse; for there I shall go if thou press the suit.

BARON Beauteous Blanche, I will not press the suit if it fits thee not. Another day I'll woo. *Adios. (Exit BARON, with curses on his lips.)*

ACT TWO

Scene: A lane leading to the castle. Enter BARON.

BARON This night shall Maurice be swept from my path. *(calls)* Tipcat and Slugger! *(Enter TIPCAT and SLUGGER.)* Are your weapons ready and your nerves steady?

TIPCAT AND SLUGGER They are, me lud!

BARON Good! You know your mee-an?

TIPCAT AND SLUGGER We doth.

BARON Then get thee to your hiding place and await the signal.

Exit TIPCAT and SLUGGER. Exit BARON, right. Enter BLANCHE, left.

BLANCHE My lovely Maurice, why comes he not? 'Twas here he promised to meet me. *(Enter BARON.)*

BARON Thy loved one is here. Why elevate thy sweet pug nose at me thusly! I'll give thee castles and gold galore, if thou wilt be mine.

BLANCHE Never!

BARON Then by St. Christopher thou shalt! *(He seizes her, they struggle. Enter MAURICE.)*

MAURICE Hold! rash man! *(BARON calls for TIPCAT and SLUGGER.)* Aha! thou call'st in vain! They are no more. Finding them hiding amidst the trees, I administered them a dynamite pill and scattered them at my feet.

(They struggle. MAURICE throws BARON to the ground, and places his knee upon BARON's third button.) Now, wretch, I have thee! Thy life shall be spared on one condition, that thou shall ne'er more accost the gentle Blanche. Do'st promise?

BARON I do. I do.

MAURICE Then get you gone. *(He flings BARON to the wings, then exits with BLANCHE.)*

ACT THREE

Scene: The same as Act One. Enter TWOOTS.

TWOOTS My daughter shall be Baroness Berasco. Let that rascal Maurice approach my humble dwelling, and by my big boots he shall suffer. *(Enter BARON.)*

BARON Thy daughter has again repulsed me. And more, my honour has been brought to the ground by the varlet Maurice. Cur-r-r-se him. Where is Blanche? *(TWOOTS calls. Enter BLANCHE.)*

BLANCHE Spare me, Father.

TWOOTS Thou shalt be the Baron's bride. Take her, Baron. *(BARON advances to take her, when MAURICE enters and pushes him away.)*

MAURICE Father Twoots, hear me. I can a tale unfold. I have powerful and convincing proofs that that man *(points to BARON)* is a traitor to his country. I can prove he is an accomplice of the "brawling brood," that he writes editorials for *The Globe*, and that he furnished sketches to the *New York Police News*.

TWOOTS Can this be true? *(He wrings his hands. BARON, during this denunciation, hangs his head. He makes a sudden movement, then falls. They rush to him.)*

BARON Gather round my friends, I am dying. How sweetly the birds sing, and how lovely looks the forest. Ah me! I admit all that Maurice has said, and more; I poisoned my dear kind grandmother and one maiden aunt, I cremated my two wives and – and – I– *(BARON dies, and BLANCHE, MAURICE and TWOOTS form a mournful tableaux around the body.)*

Curtain.

— • —

Director's Notes: *The Baron Bold and the Beauteous Maid*

The Baron Bold plays best when accompanied by suitable music before, during and between the scenes. Piano was the dominant instrument of the 19th century and thus prevalent in Victorian theatres. If Victorian pieces cannot be obtained, probably the most accessible accompaniment available today is the music of Scott Joplin.

This play is, of course, over the top in every respect. Actors should be coached to exaggerate with the worst assaults to the realistic style that they can muster. Facial and hand reactions, and the comic timing of these gestures, are skills that need rehearsal. The cast list of characters omits the two hired killers, "Tipcat" and "Slugger," and a smaller cast of four can ignore them as well in a performance, if so desired. "Baron Berasco" has some interesting ways with a vowel sound – but a creative actor can use them to his advantage to help create the mustache-tugging villain. Lastly, with less experienced actors in particular, it would be advisable to rehearse the physical comedy of the scenes, notably the "flinging" of the "Baron" to the wings by "Maurice" at the end of Act Two.

SCENE SEVEN

The Sweet Girl Graduate

"Refused! I knew it! The crass ingratitude of haughty man…" Sarah Anne Curzon herself must have muttered these sentiments—the opening lines to her most famous play—many times in her career as Canada's leading suffragist of the Victorian era. A founding member of the Toronto Women's Literary Club, and frequent contributor of essays, verse and fiction to journals of the time (and the editor of one such journal herself), Curzon was very familiar with the obstacles of gender. [17]

Not the least of these obstacles in the early 1880s was the stubborn refusal of the University of Toronto to admit women. To remedy the situation, Curzon turned her considerable editorial expertise to drama, and in 1882 published what she termed "A Comedy In Four Acts" titled *The Sweet Girl Graduate*. [18] Her satire had the effect she had hoped; on October 2, 1884, the Provincial Legislature passed an Order-in-Council requiring the University to accept female applicants for the first time.

The obvious political success of *The Sweet Girl Graduate* encouraged Curzon to attempt, toward the end of the 1880s, a serious historical drama based on the heroine of the War of 1812, Laura Secord. The play was accompanied by a series of essays and historical accounts of this period, which shows Curzon's commitment to both feminist and nationalist goals. Celeste Derkson explored this conjuncture expertly in her critique of *Laura Secord, the Heroine of 1812:* "Curzon was a member of several historical societies that had overtly nationalistic aims. She was dedicated to promoting interest in Canadian history and in seeing that women were written into that history prominently." [19] The critic concluded, "Curzon's text vacillates between adherence to colonial patriarchal ideology and the desire to give women a voice in policymaking, between stretching—even transgressing—gender limitations and reasserting them." [20]

The beginnings of these important themes were clear in *The Sweet Girl Graduate*. It was evident that Curzon used her dramas as extensions of her essays and editorials. Her play was not another short, pseudonymous, satirical jab at society for the passing amusement of her readers, but rather a forum for argument that was both entertaining and purposeful; she used dialogue as she used the essay, to dispel popular counter-arguments as well. This was the reason for the longer speeches and clever characterization found in scenes such as the one between Kate and her mother in Act I. Curzon brought a new dimension to Canadian drama.

— • —

Sarah Anne Curzon, author of
The Sweet Girl Graduate (1882)

THE SWEET GIRL GRADUATE

A COMEDY IN FOUR ACTS

ACT ONE

Scene One

Scugog. The breakfast-room in the house of BLOGGS, a wealthy Scugog merchant. At the table, KATE, his daughter, reading a letter.

KATE *(in much indignation)* Refused! I knew it!
The crass ingratitude of haughty man,
Vested in all the pride of place and power,
Brooks not the aspirations of my sex,
However just. Is't that he fears to yield,
Lest from his laurelled brow the wreath should fall
And light on ours? We may matriculate,
And graduate – if we can, but he excludes
Us from the beaten path he takes himself.

The sun-lit heights of steep Parnassus
Reach past the clouds, and we below must stay;
Not that our alpen-stocks are weak, or that
Our breath comes short, but that, forsooth, we wear
The Petticoat. Out on such trash!

Enter MR. BLOGGS.

MR. BLOGGS Why, what's the matter, Kate?

KATE Not much, Papa, only I am refused
Admission to the college. Sapient says
The Council have considered my request,
And find it inconsistent with the rules
Of discipline and order to admit
Women within their walls.

MR. BLOGGS I thought they'd say so. Now be satisfied;
You've studied hard. Have made your mark upon
The honour list. Have passed your second year.
Let that suffice. You know enough to wed,
And Gilmour there would give his very head
To have you. Get married, Kate.

KATE Papa, you vex me; Gilmour has no chance
And that I'll let him know. Nor have I spent
My youth in studious sort to give up now.

MR. BLOGGS What will you do? They will not let you in,
For fear you'd turn the heads of all the boys.
And quite right, too. I wouldn't have the care
And worry of a lot of lively girls
For all I am worth. *(He kisses her.)*

KATE P'raps not. papa. But yet I mean to have
The prize I emulate. If I obtain
The honours hung so tantalizingly
Before us by the University,
Will you defray the cost, as hitherto
You've done, like my own kind Papa? *(She kisses him.)*

MR. BLOGGS I guess I'll have to: they won't send the bills to you.

KATE Ah dear Papa! I'll make you proud of me
As if I were a son.

Enter MRS. BLOGGS. Exit MR. BLOGGS.

MRS. BLOGGS My dearest Kate,
How very late
You keep the breakfast things!

KATE My dear Mamma,
I had Papa
To tell of lots of things.

MRS. BLOGGS Your secret, pray,
If so I may
Be let into it also.

KATE Oh, it was just this letter, Mamma, from Mr. Sapient, telling me that the
Council won't let me go to University College to share the education that
can only be had there at a reasonable cost, because the young men would be
demoralized by my presence.

MRS. BLOGGS Kate, I am astonished at you! Have I not always said that
women do not need so much education as men, and ought to keep themselves
to themselves, and not put themselves forward like impudent minxes? What'll
men think of you if you go sittin' down on the same benches at the colleges,
and studyin' off of the same desk, and, like enough—for there are girls bold
enough for that—out of the same books? And what must the professors think
women are comin' to when they want to learn mathyphysics and metamatics
and classical history, and such stuff as unfits a woman for her place, and makes
her as ignorant of household work, managin' servants, bringin' up children, and
such like, as the greenhorns that some people take from the emigrant sheds,
though I wouldn't be bothered with such ignoramuses, spoilin' the knives, and
burnin' the bread, for anythin'?

KATE Now, Mamma, you say we have gone all over this before, and shall never
agree, because I think that the better educated a woman is, the better she can
fulfill her home duties, especially in the care and management of the health of
her family, and the proper training of her sons and daughters as good citizens.

MRS. BLOGGS You put me out of all patience, Kate! For goodness' sake get
married and be done with it. And that reminds me that Harry Gilmour wants
you to go to the picnic with him on Dominion Day, and to the concert at the
Gardens at night; and he said you had snubbed him so at Mrs. Gale's that he
didn't like to speak about it to you without I thought he might. Now, that's
what I call a real shame, the way you do treat that young man. A risin' young
lawyer as he is, with no end of lots in Winnipeg, and all the money his
father made for him up there; comes of a good old family, and has the best
connections; as may be a member yet, perhaps senator some day, and you treat
him as if he was quite beneath you. I do hope you'll just show a little common
sense and accept his invitations.

KATE   Well, Mamma, I think the real shame, as you call it, is that you, and other ladies, will allow your daughters to go about to picnics, parties, balls, theatres or anywhere else, with any man who happens to ask them, and without even so much as girl-companion, and yet you see nothing but impropriety in my desire to attend college, where all the opportunity of associating with the other sex is limited to a few lectures delivered by grave and reverend Professors, under conditions of strict discipline, and at which the whole attention of the students must necessarily be concentrated on the subject. As for unlimited opportunities for flirting, there are none; and the necessities of college life compel each student to attend to his duties while within the halls, and then go home; wherever that may be.

MRS. BLOGGS   It's no use talking, Kate, you won't alter my opinion. If they'd build another college specially for ladies, as I hear the Council is willin' to do, and put it under charge of a lady who would look after the girls, I wouldn't object so much, though, as I always say, I don't see the need of so much learnin' for women.

KATE   Well, Mamma, how much would be gained by a separate building? The Council, it is true, offer a piece of ground, within a few minutes' walk of the college, for a ladies' college, and promise to deliver lectures specially "altered to suit the female capacity." But if there was an intention of giddiness and flirtation on the part of the lady students, how much hindrance do you think the separate college would be? And if we can't understand the same lectures as our brothers, it is evident we can't understand the same books. – Rather a hard nut to crack, isn't it?

MRS. BOGGS   How rude you are, Kate! I am ashamed of you.

   Exit MRS. BOGGS in a rage.

KATE   Poor Mamma, she thinks her only child is a very *enfant terrible.*

Scene Two

   A lady's bedroom. KATE Bloggs and her cousin, ORPHEA Blaggs, in conversation.

ORPHEA   What will you do, dear?

KATE   A deed without a name!
   A deed will waken me at dead of night!
   A deed whose stony face will stare at me
   With vile grimace, and freeze my curdling blood!
   Will make me quake before the eye of day;
   Shrink from the sun, and welcome fearsome night!
   A deed will chase my trembling steps by ways
   Unknown, through lonely streets, into dark haunts!–

Will make me tremble if a child observes
Me close; and quake, if, in a public crowd,
One glances at me twice!
A deed I'll blush for yet I'll do't; and charge
Its ugliness on those who forced me to't–
In short, I'll wear the breeks.

ORPHEA Oh, Katie! You?

KATE Yes, me, dear coz.

ORPHEA But then your hair, and voice!

KATE I'll train my voice to mouth out short, thick words,
As Bosh! Trash! Fudge! Rot! And I'll cultivate
An Abernethian, self-assertive style,
That men may think there is a deal more in
My solid head than e'er comes out.
My hair I'll cut short off.

> *She looses down her abundant brown hair, and passes her hands through it*
> *caressingly.*

Ah, woman's simple pride! these tresses brown
Must all be shorn. Like to Godiva fair,
Whose heart, so true, forgot itself, to serve
Her suffering kind; I, too, must make
My hair an offering to my sex; a protest strong
'Gainst man's oppression.
Oh wavy locks, that won my father's praise,
I must be satisfied to cut ye off,
And keep ye in a drawer 'til happier times,
When I again may wear ye as a crown:
Perchance a bang.

ORPHEA 'Twould, perhaps, be best to wear some as a moustache.

KATE The very thing! then whiskers won't be missed.

ORPHEA But oh, your mannish garb! How dreadful, Kate!

KATE True; but it must be done, and you must help.

ACT FOUR

Scene One

A boarding-house dining room richly decorated with flowers and plants.
Twenty gentlemen, among whom is MR. TOM CHRISTOPHER, each
accompanying a lady, one of whom is MISS Blaggs. The cloth is drawn,
and dessert is on the table.

MR. BIGGS, B.A. *(Toronto University, on his feet)*
Ah – ladies and gentlemen, here's to our host,
And rising, as thus, to propose him a toast,
I think of the days which together
In shade, and in sunshine, as chums we have passed,
In love, and esteem, that forever must last,
Let happen what will to the weather.

In short, ladies and gentlemen, I have to propose the everlasting health and
welfare of our host, who should have been our honoured guest but for that
persistent pertinacity he exhibited in the matter, and which he does himself the
injustice to call womanish. But I am sure, ladies and gentlemen, no one but
himself ever accused our esteemed host of being womanish, and when we look
upon the high standing he has achieved in our University, the honour he confers
on his Alma Mater by his scholarly attainments and the gentlemanly character
he has won among all sorts of students, I am sure, ladies and gentlemen, we
should be doing great injustice to you all were we for one moment to admit that
he could be other than he is, an honour to Toronto University, and a credit to
his sex. I am quite sure the ladies are at this moment envying the happy woman
whom he will at no distant date probably distinguish with his regard, and it
must be satisfactory to ourselves, gentlemen, to know that it lies in our power,
as the incumbents of academic honours, to be able to bestow that reversion of
them on those who, having all the world at their feet, need not sigh for the
fugitive conquests that demand unceasing toil and an unlimited amount of gas
or coal-oil. Ladies and gentlemen, I call upon you to fill your sparkling glasses
to the honour of our host and college chum, Mr. Tom Christopher. And here's
with a hip, hip, hooray! and hands all round!

ALL   Hip, hip! Hurrah!

> *Tremendous cheering and clinking of glasses. Several are broken, and the
> excitement consequently subsides.*

MR. TOM CHRISTOPHER   Ladies and gentlemen, I thank you much.
For these your loving words. A third year man,
I came upon you fresh from nowhere;
This in itself a warranty for cold
And hard suspicion; but you received
Me with some warmth, and made me one of you,
Chaffed me, and sat on me, and lent me books,
And offered pipes, and made inquiries kind
About my sisters; and Time, who takes
Men kindly by the hand, made us warm friends,
And knit us in a love all brotherly.

MANY VOICES   Yes, brothers! brothers! we are brothers all!

A VOICE   And sisters!

MR. TOM I would say sisters too, but that I fear
My lady guests would think I did presume;
But yet I know, and knowing it am proud,
I hat most men here to-night would welcome all
The sweet girl-graduates that would fill the list
Did but the College Council set aside
A foolish prejudice, and let them in.
And now, I know a girl who long has worked
To pass the exams, take the proud degree
I hold to-day, and yet her petticoat
Forbade.

SEVERAL VOICES Name! Name! A toast! A toast!

MR. TOM I will not name her, gentlemen, but bring
Her to your presence, if you so incline;
First begging that you will not let surprise
Oust self-possession, for my friend's a girl
Of timid temper, though she's bold to act
If duty calls.

MANY VOICES Your friend! Your friend!

MR. TOM I go to fetch her, gentlemen; dear ladies all,
I beg your suffrages of gentle eyes
And kindly smile to greet my guest.

Exit MR. TOM CHRISTOPHER.

Scene Two

*The same. Enter MISS Kate BLOGGS in full dinner toilet of Reseda silk,
and carrying a dandelion and lily bouquet.*

MISS BLAGGS My cousin! oh, my cousin!

*Rushes excitedly forward and falls into hysterics on MISS Kate BLOGGS'
neck. The company gather round in great surprise.*

MISS BLOGGS Dear Orphea! Orphea, my dear! oh, water, gentlemen! Lay her
upon the couch. See! see! she gasps! Orphea, dear girl!

*The ladies are much alarmed, but MISS BLAGGS soon gives signs of
recovery, and sits up.*

ORPHEA *(in tears)* Oh, Kate! it struck me so to see you once again as you were
wont to be; those nasty ugly pants forever gone, and you a girl again.

KATE Dear friends, you look surprised.
Pray Heaven you'll not look worse when you know all.

I am indeed a girl, though you have known
Me hitherto as Thomas Christopher.
Four years ago I passed the exams, for
Us women, at your University.
Once more I passed. But when again I would,
I stumbled for the teaching that is chained–
Like ancient scripture to the reading desk–
Within your College walls. No word of mine
Could move the flinty heads of College Council.
Order and discipline forbade, they said,
That women should sit side by side with men
Within their walls. At church, or concert, or
At theatre, or ball, no separation's made
Of sexes. And so I, being a girl
Of firm and independent mind, resolved
To do as many a one beside has done
For lesser prize, and, as a man, sat at
The feet of our Gamaliels until I got
The learning that I love. That I may now
Look you all in the face without a blush, save that
Which naturally comes at having thus
To avow my hardihood, is praise, I trow,
You will not think unworthy; and to me
It forms a soft remembrance that will ever dwell
Within my grateful heart.
Can you forgive me?

MANY VOICES   We do, we must. All honour to the brave! Speak for us, Biggs.

MR. BIGGS   I cannot speak, except to ask the lady's pardon for our rough ways.

KATE   No; pardon me.

MANY VOICES   No! no! we ask your pardon.

KATE   If that, indeed, as I must need believe
From all your looks, you do not blame me much,
Endue me with a favour. It is this:
Let every man and women here to-night
Look out for these petitions that will soon
Be placed in many a store by those our friends
Who in this city form a ladies' club,
And each one sign. Nay more, to show you mean
What I, with swelling heart have often heard
You strongly urge, the rights of women to
The College privileges, get all your friends
To sign. Do what your judgment charges you

To help so good a cause, and let the lists
Of 1883 have no more names
Set by themselves as women. Let us go
In numbrous strength before the Parliament,
And ask our rights in such a stirring sort,
They shall be yielded. Then I shall know
Your brotherly and pleasant words mean faith,
And shall no more regret a daring act
That else will fail of reason.
May I thus trust?

ALL You may! You may.

KATE Then hands all round, my friends, 'til break of day.

— • —

Director's Notes: *The Sweet Girl Graduate*

In the first scene Curzon sets two wheels in motion. Kate receives her letter of rejection from the University of Toronto registrar solely because to admit females is "inconsistent with the rules of discipline and order." Kate appeals to her father, a wealthy Scugog merchant (a town just far enough north of Toronto to allow Kate the anonymity her plan requires). Mr. Bloggs, as the name suggests, is an easy mark for his quick-witted daughter, Kate. As much as the modern young actor may revel in Kate's independence, she may choke as she pronounces Kate's parting promise to him ("Ah, dear Papa! I'll make you proud of me / As if I were a son.") It was typical of Curzon that her heroines "vacillate[d] between adherence to colonial patriarchal ideology and the desire to give women a voice…"[21] In other words, in spite of its contemporary theme, *Sweet Girl* is firmly rooted in the 1880s, not the 1980s.

Once Mr. Bloggs exits, Kate has an extended and rather angry exchange with her mother. Mrs. Bloggs is a type to be sure: her limitations are indicated by the comic confusion of "mathyphysics and metamatics," and the general absence of final "g" in her "ing" words. This exchange may appear repetitive at first, but good pacing, emotion and emphasis render both the commonly held beliefs on marriage and education and Kate's radical departure from them clear. At the same time, the dialogue shows, at the end, the honest sympathy Kate feels toward her mother's view of the world.

The next scene introduces Orphea Blaggs, Kate's closely named character foil. It's her task to be dutifully shocked at Kate's plan to cut her hair and to "wear the breeks" or breeches (an actual theatre term of the time used when females were forced to play male roles on stage). Without a doubt, Orphea is the kind of daughter Mrs. Bloggs wishes she had.

The third scene of Act One (omitted) is completion of Kate's disguise as Tom Christopher, student undergraduate, the male identity she assumes during the time it takes her to complete her degree. Act Two has only one scene, set in a Toronto boarding house and is virtually Kate's soliloquy of worries about encounters with male students. Act Three is set two years later and offers the reading, by Orphea, of a letter from Kate after her "two years' farce" as "Tom" is complete and she is about to graduate. The audience learns that "Tom" has not only come first in Math and Natural Sciences, but received an honours in Classics and is a "Prizeman in German." Kate invites Orphea to her graduation as her "date," and furthermore informs the audience of her plan "to declare my sex in the most becoming manner to my fellow students"[22] at the ceremony.

Act Four is set in the dining room of the boarding house and is decorated with twenty male graduates, "each accompanied by a lady." Top graduate Tom Christopher is valedictorian and is properly introduced in the first scene by a classmate, Mr. Biggs. "Tom" then exits, to return as Kate to the astonishment of all the graduates in the last scene. It is a surprise ending not to be missed.

— • —

SCENE EIGHT

Camille, Alexandre Dumas (fils) and the career of Ida Van Cortland

It would be wrong to suggest that original, satirical playlets published in journals of the day formed the basis for Victorian theatre in Canada. It was the touring companies from Britain, the U.S., Europe and Ireland that filled the opera houses with melodrama and farce, monologues and magic. Canadian touring companies, such as the Marks Brothers and the Tavernier Company generally followed in their wake, choosing venues in towns small enough to be passed over by the likes of Sarah Bernhardt, Ellen Terry, and Sir Henry Irving.

Much of the repertoire of these Canadian companies was the standard fare. All touring company owners designed their programmes to please both the audience and the censors, who, in the words of J.M.S. Careless, "remained a powerful force in the pre-war province" of Ontario, as elsewhere in the country. Together with "the dominating power of older parent British and American cultures," the inevitable legacy of a new country built by waves of immigration, there was a "comparative dearth of Canadian-made drama..."[23]

The most adventurous of these Canadian touring stars was Ida Van Cortland. "Camille," she said, " was one of my strongest parts."[24] Van Cortland had placed *Camille* at the top of the company's playbill, and made Marguerite Gautier, a Paris prostitute dying of consumption, a favourite, tragic role. Surely there were safer choices given the moral conservatism of Victorian Ontario, but Van Cortland's career had been anything but acquiescent.

The censors dogged *La Dame aux Camelias* from its inception. Alexandre Dumas, son of the famous French writer of the same name (hence, *fils*), wrote the play in one week during the summer of 1849. His novel of the same title published a year earlier had been a tremendous success, and the play would go on to be the most successful melodrama of the century. Yet in Paris, the censors prevented *La Dame aux Camelias* from being performed until the change of government in 1852.

In many respects, Ida Van Cortland's life and career dared convention as well. As a teenager, she had been the only member of her family to survive the Great Chicago Fire of 1871. By the age of twenty-three, she had immigrated to Canada and had become a member of Mrs. Morrison's Grand Opera in Toronto. There, as a single woman in a new city, she managed a thirty-week season of nightly theatre. Mrs. Morrison's proved fertile ground for training as a professional actress. Van Cortland began as a member of the "ballet," which she herself later described as "the lowest rung of the ladder... the extra men and women that were always members of the company, and from whose ranks were drawn the people to fill unforeseen vacancies." The stock "ladder" was very well defined and observed "slavishly" by actors and managers alike. Van Cortland explained the "rungs," from top to bottom:

Leading man, and leading woman.
Juvenile man, and juvenile woman.
Walking gentleman, and walking lady.
The heavy man, and heavy woman (or villain and villainess).
The comedian, and soubrette.
First old man, and first old woman.
Character man, and character woman.

"…Then came the Ballet…" The fact that Van Cortland rose in her career from the lowest rung to star is progress she herself described (in all modesty) as "spectacular."

In her first season on stage at Mrs. Morrison's, Van Cortland "worked under twenty different stars… played at least forty parts, ranging from broad comedy to serious tragedy." All of these roles were small "walk-ons," carefully scrutinized by the "immediate eye of the company's stage director." This was the apprenticeship of the stock theatre. In her own words, she "learned how to walk, how to run, how to stand still—a tremendous accomplishment—how to stoop to pick up things unconsciously, things so natural and easy you would not imagine any training was required – but try to do any one of them before an audience, and see."

The successful apprenticeship of Ida Van Cortland led to supporting roles in Toronto, then New York. Here she met Albert Tavernier, a stock company actor and aspiring manager, whom she married in 1881. After a brief tour in the Maritimes with the Nannary Company, Tavernier and Van Cortland struck out on their own. The Tavernier Company, begun in 1883 and starring Ida Van Cortland, toured successfully from Montreal to Winnipeg, from Buffalo to St. Louis—and all stops between—until 1896. [25]

— • —

CAMILLE

Scene Eight

CAMILLE Leave me. *(Exit VARVILLE, c. off l. To MAD. P.)* Go find Armand, and entreat him to come to me. I must speak to him.

MAD. P. If he refuse–

CAMILLE He will not. He will seize the opportunity to tell me how he hates me. *(Exit MAD. P. c. and off l.)* What's to be done? I must continue to deceive him. I made a sacred promise to his father. It must not be broken. Oh, heaven! give

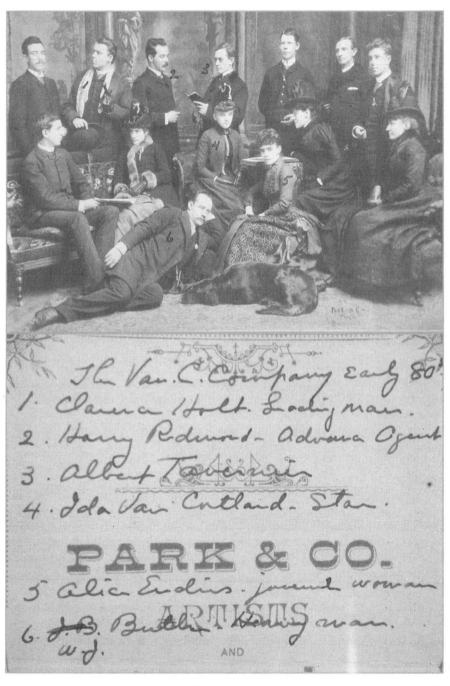

Front and back of photo card from The Van Cortland/Tavernier Touring Company, circa 1880 (Park Photographs, Brantford, Ontario). Note stock company roles.

me strength to keep it. But this duel! How to prevent it! Peril honour, life for me! Oh! No, no, no! Rather let him hate, despise me! Oh! he is here!

Enter ARMAND, c. from l.

ARMAND Madam, did you send for me?

CAMILLE I did, Armand! I would speak with you.

ARMAND Speak! I listen.

CAMILLE I have a few words to say to you – not of the past–

ARMAND Oh, no! Let that be buried in the shame that shrouds it.

CAMILLE Oh! do not crush me with reproach. See how I am bowed before you, pale, trembling, supplicating. Listen to me without hate, and hear me without anger. Say that you will forget the past, and – give me your hand.

ARMAND *(rejecting her hand)* Pardon me, Mademoiselle. If your business with me is at an end, I will retire.

CAMILLE Stay – I will not detain you long. Armand, you must leave Paris.

ARMAND Leave Paris? And why, Mademoiselle?

CAMILLE Because the Count de Varville seeks to quarrel with you, and I wish you to avoid him. I alone am to blame, and I alone should suffer.

ARMAND And it is thus you would counsel me to play the *coward's* part, and fly – fly from Count de Varville! What other counsel could come from such a source.

CAMILLE Armand, by the memory of the woman who you once loved – in the name of the pangs it cost her to destroy your faith – and in the name of her who smiled from heaven upon the act that saved her son from shame – even in her name – your mother's name – Armand Duval, I charge you leave me! *Fly – fly* – anywhere from here – from me – or you will make me human!

ARMAND I understand, Mademoiselle. You tremble for your lover—your wealthy Count—who holds your fortune in his hands. You shudder at the thought of the event which would rob you of his gold; or, perhaps, his title, which, no doubt, ere long you hope to wear.

CAMILLE I tremble for *your life*!

ARMAND You tremble for my life! Oh, you jest! What is my life or death to you? Had you such a fear when you wrote that letter? *(takes out a letter and reads)* "Armand, forget me. The Count has offered me his protection. I accept it; for I know he loves me." Love you! Oh, had he loved you, you would not have been here to-night. These were your words. That they did not kill me was no fault of yours – and that I am not dead is because I *cannot* die until I am avenged; because I *will not* die until I see the words you have graven on my brain, imprinted on the blood of him who wronged me! And should your life strings crack to part with him, he shall not live; for I have sworn it!

CAMILLE Armand, you wrong him! De Varville is innocent of all that has occurred!

ARMAND He loves you, madam! *That* is his crime – the sin that he must answer for!

CAMILLE Oh, could you but know his thoughts, they would tell you that I hate him!

ARMAND Why are you *his*? Why *here* – the plaything of his vanity, the trophy of his gold?

CAMILLE Oh, heaven! Armand! No – no! This must not be. You may retire! I have no more to say. Do not ask me, for I cannot tell!

ARMAND Then I will tell you! Because you are heartless, truthless, and make a sale of that which you call love to him who bids the highest! Because when you found a man who truly loved you, who devoted every thought and act to bless and guard you, you fled from him at the very moment you were mocking him with a sacrifice you had not the courage to make. Horses, house and jewels must be parted with, and all for love! Oh, no! that could not be! They must remain unsold, and so they did! They were returned, and with them, what? The bitter pangs of anguish and remorse which fill your breast, even while it heaves beneath a weight of gems! – the fixed despair which sits upon that brow on which those diamonds look down in mockery! And this is what the man you love has done for you! These are *his* triumphs – the wages of *your* shame!

CAMILLE Armand, you have pierced my heart – you have bowed me in the dust! Is it fit that you should die for such a wretch as you have drawn? Is it fit that you should taint your name in such a cause as hers? Remember those who love you, Armand! – your sister, father, friends, Camille! For her sake do not peril life and honour! Do not meet the Count again! Quit Paris! Forget your wrongs for *my* sake! See, at your feet I ask it in my name!

ARMAND On condition that you fly from Paris with me!

CAMILLE Oh, you are mad!

ARMAND I am indeed! I stand upon the brink of an abyss, whence I must soar or fall! You can save me. A moment since I thought I hated you. I tried to smother in my breast the truth, that it was love – *love for you*! All shall be forgotten – forgiven! We will fly from Paris and the past! We will go to the end of the earth—away from man—where not an eye shall feast a glance upon your form, nor sound disturb your ear less gentle than the echoes which repeat our tales of love!

CAMILLE This cannot be!

ARMAND Again!

CAMILLE I would give a whole eternity of life to purchase one short hour of bliss like that you've pictured now! But it must not be! There is a gulf between us which I dare not cross! I have sworn to forget you—to avoid you—to tear you from my thoughts, though it should uproot my reason!

ARMAND You have sworn to whom?

CAMILLE To one who had the right to ask me!

ARMAND To the Count de Varville, who loves you! Now say that you love *him*, and I will part with you forever!

CAMILLE *(faltering)* Yes, I love the Count de Varville!

— • —

Director's Notes: *Camille*

Dumas' play, *La Dame aux Camelias*, has several translations to English as *Camille*. One of the earliest, and the one which was the standard prompt book for Victorian productions in North America, was Matilda Heron's 1856 translation, which she produced for her own performance as "Marguerite" in Cincinnati that same year.[26] The famous New York theatrical publisher, Samuel French, unwittingly (or unscrupulously) published Heron's translation without her permission, a fact she very soon corrected in a tersely worded letter to French, dated June 24, 1856. From that date forward, Matilda Heron's name appeared on the cover of French's *Camille* as it became one of the mainstays of the Victorian stage.

Camille is set in Paris during the 1840s, at a time when France was at the height of its colonial empire, and massive amounts of wealth poured into the capital. Marguerite Gautier is an exceedingly beautiful and charming young woman, living regally among the aristocrats who have furnished her expensive apartments and attend her elegant dinner parties. She is a courtesan who coldly chooses money over love until she meets Armand Duval, and, against her better judgement, falls in love. Since she can no longer live the life she has carefully designed in Paris, Marguerite arranges to live a poor but happy existence with Armand in a country cottage. At this point, while Armand is away in Paris, his father appears and demands that Marguerite, because of her sordid past, leave his son alone. She counters that her love for his son is true, but then the old man plays a trump card: Armand's angelic sister cannot marry the man she loves because his family will not permit this marriage as a result of Armand's association with a woman of Marguerite's reputation. Seeing no way out, Marguerite reluctantly swears to Monsieur Duval she will leave Armand forever. Knowing that she will need to lie to Armand to leave him, she sends him a note that rejects his love in favour of the

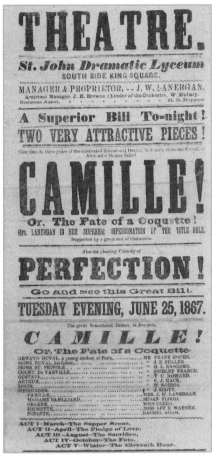

Playbill featuring *Camille*, St. John Dramatic
Lyceum, June 25, 1867.

Count de Varville, a previous benefactor whom, in reality, she despises. She returns
to Paris and sadly resumes her old life with Varville.

The previous scene is taken from Act Four and is the climax of the play. Because
the audience knows that Marguerite has lied to Armand to protect his sister, and
Armand sees only her betrayal, it is a scene that drips with dramatic irony.

The scene begins when Armand, in a jealous rage, challenges Varville to a duel.
Sensing that she must further teach Armand to "despise" her for his own safety,
Marguerite arranges a few moments alone with him. She pleads with Armand to
"Fly – fly – anywhere from here – from me – or you will make me human."
Constrained tragically by her promise to Armand's father, Marguerite struggles to
keep her true feelings from Armand. This secret finally culminates in the massive

lie neither of them wants to hear: "Yes, I love the Count de Varville!" Armand throws money at a tearful Marguerite, claiming it is her fee as a whore, and immediately challenges Varville to a duel as the scene ends. After wounding Varville, Armand flees the country. In the final act of the play, a few months later, Armand returns as a result of a note from his father who, impressed with Marguerite's honesty and suffering throughout the whole affair, has revealed to his son the true reasons behind her actions. But it is too late for anything but one final shared moment between the two lovers. Marguerite is now dying from the consumption that has plagued her from the opening scene. The play ends as she dies heroically, surrounded by Armand and the few others who know of the sacrifice she has made for love.

The role of "Marguerite" was perfectly suited to Ida Van Cortland. Like many famous actresses of her day, she built her reputation on a style strong on emotion. She recalled, "If I had to move the people, I had first to move my own heart, and many a night I have been so overcome I have been carried off the stage when the curtain fell." This concept of the actor—and her audience—who cares more for moments of high, indeed overwhelming emotion, than realism (the dominant ideal of the last century) is typical of the 19th century Romantic view of art.[27] To Victorians such as Van Cortland, the purpose of art was not to recreate or imitate nature, but to aspire to an ideal. Often this ideal was best explored blindly and irrationally, overcome by the emotions of one's heart. Although she disagreed with realism or naturalism, Van Cortland herself was aware that her romantic views were no longer mainstream by 1918:

> The modern school of acting may be naturalistic, but it often tends close upon the common-place, and unless handled with the utmost skill it is likely to be a lack of expression rather than skillful repression. It must be remembered that true art is idealistic; not the mere copying of nature.[28]

For Van Cortland and her audiences, the tragedy of Marguerite Gautier was made sublime by very profession of the heroine: a prostitute who sacrifices her love, her happiness, and her life for the well being of a person she has never met. Such martyrdom, attained by no less than a moral outcast, illuminates the ideal goodness of the human soul.

— • —

SCENE NINE

H.M.S. Parliament, or, The Lady who Loved a Government Clerk, William Henry Fuller

Many later commentators have termed Fuller's play either a parody, a farce, a comic opera, a satire, or an operetta; at the time of its first production, in February of 1880 at Montreal's Academy of Music, the programme called *H.M.S. Parliament* a *burlesque*.[29]

To a 19th century Canadian audience, as Robertson Davies noted, the *burlesque* was one of half a dozen popular styles of Victorian theatre. Burlesque audiences expected character caricature, music, a chorus and dance. "Burlesque was rowdy and irreverent, and sometimes it was dirty, as well."[30] By that Davies meant it frequently delivered a chorus of young women dressed scandalously in flesh-coloured tights (which later led to "strip" burlesque). A Victorian burlesque audience, however, "might be expected to have knowledge of the more serious drama."[31] In other words, the form was often a parody of a well-known play or opera. Fuller demanded his audience be politically aware of the issues of the day—the National Policy of the ruling Conservative government, as well as the numerous patronage scandals it had faced—and the leading politicians of the time: Prime Minister Sir John A. Macdonald (Captain Mac. A.); leader of the Opposition Grits, Alexander Mackenzie (Alexander MacDeadeye); and Minister of Finance, Sir Samuel Tilley (Sir Samuel Sillery). In addition to these luminaries, Fuller made good use of the burlesque device of comic, cross-gender roles – a male actor, for example, would play Mrs. Butterbun, and the Chorus of Senators would be men dressed as old women.

Parliament lived up to its billing. Its political and satirical style, as we have seen in most other excerpts in this chapter, was the standard form for almost all successful Canadian dramas of the time. The publication of many other Canadian political burlesques and satires—notably Nicholas Flood Davin's *Fair Grit* (1876), Jean McIlwraith's *Ptarmigan* (1895) and two others by Fuller, the *Unspecific Scandal* (1874) and *Sir John and Sir Charles* (1881)—proved the pre-eminence of this style both in journals and on stage.

Although the foreign touring companies took centre stage, Fuller cleverly used that fact to his advantage by parodying the most popular comic operetta of the era, Gilbert and Sullivan's *H.M.S. Pinafore, or The Lass That Loved a Sailor*. His sophisticated audience knew the melodies, the issues and the caricatures of *Parliament* before the curtain was raised, assuring its success. In 1880, *H.M.S. Parliament* toured nationally, playing in Ontario alone to more than twenty-four different theatres.[32] In Richard Plant and Anton Wagner's opinion, Fuller's burlesque gave the writer "one of the best records of stage production of 19th century dramatists," and made him "the most persistent and successful of the 19th century Canadian satirists."[33]

— • —

H.M.S. PARLIAMENT

or, The Lady Who Loved A Government Clerk

PREFACE

The adapter of this piece of extravagance begs to disclaim any political proclivities. He has attempted, he hopes not unsuccessfully, to get a little harmless fun out of political peculiarities and weaknesses, irrespective of party – in fact, he has endeavoured to act as much as possible after the pattern of the Irishmen at Donnybrook Fair, and wherever he has seen an available head has tried to give it a good-humoured tap, not out of any animosity, but simply for the fun of the thing. If any head should appear to come in for more than its fair share of taps, it must be attributed solely to the particular prominence of the said head, and not to any other cause. If any expression or allusion in this extravaganza should give reasonable cause of offence to any person, he will be sincerely sorry, and hereby apologizes for it in advance; but, as the epidermis of politicians is proverbially tough, he feels convinced that no offence will be taken where none is meant.

DRAMATIS PERSONAE

Sir Samuel Sillery, K.M.G.	Chief Financer of H.M.S. "Parliament"
Captain Mac. A.	Commander of H.M.S. "Parliament"
Sam Snifter	Clerk in the Sealing Wax Department
Alexander MacDeadeye	A Misanthropic Member
Tom Black	A Statistical Member
Ben Burr	A Poetical Member
Angelina	The Captain's Daughter
Mrs. Butterbun, a Monopolist	Purveyor of refreshments to H.M.S. "Parliament"

The Chief Financier's little ring of Senators and Members
Members, Clerks etc. by a full Chorus

ACT ONE

A chamber or committee room in the House of Commons. Members discovered grinding axes; others turning grindstones. On some of the axes are painted in large letters, "Section A," "Section B," "Nut-locks," "Printing Contracts," etc.

CHORUS *(sung)*
We sail the ship of State,
Tho' our craft is rather leaky;
Our grindstones swift revolve,
Tho' at times they're rather creaky.
We grind away the livelong day,
And talk in the House all night,
But if we're in luck and don't get stuck,
Our axes will soon be bright.

Enter MRS. BUTTERBUN with large basket on her arm.

MRS. BUTTERBUN *(recitative)*
Hail! gallant Members, safeguards of your nation,
I'm glad to see you at your proper station;
Relax your labours – I'll refreshments *set*,
Your axes will grind better for a *whet*.

She produces bottles of ginger beer, apples, etc. Sings. Aria.

I'm called Mrs. Butterbun, *Dear* Mrs. Butterbun,
'Tho I could never tell why,
For I sell my refreshments at very low prices,
So I'm *cheap* Mrs. Butterbun, I. ·
I supply all the Members and lobby attenders
With ginger pop, flavoured with rye;
I've apples so fruity, and oranges juicy,
For members to suck when they're dry.
Then buy of your Butterbun, cheap Mrs. Butterbun,
Members should never be *shy*.
'Tho *indeed that's a failing not often prevailing*,
Then buy of your Butterbun, buy.

TOM BLACK Well, Mrs. Butterbun, how are you today? I think I'll take a bottle of ginger pop, with the old rye flavour. How much is it?

MRS. BUTTERBUN Fifteen cents!

TOM BLACK Fifteen cents? Why, it used to be only ten.

MRS. BUTTERBUN Ah! but Mr. Black, you forgot the N.P. – everything has gone up.

TOM BLACK Now, Mrs. Butterbun, allow me to inform you that additional duties imposed by the N.P. on the imported articles which enter into the composition of your ginger beer amount exactly to one and one-thirty-second of a mill on each bottle, and, consequently, you are not justified in increasing your price fifty percent. I showed this clearly in my last leading article.

MRS. BUTTERBUN Can't help that, Mr. Black. I've got a monopoly like some of the big manufacturers, so, if you don't like to pay fifteen cents, you'll have to go without.

TOM BLACK *(aside)* Oh! confound the N.P. if this is going to be the game – it's all very well in theory, but I don't see the fun of paying fifteen cents instead of ten for my ginger beer – they'll have to increase our sessional allowance at this rate.

BEN BURR What about apples, today, Mrs. Butterbun?
An apple sweet,
I think 'tis meat
That I should eat.
That's poetry, Mrs. B. You ought to give me one for nothing for such an exquisite stanza.

MRS. BUTTERBUN Certainly, Mr. Burr; here is one.

BEN BURR But this is rotten, Mrs. Butterbun.

MRS. BUTTERBUN So is your poetry, Mr. Burr, so that's all right.

BEN BURR Are you aware, profane woman, that I am the Poet of Canada? that the roar of the mighty cataract, beside which I have been nurtured, finds an echo in my verses? Do you not know that I am to be appointed the Poet Laureate of the Dominion?

MRS. BUTTERBUN Very likely, Mr. Burr; they've been making many queer appointments lately, but if you want the apples you had better take them; they are two for ten cents.

BEN BURR Two? Why, they used to be three.

MRS. BUTTERBUN Dear me, gentlemen, I'm surprised at you. You seem to forget all about the N.P. Why, what was it for if not to put up the price of everything?

BEN BURR Oh! This is too much. *(aside)* I begin to think the N.P. is a sell, only I don't like to say so.

Enter Alexander MacDEADEYE.

MacDEADEYE I have thought it often – the N.P. is a sell.

All recoil from him, with expressions of horror.

MRS. BUTTERBUN   Why, what's the matter with the man? He looks miserable.

TOM BLACK   Don't take any notice of him, it's only poor Alec MacDeadeye – he's rather cantankerous. He used to be commander of this ship, but now he's degraded, and he's only an ordinary chap like the rest of us, and it preys upon him.

MacDEADEYE   Preys upon him! nae doot it does. How would you like it yoursel, after being captain of the ship to step down to be joost a common member of the crew?

TOM BLACK   Well, Alec, you ought to have been more civil when you were skipper, and then, perhaps, you'd have been in command now.

MacDEADEYE   Ah! that's it! – Joost because I would na condescend to humbug ye, ye turn me oot! Weel, weel, ye'll get enough humbug before ye're done, and as for the N.P., I'm joost fairly sick of it.

ALL   Oh! oh! oh!

BEN BURR   MacDeadeye, I would not wish to be hard on a man that's down, but such sentiments as yours are a disgrace to the ship.

MRS. BUTTERBUN   *(recitative)* But tell me who's yon clerk, whose roseate nose bespeaks a love of beer – or something worse?

TOM BLACK   That is the smartest clerk in all the House, Sam Snifter.

MRS. BUTTERBUN   Oh that name! Remorse! Remorse!

Enter SAM Snifter.

SAM   *(madrigal)*
The Government clerk
Loved the great chieftain's daughter.
He daren't propose,
For he could not support her,
He sang "my scanty pay."

ALL   He sang "his scanty pay."

SAM   The lowly youth
For his love did vainly sigh,
And spent too much
On bitter beer and rye.
He sang "my scanty pay."

ALL   He sang "his scanty pay."

SAM   *(recitative)*
Thanks, gentlemen, for this your kindly chorus,

But choruses yield little sustentation;
If you would kindly get my *pay* increased,
That would indeed be genuine consolation.

MRS. BUTTERBUN *(aside)* Beer and old rye must be his consolation.

ALL Yes, yes; old rye must be his consolation.

TOM BLACK But, my dear fellow, you are *too* ambitious. You can't expect the Captain's daughter to look favourably on a third-class clerk in the sealing wax department.

MacDEADEYE If ye'd ony perlitickal influence, noo, there might be a chance for ye; but, the Captains of such craft as ours don't give onything away unless they get some votes for it.

ALL *(recoiling)* Shame! shame!

SAM It's strange that the daughter of a man who commands *H.M.S. "Parliament"* may not love another who is in the same service, although in a humble capacity. For a man in this great and glorious country may rise to any position, – *if he's only got cheek enough.*

MacDEADEYE Ah! mon, cheek's a grand thing. If I'd had mair cheek I might have been Captain still.

TOM BLACK MacDeadeye, I don't want to be hard on a man who has seen better days; but such a sentiment as that is enough to make an honest politician shudder.

BEN BURR But see, our gallant Captain approaches – "bring on the banquet" – I mean, let us greet him as so great a chieftain deserves.

> *Enter CAPTAIN – cheers.*

CAPTAIN *(song)* I am the Captain of the "Parliament."

ALL And a right good Captain *he.*

CAPTAIN You're very, very good,
And be it understood
I've a large majori*tee.*

ALL We're very, very good,
And be it understood
He's a large majori*tee.*

CAPTAIN In debate I'm never slack,
Howe'er the foe attack;
And I'm good at repar*tee,*
I never, never say

A thing that's not *O.K.*
Whatever the temptation be.

ALL What! never?

CAPTAIN No; never.

ALL What! *never*?

CAPTAIN Hardly ever.

ALL What he says is always quite O.K.!
Then give three cheers to show our senti*ment.*
For the truthful Captain of the "Parlia*ment.*"

CAPTAIN I do my best to satisfy you all.

ALL But some of us are *not* content.

CAPTAIN I'll anticipate your wishes,
And see some loaves and fishes
Are served out to the malcontent.

ALL He'll anticipate our wishes,
And see some loaves and fishes
Are served out to the malcontent.

   All rub their hands rejoicing.

CAPTAIN The position which I fill
Abuse I never will
Whatever the emergen*cee.*
Corruption is a thing
I detest like anything–
And it never has been charged to me.

ALL What! never?

CAPTAIN *(confidently)* No; *never.*

ALL What! *NEVER*?

CAPTAIN Well, *very seldom.*

ALL Very seldom has been charged to *he,*
Then give three cheers to show our sentiment
For the *moral* Captain of the "Parliament."

   Exeunt all but CAPTAIN.

— • —

Director's Notes: William Henry Fuller, *H.M.S. Parliament, or, The Lady who Loved a Government Clerk*[34]

Students will enjoy performing this opening scene to *H.M.S. Parliament* after they are well acquainted with the opening lyrics and melodies of Gilbert and Sullivan's *H.M.S. Pinafore*. Fortunately, there are many websites devoted to the latter. One of the best, [http://math.boisestate.edu/gas/pinafore/web_opera/operhome.html] provides both the lyrics and midi music free of charge, thanks to Boise State University. There are many others, as any simple search will reveal.

Fuller parodies both the order and lyrics of the original songs closely, providing much of the humour and enjoyment in this opening scene, which begins with the Chorus of Members grinding the axes of patronage, and ending with the introductory song of Capt. Mac. A., I am the Captain of the Parliament. The song equivalencies are as follows:

1.   Chorus: "We sail the ship of State." ("We Sail the Ocean Blue," Song No. 1, Act 1)

2.   Mrs. Butterbun: "Hail, gallant members, safeguards of your nation." ("I'm Called Little Buttercup," Song No.2, Act 1)

3.   Mrs. Butterbun: "But tell me who's your clerk." ("But Tell Me Who's This Youth," Song No. 2a, Act 1)

4.   Sam: "The government clerk/Loved the great chieftain's daughter." ("The Nightingale," Song No.3, Act 1)

5.   Captain: "I am the Captain of the *Parliament*." ("My Gallant Crew," Song No. 4, Act 1)

It is also very common in the staging of a Gilbert and Sullivan comic operetta to devise movement or comic gesture especially for the chorus during their singing part. A simple cardboard and paper set can easily be assembled based on pictures culled from the websites.

— • —

ENDNOTES to Chapter Two: The Baron Bold

1   J.M.S. Careless, "The Cultural Setting: Ontario Society to 1914" in Anne
    Saddlemyer, ed. *Early Stages: Theatre In Ontario 1800–1914* (Toronto:
    University of Toronto Press, 1990), 18–51.
2   Richard Plant and Anton Wagner, "Introduction: Reclaiming the Past" in Anton
    Wagner and Richard Plant, eds., *Canada's Lost Plays, Volume One: The
    Nineteenth Century* (Toronto: CTR Publications, 1978), 6.
3   Richard Plant, "Drama in English" in Eugene Benson and L.W. Conolly, eds.
    The Oxford Companion To Canadian Theatre (Toronto: Oxford University
    Press, 1989), 151.
4   Rota Herzberg Lister, "Sarah Anne Curzon" in *The Oxford Companion To
    Canadian Theatre*, 127.
5   See Murray D. Edwards, "The Marks Brothers" in *The Oxford Companion To
    Canadian Theatre*, 332–33.
6   Ida Van Cortland, "Address to the University Women's Club of Ottawa" circa
    1918 in the *Taverner Collection*, Archival Collections, Toronto Reference
    Library Performing Arts Centre, Toronto Public Library. All quotations from
    Ida Van Cortland are from this source.
7   For an account of this venture see Wayne Fulks, "Albert Tavernier and the
    Guelph Royal Opera House" in *Theatre History in Canada*, Vol. 4 No.1
    (Spring, 1983), 41–56.
8   Alexandre Dumas, fils, *Camille, A Play In Five Acts*, transl. Matilda Heron
    (New York: French, 1889).
9   William Henry Fuller, *H.M.S. Parliament, or, The Lady who Loved a
    Government Clerk* in Anton Wagner and Richard Plant, eds., *Canada's Lost
    Plays, Volume One: The Nineteenth Century*, 158–93.
10 Plant, "Introduction: Reclaiming the Past," 13.
11 Careless, 32.
12 Richard Plant and Anton Wagner, "Introduction," 15.
13 "C.P.M." "Society Idyls" in *Grip*, Vol. 17, No.11 (July 30, 1881).
14 Donald Creighton, *John A. Macdonald, The Old Chieftain* (Toronto:
    Macmillan, 1955), 299–310.
15 Anne Saddlemyer, "Introduction" in Anne Saddlemyer, ed. *Early Stages:
    Theatre In Ontario 1800–1914*, 8.
16 "Titus A. Drum" "The Baron Bold and The Beauteous Maid" in *Grip*, Vol. 23,
    No.1 (July 5, 1884).
17 Lister, "Sarah Anne Curzon," 127.
18 Sarah Anne Curzon, "The Sweet Girl Graduate" in *Grip-Sack*, Vol. I, 1882,
    122–37.
19 Celeste Derkson, "Out of the Closet: Dramatic Works by Sarah Anne Curzon
    Part One: Woman and Nationhood: Laura Secord, The Heroine Of 1812" in
    Theatre Research In Canada/ Recherches Theatrales au Canada, Vol. 15, No. 1
    (Spring/ Printemps 1994), 6.

20   Ibid., 19.

21   Derkson, 18.

22   Curzon, 131.

23   Careless, 48–50.

24   All references to Van Cortland, from her "Address to the University Women's Club of Ottawa," 1–9.

25   Kathleen Fraser, "Ida Van Cortland" in *The Oxford Companion To Canadian Theatre*, 575.

26   See "The True Camille," a note on the inside cover of Dumas, *Camille*, transl. Matilda Heron (above). Heron claims to have first published her translation in Cincinnati, in April of 1856.

27   Norman A. Bert, *Theatre Alive! An Introductory Anthology of World Theatre* (Colorado Springs: Meriwether Publishing, 1994), 275–76.

28   Van Cortland, "Address...," 3.

29   Plant and Wagner, "Introduction," 12–13.

30   Robertson Davies, "The Nineteenth Century Repertoire" in Saddlemyer, *Early Stages,* 114–16.

31   Ibid., 115.

32   Murray D. Edwards, "William Henry Fuller" in *The Oxford Companion To Canadian Theatre*, 218.

33   Plant and Wagner, "Introduction," 13.

The Dominion

Years

Theatre and indigenous drama were often at odds with one another in the Dominion of Canada from the 1920s to the 1950s. During this time, the Little Theatres, amateur groups across the country, sustained theatre art, and the annual Dominion Drama Festival (1932–1970) was their national showcase. Yet the DDF was both a blessing and a curse.

The Dominion Drama Festival furnished mid-century theatre in Canada a much needed profile, giving many amateurs a national audience during the time when movie houses had replaced the opera houses; however, it was also innately colonial and elitist and, in spite of occasional efforts to the contrary, did as much to prevent an indigenous professional theatre as encourage one. Even Betty Lee, advocate and historian of the DDF, admitted, "many observers believe… the rise of the Golden Age of amateurism may have blocked the evolution of the professional system." [1] Robertson Davies, frequent playwright, director and committee member of the Festival, concluded much the same: "Though the DDF never succeeded in bringing a Canadian drama into being, it kept the whole country aware of what was being done in world theatre." [2] Nonetheless, the Festival *was* at the centre of the Canadian theatre world, especially during the decades that shouldered World War II.

The 1920s were a time of Canadian cultural nationalism, largely as a result of the colonial nation's own dramatic entrance onto the world stage after its contribution to World War I, and partly because this was an era of artistic innovation worldwide. This new nationalism naturally found expression in the arts. Painters of the now famous Group of Seven, and Tom Thomson, searched for the spirit of Canada in nature; a notable group of six Canadian poets published an anthology, called *New Provinces*, with a similar artistic treatise; theatre artists such as Roy Mitchell, Merrill Denison, and Herman Voaden attempted a national voice using drama. [3] When the Depression years took hold of Canada, a third group—from the radical Left—joined in the struggle to articulate a national drama by using the modern form of political theatre known as agitprop. This was theatre that aimed to engage their audience in the struggle for a more just society, and harkened back to the gentler satires of *Grip* magazine, and the Canadian predilection for the drama of politics.

In spite of all this creativity, the cultural establishment of Canada, moulded by its long, colonial past, endorsed the familiar British, or embraced the ubiquitous U.S. cultural exports as it had always done. Neo-colonialism had its price. By 1931, both Mitchell and Denison, two of the most visionary talents of the time, had left Canada for the U.S. [4] They had been frustrated by the same artistic indifference and resistance to innovation encountered time and again by Herman Voaden, another advocate of a Canadian national theatre, in the DDF competitions, where all of his expressionist dramas clearly mystified the foreign adjudicators (yet local reviewers had embraced Voaden's ideas). [5] And, although a socialist drama from Vancouver

won the 1936 DDF competition—momentarily crossing paths with the elite—police
in Toronto in 1933 and Winnipeg in 1934 banned *Eight Men Speak*, "Canadian
agitprop's greatest success."[6] The DDF and the "golden age of amateur theatre"
may have supplanted the perennial roots of a hardy national drama with its annual
display of imported colours.

Yet, as Robertson Davies, one indigenous playwright who did take root and
thrive under the auspices of the DDF and another preeminent talent of this period,
correctly concluded, the Festival "kept alight a flame."[7] Davies, of course, was
right; the cultural impact of the Festival on Canada cannot be ignored.

The Governor General of Canada, the Earl of Bessborough, had first lit this flame
after arriving at the start of the Depression to assume vice-regal duties. To
Bessborough (a lover of drama who had built "the best equipped private playhouse
in the kingdom" on his estate in England),[8] the Canadian theatre scene appeared
dismal: "When I arrived in 1931, I found road company activity dead. Theatres had
been taken over by film companies. Depression had practically killed touring by
professional companies from abroad."[9]

Such public despair for drama from the King's representative did not go unnoticed.
It wasn't long before Lord Bessborough, who had made his millions selling
margarine, was quickly buttered by members of the Canadian Little Theatre scene.
In spite of the first impressions of the Governor, amateur theatre *was* flourishing,
albeit in nodes, throughout the country by 1931.[10] The Governor's idea (which
had really been suggested for years by Herman Voaden and others) was the
establishment of an annual national amateur drama competition. Bessborough
proposed to the Prime Minister to unify Little Theatres, such as those in Saskatoon
and Montreal, the Ottawa Drama League, and Toronto's successful Hart House
Theatre, by assembling an aristocratic committee of politicians, university
presidents and dignitaries (notably Vincent Massey) to create the Dominion Drama
Festival, with himself as its sole patron. After a rigorous round of provincial
competitions, the regional winners competed in Ottawa for the Bessborough
Trophy – cultural silverware that would rival, he felt, the athletic ones donated by
his two predecessors, Lord Stanley and Lord Grey, to national hockey and football,
respectively.

The DDF, which lasted from 1932 until 1970, had its critics. Most despaired its
elitism, some (like Canadian playwright John Herbert) labelling the DDF executive,
as "socializing dilettantes."[11] The Festival's colonial predilection for foreign drama
was well known, as was its preference for adjudicators from Britain or France.
It took all the nationalism of Canada's Centennial year of 1967 for the Festival
organizers to require only Canadian plays, albeit for that year only.

In spite of these valid criticisms, most commentators agree that the DDF did more
to encourage Canadian drama than discourage it, especially during the lean years
of the 1930s and 1940s. Herbert Whittaker, Toronto critic, scholar, and DDF
adjudicator concluded:

> While the DDF can be faulted for emphasizing too strongly the values of foreign theatrical repertoires, it nonetheless made a great and significant contribution to Canadian drama and theatre. Unsubsidized, scattered across a vast country, the amateur theatre the Festival nourished was the bridge to the new professionalism of Canadian theatre of the 1960s and beyond. [12]

Approximating the twin mandate of CBC Radio and later Television, from its inception the DDF encouraged plays in both French and English. In addition, it provided a forum for a wealth of successful Canadian writers, directors, stage technicians and actors from both cultures, including Robertson Davies, Gwen Pharis Ringwood, Gratien Gélinas, and Marcel Dubé. As the Canadian government began to take its role in the arts in the 1950s—through the mandates of the Canada Council and the CBC—these professionals grew roots outside amateur circles, populating the stages of Canadian touring companies (like Crest Theatre) and professional houses (like the Stratford and Shaw Festivals) and the sound stages of the CBC.

Of the five scenes that follow, three were DDF finalists. Patricia Joudry's *Teach Me How To Cry* won the Best Play Award in 1956. Denison's play, *Brothers in Arms*, was such a Festival favourite to be considered "an old perennial." [13] Robertson Davies, better known as a novelist, wrote nine full-length plays and five one-act plays, many of which were produced at DDF festivals. He won Best Canadian Play in 1948, served the Festival in many capacities and, like Joudry, made the transition from amateur to professional stage, and to CBC Radio and Television. *Eight Men Speak*, because of its controversial content, never saw a second performance, let alone a Festival final, but other socialist dramas did compete and impressed adjudicators. Harley Granville-Barker gave the top play award to a Canadian social drama, *Twenty-five Cents*, in 1936. And, although Herman Voaden's expressionistic drama *Rocks* was "ruled out" by adjudicators of the 1933 Festival because of its non-realistic, expressionistic style, Voaden himself, by virtue of his talent as a Little Theatre author and director (and critic of the DDF) [14], was unmistakably part of this tradition as well.

Brothers In Arms, *Hill-Land*, and *At My Heart's Core* all dealt with the issue of life in the Canadian wilderness, and the romantic mythology of the Northland. Each playwright had a remarkably different answer to this popular notion at the time that the Canadian identity was a response to a pioneer life in the harsh, unforgiving wilderness.

Denison's satire did its best to unseat this romantic ideal. The play is set near his family estate on Lake Mazinaw (now Bon Echo Provincial Park). In 1921, this area was the backwoods of Ontario. Denison's dialogue between a patronizing Toronto businessman, his idealistic wife, and a rural backwoodsman, *Brothers In Arms*, satirized the notion that the rugged, unforgiving nature of the Canadian North had built a breed of people with the strength of spirit to match the Northland. Denison continued this theme for several plays, comedies and dramas, at Hart House Theatre in Toronto. Indeed, his first publication of his plays he called *The Unheroic North*.

Herman Voaden, like the painter, Tom Thomson, and the poet, A.J.M. Smith, promoted the notion of the heroic land, in his plays of the 1930s. *Hill-Land* showed settlers (ironically only one Ontario county to the west of Denison's Lake Mazinaw) bravely overcoming death and climate to take ownership of the harsh northland. As Anton Wagner noted, Voaden's plays "…are marked by a search for a dramatic style that would express his romantic idealism and belief in the invigorating vitality of Canadian nature." [15]

Robertson Davies, writing some twenty years after Voaden and thirty-five years after Denison, sided more with Denison than Voaden in *At My Heart's Core*. Davies portrayed the lives of three famous Canadian female pioneers, Susanna Moodie, Catherine Parr Traill and Frances Stewart during the Mackenzie Rebellion of 1837. Davies' setting was the backwoods of Lakefield, a century before, but only a few miles south of settings in Voaden and Denison. Without Denison's satire and Voaden's idealism, Davies saw the backwoods as an obstacle to personal fulfillment; he cleverly denounced the limitations that a life in the wilderness placed on creative and gifted individuals – namely Moodie, Traill and Stewart. This was a theme he repeated frequently in his many works, most directly his collection of essays, *A Voice From the Attic*. [16] If, in other works, the landscape was not the villain, then the lack of wit, culture and imagination of its citizenry prevented the gifted individual from exploring his full potential. All Davies' writing (and *At My Heart's Core* was no exception) has high expectations of the reader. "A book is a mirror. When a monkey looks in, no apostle can look out," [17] Davies was fond of saying. If audiences were up to the challenge—and those of the DDF were charmed for years—there is no more intellectually rewarding writer in Canadian literature.

Thus, drama during the Dominion period was characteristically Canadian: a creative, original heart beating within a Neo-colonial body – the genius of indigenous playwrights like Denison and Voaden was abruptly shaken by the tendencies of the DDF to promote British and French tastes, which, while it fostered talents like Davies and Joudry, ignored the social realities of the country and all but failed to recognize the rumblings of agitprop. However, from Denison's attempt to write the first consciously Canadian play in 1921 to the finely crafted works of Davies in the 1950s, Canadians began to see in the DDF the beginnings of a truly professional, national theatre.

SCENE TEN

Brothers In Arms, Merrill Denison

Vincent Massey and his "stage-struck younger brother, Raymond"[18] were both destined, by talent and by wealth, for greatness. Vincent became a diplomat, then Canada's first native-born Governor General, a patron of the arts, and chairman of the influential Massey-Levesque *Report* on Canadian arts and science in 1951; Raymond went to the stages of Broadway, followed by a career of seventy Hollywood films, and is most remembered for his portrayal of Abe Lincoln.

But, in 1919, both men were enthralled with their new theatre. Built in the basement of the student centre at the University of Toronto with money from the Massey Foundation, it was named Hart House, after the Massey patriarch, Hart Massey. The little theatre provided an "intimate playhouse, seating 450, with proscenium stage and excellent acoustics, offered outstanding facilities for actors, technicians, and audiences."[19] Vincent Massey was determined to run highly professional amateur productions at Hart House; thus "it had a great influence on the Little Theatre movement in Canada."[20] He hoped his theatre would be a Canadian version of Ireland's successful Abbey Theatre, which inspired the Irish nationalism of Synge and Yeats.

Massey recruited Roy Mitchell to be his first director, largely because of Mitchell's experience in New York Little Theatre and his originality in the use of stage imagery and colour. Mitchell turned to future Group of Seven artists Arthur Lismer, Lawren Harris, and A.Y. Jackson to express his ideas in set design, assisted by Merrill Denison, a trained architect. Mitchell soon realized that in Denison he had found more than another remarkable set designer – he had discovered Canada's first original playwright.

Since Hart House, like Dublin's Abbey, had a national theatre as its goal, Mitchell was desperate in his second season to find suitable material for an all-Canadian bill. He locked Denison in a room adjacent to Hart House with only sandwiches, paper and pen, telling him he wasn't to come out until he had written a Canadian comedy. Merrill Denison emerged a day later with his first play, *Brothers in Arms*. It was a gem: a one-act satire on life in the "backwoods" featuring a cast of four – a frustrated Toronto businessman and his dreamy wife, foiled in their rush to leave the wilderness by two lethargic country woodsmen, Syd and Charlie. In the original production at Hart House in April 1921, Merrill Denison even played the role of Charlie. *Brothers in Arms* became a Little Theatre "standard," and by 1971 had counted more than 1500 performances.

Mitchell left Hart House after two years as artistic director and, in 1927, left Canada for New York. Renate Usmiani remarks: "Mitchell encountered a great deal of indifference, if not resistance, to his avant-garde views." In summing up his achievements, Usmiani is unequivocal: "Mitchell represents the most prophetic voice in Canadian theatre history, anticipating the work of Antonin Artaud, Tyrone Guthrie, Peter Brook, and Jerzy Grotowski as well as developments in Canadian theatre of the 1960s." [21]

Merrill Denison stayed on writing plays for Hart House for several seasons and in 1923 published *The Unheroic North*, a collection of four of these efforts: two satires, *From Their Own Place* and *Brothers in Arms*, followed by two naturalistic dramas, *Marsh Hay* and *The Weather Breeder*. Each was a variation of the city versus country theme of his first play, and each had played successfully at Hart House. Vincent Massey also published a play anthology, an impressive two-volume collection titled *Canadian Plays From Hart House*, which contained three of Denison's plays. But, as Alex Leggatt has remarked, Denison's skill as a dramatist stood out "in high relief" to the other Canadian authors:

> There is a distinctive voice, dry and sardonic. The plays are well-constructed, not just with the cleverness of a writer who has learned the basic tricks, but with the authority of one who knows what he wants to do with his medium. Most significant, there is a strong sense of community. Denison has staked out a particular territory—the unheroic North—and made it his own. [22]

Merrill Denison's *unheroic* North, based on the "backwoods" of eastern Ontario near his family estate on Lake Mazinaw, demystifies in one comic act a predominant theme in Canadian arts and letters for a hundred years – the romantic ideal of the Northland.

— • —

BROTHERS IN ARMS

DOROTHEA is sitting on the bench, Altrus BROWNE kneeling beside her. Neither of them see SYD White enter. SYD is a backwoodsman. He is wearing an old army tunic, a nondescript cap covered with red and his trousers are thrust inside a pair of heavy boots. He observes the pair on the bench, nods toward them and turns to place his gun against the wall. At the sound of the gun falling, DOROTHEA starts and BROWNE raises quickly to his feet.

DOROTHEA Oh!

BROWNE *(importantly to SYD, who is going on with his work)* My name is Browne. Major J. Altrus Browne. Mr. MacDougal told me that I'd find the man who drove me up from the station here.

SYD *(mildly interested)* Oh, he did, eh? *(looks at the stove)* Fire's kinda low, eh? *(goes to the corner and gets some wood)* You couldn't find no wood I spose, to put on it. We jest rip a board off'n the floor. *(going to the stove)* Saves a feller quite a bit of time.

BROWNE *(trying to impress SYD)* I received a very important business communication this morning which makes it imperative that I return to Toronto to-night.

SYD Oh, got to go back, eh?

DOROTHEA And I do wish he would stay longer. But the Major is a business man, you know. *(She is trying to fit SYD into innumerable roles in fiction.)*

SYD Oh, he is, eh? *(filling his pipe)* Kinda dark in here. *(looks around)* A feller might have a bit of light. *(gets up and prowls around)* There was a lantrun some place around here with the chimley cracked.

BROWNE *(impatiently and imperiously)* Never mind the lantern. We'll only be here a few moments, anyway.

SYD *(still searching under the beds)* Won't do no harm to have a bit of light. *(He finds the lantern and lights it. The globe is so sooty that just a glimmer shows.)* There, kinda helps make the place more cheerful.

BROWNE Where is the man who drove us up from the station?

SYD *(hanging the lantern and sitting down behind the stove)* Well, that's kinda hard to say. When was it he druv you up?

BROWNE Last Tuesday.

DOROTHEA *(helpfully)* And it rained the whole way. I loved it.

SYD *(politely)* Kinda wet, eh? *(to BROWNE)* Last Tuesday? That must a been Charlie druv you up.

BROWNE It doesn't matter what his name is. What I want to know is when he will be back.

SYD Charlie it was. Charlie Henderson. That's who it'd be. He aint here.

BROWNE Yes! Yes! Yes! But when will he be here?

SYD *(lighting his pipe)* Well, that's kinda hard to say. The lads went over to Wolf Lake this mornin.

BROWNE This Charlie is with them?

DOROTHEA *(to SYD)* You know, I think your camp is adorable. It's so simple and direct. So natural. *(with appropriate gestures)*

SYD *(to DOROTHEA)* This here place?

DOROTHEA Yes. Oh! I love it.

BROWNE Dorothea!

SYD *(observing BROWNE walking near the corner by the head of the beds)* That floor aint none too good since we've been usin it for the stove.

BROWNE Never mind about me. *(exasperated)* When will these men be back from Wolf Lake?

SYD Well... that's kinda hard to say. It's most ten miles over there and the trail aint none too good. But I figger they ought to be comin in most any time now.

BROWNE And this fellow Henderson will be with them?

SYD No... he won't be with them. That is, it aint likely.

BROWNE Can't you understand that I have only five hours to catch that midnight train at Kaladar. And that I must find this fellow Henderson to take me down.

DOROTHEA *(to SYD)* And I simply hate to think of going back so soon.

SYD Shame you can't stay 'til the end of the huntin season. He might kill a deer.

BROWNE Dorothea! Will you please try and keep quiet. Now *(to SYD)* when will Henderson be back? Answer me definitely.

> *SYD is cleaning his gun for several successive speeches. This adds to the hopelessness of BROWNE's position)*

SYD Well... that's kind of hard to say. He went still huntin over back of the big rock...

BROWNE *(almost frantic)* Yes, but you must know when he'll be here. I've got to have him drive down to that train to-night.

SYD Oh... you want him to drive down to catch the midnight?

BROWNE Yes, yes, yes. When will he be back?

SYD Well... if he went back of the big rock he'd most likely leave about dark...

BROWNE It's been dark half an hour. How long would it take him to get back?

SYD I figger it'd take him about half an hour if he had a boat.

BROWNE Half an hour, eh? Should be here, then, soon. *(thinks)* Did he have a boat?

SYD No... he didn't have no boat.

BROWNE *(infuriated)* What in heaven's name are you talking about a boat for if he didn't have one?

DOROTHEA Don't be impatient, dear.

SYD As I was sayin. If he had a boat...

BROWNE *(screaming with rage)* But you said he didn't have one.

DOROTHEA *(helpfully)* But, dear, if he did have a boat.

BROWNE Dorothea! Will you kindly keep quiet and leave this to me? *(to SYD)* Now, if it's within the range of human possibility, will you tell me when you expect Henderson back here?

SYD *(laying down his gun and doing his best to be explicit)* Well, I figger it this way. If he had a boat...

DOROTHEA *(patiently)* He means that if he had a...

BROWNE *(disgustedly)* Let's forget about the boat. On foot, how long would it take him to get over here? Don't you realize that he's got to take me to that train? Will he be back in ten minutes? Twenty minutes?

SYD Well... it's kinda hard to say. He mightn't have went back of the big rock at all. He might have picked up a fresh track and followed it west. But that aint likely because most of the deer's scared off'n this side of the lake.

DOROTHEA Oh! What scared them?

BROWNE Dorothea! How many times must I ask you to keep quiet and not interrupt? I must find out when we can get out of here. *(to SYD)* You feel sure that he went back of the big rock?

SYD I figger that's most likely where he's went. And if he couldn't have got the loan of a boat...

BROWNE He might have borrowed a boat then?

DOROTHEA *(helpfully)* Why, yes dear, he might have *borrowed* a boat.

BROWNE Is there some place that he might have borrowed a boat?

SYD No... there aint.

DOROTHEA You see, dear, he couldn't have got a boat anyway.

BROWNE Good God!

SYD Aint no one's got a boat over here except Levi Weeks and he's got his'n up to Buck Lake.

BROWNE *(striding over to SYD)* Look here, we've established this point. He wouldn't have gotten a boat.

SYD Well... I wouldn't go as far as to say that. He might...

DOROTHEA Dear, won't you sit down?

SYD Yes, you'd best to sit down. That floor aint none too good.

BROWNE Never mind about me. I can look out for myself all right.

DOROTHEA But do be careful, dear.

BROWNE Dorothea! *(to SYD)* Now let's find out about your friend Charlie.

SYD He aint no particular friend of mine. Kind of a brother-in-law, it seems to me. His half-sister Nellie married my stepbrother Aligan. My father's...

DOROTHEA Why, you're related then.

BROWNE Dorothea! *(pleadingly)* Do keep quiet. *(to SYD)* He could walk back in an hour couldn't he?

SYD He might. But it'd depend on whether he got a deer or not. If he got a fawn and it wasn't too much to heft, he'd most likely try and drug it out.

BROWNE From what I've seen of this country, it's likely he never saw a deer.

DOROTHEA Why, Altrus, they catch lots of wild things in the wilds.

SYD Well... if he didn't get a deer the chances is he'd stay in the bush all night.

BROWNE Do you mean to say that there is a possibility of his not returning at all?

DOROTHEA We'd have to stay over then, wouldn't we?

SYD *(laughing)* I figger you would. He often stays out all night when he's still huntin. It aint likely though. Charlie most often gets his deer. He ought to be here most any time now... if he's a comin at all.

DOROTHEA I almost hope he doesn't come. You know, this is the first trip we've had together since we've been married. Since Altrus left his battalion.

SYD You're his woman, eh? Married?

BROWNE Dorothea, do shut up. Can't you realize what twenty-five thousand dollars means to us? *(She pouts.)*

SYD *(seriously)* If you'd really wanted to have gone you should a went this morning.

BROWNE I didn't know 'til four o'clock. *(angrily)* I should never have come up into this God-forsaken hole at all.

SYD *(mildly remonstrative)* This place aint bad. The deer's about scared off what with the Finches runnin hounds all the year around but they's still some left.

BROWNE *(disgustedly)* I'm not talking about the hunting. I'm talking about the distance it is from the railroad.

DOROTHEA That's why I love it. It's so far from everything.

SYD Might be another twenty miles and do no harm.

DOROTHEA *(excitedly)* Oh, Altrus. He loves the wild virgin country, too. Far, far from the civilization... and phones... and motors.

BROWNE I'd give a lot to see one, just one, now.

SYD It's quite a ways from them things, but I figger it's just as well. Keeps folks out a here in the summer. City folks is a kinda bother.

DOROTHEA I know, They encroach on the freedom of your life.

SYD They's always tryin to get a feller to work. One way and another they figger they's doin a feller a favour to let him work for 'em.

DOROTHEA I know, you want to be left alone to lead your own simple life.

BROWNE *(who has been walking like a caged lion and has neared the dangerous corner)* Simple is right. Now look here. I'm going to give Henderson ten minutes more.

SYD He might be back in ten minutes. If he got a deer and didn't try to drug it out with him. *(pause)* And he comes by the lower trail, *(pause)* and he didn't stop down to the MacDougals' to listen to that there phonograph. I'd figger he'd most likely be about…

— • —

Director's Notes: *Brothers in Arms*

Toronto businessman J. Altrus Browne urgently needs a ride to the train station in Kaladar, some twenty miles away from the wilderness retreat where he and his wife, Dorothea, have been vacationing. They have come to the cabin of Syd White, backwoodsman, to get a ride from Charlie, the man who drove them into the wilderness in the first place. Finding no one home, they wait, Altrus pacing the wooden floor impatiently but cautiously, since many of the floorboards have been torn up to be used as firewood by the lackadaisical Syd. The entire act of this one-act play is the conversation among these three comic types, as Altrus' attempts to find out where Charlie is and if he will arrive soon enough to drive him to the train station on time to save a Toronto business deal worth $25,000. Of course, when Charlie does arrive at the end of the play, we all learn that Syd could have driven to the station, if Altrus had only asked.

The comedy in this scene is created by the urban urgency of Altrus Browne, constantly frustrated by the mind-numbing indifference of the backwoodsman, Syd White. It is a classic comic duet (like Ralph's battles with Norton in "The Honeymooners"). Browne's wife, Dorothea, (like Gleason's Alice) simply adds to her husband's comic vexation with her frequent attempts to help Altrus "understand." Dorothea's idealism is really Denison's point – a theme that he explores in all four of his "unheroic North" plays. Her romantic view of the wild— the nobility of the simple woodsman's life, living in spiritual harmony with nature—Denison knew from his childhood in the backwoods of Lake Mazinaw was pure bunk. In his view, as Alex Leggatt notes, "They're all fourth generation, inbred pioneer stock gone to seed. All the good ones have had the guts to get out of the country. Only the dregs remain."[23] Yet the romantic ideal of the North, true and strong, was as firmly rooted in Canadian culture of the time as it was in dreamy tourists such as Dorothea. It is testimony to Denison's wit and perception that he was able to skewer the belief so sharply.

It is tempting to play Syd as the sly country bumpkin who tricks the city slicker with a wink and a nod. Denison has other characters who have this subtext, but not in this play. For Syd, the presence of city folk in his cabin is quite simply, as he says, "…kinda a bother." There is plenty of room for comic exaggeration in Syd's dialect and in his lugubrious delivery – and in discovering Denison's keen sense of comic timing. Dorothea is comically exaggerated with numerous "artsy" gestures and sighs, coupled with mock anger or a similar comic reaction to her husband's admonishments. Altrus is simply a pompous, misunderstood man, frustrated by all those around him – and obviously there is *nothing* comic about that dilemma.

— • —

SCENE ELEVEN

Eight Men Speak, Oscar Ryan, Frank Love, E. Cecil-Smith and Mildred Goldberg

In addition to the creations of Hart House and the DDF, Canadian theatre was invigorated by an infusion of revolutionary culture from the Left during the 30s. It was a response dictated by the Depression itself, which was a reality rarely reflected on the stages of Little Theatres across Canada.

Organizations such as Vancouver's Progressive Arts Players and Toronto's Progressive Arts Club (later, Theatre of Action) created a vital Worker's Theatre network in Canada. The movement peaked in 1933 when, "over sixty towns, villages, and cities in Canada"—including tiny farming communities such as Rycroft, Alberta and Finland, Ontario—had socialist arts clubs. [24]

These clubs were essentially an attack by the unemployed on the despair and repression of the era. In part, they were a cultural revolt as well, inspired by the elitist and colonial tastes of amateur theatre organizations such as the Dominion Drama Festival, whose fare of bourgeois British melodrama didn't speak to the realities of the Depression. More importantly, Worker's Theatre was also very much a product of the Canadian immigrant experience: its innovative techniques of choral mass chant and audience involvement were taken from the agitation-propaganda ("agitprop") theatres of 1920s Germany; quite often its directors (such as David Pressman of the Toronto Club) were versed in *An Actor Prepares*, the handbook of Russia's brilliant director, Stanislavski. Significantly, though, Worker's Theatre rested on the theatrical traditions of Yiddish, Ukrainian, Polish, Finnish and other immigrant societies upon whose experience and cultures it was built and in whose union halls it was staged. Lastly, Canadian agitprop was linked organically to elements of Canadian theatre that existed both before and after that remarkable decade, namely a taste for political satire and a desire to reflect Canadian realities rather than foreign ones.

Frank Love, an out-of-work electrician and trade unionist in Toronto began to write plays to counter the despair of living on welfare. His first play, *Looking Forward*, was written to advocate the necessity of unemployment insurance. Frank Love's message was simple: to portray real people on stage, then to advocate political action over "Drop dead" despondency. Toby Gordon Ryan interviewed him about his play in her invaluable memoir of the era, *Stage Left*:

> The actors had only a short time to get the message across. The daughter was an advocate of insurance and the father – he was an advocate of "Drop dead." But you have some of the same attitude today. There are people who say, "What the hell difference does it make what I do? It's not going to change anything." There were people like that then too.

> I think the audience felt they were real, all right. They saw themselves on the stage. Most of the people in the audience were out of work, or so close to being out of work that a lot of them were on welfare. They were just going through that themselves and they didn't consider it a propaganda play.[25]

The government, however, *did* see Love's plays as propaganda. Progressive Arts Club members were constantly followed, detained, bullied, and censored by the "Red Squads" of city police forces, and by the RCMP, operating under the authority of the infamous Section 98 in Canada's Criminal Code.

Eight Men Speak, co-authored by Love, was Canadian agitprop's "greatest success" according to Robin Endres.[26] The play had a distinctly Canadian subject: the repeal of Section 98. This was legislation from the time of the Winnipeg General Strike, resurrected by Prime Minister Bennett in 1931 in order to conduct a mass arrest of Communist Party members. In Oscar Ryan's words, under Section 98, "...anybody could be arrested for almost anything – doing anything or doing nothing."[27] After the arrest and imprisonment for five years of Party organizers, the leader of the Party, Tim Buck, was shot at, while in his prison cell, by a guard at Kingston Penitentiary. The injustice of this incident became the impetus for the controversial drama. After one performance for 1500 at the Standard Theatre, police effectively banned the show in Toronto by threatening to revoke the licenses of the theatre owners. Later, Winnipeg police used the same tactic to stop a performance at that city's famous Walker Theatre.

Agitprop was a cultural revolt as well. Oscar Ryan, one of the founders of Toronto's Progressive Arts Club and another author of *Eight Men Speak*, remembered:

> Those who came together in PAC were dissatisfied with the established cultural values of the country. We felt that literature, the graphic arts, theatre, etc., were merely reflections, and usually imports, from the United States and Great Britain.

> We thought two things – one, that we would like to see a more genuine Canadian reflection in the arts. But even more, because of the times we were living in, we especially wanted a more radical... a more critical attitude to the society we lived in – and we didn't find such a viewpoint too prevalent. We felt that too few culturally active people were interested in social questions.[28]

Avrom Yanovsky, a member of Toronto's PAC as well, shared Ryan's commitments. He used to perform "comic chalk-talks"[29] using his skill at political cartooning to charm the audience. (Interestingly, Yanovsky revealed to Toby Ryan that the idea was originally used by John Bengough, the editor of *Grip* magazine, which was, as we have seen in the previous chapter, a vital provider of many political satires in Victorian Canada.) Ryan's play, *Eight Men Speak*, the first to use the international, agitprop style "in a specifically Canadian way,"[30] was in part a response to existing, Little Theatre styles.

A quick look at the typical Dominion Drama Festival productions of the time show why artists such as Ryan and Yanovsky—finding their views not "too prevalent"—turned to satire and its more revolutionary cousin, agitprop. The contemporary irrelevancy of typical DDF productions, such as *The Old Trouper*, presented by the Theatre Guild of Saint John at the DDF Finals in 1936, was obvious even to the British adjudicator of the time, Harley Granville-Barker. His comments on *The Old Trouper* were trenchant: "The actors are wasting their time and yours when they produce such a play. It is not like anything in heaven or on earth."[31] Granville-Barker wisely gave two of the three top play awards that year to socialist productions: Canadian Eric Harris' *Twenty-Five Cents*, about a Canadian family on welfare, and the Vancouver Progressive Arts Club's production of Clifford Odet's *Waiting For Lefty*, the most successful play of Worker's Theatre movement.

This singular moment of détente between the theatre of the establishment and its rebellious opposition was not to be repeated – at least until the partial revival of agitprop style among the Collective creations of the 1960s. It is worth noting that even now in the two most accessible sources on theatre history during the Dominion period—Betty Lee's account of the DDF in *Love and Whiskey*, and Toby Gordon Ryan's *Stage Left*, a memoir of the Worker's Theatre—each side ignores the contributions of the other. Lee, in particular, in her history subtitled, *"The Story of the Dominion Drama Festival and the Early Years of Theatre in Canada, 1606 to 1972."* makes no mention at all of Worker's Theatre at the 1936 DDF or elsewhere, whereas Ryan devotes two chapters to the movement.

— • —

EIGHT MEN SPEAK

ACT IV

The scene is in the interior of a large cell. Across the entire front of the stage stretch bars. About three paces behind bars, a long bench on which the EIGHT sit. They are wearing regulation convict uniforms and caps.

C.L.D.L *(her voice comes clearly from the wings)* We call eight witnesses from Kingston Penitentiary – Tim Buck, Tom Ewen, Matthew Popovich, Tom Cacic, Malcolm Bruce, Sam Carr, John Boychuk, Tom Hill.

BUCK *(leaning forward slightly)* Workers of Canada!

ALL The Eight speak…

EWEN from their cells,

POPOVICH …where they lie rotting.

CACIC Because they led the Canadian working class,

BRUCE against hunger,

CARR against wage cuts,

BOYCHUK *(his voice growing in power)* against imperialist war.

HILL *(continuing this upward rise)* against terror!

ALL Terror! *(pause)*

BOYCHUK Workers' meetings are disrupted. Women and children run screaming out of the way of horses' hoofs. Choking gas fills the nostrils of workers.

EWEN *(quickly)* Beat them!

HILL Run them down!

BRUCE *(sneeringly)* It doesn't matter. They are only workers. They must not be allowed to speak. *(pause)*

BUCK But...

ALL *(with force)* ...they *will* speak! *(pause)*

BOYCHUK Section 98...

POPOVICH ...the capitalist manifesto that protects a cowardly capitalism from hearing itself denounced, – that outlaws the Communist Party, fighter for the right of workers to live, – that jails its leader...

ALL ...*our* leader, Tim Buck! *(On the name of Tim BUCK, their hands all come up in the red salute.)*

BUCK *(rising from bench and stepping up to bars)* When I was free I was a slave in a machine shop. Now I am in Kingston in a machine shop, driven at the point of a gun. My parents were workers. *I* am a worker. I *led* the workers. *(He speaks quietly and convincingly.)* The bosses jailed me. From my cell today I lead the working class. The bosses are not satisfied merely with jailing me. They want my life. On my cell wall today can be seen the marks of five bullets. The cowards! This is how they meet their problems. Death for all who oppose them. Working class of Canada! Your leaders are being treated like criminals of the worst type. I appeal to you – *(remains standing at bars)*

BOYCHUK Will you let them be murdered? *(pause)*

HILL The terror shows itself in attempts to suppress trade unions – unions organized by workers – the bosses know that the strike is a strong weapon in the hands of workers.

ALL In Princeton...

HILL *(continuing)* ...Section 98 was used to jail Arthur Evans, leader of the striking coal miners.

ALL In Stratford…

HILL …Troops and tanks were called in to terrorize the strikers and crush their struggle. *(pause)*

BOYCHUK The struggle led from a prison cell,

ALL By our fighter, Tom Ewen.

EWEN *(rising and joining BUCK at the bars)* A blacksmith, trade unionist, sentenced to five years in Portsmouth Penitentiary. I call upon you, trade unionists of Canada! A hundred years ago, in Queen's Park, Toronto, workers demonstrated for their trade union rights. These rights are in danger today. *(pause)*

ALL Hounding…

POPOVICH …of foreign-born workers.

BUCK In Manitoba,

CACIC …the offices of the Workers' Benevolent Association were raided at the instigation of Ukrainian fascists.

BRUCE To break the growing militancy of the foreign-born workers and poor farmers.

CARR Under the leadership…

ALL …of our comrade, Matthew Popovich.

POPOVICH *(rises and steps forward to bars)* When I was a child in the Ukraine, my father, a poor peasant, used to teach me simple lessons of the class struggle. I came to Canada and taught these same lessons to my oppressed fellow workers. Now I am in Kingston Penitentiary, serving five years. *(rallying)* Foreign-born workers! Canadian workers! Will you see our lives burnt out and your ranks broken to save a dying capitalism?

BOYCHUK Have you the will to save the working class? *(pause)*

CARR The terror stops at nothing.

BOYCHUK Exploiters have no conscience.

BRUCE Workers are beaten…

CARR …jailed!…

BOYCHUK …murdered!…

HILL …and deported! *(pause)*

BUCK Today they plot the death of

ALL …Tom Cacic!

EWEN Coal miner…

HILL ...lumberjack.

CACIC *(rising and stepping up to bars)* First they jail me. Then, on the word of a rich broker, a crook, they send me to the hole, on bread and water. Brokers go free at half time! But forty days are added to my sentence. They steal forty days of my liberty. Then they devise a new torture. They order me deported to fascist Jugo Slavia. They know it means my certain death. And they want forty more days to gloat over me. Workers, you can put an end to this! *(He points through the bars to the audience.)*

ALL *(pointing)* Will you? *(pause)*

BUCK Terror is being used to crush freedom of speech...

EWEN ...freedom of thought...

POPOVICH ...To crush the working class press, to jail...

ALL ...Malcolm Bruce, our voice!

BRUCE *(rising and stepping up to bars)* I fought side by side with Big Bill Haywood. I worked in the mines, and as a carpenter. I wrote down the painful words of my exploitation, of your misery, so that thousands could read it, – and fight against it.

BUCK Through unity!

ALL To struggle! *(pause)*

BOYCHUK Terror is being used against the youth of Canada. Young workers are being prepared for the imperialist war, to be sacrificed as cannon fodder to the hungry god, capitalism. Joe Derry, young worker, called upon the youth to resist war. He was arrested. His trial draws near. Section 98 may send him to a Kingston cell...

ALL ...With Sam Carr.

CARR *(rising and joining others at the bars)* To my enemies, a number in a prison cell. To the workers, a comrade! My father was murdered by white guards in the Ukraine. I came to Canada. I worked in shops. When unemployment emptied the shops, I organized the unemployed. For all that, I was thrown into Kingston. Young workers, will you allow yourselves to be herded into slave camps?

ALL Or will you fight back? *(pause)*

BUCK Terror is being used against militant workers in the shops...

POPOVICH ...who fight for better wages...

BRUCE ...for decent conditions...

HILL A worker in the shop...

ALL John Boychuk!

BOYCHUK *(rising and stepping up to bars)* A tailor in the shop, a worker at the bench when they arrested me, I worked in sweat shops. I fought against sweat shops. And for that I am in Kingston. That makes me a criminal. Factory workers, exploited workers, your support means success in our fight for justice.

ALL Workers' justice. *(pause)*

EWEN In the mines, in the metal plants, terror shields the bosses' profits.

CACIC Coal miners are murdered at Estevan...

CARR ...A gunboat is sent to Anyox...

CACIC ...Arthur Evans is kidnapped...

CARR ...Force! Violence! Murder!

BUCK An organizer of the northern metal miners...

POPOVICH ...is jailed.

ALL Tom Hill!

HILL *(rising and stepping up to bars)* I went from town to town in the North. And everywhere I went I was followed by police agents, watching me, trailing me when I went into the miners' huts. The gold barons had me arrested, had me sent to prison. You miners who dig gold, organize and fight...

ALL ...For our release! *(pause)*

BUCK In Kingston pen,

EWEN Unsanitary conditions undermine our health.

POPOVICH We are denied communication with fellow beings...

CACIC ...denied the right to study and to read...

BRUCE ...hounded...

CARR ...spied upon...

BOYCHUK ...tormented...

HILL ...damned!...

BUCK Capitalism seeks to cow us.

HILL But capitalism does not know our strength!

POPOVICH We will not capitulate.

BOYCHUK For behind us lies the strength of the strongest class of all.

ALL THE WORKING CLASS!

BUCK Workers!

CARR *(pointing out through bars)* In your support lies the strength.

BOYCHUCK *(pointing out through bars)* In your support lies the will.

POPOVICH *(pointing out through bars)* In your support lies the power.

ALL To free yourselves.

CARR To free the working class.

BOYCHUK ...from the chains that bind it. *(pause)*

ALL *(quietly but tensely)* Eight men speak!

> *Here the blue border lights dim out and a full red light is flashed on scene.*

BUCK Smash Section 98!

ALL *(a little louder)* Eight men speak!

POPOVICH Smash the iron heel!

ALL *(still more power in their voices, but very tensely)* Eight men speak! *(taking a step forward and pointing through bars)* ...to you!

> *Curtain.*

— • —

Director's Notes: *Eight Men Speak*

Agitprop theatre was designed to motivate; audiences were expected to change their society after a performance. Toby Ryan sees this quality as not only the potency of agitprop, but essential to theatre itself:

> The audience reaction was very emotional—cheering, laughing, booing—as their involvement grew. There was active rapport and participation between actors and audience, such as I have always believed good theatre should have. Without this, theatre becomes an exercise in escape and one never knows what the audience is feeling, or whether they are even entertained. [32]

Ryan had first seen agitprop as it was performed in New York by the German language group Prolet-Buhne, the first company to perform this style in North America. Robin Endres describes this style:

> A raised platform at a rally was about as close as an agitprop skit came to a stage. Generally, they were performed on street corners, at demonstrations or picket lines. Mobility was inherent in the nature of the propaganda objective, but other factors such as the lack of funds and police

harassment accounted for the speed with which a troupe could pack up, move, and perform again. All props and costumes (lighting and scenery were of course dispensed with) had to be extremely simple and portable. Performers usually wore a basic uniform which was supplemented with scarves, collars, top hats and so on. Props were such items as sticks to depict police batons and prison bars, red ribbon to be used as red tape, or even a placard borrowed from a demonstrator on the spot.[33]

Eight Men Speak is in episodic agitprop style. Acts I and II offer vignettes of the reaction to Tim Buck and the Communist Party arrest by several groups, including the corrupt Superintendent of Penitentiaries, the propaganda of the press and radio, and the easy manipulation of a trial judge by the RCMP. Act III then turns the tables and presents a mock trial where Guard X, presumably responsible for the shots fired at Tim Buck while in his cell, is in the Prisoner's Box. The prosecuting attorney is an organizer for the CLDL (the Canadian Labour Defence League). She "is dressed quietly, in a neat suit; her attitude is one of entire confidence in her case." Her opponent is the attorney for the defense, "CAPITALISM… a well-fed, paunchy individual, quite bald and red-faced."[34] The final scene of Act III is a mimed reenactment, in flashback, of Guard X firing five shots at the unarmed Tim Buck, imprisoned in his Kingston cell.

Act IV is, within the play within the play, the calling of the eight imprisoned Communists as "witnesses" by the CLDL attorney. This is the scene included here. Each prisoner tells his story, and the cast uses the agitprop techniques of choral speech and chant. The rehearsals for this scene are perfect opportunities for lessons in vocal variety; that is, variety of tone and pitch, volume and articulation, pace and rate, pausing and inflection. The challenges presented to an actor's timing make themselves evident on first read-through: abrupt changes from a single voice to "All" and short, half-line utterances from several actors in sequence require coaching throughout the scene. Fortunately, the emotions of the scene—anger and a sense of injustice—are easy to find in most young actors.

— • —

SCENE TWELVE

Hill-Land, Herman Voaden

This is a beauty
of dissonance,
this resonance
of stony strand,
this smoky cry
curled over a black pine
like a broken
and wind-battered branch
when the wind
bends the tips of the pines
and curdles the sky
from the north.

This is the beauty
of strength
broken by strength,
and still strong.[35]

These concluding stanzas to "The Lonely Land" by Canada's modernist poet A.J.M. Smith summarized one prevalent early 20th century belief in a distinct national character. Smith's famous poem was a reflection of Tom Thomson's picture, "The West Wind" – the artist's attempt to paint an epic statement on the character of Canada. According to critic Barry Lord, Thomson's "The West Wind," "…has become a national emblem. Its theme is the staunch resistance of the trees to the unremitting harsh winds…. The tree in the wind is a symbol of the tenacious grasp on the land and on life that our nation has maintained. Like the tree, Canadians have had to fight to survive."[36] Whether or not this image of "the true North strong and free" accurately plumbed the national character, such an ideal was popular in Canadian arts and letters, especially in the 1920s. What Smith and Thomson attempted in poetry and painting, Herman Voaden expressed using the medium of theatre. Where Merrill Denison was satirical in his dramas, Voaden was just the opposite, sensing in the North the essence of the nation.

Stylistically, Voaden's expression of the Canadian character tried to combine the effects of painting and poetry with the sister arts of music and theatre. This synaesthetic style he termed *symphonic expressionism.* He defined his theory in a programme note for *Hill-Land,* beginning with the words of the Spanish philosopher, George Santayana:

The Symphonic Theatre

"That a man is unhappy, indeed, who in all his life has had no glimpse of
perfection, who in the ecstasy of love, or in the delight of contemplation,
has never been able to say: It is attained. Such moments of inspiration are
the source of the arts, which have no higher function than to renew them."
—Santayana

The symphonic theatre should seek to recreate these moments in which
perfection is glimpsed – these moments of intuitive illumination. This it can
do by intense, slow, and lovely picturization – by translating ordinary
stage movements into those of ritual and rhythm, by introducing music,
dance, and choral comment to sustain and lift the moment to complete
significance. [37]

Voaden found inspiration for his aesthetic in German expressionism and Wagnerian
opera, but it was firmly rooted in the 19th century tradition of Romanticism. This
same aesthetic we have seen in Chapter 2 expressed by Victorian actress Ida Van
Cortland: "It must be remembered that true art is idealistic; not the mere copying
of nature." Van Cortland aspired to give her audience glimpses of ideal love (or
sacrifice, or betrayal). Similarly, Voaden believed "art should draw men not as they
are, but as they ought to be." [38] To this end, he sought (through expressionism)
moments of insight in his dramas which would inspire an "intuitive illumination"
using "intense, slow, and lovely picturization." Both artists believed Santayana's
"moments of inspiration" can recreate for an audience "moments in which
perfection is glimpsed." The Van Cortland and Voaden philosophy was then
the polar opposite of the skepticism of Merrill Denison.

Unlike Denison, who left Canada as frustrated by its cultural institutions as his
colleague, Roy Mitchell, Herman Voaden persisted with his ideals. His symphonic
plays—*Rocks* (1932), *Earth-Song* (1932), *Hill-Land* (1934), *Murder Pattern* (1936)
and *Ascend the Sun* (1942)—place him, according to Anton Wagner, among only
a handful of playwrights, including Merrill Denison and Robertson Davies, who
have in the 20th century made "significant contributions to Canadian theatre and
culture." [39]

Ironically, Voaden was vetoed by the DDF. Adjudicators "criticized the dramatic
effectiveness of Voaden's plays in the 1933, 1935, 1936, 1938 and 1939
competitions." [40] His first entry, *Rocks*, was "ruled out" of competition entirely.
Toronto newspaper critics responded to the foreign adjudicators with their own,
far more perceptive assessments of Voaden's work:

In the Toronto regional festival, Herman Voaden's highly original and
intensely Canadian play *Rocks*, which wholly discards standard realistic
methods of production in favour of the most modernistic art-of-the-theatre,
was simply ruled out by the adjudicators because, as they frankly stated to
the audience, there was absolutely no provision in the marking system for
properly evaluating a presentation of this kind. Yet surely our national
drama festival does not wish to close the books with the year 1900,
refusing any consideration to 20th century stagecraft. [41]

One can only imagine Voaden's patience—especially with the DDF—an organization he had helped to found.

Today, the most thorough and recent assessment of Herman Voaden and his work can be found in Anton Wagner's *Vision of Canada*. Wagner, a respected theatre academic and commentator, concludes:

> Herman Voaden's dramas constitute an artistic, religious, and communal celebration of "place," the Canadian natural environment, and the bond that unites men and women with nature and themselves.... Unlike Merrill Denison's satires and realistic dramas, Voaden's works depict a romantic, ideal vision of Canadian society. [42]

By grounding his idealism firmly in the soul of Haliburton County, Voaden created an expression wholly unlike its antecedents. In Richard Perkyns' view, *Hill-Land* "is one of the most neglected masterworks in Canadian drama." [43]

— • —

The stylized altar from the Central High School of Commerce
production of *Hill-Land* by Herman Voaden, 1934.

HILL-LAND

THE SINGER *(to music and a solo dance, restrained in character)* Summer comes to the hill-land.

RACHEL is seen, standing downstage centre.

THE LYRIC VOICE Rachel, who was lovely in childhood, has fulfilled her promise. Beautiful she is, clear and gentle. She has grown in the clean wonder of the rock-land.

RACHEL *(speaking very slowly and purely – as if to herself)* He needs me. I love him. I am a woman, already. In my heart he shall find rest, and faith.

Music.

NORA *(enters from upstage right)* Are they not home from church yet?

RACHEL No. It's not likely they'll be here 'til dark.

NORA *(sitting, after a pause, knitting)* This is different land from Devonshire. There, fifteen minutes walk took me to another village, with a dozen cottages along the way. Here the same walk takes one to another house. *(dreamily)* It doesn't matter. This North will yet be the heart of the new land.

RACHEL I should like to know the way. *(pause)* Will you listen, now, in the twilight? I should like to be greater than my fears. But I can't escape them. Mother was the same. She wanted to be happy. She cried fiercely for her happiness. Yet there was something in her way. Always she feared. And when my father went she couldn't endure being alone. So she stepped free.

THE LOW CHORUS *(quietly)* Into the silence.

Music. NORA listens.

RACHEL One night my father came home from following his trap lines. It was late. He was very quiet. There was something strange about him. Mother tried to make him tell what had happened. He smiled and said it was nothing. *(Music responds to her words and lifts the tension.)* She had always feared he would not stay by her. She feared he would go into the woods, away from her. And the autumn, when the trees wore their brightest colours, he went.

THE VOICE OF PITY *(with great compassion)* Into the dark woods.

THE HIGH CHORUS *(echoing the words in silence)* Forever.

THE LOW CHORUS Forever.

RACHEL He is strong, my father. And he loved the North. But there was something here that even he was not a match for. One day he knew it would get the better of him. He knew he would go one day and would not come back. *(pause)* The only thing that worried him was leaving Mother. He wasn't afraid for himself.

THE NARRATOR The strong of soul go forth in their might, knowing they shall not return.

RACHEL *(quietly)* They said it was a heart attack. I don't know. I only know she could not forget. And one must forget at last. Is it not so?

NORA *(smiles)* One learns at last to remember, and be free.

RACHEL She never did. They had always been – like one. She thought that was the way to go on – just being one.

THE FATALIST Strange are your ways, O immortal love!

THE COMMENTATOR It is often so. In the depth of his sorrow man seeks release in the incurious shadow, in the final silence. There are hopes he will find...

THE FATALIST Nothing! There is nothing beyond the shadow and silence. Nothing!

His voice dies away in hollow and mournful insistence.

THE LOW CHORUS The vast broods about them. They live in the midst of the great distances. They know the cry of inalienable loneliness.

RACHEL I was just a girl. But I remember that winter. I remember how terrified she was. The two of us were alone. The wind went storming through the long nights.

THE NARRATOR The dark North hurtled along the wind.

THE HIGH CHORUS Storm – storm.

THE LOW CHORUS Storm – storm – storm.

RACHEL She would wheel suddenly, with a startled look, as if she saw something. She was hunted, like a wild thing in the woods. *(pause, then in a lower voice)* At last she arranged that we should go south, to visit my uncle, who lived in the city. I know now. It was I alone who was to go south. She was going to stay with my father. She was going to join him, to be with him. *(pause, then she speaks with difficulty)* The night before my uncle was to come for us, I went to bed early. She said she was coming. It was bitter cold. The wind shrilled through the pines.

THE VOICE OF HOPE Brave is he who will dare the whistling wind, the stamping dark.

All elements lift into greater and more imminent tension and terror. Yet they remain controlled. There is no frenzy.

RACHEL The snow was deep, deep.

Music, light climax, and then subside. There is a complete change of light and musical tonality. The DANCERS relax.

(quietly) They found her the next morning about half a mile from the house. *(pause)* I've never gone back there, to the far North – never. I never shall.

The music begins again—more serenely—like a slow dirge. Then it ceases.

And yet I love this land. It is mine. Here I belong. Is it not beautiful, now in the early evening? If only it were not so lonely! Even to come this far north after years in the south awakens old memories.

THE VOICE OF ECSTASY To go up and down over the twisting, rocky roads – to come again into the circle of hills, the land of uncounted waters.

RACHEL Once you have known the hill-land it claims you for its own. You are part of it.

NORA It takes a new kind of strength to belong here. You've got to be clean and sturdy and austere, like a god. Or the early frost will numb you, and the wintry cold and loneliness will rob you of hope. And there's beauty here. It's not the soft, misty kind the poets in England sing about. It's perilous unless you are strong. But if you're strong and can live it, then you'll rejoice and be free.

RACHEL I shall try.

NORA Paul needs you. You must conquer your fear. You must be certain, proud, and strong in courage.

THE NARRATOR Sombrely the day dies.

THE LYRIC VOICE The darkness falls quietly, billowing softly over the pine-slopes and the hills of cedar. There is no colour, no lament.

NORA Listen, they are coming.

PAUL and his MOTHER enter.

JEAN Home again.

NORA Did you walk?

JEAN No. They drove us. We walked in from the road.

RACHEL It is getting dark. Shall I light the lamp?

JEAN Yes, Rachel, if you please.

No words are spoken. The music echoes again the lamp theme of hope.

THE COMMENTATOR Go, young lovers, into the night. Go young gods, toward the glory that shall be yours.

THE HIGH CHORUS The earth trembles and is afraid of its loveliness.

THE LYRIC VOICE The white moon hangs above the shadowy forests and jewels a myriad lakes to shine like stars, sown in the dark wonder of the north earth…

PAUL *(his manner natural)* Would you like to go for a walk?

RACHEL Yes. The night is lovely. Yes.

Music.

NORA Go, children.

JEAN   Nora and I will sit here and talk for a while. When we go to bed we'll turn the lamp low.

> *The music plays triumphantly, prophetic of the glory to come. NORA and JEAN sit quietly. The light darkens on them, the altar light fades. The DANCERS draw the opening curtains aside in slow ecstatic worship of the night. Blue darkness. There is a pause, as the music plays. Then PAUL and RACHEL are seen, moving upward toward the highest elevation on the stage. PAUL helps RACHEL up a step. Together they watch the night.*

THE NARRATOR   The moon is bright upon them. They watch in an earth trance of silver.

THE VOICE OF HOPE   The witchery of the calm warm night amazes them.

THE NARRATOR   Mystery has settled upon them.

THE LYRIC VOICE   Still is the wide lake,
Still are the hills.

THE VOICE OF ECSTASY   The lake is a mirror that tilts toward them, flashing the white slow flame of the moon in their eyes.

THE COMMENTATOR   They are quick to answer the lonely rapture of the North-land. They shall be as gods in their worship of its loveliness.

PAUL   *(after a pause, with music)* This is the hill where Mother and Father used to come. Where they first promised. In us the flame burns on.

THE VOICE OF PITY   Children of passion. Children of pain and glory.

PAUL   And Peter and I, too. Long ago. *(music)* On this night, summers past, I should have been unhappy. Tonight you watch beside me. I am content. I can almost think quietly now, of Father and Peter.

RACHEL   I want to help you, Paul. You have suffered so much. I too, have much to remember. But I believe we shall be different. I believe in you.

PAUL   Rachel!

RACHEL   Paul!

THE COMMENTATOR   In this belief shall man put on godhood.

PAUL   This shall be a sign, that we are one with all about us. That we shall go on…

> *They kiss. Music plays tenderly, triumphantly. Light glories on their faces. RACHEL's hands are flung out. PAUL's arms are about her waist.*

THE COMMENTATOR   These are their vows. They shall lift clear of life. Paul shall not forget his grief, and Rachel her fear. Death shall not touch them.

PAUL Long ago this brightness flashed upon me first. I have come steadily toward it.

THE VOICE OF ECSTASY The beauty of the moonlight is a song in Rachel's heart. The strength of Paul is a song in Rachel's heart.

PAUL Your face – in the light!

THE LOW CHORUS A moment of ecstasy, a moment of peace!

THE COMMENTATOR They have come to the inner mystery. They deepen into the immortal earth-rhythm.

PAUL No face so beautiful... in all the world.

THE COMMENTATOR Her beauty is a sign and call of earth's loveliness, which he praises in his worship.

PAUL Come, let us sit here. *(music)* Why do you smile?

RACHEL Paul.

She laughs.

THE VOICE OF ECSTASY This laughter is moonlight cadence.

THE LYRIC VOICE They are lost in wayward silver dreams.

PAUL The moon watches your face.

THE COMMENTATOR Minutes pass. Hours. An eternity.
Tonight these are moon-spirits.
Their imaginings are tangled in a web of iridescent light.
Their eyes flash with the youngest laughter.
Of all the spirits that are happy
In the fantastic moon-world of this summer night.

THE VOICE OF ECSTASY Deep and still is their rapture.

THE NARRATOR This is the first singing of the song of their divinity.

THE COMMENTATOR *(jubilantly)* And so it has happened. The glory in Paul flames with love into godhood.

THE FATALIST This cannot last. There will be an end to this young glory.

THE COMMENTATOR No! To all Eternity this Moment lasts on. Strong in their love, and in the earth... their love, and in the earth they touch and know, they shall not fear the shadow and the silence. They shall lift clear of death, into their timeless god-life.

THE HIGH CHORUS *(extending worshipping arms toward the lovers, while the music grows in triumph)* They shall lift clear of death, into their timeless god-life.

THE LOW CHORUS Into their timeless god-life.

PAUL Rachel!

RACHEL Paul!

Light fades into darkness, and the music ceases.

— • —

Director's Notes: *Hill-Land*

Herman Voaden's Haliburton County is only an hour west of Denison's Lake Mazinaw, yet its people and its vision as portrayed in *Hill-Land*, are not anything like Denison's comic backwoodsmen, Syd and Charlie. Voaden himself explained that he chose to ground his play in an actual place (with the semblance of a plot) over criticisms that both *Rocks* and *Earth-Song* had been too difficult to follow. The conscious choice also brought his aesthetic theory closer to home; these lofty ideals now became an expression of the Canadian pioneer spirit:

> So I turned to the Haliburton I knew well, and wrote a play about *real* people [Voaden's emphasis] – three generations of a family that had settled there. In creating Paul, the young hero of the third generation, and Nora, his grandmother, I expressed my hope for the new man in a new land" [44]

The young lovers, Paul and Rachel, understand the beauty of the new land in ways that their parents could not. Nora represents these older, pioneer generations who remain spiritually rooted in the "faraway hedges and the quiet lanes" of England. Jean is Nora's daughter. Described in the stage directions as "weary, sensitive and tragic," Jean represents the generation beaten by the inhospitable North. Only Paul is able to combine Nora's strength of character with youthful idealism to eventually embrace the new land.

The characters, as Richard Perkyns suggests, are like roles in a medieval morality play where each part was allegorical, as the description above might indicate. Thus the Choral Voices, especially the Commentator and the Fatalist, sitting on elevated seats to the left and right of the proscenium, play roles of Life and Death, while the other voices of the Greek-like chorus, moving and chanting from various parts of the stage, fulfill their respective roles in the allegory.

There are two acts in *Hill-Land*. Each act has four scenes, representing Spring, Summer, Autumn and Winter; the cycle of seasons is thus reflected in the structure and action of the play. In Act 1, Scene 2, it is Summer: an appropriate time for the young hopefuls, Paul and Rachel, to consummate their love (or as Voaden prefers it, "to plight their troth. In these days of explicit love-making in print and on screen," he continues, "it is good to read: Sweet the soft yielding of your body/Flowing into the tides of my strength…"). [45]

In the previous scene, the audience has learned that Paul's brother, Peter, drowned while the two young boys were swimming; in this scene we learn that Rachel, a young teacher whom Paul has just met, has suffered as well from the harshness of the Northland, losing both her parents. Yet, Rachel, like Paul, both hates and loves the land, recognizing its beauty and her own sense of belonging. This contradiction is typical of Voaden who understands that, as in the changing of the seasons, life can only be reborn in death.

The dialogue is only a small part of the scene, however, and most rehearsal time should be spent on directing both the voices of the High and Low (pitch) Choruses, their movements as the singers and dancers, and the music and lighting which rises and fall to reflect the emotions on stage. The set should ideally have a cyclorama to re-create the importance of the lighting effects as an emotional element of the drama, and a set of steps or riser to give the necessary elevation for Rachel and Paul. Students will find it a challenge to design both the light- and soundscape required throughout the scene. Needless to say, it is a drama in which skill, patience and timing will be well rewarded.

— • —

SCENE THIRTEEN

At My Heart's Core, Robertson Davies

In the opinion of many critics, it was the plays of Robertson Davies that best characterized the Dominion years: *The Oxford Companion to Canadian Theatre* simply states "...Davies' dramatic contribution to mid-century Canadian theatre surpassed that of any other playwright...."[46] Other academics extended the praise to Davies' more famous non-dramatic works, including the Deptford trilogy of novels, saying the author was "widely recognized as one of the most versatile and accomplished literary figures in Canada."[47] They acknowledged the contributions Davies made to the arts over the course of the century, including histories of the Stratford Festival, a report on the state of Canadian theatre to the far-reaching Massey Commission, and his intellectual preeminence later in life as the Master of Massey College at the University of Toronto, among many other achievements in the world of *belles lettres*.

Davies' contributions to the Dominion Drama Festival, particularly in the late 1940s and early 1950s, were exceptional. Many finals during these years had Davies, as a director, competing against himself as a playwright – and often he won in both categories. He then wrote a successful novel about the experience. His 1952 work, *Tempest-Tost*, offered a humorous exposé of the amateur world of the DDF, and, according to one historian, "must stand as the finest record of the amateur theatrical experience." In many respects, Robertson Davies and the DDF were a perfect match: "ever excoriating the shoddy, this playboy of the eastern world surely used the festivals as they should be used, giving to them much more than he took."[48] Davies was the Canadian playwright the DDF had been searching for since its inception: he was Canada's George Bernard Shaw.

At My Heart's Core was specifically written for the 1950 Peterborough Centennial. Its theme and characters expressed the two concerns of Davies the writer through-out his career: the obstacles that an unsophisticated and uncultured landscape—geographic or human—imposed on the creative potential of an individual, and secondly, the necessity of discovering this potential by beginning "the long, solitary task of perfecting himself."[49] In general, Davies' plays and early novels explored the first social theme. Later in his career his most famous novels, such as *Fifth Business* and the rest of the Deptford trilogy, delved into the psychological one, using an allegory of Jungian archetypes.

The effect of the Canadian North on the lives of pioneers was thus a theme common to *Brothers In Arms, Hill-Land* and *At My Heart's Core*. Each playwright had a different interpretation of the "heroic North." Whether these writers satired, romanticized or intellectualized it, the Canadian North played a significant role in each drama.

— • —

AT MY HEART'S CORE

ACT TWO

When the curtain rises it is plain that dinner has been over for some time, but the ladies and their guest are still seated around the table, and their high spirits are in marked contrast to what they showed at the end of Act One. PHELIM still sits in the doorway, gloomy and disgruntled.

CANTWELL I really must stop talking. I have been monopolizing the conversation abominably.

MRS. STEWART On the contrary, sir. I hope that you will continue, for I have not been in such good spirits since my husband went to York.

MRS. TRAILL I have often reflected that the conversation of ladies alone is like a peal of bells without the support of the great bell; it readily becomes a clangour.

CANTWELL You are hard upon your sex, madam. You cannot conceive what pleasure it gives me, in this backwoods place, to hear my native tongue spoken with so much of that charm and delicacy which only ladies can impart to it.

MRS. MOODIE You flatter us, Mr. Cantwell, upon a point which is very near to our hearts. We hear the Yankees, and the Irish, and many good, humble people, but it is rarely that we hear English spoken in a fashion that recalls the society to which we were accustomed to in our better days.

CANTWELL Better days, madam?

MRS. MOODIE Earlier days, I should have said.

CANTWELL But you think of them as better days, and you are right to do so. None of us need pretend, I think, that this is the pinnacle of existence, though warmer hospitality and more charming society than I now enjoy will hardly be met with anywhere. Your fashion of treating a guest, Mrs. Stewart, speaks eloquently of the Ireland which we both know.

MRS. STEWART When were you last in Ireland, sir?

CANTWELL A month less than two years ago I was the guest of Lord Rossmore.

MRS. STEWART Rossmore? You know him well?

CANTWELL Intimately. I think we have other friends in common. The Wallers and the Beauforts have spoken of you; Miss Edgeworth also honours me with her friendship.

MRS. MOODIE Maria Edgeworth? How I envy you!

CANTWELL She sends all her new books to at least one friend in Upper Canada, for she told me so herself.

MRS. MOODIE Yes, to Frances. We all read them greedily. They are a breath of a greater world to us here. We have little enough time to read, but half an hour now and then gives the mind something to feed on during the endless hours of sewing, mending, cooking, candle-making, preserving, gardening – all the tasks that devour our time in this Ultima Thule* of civilization.

CANTWELL It is, indeed, a demanding life. So much so that I am giving it up. And if I may say so, I think that many others might be wise to give it up, as well.

MRS. STEWART There are many others who cannot give it up, sir.

MRS. MOODIE And many who would be too proud to do so.

CANTWELL It is well to rid oneself of the folly of being too proud to do what is sensible.

MRS. TRAILL You are probably aware, sir, that our husbands are retired officers, who have their way to make in the world.

CANTWELL And who are trying to make it as farmers upon land which has not been farmed before, without previous knowledge of farming. That is very hard.

MRS. TRAILL You may well say so.

CANTWELL I have watched some of those officers here in Upper Canada following the plough, and whenever they rest—which it must be said to their eternal credit is rarely—they always come to a halt facing east. I think that without knowing it they are looking toward England, as they wipe the sweat from their brows.

MRS. TRAILL I would rather not talk about it.

CANTWELL Forgive me; I had not realized…

MRS. STEWART *(bridging the difficult moment)* I have a guilty conscience about Phelim. He must be growing very cold. I'll take him a cup of tea.

MRS. MOODIE But Frances, you are punishing Phelim for his wickedness and trying to bring him to a better frame of mind. How can you do that and give him cups of tea at the same time?

MRS. STEWART Set it down to the Irish irrationality, Susanna.

CANTWELL It is the sort of irrationality which makes our system of government endurable. If we will not permit people to run their own affairs, we are obliged to be very kind to them to make up for it.

---

* The highest or farthest point that could be reached.

MRS. STEWART If you will spare me any further philosophical observations and pithy generalities, I shall take Phelim his tea now.

CANTWELL I most humbly ask your pardon, madam.

MRS. STEWART Pray do not; I like your conversation very much. I thoroughly enjoy having a gentleman about the place to moralize and utter weighty apophthegms* while I do as I please.

CANTWELL I shall accompany you.

MRS. TRAILL And I. I feel the want of air.

MRS. MOODIE I shall come too. I want to see how the man who called me a petticoated grenadier is enduring the cold.

During these speeches, they have gone out-of-doors.

MRS. STEWART Phelim, I have brought you a cup of tea.

PHELIM Is it gentry tea, or common folks' tea?

MRS. STEWART It is the last of the pot and strong enough even for you, I think.

PHELIM I don't know as I ought to take it.

MRS. STEWART Do, and oblige me. It is very hot.

PHELIM Well, if it's to oblige you, ma'am. I don't mind draining it through me, but don't think it'll soften me heart.

During this, SALLY and HONOUR, indoors, clear the table.

MRS. STEWART I'm sure it won't but if you are determined to stay here I cannot allow you to freeze to death at my door.

PHELIM How wise ye are! Himself would skelp ye if ye treated me bad. I'll be waitin' here 'til he comes.

MRS. STEWART Compose yourself for a long wait, then, for I do not expect Mr. Stewart for many days.

PHELIM He's away to fight the revolution, I suppose?

MRS. STEWART Yes.

PHELIM A big help he'll be, and him with that delay in his right leg. There'll be great times in York, I'm thinkin', and all of them fine fellas there spoilin' for a fight. I wish to God I was with 'em. Sure there's no time like wartime for larkin'. Drunk every day before noon they'll be.

He pours a generous dollop from his bottle into the hot tea, and drinks it at a gulp.

---

* A short, forceful saying; aphorism.

CANTWELL And which side would you favour, Phelim, if you were there?

PHELIM The side the bards has always been on – both sides at once. Sure, I'd make songs o'victory for the conquerors, and take sup with them, and I'd fashion laments for the vanquished, and take a sup with them. It's what ye call the impartiality o'the artist – rejoice and mourn with everybody and hit both sides a good clout if ye can.

CANTWELL Your philosophy of art differs from Mrs. Moodie's. She has written vigorously in support of the government side.

PHELIM The gentry ladies are all on the government side. The Queen's proclamation was hardly dry before Moodie and Traill were squeezin' themselves into their old uniforms, and scourin' up their swords with sand, and shoutin' around in hoarse voices the way ye'd think the trees was all sojers. Hasn't this revolution been a glory and a blessed gift to them! Back to sojerin', and away from this cursed spot, and away from their wives and their debts. They've a right to be yellin' for the revolution, I'm tellin' yez.

CANTWELL You should not speak so before Mrs. Moodie and Mrs. Traill.

PHELIM If none of us ever spoke but as we should it's little talkin' there'd be.

MRS. MOODIE Let him say what he pleases. He is railing so bitterly because he is on the losing side in the little battle that is being fought right here.

PHELIM Go on! Pity me if it does ye good! But I told you this morning, me fine madam, and I tell ye again that you and me is both in one losin' battle. We're the songbirds that aren't wanted in this bitter land, where the industrious robins and the political crows get fat, and they with not a tuneful chirp among the lot of 'em!

MRS. TRAILL How odd that poets are such bad naturalists! There are songbirds all about you, you foolish old man! Come Susanna, I am going inside. It is colder than I thought, and you have no shawl, my dear.

MRS. MOODIE Phelim, if you think to hurt me, you must use a hickory club. I am an author, and I have winced under the lash of professional criticism. Words are powerless upon me.

> *She and her sister go into the house.*

CANTWELL Shall we follow them?

MRS. STEWART Just a moment, Mr. Cantwell; I want a few more moments in the sunshine. Shall we walk in this direction?

PHELIM Ah, ye want to say somethin' them two mustn't hear.

> *They ignore him, and walk to the right, out of his earshot.*

MRS. STEWART It embarrasses me to find that we have friends in common, Mr. Cantwell. I feel that I have been shamefully rude and neglectful toward you and your wife. I should have called upon her many months ago.

CANTWELL There is no cause for embarrassment, I assure you. We did not show ourselves friendly. And Mrs. Cantwell needed a period in which to accustom herself to domestic life. I presume that you know why that was so?

MRS. STEWART I know nothing about it.

CANTWELL You heard the rumours about us, surely.

MRS. STEWART I pay no attention to rumour.

CANTWELL But in this case the rumour was the truth. Mrs. Cantwell was a novice in a nunnery in Cork. She was forced into that position because her parents did not want her to marry me. I rescued her, and brought her here. She was not anxious to meet many people for some months. But now we are returning to Europe.

MRS. STEWART To Ireland?

CANTWELL To Italy.

MRS. STEWART If it had been to Ireland I should have asked you to take some messages to friends there.

CANTWELL To Miss Edgeworth?

MRS. STEWART To her, of course, and to Lord Rossmore.

CANTWELL Rossmore travels a great deal; I may well see him on the Continent. What shall I tell him?

MRS. STEWART *(after some hesitation)* Oh, give him my good wishes.

CANTWELL Nothing more?

MRS. STEWART What more should there be?

CANTWELL I knew Rossmore intimately. Not long before I left Ireland we were together in a day's hunting. He was thrown from his mount at a rather dangerous leap, and when he did not rise at once I feared that he might have broken his neck. There were no others near, and I knelt to examine him; his pulse beat faintly, and I opened his shirt to listen to his heart. Around his neck, on a chain, was a locket; in it was a lock of hair and a miniature of a beautiful young woman.

MRS. STEWART You opened it?

CANTWELL I did, madam.

MRS. STEWART Was not that a breach of confidence?

CANTWELL No; it was a friendly precaution. If he had been dead I should have removed the locket at once. For the portrait was not that of Lady Rossmore. Men do such things for one another, you know.

Pause.

MRS. STEWART Do you tell that story to many chance acquaintances?

CANTWELL I have never told it to anyone but yourself, for you alone have the right to know it.

MRS. STEWART Why have you told it to me?

CANTWELL Because it piques my sense of the incongruous to know of this link between a world of brilliant fashion and the backwoods of Canada.

MRS. STEWART There is no link, I assure you.

CANTWELL With the best will in the world, madam, I do not believe you. Indeed, I have seen that picture; I cannot believe you.

MRS. STEWART Is my assurance nothing?

CANTWELL You gave stronger assurance of the truth of my suspicion when I mentioned Rossmore at the table. And there is more colour in your cheek now than you know. And can you deny that you asked me to remain here with you outside the house to quiz me about him? I am not a simple man, Mrs. Stewart; I can see through a brick wall with tolerable clarity.

MRS. STEWART If once there was a strong attachment between Lord Rossmore and me, you have no right to suggest that it endures still. I was curious about a former friend, that is all.

CANTWELL A friend who still cherishes your memory very dearly. Do not think that I imply anything discreditable to either of you, or injurious to Lady Rossmore, who is my friend, too. But when I see her once again in the midst of that brilliant and fashionable society, with the light of a hundred candles falling upon her jewels, shall I be able to repress a thought of you, sitting on a rush chair by the light of a backwoods fire?

Far away the note of a horn is heard, clear and mysterious in the still December air.

MRS. STEWART I do not know Lady Rossmore, nor do I envy her her jewels or her friends.

CANTWELL I am sure that you do not. And yet how well you would become such a life!

MRS. STEWART I? You are absurd.

CANTWELL No. You are beautiful, highly born, witty, and possessed of that wonderful generosity of spirit—that quality of *giving*—which raises beauty and charm to the level of great and holy virtues. What need has the backwoods of these things? You should not be here. You chose wrongly.

MRS. STEWART I cannot permit you to say more. Do not follow me.

Agitated, she goes out left, passing PHELIM, who raises his head slightly. CANTWELL watches her reflectively, and then goes into the house. His step is jaunty and he hums an Irish air under his breath.

— • —

Director's Notes: *At My Heart's Core*

At My Heart's Core argues that the obstacles of the pioneering life can prevent the true fulfillment of three famous pioneer women: Catherine Parr Traill, Susanna Moodie and Frances Stewart. Traill is an accomplished naturalist; Moodie is an essayist, and Stewart, a gentlewoman, is sophisticated and kind-hearted. All three are neighbours, living in the backwoods near Peterborough during the Rebellion of 1837. (Their husbands are absent, being engaged at York, fighting the rebels.) These three women are challenged by a rakish visitor, Edmund Cantwell, playing the role of devil's advocate, "in a manner reminiscent of Bernard Shaw"[50] As his surname suggests, Cantwell tempts all three ladies with his silver tongue, bedevilling into their hopes and dreams to discover unfulfilled lives, and genius wasted by the mindless drudgery required to survive in the backwoods.

This excerpt is from Act 2 and is the key scene in this three-act drama. At the end of Act 1, in which the audience learns of a comic subplot involving Mrs. Stewart's lower class neighbours, Phelim and Honour Brady, and Edmund Cantwell barely convinces the ladies that they need his protection from Phelim Brady, who has been banished outside the cabin (though still visible on stage left) until Mr. Stewart returns from York and can solve the problem between Phelim and his new wife and baby who have sought refuge within. As Act 2 opens, though, Cantwell has obviously charmed all three women immeasurably over lunch. They wander outside, and after a brief comic exchange with Phelim over the rebellion, the heart of Davies' drama takes shape. One by one, Cantwell convinces the women that their talents—and lives—are being wasted in the wilderness and they should return, as he is, to the civilization they left behind.

It is Mrs. Stewart that Cantwell approaches first, tempting her with news of a previous lover, the aristocratic Rossmore, and all the delights of the "brilliant and fashionable society" that she left for a meagre life in the backwoods. To add to the devilish portrait of Cantwell, the audience later learns that he may have invented the details of the locket. Whether fact or fiction, the devil has indeed tempted Mrs. Stewart, and she exits, obviously upset, while he "watches her reflectively" and then, with a jaunty step and whistling an Irish jig, sets his sights on Mrs. Traill and Mrs. Moodie. Cantwell then repeats the temptation on each, tailoring his words to exploit the longings of each character. Act 3 offers a quick resolution to the play, with the return of Mr. Stewart, a jovial but imposing figure, who learns just enough of the story to dismiss Cantwell and resolve the details of the comic subplot involving Phelim Brady.

"Davies appears to be writing within a tradition of British comedy: most of his characters are highly literate; they still speak with the grace and elegance of the early 19th century cultured class of society from which they have emigrated."[51] The best advice for acting the main characters is to see a play by Shaw – or at least watch Rex Harrison in *My Fair Lady*. By observing the vocal habits of Prof. Higgins, students will understand better the style of British comedy from which Davies draws his inspiration.

— • —

SCENE FOURTEEN

Teach Me How To Cry, Patricia Joudry

Western Canada produced playwrights as talented as those in the east, most notably, Gwen Pharis Ringwood, whose *Still Stands the House* and *Drum Song* trilogy won numerous awards, and Patricia Joudry, whose drama of adolescent love, *Teach Me How To Cry*, won the top trophy at the 1956 DDF finals and went on to further fame in London's West End (as *Noon Has No Shadows* in 1958) and Hollywood (as Universal Studios' *The Restless Years* in 1959).

Both Ringwood and Joudry got their start in radio. Joudry's first version of *Teach Me How To Cry* (1953) had been a part of Andrew Allen's influential drama series "Stage" on CBC Radio, and she soon expanded to writing for television and the stage in Canada, Britain and the U.S. Although Patricia Joudry's contribution to Canadian theatre history was not as well documented as Ringwood's, Joudry "writes perceptively and expresses a variety of contemporary social concerns with clarity and insight." Moreover, "many of her observations on marriage, child-rearing, and woman's identity were clearly in advance of her time." [52] *Teach Me How To Cry* enjoyed international success for these reasons.

Joudry's play was concerned with the stifling morality of the small town. Her theme was the same one tackled by Margaret Laurence in her classic novel, *The Diviners* (a work some small towns still have difficulty accepting), and by Alice Munro in her many famous short stories. The same theme has been the subject of Canadian satire as well, most memorably in Stephen Leacock's *Sunshine Sketches of a Little Town*. Since a great many Canadians grew up in the small-town environment, especially before mid-century, it was no wonder the shortcomings of this setting became a major theme for Canadian writers.

— • —

TEACH ME HOW TO CRY

ACT I

Scene 4

After a pause, lights come up on the ruins of the bandstand, on raised platform U.S. Trees, a small bench R. The mood is lonely and desolate. The stage is empty.

WILL'S VOICE *(after a moment, offstage R.)* Here – this looks like the way.

MELINDA *(off R.)* I'm frightened.

WILL Yeah – this is it all right. *(He emerges from R., leading to her by the hand. She is carrying a book. He wears a jacket or coat.)*

MELINDA Will, we shouldn't.

WILL Shouldn't what?

MELINDA Come here.

WILL Why not? It's only a place. *(They walk C., look around.)* An old run-down place. I bet there aren't any ghosts at all.

MELINDA *(shudders a little)* It feels as if there are.

WILL Do many people come here?

MELINDA No. Hardly anyone. And we shouldn't either. It's a terrible place.

WILL Listen, I told you what my parents said, didn't I?

MELINDA Why did they say you can't see me?

WILL It's just them. It's what they're like. We can't hang around town. So where else is there?

MELINDA *(looking around, softly.)* It's just the way I pictured it.

WILL How – how did it get burned down?

MELINDA I don't know.

WILL *(watching her)* Don't you?

MELINDA People whisper about it—it must have been something terrible—but I don't get to hear things always.

WILL Did you tell your mother anything about me?

MELINDA No. *(looks down at her hands)*

WILL *(a step toward her)* You did, didn't you?

MELINDA Yes. She – she doesn't like me going out with boys. And you – it's your father – What's so terrible about being a salesman?

WILL I don't know. You'd have to ask my mother, she knows all about it. We'll come here, see? Every day. I've got it all figured out.

MELINDA What will we do?

WILL *(goes over to bandstand steps, tests them)* We'll talk. And just sort of be together.

MELINDA *(Now she smiles and hugs book to her.)* And you can hear my lines for me.

WILL Have you got the whole scene memorized?

MELINDA *(looks at book)* I've got the whole play memorized. *(to him)* But I only need to know the scene for the audition. It's beautiful. The best scene in the play. *(She looks around.)*

WILL *(indicates a section of the bandstand, smiles)* And this could be the balcony.

MELINDA *(She runs over to it and up a few steps to a small platform section. Up there, her excitement changes to a feeling of loneliness. She looks down at him.)* I wish you were in the play.

WILL I'll sit in the front row. Every night! *(He goes to bench, sits back, watching her with assuring admiration.)*

MELINDA *(looks front, fearfully)* They'll – they'll all be there. Looking at me.

WILL Sure. And you'll be beautiful. *(a slight pause)* Melinda.

MELINDA What?

WILL I was just saying your name. It has a nice sound. I think Melinda is a pretty name. Prettier even than Juliet.

MELINDA *(darkly)* I don't. I think Melinda is a terrible name.

WILL A name isn't so very important anyway. I knew a fellow once called Stupanski and the kids used to call him Stoop. Or sometimes Stupid. He wasn't though. He was smart. That was his name, that's all. Melinda – at least Melinda is your own name. Guess where my mother got the idea for my first name from? *(During above speech, he comes over to her, stands on steps, looking up at her.)*

MELINDA William. *(He points to the book she's holding.)* Oh!

WILL *(grins)* Yeah. If a guy called Shakespeare had come along ever and asked her to marry him, I bet she would've. Then she could have called me Will Shakespeare. She would have liked that.

MELINDA Are you going to be a poet for a living?

WILL *(wanders R. across stage)* No, they don't make any money.

MELINDA Do you want to make a lot of money?

WILL No, but my wife will probably want me to.

MELINDA Why marry her then?

WILL Because I'll want to, I guess. *(thunder)*

MELINDA It's cloudy. It's going to rain. Do you like rain?

WILL I don't mind it.

MELINDA *(with inner intensity.)* I love it. I love it better than anything in the world. I like to be out in it. When it rains in the night, I get up and sit looking at it, and want to go out in the rain.

WILL *(watching her)* I wonder why.

MELINDA *(simply)* Because it's raining. I pretend things. Sometimes that I have a friend walking with me.

WILL My father says friends are an asset. He's great on friends. Only he hasn't got any. I guess not many people have.

MELINDA Polly has lots.

WILL No, she hasn't. She hasn't got one. That's what she's afraid of.

MELINDA I think my mother had one once. But she lost him.

WILL That's too bad, to lose a friend.

MELINDA All the time, when I was a little girl, my mother waited for a letter.

WILL From her friend?

MELINDA I think so. She won't let the postman come to our house any more. She thinks it's his fault. And she doesn't want me to write to anyone. But I don't mind. I don't have anyone to write to. *(a little pause)* Will you be going away?

WILL Maybe.

MELINDA You will, won't you? *(He doesn't answer. She goes front and looks down.)* The cliff is steep. I look up at it sometimes when I'm walking home from school. If a person fell down that cliff, they'd be killed.

WILL I guess they would.

MELINDA *(straining forward... looking down)* Or if they were pushed.

WILL *(a little pause)* Or if they jumped.

MELINDA *(pulls back)* Sometimes you say terrible things!

WILL It doesn't hurt to say things, Melinda.

MELINDA *(turning on him, angrily)* It does! It does!

WILL Not if they're true.

MELINDA *(scornfully)* What does *true* mean! You don't understand the words you say. Nobody would jump over a cliff.

WILL Lots of people do. They do it all the time.

MELINDA *Because they're terrible, terrible cowards, and they don't deserve to live.*

WILL Now *you're* saying terrible things. Everybody deserves to live.

MELINDA *I don't.*

WILL *(rushes up onto bandstand, urgently)* Do you know why you say that? I'll tell you why you say things like that.

MELINDA I don't want to know!

WILL You don't want to know anything. So you don't. You don't even know who you are.

MELINDA Stop talking to me. You talk and talk and I don't understand you.

WILL *(suddenly humbled)* Sure, okay. I'll go away if you want.

MELINDA Go on then! As far away as you want. *(WILL walks to a bench.)* I don't know why we came to this terrible place. I hate it here. *(WILL sits quietly, watching her. She comes slowly down the steps.)* There aren't any flowers – nothing. There used to be music here. It was springtime, like now, only people used to come here. *(walks U.C.)*

WILL We come here.

MELINDA *(stands with back to audience)* They were in love, and they listened to the music. A band played. They were sad. I seem to know it. I seem to hear the music. *(Bring in sound of cornet, muted, playing a sad martial tune. She turns.)* It makes me want to cry.

WILL Go on then.

MELINDA No, I never cry.

WILL You look sometimes as if there are tears behind your eyes.

MELINDA *(trembling)* I'm cold – it's getting cold.

WILL Come here and sit down.

MELINDA *(She goes to the bench and sits beside him. A pause. She is quiet after her outburst.)* Do you really think Melinda is a nice name?

WILL Yes, I do.

MELINDA But it isn't as nice as Juliet. If I – If I get the part, then I'll have two whole months to be Juliet.

WILL You won't be, though.

MELINDA What?

WILL It's only pretending for a little while. When the play is over, you'll have to go back to being you.

MELINDA I wish I didn't.

WILL *(The light has been fading. Now the rain starts gently. WILL looks up.)* It's starting to rain. I'll give you my coat.

MELINDA No, you don't have to. *(He gets up and takes off his coat. She looks front, at the rain.)* It's like crying. Like the sky crying.

WILL *(Putting the coat gently over her shoulders.)* The sky knows how to cry. *(He sits and speaks with simple directness.)* Is your mother insane?

MELINDA *(a pause, shocked to her soul.)* That's – a – terrible – thing to say. *(The music is out.)*

WILL I didn't mean anything by it. I only want to know.

MELINDA Of course she isn't insane!

WILL What's the matter with her then?

MELINDA There isn't anything the matter with her! She's – she acts perfectly fine. She's just young. *(pleading)* There's nothing wrong with being young!

WILL There is if you're old.

MELINDA My mother isn't old!

WILL Mothers are old. They're old and tired. They get tired after a while.

MELINDA My mother is never tired! My mother looks after me. She's always there – for me to go home to – and we talk. I can tell her about things – I can ask her things too!

WILL What things?

MELINDA Anything! Anything at all! She helps me to understand. She knows about me– *(slight pause)* When you want to know something, you ask your mother. When you're lonely, you go to your mother and she explains things and you're not lonely any more. When you don't understand – when you're frightened in the night – when you're hurt – your mother makes things better. She puts her arms around you, and you can lean on her. You can lean on her. *(She is looking front.)*

WILL *(quietly)* You're crying.

MELINDA No, I'm not. *(She does not sound as though she's crying.)*

WILL *(still watching her)* Just silently.

MELINDA It's the rain. *(WILL slowly reaches out and touches her cheek.)*

WILL *(tastes his finger)* It's salty. It's tears all right. You don't even cry right out. *(wonderingly)* The only way you'd know they were tears is by the taste.

MELINDA They dry by themselves.

WILL They're quiet. Tears should bust out – or they're no good. Lean on me. Lean on me, Melinda, and cry right out!

> *MELINDA remains motionless, staring out front. WILL very still, watching her. Pause. Lights dim to blackout. After an instant, a flash of lightning. They are revealed clearly, and MELINDA is in WILL's arms, her face buried on his shoulder. Then a slow roll of thunder, followed by a hard crash of thunder ...*
>
> *Curtain.*

— • —

Director's Notes: *Teach Me How To Cry*

Teach Me How To Cry is basically a Romeo and Juliet story without the tragic ending. In fact, the competition for roles in the local high school production of this famous tragedy both creates the initial conflict and forms the play within a play structure of the drama.

Melinda and Will are the two lovers. Both teens lead troubled lives. Melinda's mother, Mrs. Grant, is cast aside for years by the townsfolk because she bears Melinda out of wedlock, the result of a passing romance with "a traveller" at the bandstand in the park when she herself is a teenager in the town. Immediately after the incident, the bandstand burns to the ground, and although no one is blamed, the audience suspects the arson is a desperate attempt by Melinda's mother to remove from her memory—and the town's—a reminder of her past. In fact, all she succeeds in erasing is her own mental stability. The bandstand—a charred ruin—represents for the town a symbol of immorality; it stands as a "lonely and desolate place" and is the setting for this scene.

Since Melinda's illegitimate birth, Mrs. Grant (a title she invents to acquire some respectability for Melinda) and her daughter have been leading reclusive lives. Melinda attends school quietly, innocently loving her eccentric mother, but forever at the edge of social acceptance because of her origins.

Will Henderson is also the product of a troubled environment. His father is a frustrated Willy Loman-esque salesman, driven by his wife to succeed. The Hendersons are new to the town, a fact which explains Will's disregard for the history of the bandstand and his honest attraction to Melinda. It also explains Will's father's dislike of Melinda – he is concerned that the Grant reputation will affect his chances of success in the new town. Melinda's mother, on the other hand, is afraid that a boyfriend will lead Melinda to repeat her mistake.

But, as Melinda and Will move closer together, they gain new self-respect. As Act 1 draws to a close, Melinda pushes herself to audition for the role of Juliet in the upcoming school play. Will agrees to help her with her lines; she loves the play so much that she already knows the famous role by heart. The ruins of the bandstand are their secret meeting place; however, both are unaware of the irony of the setting (although this is sensed by Melinda in a foreshadow as the scene begins).

Polly, the popular girl who always gets the lead roles, is Melinda's only competition for Juliet. When Melinda wins the role, Polly uses every device in her considerable arsenal to sabotage Melinda's first, tentative steps toward social acceptability. The climax of the play is a fight between Will and another boy, Bruce, who, goaded by Polly, insults Melinda's honour. Will is expelled from school for fighting. Although, as a sanctimonious school official explains, Will's expulsion is not because of the fight, but because of his "morals" – by defending Melinda's honour he is admitting that he, himself, is the one who has compromised her honour.

Unlike the original *Romeo and Juliet*, *Teach Me How To Cry* has a much less tragic ending (although the original option is cleverly implied in this scene.) Joudry's theme is the small-minded morality of a little town, not the tragedy of impulsive love. As Will prepares to leave town, he asks Melinda to wait for him to return when he is successful so they can marry. Like Melinda, the audience is certain he will keep his promise.

— • —

ENDNOTES to Chapter Three: *The Dominion Years*

1   Betty Lee, *Love and Whiskey: the Story of the Dominion Drama Festival and the Early Years of Theatre In Canada 1606–1972*, (Toronto: Simon and Pierre, 1982), 77.

2   Robertson Davies, xi.

3   A.J.M. Smith, "A Rejected Preface" in *New Provinces:Poems Of Several Authors*, Michael Gnarowski, ed. (Toronto: U of Toronto Press, 1976), xxvii–xxxii.

4   Renate Usmiani, "Roy Mitchell," in Eugene Benson and L.W. Conolly, eds., *The Oxford Companion to Canadian Theatre* (Toronto, Oxford, New York: Oxford Univ. Press, 1989), 343, and also, *A Vision of Canada: Herman Voaden's Dramatic Works 1928–1945*, Anton Wagner, ed. (Toronto: Simon and Pierre, 1993), 11.

5   Anton Wagner, "Herman Voaden," *The Oxford Companion to Canadian Theatre*, 584, and Wagner, *A Vision of Canada*, 24–26.

6   Robin Endres "Introduction" in Richard Wright and Robin Endres, eds., *Eight Men Speak and Other Plays from the Canadian Worker's Theatre*, (Toronto: New Hogtown Press, 1976), xxvi.

7   Davies, "Foreword" in Lee, xi.

8   Lee, 83.

9   Ibid., 84.

10 Ibid., 76–83.

11 Ibid., 271.

12 Herbert Whittaker, "Dominion Drama Festival," *The Oxford Companion to Canadian Theatre*, 144.

13 Lee, 292.

14 Ibid., 82.

15 Anton Wagner, "Herman Voaden," *The Oxford Companion to Canadian Theatre*, 583.

16 Robertson Davies, *A Voice From The Attic* (New York: Viking Press, 1960)

17 Ibid., opening quote.

18 Lee, 81.

19 Ross Stuart and Ann Stuart, "University Theatre" in Anne Saddlemyer and Richard Plant, eds., *Later Stages: Essays in Ontario Theatre from the First World War to the 1970s*, Toronto: Univ. of Toronto Press, 1997), 310.

20 Ibid., 310.

21 Renate Usmiani, "Roy Mitchell," *The Oxford Companion to Canadian Theatre*, 343.

22 Alexander Leggatt, "Plays and Playwrights," in *Later Stages*, 333–34.

23 Ibid., 334.

24 Robin Endres, "Introduction," *Eight Men Speak*, xxv.

25 This information and above, Toby Gordon Ryan, *Stage Left: Canadian Theatre in the Thirties* (Toronto: CTR Publications, 1981), 26–28.

[26]   Endres, xxvi.

[27]   Ryan, 26.

[28]   Ibid., 26.

[29]   Ibid., 44.

[30]   Endres, xxvi.

[31]   Ryan, quoting Granville-Barker, 66.

[32]   Ibid., 46.

[33]   Endres, xvi–xvii.

[34]   Ibid., 51.

[35]   A.J.M. Smith, "The Lonely Land," *New Provinces*, 72–73.

[36]   Barry Lord, *The History of Painting in Canada* (Toronto: NC Press, 1972) 128.

[37]   Voaden quoted by Anton Wagner, *Vision*, 265.

[38]   Ibid., 53.

[39]   Ibid., 10.

[40]   Anton Wagner, "Herman Voaden," *The Oxford Companion to Canadian Theatre*, 584.

[41]   Lee, 121 (quoting the Toronto *Globe*'s Lawrence Mason from a review of the first DDF final in 1933).

[42]   Wagner, *Vision*, 52–53.

[43]   Richard Perkyns, ed., *Major Plays of the Canadian Theatre 1934–1984*, (Toronto: Irwin, 1984), 24.

[44]   Wagner, *Vision*, 262.

[45]   Wagner (quoting Voaden) *Vision*, 263.

[46]   Susan Stone-Blackburn, "Robertson Davies," *The Oxford Companion to Canadian Theatre*, 132.

[47]   Perkyns, 64.

[48]   Martha Mann and Rex Southgate, "Amateur Theatre," *Later Stages*, 283–84.

[49]   Alex Leggatt (quoting Davies from his play *A Jig For The Gypsy*), *Later Stages*, 347.

[50]   Perkyns, 66.

[51]   Ibid., 65.

[52]   This fact and above: Aviva Ravel, "Patricia Joudry," *The Oxford Companion to Canadian Theatre*, 282.

A Revolution
in Quebec

Anton Wagner identified Merrill Denison and Herman Voaden as playwrights distinguished from most of their contemporaries not only by "a greater degree of dramatic talent," but by "their vision of Canada expressed in a body of dramatic works."[1] In the history of Quebec, critics in general agreed there were three dramatists who created a similar revolution in Canadian theatre in French: Gratien Gélinas, Marcel Dubé, and Michel Tremblay. All three dramatists were almost equally spaced in terms of play production during the forty years following the Second World War; all three expressed a vision of Quebec society over a volume of works; and, even though naturally Gélinas, Dubé and Tremblay interpreted their society in different ways, each confronted issues intrinsic to Quebec theatre from its beginnings.

Because all these remarkable talents merged in the mid-20th century, it is fair to wonder "why so late"? The answer defines three cultural conflicts. Francophone theatre has struggled from the fall of Quebec in 1759 to survive on an English-speaking continent. Thus, Quebec culture has been largely *survivance-resistance* – not a healthy state for creativity. Secondly, as Elaine Nardocchio points out, French culture in Canada has also had its own internal battles, stretching back to colonial days: "…for well over 300 years, Quebec theatre was dominated by Church and State, the latter more recently replacing the former in both its supportive and its censoring functions."[2] This repression extends from the workplace, where Francophones formed for many years an alienated working class in a province run by English-speaking interests, to deep within the Quebec family itself, ruled by a mutually dependent Church and State aiming to keep its citizens in a state of devoted, rural poverty, unfamiliar with the material temptations of urbanization. All these tight bonds are not broken until the Quiet Revolution, a time of reform in education, politics, religion, and culture, which begins after the death of Maurice Duplessis in 1959.

For these reasons, historical and religious dramas are the most popular, or the only acceptable, form of theatre until well into the 20th century, although exceptions— such as Marc Lescarbot's diversion of 1606, *Masque de Neptune*—do exist. Joseph Quesnel, a French commander captured by the British then later released, wrote several comedies at the very beginning of the 1800s. These were staged for the amusement of the Francophones of Montreal and officers of the British garrisons (most of whom spoke French) who themselves frequently staged garrison productions of Molière.[3] Later in the century, the historical plays of Louis Fréchette, *Felix Poutre* (1862) and *Papineau* (1880), spoke to the nationalist feelings aroused by the Papineau Rebellion of 1837. Foreign touring stars, such as Sarah Bernhardt, visited Montreal as often as Toronto in the 1880s. Although in Quebec, the Bishop of Montreal warned his parish not to attend Bernhardt's performances that he deemed immoral.[4]

Similarly, during the early years of the 20th century, amateur theatrical societies, or *Cercles,* were as popular in Quebec as in English Canada. And, a few indigenous playwrights did compete in festivals such as the Earl Grey Competition and later the Dominion Drama Festival; however, "the first thirty years of the 20th century saw very few playwrights whose plays did not fall into oblivion soon after their performance."[5] Catholic colleges, led by enterprising clergymen, such as Father Emile Legault and, later, Father Gustave Lamarche, dominated both theatre training and indigenous playwrighting well into the mid-century with the "goal of promoting Christian theatre."[6] This direction was met with the approval of both the Church and the State under Maurice Duplessis, the premier of Quebec from 1936 to 1959; however, to many Quebecois, the Duplessis "reign is still referred to as *la Grande Noirceur* (The Great Darkness)."[7]

The first playwright to emerge from the darkness was Gratien Gélinas. He did so under the auspices of a new theatrical medium that in Quebec, in particular, during the 1930s commanded a very large, working class audience – radio. Although Montreal, for example, had only three theatres in 1932, more than 72 percent of households had a radio. With little competition from elsewhere on the Anglophone continent, a good radio show in French could entertain hundreds of thousands nightly.[8]

Gélinas invented Fridolin, a radio character who was "a street-smart adolescent from Montreal's East End slums." His working class language and dilemmas were documented in a weekly serial known as *Les Fridolinades.* Wearing short pants and a Montreal Canadiens hockey sweater, carrying a slingshot (aimed at society), Fridolin became an instant, then decade-long (1937–1947) success with Quebec audiences:

> Week by week Fridolin's struggling acceptance of the facts of provincial
> and national life, his cocky determination to survive and dream in the face
> of hardship and disillusion, and his capacity for optimism and laughter in
> life's gloomiest moments came to epitomize for audiences all that was best
> in French-Canadian character. Not the least of Fridolin's charms was his
> frankly colloquial Quebec French.[9]

Fridolin's "cocky determination" was matched only by his favourite response to his lot in life—"*eh souffrance!*"—the badge of *survivance-resistance* of the Quebecois. Gélinas brilliantly deepened Fridolin in his most famous creation for the theatrical stage, the tragic character, Tit-Coq. To many, the first production of *Tit-Coq* at Montreal's Monument National Theatre, 1948 (with Gélinas in the title role), "can be considered as a conclusion and as a beginning in the history of Quebecois theatre."[10] It made Gratien Gélinas "Father of the French-Canadian national theatre,"[11] and his drama a "role-model" for Quebec playwrights to come.[12]

If the Thirties and Forties belonged to Gélinas, then Marcel Dubé dominated the next two decades. Like Gélinas, Dubé first wrote plays for a medium other than the stage, namely the icon of the modern era, television. Some twenty years younger than Gélinas, Marcel Dubé was "both a product of... and a catalyst for" French

Canadian television and theatre. To date he has written more than forty plays for television, radio and the stage. [13]

Dubé's career in the theatre jump-started when his first full-length drama, *Zone*, won best Canadian play at the Dominion Drama Festival of 1953 – the first Quebec play to have captured this distinction. *Zone* was about the teenage members of a Montreal street gang who smuggle cigarettes from the U.S. Led by "Tarzan," who essentially martyrs his life for their survival, the teen characters of *Zone*, like Tit-Coq, struggled unsuccessfully against lives dispossessed of a future by virtue of their birth in the working class "zone" of Montreal's East End. Dubé's characters, again like Gélinas', represented the historical struggle of Quebec society and culture to survive meaningfully within North American society. It was this theme that gave both playwrights "a vision of Canada beyond their contemporaries."

Although Tit-Coq and Tarzan spoke a dialect found in the slums of East End Montreal, their words were not laced with swearing. Conservative Montreal audiences were not at all used to hearing plays entirely in colloquial French – until they heard Michel Tremblay's characters. In 1968, Tremblay's cast of fifteen "sisters-in-law" rattled Quebec audiences with their unconstrained use of *joual*, or Quebecois French, in the first production of his play, *Les Belles-soeurs*. As one journalist wrote in his review: "it is the first time in my life that I hear in a single evening so many curses, swear words, four-letter words, and bathroom expressions...." [14] This production caused a revolution in Quebec theatre – and changed Quebec culture:

> Never before had there been a play that used *joual* so exclusively and that so clearly and aggressively presented life on the wrong side of the tracks in Montreal.... Regardless of their personal language preferences, everyone agreed that Tremblay's vibrant use of *joual* and his re-creation of its squalid context established a new image of the Quebecois and the common linguistic bond that unites many of them. *Joual* soon came to be commonplace in Quebec theatre as well as in Quebecois novels and poetry. [15]

But *Les Belles-soeurs* was much more than a linguistic experiment; it was the world of the Quebecois in Montreal, from the rue Fabre in the East where Tremblay was born, to the sordid bars of rue St. Laurent: it brought the East End victims of Gélinas and Dubé to the 20th century neon freedoms of "The Main," where French and English Montreal, and indeed the two solitudes of Canada, met. The play, which brilliantly used in many instances the devices of the classical Greek stage as well, introduced an entirely female cast who expressed a "symphony of frustrations" [16] about being poor, alienated and repressed. Many of these characters were explored further in the nine other dramas of Tremblay's *Belles-soeurs* cycle of plays, which ended ten years later in 1977 with *Damnée Manon, Sacrée Sandra*. Tremblay's play cycle was an artistic expression of the Quiet Revolution – the nationalist movement of the 1960s in Quebec that brightly and garishly illuminated *la Grande Noirceur* and brought Quebec into the modern world. Elaine Nardocchio explains:

> In all his plays of the sixties and seventies, Tremblay sought to point out and denounce the social and cultural failings of a repressed and frustrated minority. His work also defended the right of the Quebecois to seek a better material and cultural role in the modern world.... His view of the Quebec community would inspire a whole generation of writers and actors in the seventies. [17]

One of those who Tremblay inspired wrote the final scene selection in this chapter. *The Coronation Voyage* (*Le Voyage du Couronnement*), written by Michel Marc Bouchard and first performed in 1995, was set aboard the *Empress of France* during a transatlantic crossing in 1953. The drama dealt with many of the issues raised by Bouchard's more illustrious Quebec predecessors: the conflict within a family, in this case between father and sons, historical fact and fiction, and the true nature of identity. The structure of *The Coronation Voyage* possessed a musical symmetry reminiscent of *Les Belles-soeurs*, and had clear thematic links to the plays that shaped theatre in Quebec.

SCENE FIFTEEN

Tit-Coq, Gratien Gélinas

The success of *Tit-Coq* is its identification of two themes dear to the hearts of postwar Quebecois audiences: the appeal of the large, comfortable, traditional family, and the cocky determination of the protagonist, *à la Fridolin*. At the beginning of the three-act play, young soldier Tit-Coq, because of his illegitimate birth and orphanage upbringing, has plenty of the latter but desperately desires family. When he meets, on a weekend pass, Marie-Ange and her idyllic tableau of aunts, uncles, brothers, and parents, Tit-Coq is in heaven; however the prize of legitimacy is snatched from his immediate grasp by conscription, and he nobly postpones their marriage until he returns from overseas. Of course, Marie-Ange, in spite of her devotion to Tit-Coq, is convinced by family and friends to marry another in his long absence. The hero returns, bitterly convinced more than ever that *souffrance* is his only birthright.

One of the most perceptive interpretations of the play comes from Renate Usmiani. Although acknowledging, as all critics do, that Gélinas' play represents a cultural watershed for Quebec theatre, she views *Tit-Coq* as also the product of traditional conservative values, mainly because of its production under the Duplessis regime.[18] Marie-Ange's family, the ideal world for the hero, is rooted in the culture and folklore of traditional Quebec, known as *terroir* literature, where the bucolic pleasures of rural village life, orthodoxy, and humble acceptance of one's lot in life are themes of the artist. Elaine Nardocchio agrees:

> Tit-Coq is the only character fighting what those around him accept stoically – the Jansenistic attitude that what will be will be and that one should be thankful for what one has. Tit-Coq's lonely search for identity and his constant struggle against his social inferiority are shown to be futile and senseless.[19]

Tit-Coq's fight to become accepted in society, to legitimize his birth, is a key element in both the plot and the symbolism of the play. When he angrily confronts Marie-Ange in the final scene and convinces her to leave her ill-chosen husband for a life with him, the man she confesses she loves, he is thwarted by his own past. A priest, Padre Phillipe, persuades Tit-Coq that his plan will only result in more illegitimate children, more bastards like him, because the Church would never sanction Marie-Ange's divorce. Family is Tit-Coq's dream, and he exits a tragic figure, without his love, more alone than ever.

But, the "bastard motif" also applies symbolically to Quebec's position in Canada. Tit-Coq will remain a second class citizen, it is his birthright, and his struggle represents "the embodiment of the alienation and lack of identity felt by the Quebecois."[20]

It is easy to see why *Tit-Coq* deserves the audiences it has earned. On the one hand, it is a compelling melodrama; on the other, it embodies the vision of an entire society.

— • —

Désilet and Padre confront Tit-Coq (played by Gratien Gélinas) and Marie-Ange. May 1948, Montreal, Quebec.

Tɪᴛ-Coq

Scene Seven

GERMAINE's room, the next evening, same setting as the last scene of Act One; however, certain accessories and pieces of furniture have changed as a result of MARIE-ANGE's departure.

GERMAINE, alone on the stage, is at the telephone.

GERMAINE *(nervously)* Yes, eh?... Well.... Well, you know, Jean-Paul, the "Maybes" and the "You-should-haves," it's too late for that. Besides, I've been thinking it over all day, me too, and I see no other way out. If Marie-Ange had refused to meet him, just imagine the rumpus he could have raised. While this way he'll see her, get it off his chest, and then, as he said yesterday, be gone and done with.... No, you better keep out of it. You know you'd only stir up more trouble.... All right, what's all this you could fix? Oh! Break his back, break his back, a crazy argument that is.... Why don't you keep your shirt on and... *(doorbell rings)* Wait! The doorbell. *(presses the release button)* Must be her. Hold the line... *(She opens the door and takes a quick glance down the stairway, returning to the telephone.)* Yes, it's her, excuse me.... My God, my God!... *(worn down)* Well, all right! *(low)* But mind what you say to her. She must be upset enough already.

MARIE-ANGE has just entered. She is pale and leans on the doorframe.

GERMAINE What's wrong?

MARIE-ANGE I just caught a glimpse of him.

GERMAINE Where?

MARIE-ANGE Watching for me from the corner.

GERMAINE *(hand over the mouthpiece)* Well! Swoon some other time, Jean-Paul's on the line. He wants a word with you.

MARIE-ANGE No, I won't listen to him again.

GERMAINE *(at the telephone)* See here, Jean-Paul, he's already on the corner... *(beside herself)* My sweet God! You should realize we're both rattled enough as it is.... Oh, go to the devil, if you're so stupid! *(She hangs up violently.)*

MARIE-ANGE *(has let herself drop into a chair)* He's right. I should never have come.

GERMAINE Poor kid, you know you had no choice.

MARIE-ANGE I'm scared...

GERMAINE Why, no, don't worry! He won't hurt you.

MARIE-ANGE *(to herself)* It's not him I'm scared of.

GERMAINE *(bursting out)* Now, buck up, you! This is no time for hysterics! *(In her way, she is as upset as MARIE-ANGE.)* After all, what's he got so much against you? Just let him yell and rave at you to his heart's content. Admit everything. With firecrackers like that, it's the easiest way out.

A curt ring of the doorbell.

(starting) My God, if he finds me here, he'll skin me alive. *(She throws a woolen vest around her shoulders.)* So I open the door for him and go upstairs to Mrs. Lassonde's. If you need me, bang on the pipe twice; I'll come right down. *(She presses the release button.)* And don't worry, huh? I've promised a mass for the souls in purgatory if it works out for the best. *(She goes out, leaving the door half open.)*

TIT-COQ appears, eyes wicked, and bears straight down to front stage, where MARIE-ANGE is seated, right. A pause. He wants to speak, but a growing emotion, which he fights with all his strength, paralyzes his throat. They are now gripped in a leaden silence.

MARIE-ANGE *(after a few unending seconds, almost inaudibly)* Say something, please!

TIT-COQ *(trying to get a grip on himself)* I came here to slap your face… but since I set foot in this room… *(As he cannot find words, he makes a gesture indicating he is lost. A pause. Then in a voice at first ill-assured which, while he is progressively regaining self-control, will harden to cold anger.)* But if there's justice on this earth, at least you must know you're a little slut! *(He has turned toward her.)* A little slut, for making a fool of a poor sucker like me for two years, swearing you loved me. It was as cheap to make me swallow that as bashing a baby. You're a slut! And I'm sorry I did you the honour of respecting you then like a blessed virgin, instead of making you like the first girl to come along. *(taking the album from his blouse)* I've brought this back. In case you've forgotten it with the rest, it's the family album you gave me when I left…. Up to a week ago, I'd rather have lost an eye than part with it. But today I realize it's nothing but a bunch of dirty cardboards. *(He throws it on the couch.)* Dump it yourself in the ashcan! Now, I've got nothing of yours left. As for your damn memory, I'll manage somehow to scour that off my heart, by pounding it into my head that women as faithful as you, they hang around on every street corner! *(He moves toward the door.)*

MARIE-ANGE *(Without a gesture she has listened to it all, head bowed.)* No!… Don't go like that. Wait… wait a second. *(TIT-COQ stops, turned to the rear. After a while she continues almost inaudibly.)* Forgive me.

TIT-COQ *(remains a moment taken aback)* It's easy to say "Forgive me" when the damage is done… and well done.

MARIE-ANGE It won't change anything, I know.

TIT-COQ I'll never forgive you for lying to me all that time… lying with your head snug on my shoulder.

MARIE-ANGE I didn't lie to you.

TIT-COQ Stop cringing to me. I won't make trouble! Your little golden happiness, I'll not be the one to break it, because I'm going to vanish like a stone in a lake. If you've done any wrong, life will punish you somehow. I won't.

MARIE-ANGE I'm punished enough as it is, don't worry.

TIT-COQ Punished?

MARIE-ANGE I'm as miserable as you are, if it consoles you.

TIT-COQ Miserable? *(a pause while he tries to understand)* So you're unhappy with him? What does this rhyme with?… He doesn't love you, eh? He doesn't love you?

MARIE-ANGE He loves me.

TIT-COQ Then why are you unhappy?

MARIE-ANGE *(who fears she has said too much already)* That's all I have to say.

TIT-COQ When a woman's unhappy after six months of marriage, it doesn't take a fortune-teller to know why. If he loves you, then it's you that don't love him. *(pressing)* There's no other way out: it's you that don't love him! *(MARIE-ANGE hides her face in her hands.)* You don't love him! That squares me with him... the swine. Why, of course! It had to be so. He could not possibly make you happy. *(turning toward her)* So, if you don't love him—if you could not love him—it might be... you love somebody else?

MARIE-ANGE I beg you, go away!

TIT-COQ It might be you still love somebody else? Somebody you've never lied to? I must have the truth, the truth and all of it. I must! *(MARIE-ANGE breaks into sobs.)* If it's true, say it... say it, for God's sake.

MARIE-ANGE *(in spite of herself)* Yes, I love you... I love you. *(A pause while she weeps. He remains thunder-struck by the confession.)* I'm going mad thinking about you... I'm going mad!

TIT-COQ Marie-Ange, Marie-Ange!... Why didn't you wait?

MARIE-ANGE I don't know.... I don't know...

TIT-COQ Why?

MARIE-ANGE I wanted to wait... wait as long as I had to, in spite of the empty space in my mind from never seeing you, or hearing your voice or kissing you...

TIT-COQ Me neither, I couldn't see you, nor kiss you.

MARIE-ANGE You had only yourself to fight against. While me, instead of helping me stand up, everybody was pushing me down, everybody, driving me crazy with objections, wishing I'd never met you, swearing that I was wrong to wait, too young to know if I really loved you.... Repeating in all tones from every side, that this war would never end, that you'd forget over there, and never come back to me...

TIT-COQ Sons-of-bitches!

MARIE-ANGE Making me doubt you as I might have doubted there's a heaven above, so they could force me into the arms of another man.

TIT-COQ I knew it... I knew they'd gang up to try and break us apart. I was sure of it.

MARIE-ANGE And then, one horrible night, when I was sick with the fright of giving in, they won. I broke my promise... my promise not to dance 'til you came back... I went, I danced liked a mad one. And God punished me. From then on, everything about our love went black…. When I came back to my senses, it was too late, even if I cried all the tears of my eyes… I'm so sorry, Tit-Coq, so sorry!

TIT-COQ So it's a nightmare we've had. We dreamed we'd lost each other for life, but we just woke up screaming to find it wasn't true… it wasn't true.

MARIE-ANGE *(hands icy)* What do you mean?

TIT-COQ I'm taking you back, understand? I'm taking you back.

MARIE-ANGE No, don't say that.

TIT-COQ If you still love me, it's all that matters. And you're still mine, mine, and only mine.

MARIE-ANGE No, no! It's too late… too late, you know it is.

TIT-COQ It's not too late, not yet.

MARIE-ANGE I deceived you stupidly, I don't deserve you anymore.

TIT-COQ It wasn't your fault: you just proved it. *(as much for himself as for her)* Wasn't your fault, you hear? I believe you, Marie-Ange, I believe you. And I believe you when you say you never loved him, the other one.

MARIE-ANGE But him… he loves me!

TIT-COQ You can't live your life out with the dirty sneak who took you in your sleep without bothering to find out if you really belonged to him. Who disappointed you… by being content with your body and to hell with the rest! While myself, I love you and I'll make you happy, you know it, happy as a woman can be happy!

MARIE-ANGE Just realize what you're asking…

TIT-COQ He'll still have a whole family around him…. But for me, there's no one in the world, except you.

MARIE-ANGE *(weakening)* Please.

TIT-COQ Without you I'm lost, Marie-Ange. If you don't give me a hand, I sink like a drowning man.

MARIE-ANGE You know I'd do anything for you. But all this, it's happened so quick. Give me time to think.

TIT-COQ Time? No! Time has worked against us long enough. Time, that's our enemy. That's the villain in our picture. We won't give him another chance to…

The doorbell rings.

MARIE-ANGE *(in a panic)* It's Jean-Paul! *(Swiftly, TIT-COQ goes and glances down from the balcony door.)* I told him not to come.

— • —

Director's Notes: *Tit-Coq*

Two compelling scenes from *Tit-Coq* occur at opposite ends of the play. The first date between Tit-Coq and his new girlfriend, Marie-Ange, is only three pages of text, but it conveys all the tenderness and the innocence of a first, yet decisive romantic moment. The audience knows when this scene is over that Tit-Coq has finally found his family and that Marie-Ange as well, completely charmed by his presence, has discovered her ideal love. Its antithesis is the final meeting between the two lovers, when Tit-Coq has returned from the war after hearing the news of Marie-Ange's marriage to an old suitor, Leopold Vermette. However, the latter scene makes greater demands on both actors, because the text demands such a range of emotions.

This scene begins with Germaine, Marie-Ange's roommate until the marriage to Leopold, desperately explaining to Jean-Paul, the brother of Marie-Ange and Tit-Coq's best friend (again, until the betrayal), that her apartment will be the setting for the final airing of Tit-Coq's rage. The dramatic tension, raised to a high level already by the first part of the act, in which Tit-Coq vented his bitterness in scenes with everyone *but* Marie-Ange, is now compounded by the audience's realization that the lovers will have only a short time to resolve their dilemma before the arrival of Jean-Paul and the Padre, the voices of tradition. Also, the audience is aware that Tit-Coq's despair has driven him to drink heavily and to threaten others, and thus, after Germaine's flippant remark to Marie-Ange, "He won't hurt you," we anticipate tragedy.

But, it is Marie-Ange's reply to Germaine that is most revealing of what is to come: "It's not him I'm scared of." She doubts her own resistance to turn away again from the man with whom she devotedly exchanged love letters for the lonely years of his absence before she was shamed into marrying Leopold, a suitor she had constantly and rudely rejected. When Tit-Coq bitterly throws down her family album that he has carried through the war, they both know she cannot resist the truth any longer.

Following this scene it is the Padre, who enters behind Jean-Paul, who defuses the scene with cold Jansenistic logic. He dismisses Jean-Paul to avoid a fistfight with Tit-Coq and, alone with the two lovers, advises them of the full extent of the circumstances surrounding their decision to run away together. First, he counsels they will never be able to marry because, unless Marie-Ange can prove Leopold has been unfaithful, even a court of law won't grant her a divorce, let alone the Church. Then, turning his argument to Tit-Coq, he calmly reminds him of an earlier conversation. Tit-Coq once confided to the Padre that the reason he didn't marry

Marie-Ange before he left for the war was because "he wanted from the first day to kiss the child you would give him." Tit-Coq did not want a child, like him, who would never know his father. Marie-Ange succumbs at this point, and in a climactic moment, she levels Tit-Coq with her insight: "You wouldn't want him, that child… because he'd be like you, a…" Tit-Coq's hand covers her mouth before she can finish, and by his acquiescence brings both the plot and the theme to resolution at once. No matter how cocky and determined Tit-Coq is, he is no match for the fate God has dealt him. He has nothing left, and whispering "Adieu" "almost inaudibly," Tit-Coq exits in painful defeat. [21]

SCENE SIXTEEN

Zone, Marcel Dubé

Critics commonly divide Marcel Dubé's playwriting career into two periods. His first plays for the stage—and one must remember that Dubé wrote more than twenty-five full-length plays for television and thus, was one of the few Quebec writers at this time to make a living from his craft—deal with the same East End Montreal milieu first seen in Gélinas, and further explored later by Tremblay. These dramas of the young and dispossessed, namely *Zone* (1953), *Un Simple Soldat* (1958), *Le Temps des lilas* (1958), and *Florence* (1960) are contrasted with the plays of the 1960s, such as *Les Beaux Dimanches* (1968), which deal with the more affluent families of the new Quebec upper middle class, created by the economic reforms of the Quiet Revolution. If the dilemma facing the rich is not the struggle to survive, they do share a spiritual need to find meaning in their lives that are besotted with alcohol, materialism, and marital infidelity. Dubé regretted the loss of traditional family and religious values. [22] Thus, "the student of Dubé's plays can trace in them the socio-economic and cultural development of French Canadian society through the fifties and sixties." [23]

Dubé, whose themes, like those of Gélinas or Tremblay, tend to reveal the alienation and despair found in modern Quebec, is also viewed as less of an innovative playwright than either of the former pair. [24] As with the street gang in *Zone*, life is a dilemma for the poor because they have no share of the wealth, nor do they have any means of improving their lot. For them, it is *survivance-resistance* revisited. On the other hand, for Dubé, the unbridled pursuit of goods and pleasure by the *nouveau riche* leave marriages broken and the traditions of family destroyed. Yet, as Gélinas owned the suffering souls of the poor, Tremblay would claim the family as his domain, and dissect masterfully its spiritual anguish.

Marcel Dubé's strength, other than to consolidate these themes in a remarkable *oeuvre* of more than forty full-length plays, is his ability to create dramatic tension, television-style, with as few words as possible. His dramas are starkly realistic; unlike Tremblay, no characters step out of role to chant, soliloquize, or transform themselves into an idea. The characters of *Zone* all have straightforward intentions and obstacles – within the first few minutes the audience knows why they steal and what they want. In the remarkable second act, set in a grim police interrogation room, complete with bare light bulb, a wooden stool, and trenchcoated cops, the audience enjoys a dramatic tension that rivals any example of the genre that Hollywood can offer.

— • —

ZONE

TARZAN Let me go now, I told you everything. I'll give you the details tomorrow. I'm too tired now. *(He rises.)*

LEDOUX You should sit when you're tired. Sit down.

TARZAN *(uneasy)* What more do you want?

LEDOUX Nothing much, don't get excited.

CHIEF What time did you cross the border today?

TARZAN I don't know. I crossed three times.

CHIEF The *first* time, about what time was that?

TARZAN It was very hot, close to noon I'd say.

LEDOUX The second time?

TARZAN Three o'clock, maybe?

CHIEF And the last?

TARZAN I don't remember.

CHIEF You must remember. What time was it?

TARZAN Probably about six. *(He rises.)*

LEDOUX Not so fast, sit down. Relax. *(sits him down)*

CHIEF Did you meet anyone in the woods?

TARZAN No.

LEDOUX That's strange. Since the war, the border hasn't been watched as carefully as it is now.

CHIEF If you'd met a border guard, what would you have done?

TARZAN I don't know. I would've hidden.

CHIEF Have you ever hidden from a border guard before?

TARZAN Often.

LEDOUX Are you armed when you cross the border?

TARZAN No.

CHIEF How many cigarettes did you bring across today?

TARZAN A lot.

CHIEF How many?

TARZAN Thirty thousand.

CHIEF Without a gun?

TARZAN Without a gun.

CHIEF You take risks.

TARZAN That's my choice.

CHIEF You risk your life too, you know.

TARZAN It's my life.

CHIEF Very noble, but your cause is rotten.

TARZAN Fighting for your life is not a rotten cause!

LEDOUX And since you enjoy taking risks, you steal across unarmed?

TARZAN Yes.

CHIEF We believe you. That's just about all we wanted to know. *(pretends that his dossier is complete)* So, when you saw the border guard, you hid, eh?

TARZAN Yes.

CHIEF Oh no, you just said you didn't see him.

LEDOUX *(sits him down roughly)* You mustn't start lying to us again, my boy. Too bad. Things were going so well. Now we've got to start all over again.

CHIEF Did he see you?

TARZAN Who?

LEDOUX The border guard.

TARZAN No.

CHIEF What time was it?

TARZAN During the second trip, about three.

CHIEF If he'd seen you, would you have fired at him?

TARZAN No, I wasn't armed!

LEDOUX What *would* you have done?

TARZAN I don't know. I'd have let him approach.

LEDOUX And you'd have tried to disarm him?

TARZAN Maybe.

CHIEF But he didn't see you?

TARZAN No.

LEDOUX He was a Canadian, right?

TARZAN No, American.

LEDOUX　That's what I meant.

CHIEF　That's right, an American was killed…. Was he a big man?

TARZAN　Medium.

CHIEF　Fat?

TARZAN　Thin.

LEDOUX　Was he old?

TARZAN　About thirty, maybe.

CHIEF　Then you had a good look at him, right?

TARZAN　He walked close by me.

CHIEF　The colour of his eyes?

TARZAN　Black.

CHIEF　Well! You say he didn't see you, yet you saw the colour of his eyes!

TARZAN　I saw his eyes: two big black eyes.

CHIEF　He must've been pretty absent-minded not to have seen you.

LEDOUX　He was probably singing a little tune to pass the time of day.

CHIEF　That's it, eh?

TARZAN　I don't know.

CHIEF　What time was it?

TARZAN　Three o'clock.

CHIEF　And the first trip?

TARZAN　At noon.

CHIEF　And the last?

TARZAN　At six.

CHIEF　*Where* were you coming from?

TARZAN　From Landmark Road two miles from the American border.

CHIEF　Where were you going to?

TARZAN　A truck waits for me at the side of the road about a mile from the Canadian side.

CHIEF　The truck driver's name?

TARZAN　*(He hesitates.)* It's… I'm the driver. I rent the truck.

CHIEF　So you walk three miles?

TARZAN　Yes.

LEDOUX Three miles there, three miles back, you walked six miles.

TARZAN Yes.

LEDOUX And eighteen, in all, to make three trips.

TARZAN Yes.

LEDOUX Pretty fast considering you have to go through the woods.

CHIEF You certainly weren't taking many precautions.

TARZAN I'm used to it. I know my way.

CHIEF Maybe you don't actually cover three miles each time?

TARZAN Maybe not.

LEDOUX And all you saw was a border guard.

TARZAN Yes.

LEDOUX Are you sure he didn't see you?

TARZAN Yes.

CHIEF Why?

TARZAN I don't know. I don't know anymore… you're asking too many questions.

LEDOUX How come he didn't see you?

CHIEF I suppose he was too far away.

TARZAN That's right, he was too far away.

LEDOUX No, just a minute ago, you said you saw him from up close. You even knew the colour of his eyes.

CHIEF Was he near you, or was he far away?

TARZAN He was… neither near… or far.

LEDOUX Then he wasn't anywhere! Come on, answer! Did he walk by or didn't he?

TARZAN He walked right in front of me. I was hiding, that's all.

LEDOUX Was he big?

TARZAN Yes.

LEDOUX You just said he was medium.

CHIEF Why did you say he was medium? I suppose from far he looked big, and from near he looked medium. Distance changes your perspective. But he can't be near and far at the same time, so he can't be big *and* medium.

LEDOUX It doesn't make sense. It's one or the other.

CHIEF Was he fat?

TARZAN Thin.

CHIEF What time was it?

TARZAN Three o'clock.

LEDOUX He saw you and you fired at him.

TARZAN No, I wasn't armed.

CHIEF Why did you say you carried a .38?

TARZAN I didn't say that.

LEDOUX Yes you did.

CHIEF At the beginning of your testimony you said: "I always carry a .38 when I cross the border."

LEDOUX You don't remember?

TARZAN I said that I risk it and cross without a gun.

CHIEF You have a bad memory.

LEDOUX You're confused, my boy.

CHIEF Soon we won't know what you said and what you didn't say.

LEDOUX And neither will you.

CHIEF Come on, refresh your memory – you always need to do that.

LEDOUX Here, let me help you out…. When did you cross the first time?

TARZAN At noon.

CHIEF And the second?

TARZAN Three o'clock.

LEDOUX And the last?

TARZAN Six!

CHIEF That's right. Interesting how the number six keeps turning up. Six miles there and back, six hours for three trips, the last trip was also at six.

LEDOUX And the border guard was six feet tall.

CHIEF That's true, he was six feet tall.

LEDOUX And you said he was thin, eh?

TARZAN No.

CHIEF Yes, that's what you said: thin, with black eyes.

TARZAN Yes, his eyes were black, I saw them. I told you. I remember that.

CHIEF Then he wasn't too far when he went by?

LEDOUX Maybe he was even close?

CHIEF Very close?

TARZAN Yes.

CHIEF And the sun was shining?

LEDOUX Pretty afternoon sunshine?

TARZAN Yes... the sun was shining... or rather it wasn't, it was close to evening.

CHIEF Then it wasn't three o'clock?

LEDOUX You just said you saw him during the second trip.

CHIEF But if it wasn't evening, then it must've been during the last trip at six then.

TARZAN No.

CHIEF So when was it?

TARZAN I don't know, I don't know.

LEDOUX Admit it, you fired at him. Everything was in your favour.

TARZAN No.

CHIEF Yes.

LEDOUX With a .38.

TARZAN No! No! No!

CHIEF With a .38 at point-blank. He died immediately.

TARZAN That's not true.

LEDOUX What? That he didn't die immediately?

TARZAN That I fired at him. That's not true.

CHIEF Afterwards, you saw that his eyes were black.

TARZAN No.

LEDOUX Yes. He bled a lot. You were afraid, it was your first crime.

TARZAN No.

CHIEF Where did you put your gun?

TARZAN I didn't have a gun.

CHIEF We must have the murder weapon.

TARZAN You won't have it.

CHIEF Then you confess.

TARZAN No, You're forcing me to talk and I'm saying things that aren't true.

LEDOUX The truth's coming out now.

CHIEF We must ask a lot of questions to get at the truth!

LEDOUX We must question you to the bitter end. We must break down all of your resistance.

CHIEF Confess!

LEDOUX Confess!

CHIEF Confess, Tarzan!

> *The CHIEF moves towards the back wall. He presses a button. A very strong reflector on the ceiling I lit and beamed on TARZAN's head.*

TARZAN I didn't do it!

> *LEDOUX seizes TARZAN by the hair and shoulders. He holds his face in the beams.*

Not the light... not the light... I'm not a murderer!

CHIEF Look straight into the light, it tells the truth.

TARZAN Turn it off, turn it off!

LEDOUX Some criminals can't stand the light...

CHIEF Because they're afraid.

TARZAN Turn it off, turn it off!

CHIEF Confess!

TARZAN You're driving me crazy, turn off the lights!

LEDOUX Confess!

CHIEF Tell us you killed him!

TARZAN *(in one loud scream)* Yes, I did it!... Turn it off... I did it, I did it!

> *The CHIEF turns off the light. LEDOUX releases TARZAN, who slumps down in the chair, covers his face with his hands, and sobs. We hear fragments of TARZAN's speech.*

He walked by... he looked into my eyes... he opened his mouth to speak... I fired!... He fell... he fell like a tree... he couldn't cry out... he couldn't speak, his words were caught in his throat...

> *He sobs. A long silence. The tension is broken.*

CHIEF *(softly)* Take him away.

> *TARZAN rises automatically.*

Do you have anything to add?

TARZAN No... that's all... Ciboulette... release her... let her go...

CHIEF The others will be released tomorrow. After your trial, they won't feel like starting over again.

TARZAN Ciboulette.... Tell her... tell her that I... no, don't tell her nothing.

CHIEF Take him outside. *(LEDOUX leads him out.)*

> *LEDOUX exits. The CHIEF shows visible signs of fatigue. He sits at his desk and files away his papers. Then, after several moments he lifts the receiver and dials.*

Hello! Get me Inspector Spencer, in Plattsburg, please.

> *As the scene ends, the harmonica plays its melancholy music. The music fades into the stillness of the night.*

— • —

Director's Notes: *Zone*

Zone has a cast of five young actors and two adults. Tarzan, the older, respected leader of the gang, is late returning to the hideout from a smuggling operation, his gang—Ciboulette ("Celery"), Passe-Partout ("Skeleton Key"), Tit-Noir and Moineau—anxiously await his arrival. As they discuss what could have gone wrong, they reveal that one of their gang—Passe-Partout—has been breaking Tarzan's rule – not to steal.

By smuggling cigarettes from the U.S. and selling them duty-free to acquaintances, Tarzan's East End teenage street gang manage to create meaningful lives for themselves. Ciboulette, the only female gang member, distinguishes immediately the difference between smuggling operation and common theft. She admonishes Passe-Partout, a gang member who later in the play betrays them to the police, for not having a factory job like the others to show the police "that we live ordinary lives."

> CIBOULETTE I'm not a crook. Selling cigarettes on the black market isn't stealing.
> PASSE-PARTOUT It's stealing from the government, it's stealing from society.
> CIBOULETTE We're cheating them. We're not stealing. It's not the same.[25]

For most of the gang, smuggling is the only legitimate means of "cheating" the society that has trapped them into the "ordinary lives" of minimum wage labour, endless poverty, and violent, broken, alcohol-ridden families. For all but Passe-Partout, smuggling money allows them once again to dream of escape. For Tit-Noir, escape means more education; for Ciboulette, it means a decent life with Tarzan free from the despair and poverty she knows at home. Thus, when Passe-Partout's reckless, petty crime leads to his inadvertent theft of an undercover policeman's wallet, Passe-Partout not only betrays the smuggling gang but destroys their dreams as well.

The two remaining characters in the cast are the Police Chief and Detective Ledoux, a hard-nosed undercover cop and owner of the wallet. After catching the thief, Ledoux is quick to suspect he has stumbled onto smugglers, and he hauls them all down to the police station, where he and the Chief interrogate each one. The stakes are raised when it is revealed that a U.S. border guard has been shot in a botched smuggling attempt that afternoon. It is Passe-Partout who, Judas-like, links Tarzan to the crime in an effort to save himself.

Having bullied Moineau, then Tit-Noir, Ciboulette and Tarzan—none of whom would tell him a thing—a frustrated Ledoux calls in Passe-Partout. Thrown out of the gang by Tarzan earlier in the day for his stealing, he confesses everything about Tarzan's smuggling ring on the vague promise that he will escape prosecution, and to get revenge on his leader. A clever Ledoux then holds Passe-Partout just long enough for Tarzan to suspect he's looking at his betrayer as he is called back to the "gloomy and bare" room by Ledoux for further interrogation.

Ledoux and the Chief stalk their victim with patience. The police need a full confession from Tarzan that he killed the border guard that afternoon. Having planted a doubt in Tarzan's mind that perhaps, like Passe-Partout, the rest of his gang has broken their loyalty and sensing that Tarzan has lowered his guard, both men go in for the kill. Their rapid-fire questioning (requiring plenty of rehearsal) and clever manipulation of the facts finally corner Tarzan, who is forced to confess. Before he is led away, Tarzan all but proclaims his love for Ciboulette in a final, desperate act of loyalty to their cause. It is Tarzan who emerges the hero of the play ("Fighting for your life is not a rotten cause"), and in the third act he escapes captivity long enough to return to Ciboulette before he deliberately walks into a police trap, sacrificing his own life for her survival. The Chief's parting shot at Tarzan regarding the future of Ciboulette and the gang ("After your trial, they won't feel like starting over again.") echoes ironically at his death. Elaine Nardocchio summarizes this important theme:

> The young smugglers in *Zone* have tried to build a dream for themselves from which they are rudely awakened by the death of Tarzan. They must now return to face the harsh reality of dead end jobs, endless poverty, humiliation, and a closed world from which there is no apparent escape.[26]

Although, unlike Tremblay's characters, Tarzan, Ciboulette, Ledoux and the others never become anything other than realistic portrayals of their time and place, they do remind the audience forcefully of the ethics of *survivance-resistance*, a dominant motif in the works of all three wise men from Quebec: Gélinas, Dubé and Tremblay.

— • —

SCENE SEVENTEEN

Les Belles-soeurs, Michel Tremblay

During the 1970s, it was the plays of Michel Tremblay that expressed both the hopeless lives of Dubé's impoverished East End street gang, and the tragic struggle of Tit-Coq to overcome his fate as a second-class citizen. Yet, where his predecessors saw plight, Tremblay offered fight; the hard-working characters of Tremblay's world emerged defiant, courageous, and renewed by the struggle. Tremblay took the same East End setting, characters and themes, and gave them something more – their own language. Then, by using the structures of classical, and the metaphors of modern theatre, Tremblay made universal their conflict, their despair, and their victories.

Tremblay grew up in East End Montreal, the son of a linotype operator, in a household filled with the voices of the working class mothers of rue Fabre. He had two passions as a student: reading the texts of classical Greek theatre and watching television. Both media would prove useful to his later career, as he was able to combine the choral techniques learned from Aeschylus with the psychological appeal of U.S. drama, found in the plays of naturalist playwrights such as Tennessee Williams. [26] But, it was the female voices of rue Fabre that would provide the inspiration for his most famous play.

Les Belles-soeurs is a portrait of the lives of fifteen women who live in small tenement apartments framed by the narrow alleys and circular stairs that lead to the streets of East End Montreal. In fact, there are four sisters and one sister-in-law, and the other characters are neighbours of Germaine Lauzon. She wins a grocery store coupon lottery, making her the envy of her impoverished "sisters," who are invited to help her paste her prize of a million "gold bond stamps" into booklets so she can buy the entire catalogue of prizes. As the stamp-pasting party progresses, the audience sees that Germaine and her "sisters" "all share a life so similar that they might as well be members of the same family." [27] Their despair is expressed in one phrase: *la vie plate,* the dull life (or, more colourfully, "this god-damn rotten life!") Their days are filled with the domestic routines of the poor: washing, ironing, shopping, childcare. The only thing that breaks the monotony is the weekly bingo, which is thus elevated to the level of a religious experience. *Maudite vie plate* ("damn dull life") becomes the central choral chant to Act 1; the "Ode to Bingo" its counterpoint in Act 2.

Maudite vie plate is the central theme of this and many other of Tremblay's rue Fabre plays, such as *A Toi, Pour Toujours, Ta Marie-Lou* (Forever Yours, Marie-Lou) in 1973, and *Bonjour, la, bonjour* in 1974. Tremblay's later play cycle, those dealing with the bars, clubs and denizens of the rue St. Laurent (the "Main"), further develop this motif in a way not found in either Gélinas or Dubé. Rather than stating their despair, simply frustrated and made impotent by the lack of alternatives (like Dubé's street gang), these characters inevitably find a way out, many through the freedom of honest sexual expression. *Hosanna*, whose main character is a transvestite, is such a play; however, as the playwright moves away from the world of rue Fabre, his characters become less realistic and more symbolic.[29] Tremblay reveals the universality of *la vie plate*, which vastly broadens his appeal but, like all universal questions, inevitably belies an easy answer.

This universality is accomplished mainly by Tremblay's ability to use the techniques of classical theatre. Through the use of Greek chorus, a large cast that by and large remains on stage throughout the play, and a series of individual monologues and dialogues performed while other characters freeze in half-lit tableaux, Tremblay takes his audience from the local realism of Germaine Lauzon's apartment into the realm of the classics.

> His style brings together the two polar opposites of the theatrical tradition: naturalism, the attempt to create the illusion of a slice of "real life" on stage, and theatricalism, the use of devices frankly intended to remind the spectators that they are watching a "performance."[30]

The realism of the scene is rooted in the earthiness of the dialogue; yet these same words, spoken solemnly in chorus or in plaintive monologues, also raise the performance far beyond the lives of the sisters who argue around Germaine's kitchen table. The language of the play cannot be ignored, yet it is easy to regard the play, as many early reviewers do, as sensational, and miss complex elements of *Les Belles-soeurs'* classical, even musical structure. The playwright's choice of language is the catalyst for the themes of the play, and came to him in a moment of creative insight. Tremblay recounts that, after seeing two films made in Quebec that used foreign classical French, he realized the obvious – French drama should be written in the language of Quebec, not France. Inspired by this idea, he then wrote *Les Belles-soeurs* in a matter of three weeks.[31]

Viewed on the plot level this is a play about Germaine Lauzon, her envious friends, and a million stamps. After seeing or performing the play, actors may sense what many critics have agreed: *Les Belles-soeurs* is a play that created a revolution, turning French-language theatre into Quebecois theatre.[32]

— • —

LES BELLES-SOEURS

ACT ONE

LINDA Lauzon enters. She sees four boxes in the middle of the kitchen.

LINDA God, what's that? Ma!

GERMAINE Is that you, Linda?

Michel Tremblay's *Les Belles-soeurs* original cast,
Théâtre du Rideau Vert, Montreal, August 1968.

LINDA Yeah! What are all these boxes in the kitchen?

GERMAINE They're my stamps.

LINDA Already? Jeez, that was fast.

GERMAINE Lauzon enters.

GERMAINE Yeah, it surprised me too. They came this morning right after you left. The doorbell rang. I went to answer it and there's this big fellow standing there. Oh, you'd have liked him, Linda. Just your type. About twenty-two, twenty-three, dark curly hair. Nice little moustache. Real handsome. Anyway, he says to me, "Are you the lady of the house, Mme. Germaine Lauzon?" I said, "yes that's me." And he says, "Good, I've brought your stamps." Linda, I was so excited. I didn't know what to say. Next thing I knew two guys are bringing in the boxes and the other one's giving me this speech. Linda, what a talker. And such manners. I'm sure you would have liked him.

LINDA So, what did he say?

GERMAINE I can't remember. I was so excited. He told me that the company he works for was real happy I'd won the million stamps. That I was real lucky… Me, I was speechless. I wish your father had been here, he could have talked to him. I don't even know if I thanked him.

LINDA That's a lot of stamps to glue. Four boxes! One million stamps, that's no joke!

GERMAINE   There's only three boxes. The other one's booklets. But I had an idea, Linda. We're not gonna do this all alone! You going out tonight?

LINDA   Yeah, Robert's supposed to call me…

GERMAINE   You can't put it off 'til tomorrow? Listen, I had an idea. I phoned my sisters, your father's sister and I went to see the neighbours. And I've invited them all to come and paste stamps with us tonight. I'm gonna give a stamp pasting party. Isn't that a great idea? I bought some peanuts, and your little brother went out to get some Coke…

LINDA   Ma, you know I always go out on Thursdays! It's our night out. We're gonna go to a show.

GERMAINE   You can't leave me alone on a night like this. I've got fifteen people coming…

LINDA   Are you crazy! You'll never get fifteen people in this kitchen! And you can't use the rest of the house. The painters are here. Jesus, Ma! Sometimes you're really dumb.

GERMAINE   Sure, that's right, put me down. Fine, you go out, do just as you like. That's all you ever do anyway. Nothing new. I never have any pleasure. Someone's always got to spoil it for me. Go ahead Linda, you go out tonight, go to your goddamned show. Jesus Christ Almighty, I'm so fed up.

LINDA   Come on, Ma, be reasonable…

GERMAINE   I don't want to be reasonable, I don't want to hear about it! I kill myself for you and what do I get in return? Nothing! A big fat nothing! You can't even do me a little favour! I'm warning you, Linda, I'm getting sick of waiting on you, you and everyone else. I'm not your servant, you know. I've got a million stamps to paste and I'm not about to do it myself. Besides, those stamps are for the whole family, which means everybody's gotta do their share. Your father's working tonight but if we don't get done he says he'll help tomorrow. I'm not asking for the moon. Help me for a change, instead of wasting your time with that jerk.

LINDA   Robert is not a jerk.

GERMAINE   Sure, he's a genius! Boy, I knew you were stupid, but not that stupid. When are you going to realize your Robert is a bozo? He doesn't even make sixty bucks a week. All he can do is take you to the local movie house Thursday nights. Take a mother's advice, Linda, keep hanging around with that dope and you'll end up just like him. You want to marry a shoe-gluer and be a strapper all your life?

LINDA   Shut up, Ma! When you get sore, you don't know what you're saying. Anyway, forget it… I'll stay home…. Just stop screaming, okay? And by the way, Robert's due for a raise soon and he'll be making lots more. He's not as dumb as you think. Even the boss told me he might start making big money 'cause they'll put him in charge of something. You wait. Eighty bucks a week is nothing to laugh at. Anyway... I'm gonna go phone him and tell him I can't go to the show.... Hey, why don't I tell him to come and glue stamps with us?

GERMAINE Mother of God, I just told you I can't stand him and you want to bring him home tonight. Where the hell are your brains? What did I do to make God in heaven send me such idiots? Just this afternoon, I sent your brother to get me a bag of onions and he comes home with a quart of milk. It's unbelievable! You have to repeat everything ten times around here. No wonder I lose my temper. I told you, Linda. The party's for girls. Just girls. Robert's not queer, is he?

LINDA Okay Ma, okay, don't flip your wig. I'll tell him not to come. Jesus, you can't do a thing around here. You think I feel like gluing stamps after working all day?

LINDA starts to dial a number.

Why don't you go dust the living room, eh? You don't have to listen to what I'm going to say.... "Hello, may I speak to Robert?... When do you expect him?... Okay, will you tell him Linda phoned?... Fine, Mme. Bergeron, and you?... That's good.... Okay, thanks a lot. Bye."

She hangs up. The phone rings right away.

"Hello?"... Ma, it's for you.

GERMAINE *(entering)* Twenty years old and you still can't say "One moment please" when you answer a phone.

LINDA It's only Aunt Rose. Why should I be polite to her?

GERMAINE *(putting her hand over the receiver)* Will you be quiet! What if she heard you?

LINDA Who gives a shit?

GERMAINE Hello? Oh, it's you, Rose.... Yeah, they're here.... How 'bout that? A million of 'em! They're sitting right in front of me and I still can't believe it. One million! One million! I don't know how much that is, but who cares? A million's a million.... Sure, they sent a catalogue. I already had one but this one's for this year, so it's a lot better. The old one was falling apart.... They've got the most beautiful stuff, wait 'til you see it. It's unbelievable! I think I'll be able to take everything they've got. I'll re-furnish the whole house. I'm gonna get a new stove, new fridge new kitchen table and chairs. I think I'll take the red one with the gold stars. I don't think you've seen that one.... Oh, it's so beautiful, Rose. I'm getting new pots, new cutlery, a full set of dishes, salt and pepper shakers.... Oh, and you know those glasses with the "caprice" design. Well, I'm taking a set of those, too. Mme. de Courval got a set last year and

she paid a fortune for them, but mine will be free. She'll be mad as hell....
What?... yeah, she'll be here tonight. They've got those chrome tins for flour
and sugar, coffee and stuff.... I'm taking it all, I'm getting a Colonial bedroom
suite with full accessories. There's curtains, dresser-covers, one of those things
you put on the floor beside the bed.... No, dear, not that.... New wallpaper....
Not the floral, Henri can't sleep with flowers.... I'm telling you Rose, it's
gonna be one beautiful bedroom. And the living room! Wait 'til you hear
this.... I've got a big TV with a built-in stereo, synthetic nylon carpet, real
paintings.... You know those Chinese paintings I've always wanted, the ones
with the velvet?... Aren't they though? Oh, now get a load of this.... I'm gonna
have the same crystal platters as your sister-in-law, Aline! I'm not sure, but
I think mine are even nicer. There's ashtrays and lamps.... I guess that's about
it for the living room... there's an electric razor for Henri to shave with, shower
curtains. So what? We'll put one in. It all comes with the stamps. There's
a sunken bathtub, a new sink, bathing suits for everyone.... No, Rose, I am
not too fat. Don't get smart. Now listen, I'm gonna re-do the kid's room,
completely. Have you seen what they've got for kids' bedrooms? Rose, it's
fabulous! They've got Mickey Mouse all over everything. And for Linda's
room.... Okay, sure, you can just look at the catalogue. But come over right
away, the others will be here any minute. I told them to come early. I mean it's
gonna take forever to paste all those stamps.

MARIE-ANGE Brouillette enters.

GERMAINE   Okay, I've gotta go. Mme. Brouillette's just arrived. Okay, yeah....
Yeah.... Bye!

MARIE-ANGE   Mme. Lauzon. I just can't help it, I'm jealous.

GERMAINE   Well, I know what you mean. It's quite an event. But excuse me for
a moment, Mme. Brouillette, I'm not quite ready. I was talking to my sister,
Rose. We can see each other across the alley. It's handy.

MARIE-ANGE   Is she gonna be here?

GERMAINE   You bet! She wouldn't miss this for love nor money. Here, have
a seat and while you're waiting, look at the catalogue. You won't believe all the
lovely things they've got. And I'm getting them all, Mme. Brouillette. The
works! The whole catalogue.

GERMAINE goes into her bedroom.

MARIE-ANGE   You wouldn't catch me having luck like that. Fat chance. My life
is shit and it always will be. A million stamps! A whole house. If I didn't bite
my tongue, I'd scream. Typical. The ones with all the luck least deserve it.
What did Mme. Lauzon do to deserve this, eh? Nothing. Absolutely nothing!
She's no better-looking than me. In fact, she's not better period. These contests
shouldn't be allowed. The priest the other day was right. They ought to be
abolished. Why should she win a million stamps and not me? Why? It's not

fair. I work too, I've got kids, too, I have to wipe their asses, just like her. If anything, my kids are cleaner than hers. I work like a slave, it's no wonder I'm all skin and bones. Her, she's fat as a pig. And now, I'll have to live next door to her and the house she gets for free. It burns me up, I can't stand it. What's more, there'll be no end to her smart-assed comments 'cause it'll all go straight to her head. She's just the type, the loud-mouthed bitch. We'll be hearing about her goddamned stamps for years. I've a right to be angry. I don't want to die in this shit while madame Fatso here goes swimming in velvet! It's not fair! I'm sick of knocking myself out for nothing! My life is nothing. A big fat zero. And I haven't a cent to my name. I'm fed up. I'm fed up with this stupid, rotten life.

During the monologue, GABRIELLE Jodoin, ROSE Ouimet, YVETTE Longpre and LISETTE de Courval have entered. They take their places in the kitchen without paying much attention to MARIE-ANGE. The five women get up and turn to the audience.

THE FIVE WOMEN *(together)* This stupid, rotten life! Monday!

LISETTE When the sun with his rays starts caressing the little flowers in the fields and the little birdies open wide their little beaks to send forth their little cries to heaven...

THE OTHERS I get up and I fix breakfast. Toast, coffee, bacon, eggs. I nearly go nuts trying to get the others out of bed. The kids leave for school, my husband goes to work.

MARIE-ANGE Not mine, he's unemployed. He stays in bed.

THE FIVE WOMEN Then I work. I work like a demon. I don't stop 'til noon. I wash.... Dresses, shirts, stockings, sweaters, pants, underpants, bras. The works. I scrub it, wring it out, scrub it again, rinse it.... My hands are chapped. My back is sore. I curse like hell. At noon, the kids come home. They eat like pigs, they wreck the house, they leave. In the afternoon I hang out the wash, the biggest pain of all. When that's finished, I start the supper. They all come home. They're tired and grumpy. We all fight. But at night, we watch TV. Tuesday.

LISETTE When the sun with his rays...

THE OTHERS I get up and I fix breakfast. The same goddamn thing. Toast, coffee, bacon, eggs. I drag the others out of bed and I shove them out the door. Then it's the ironing. I work, I work, I work, and I work. It's noon before I know it and the kids are mad because lunch isn't ready. I make 'em baloney sandwiches. I work all afternoon. Suppertime comes, we all fight. But at night, we watch TV. Wednesday. Shopping day. I walk all day, I break my back carrying parcels this big, I come back home exhausted. But I've still got to make supper. When the others get home I look like I'm dead. I am. My husband bitches, the kids scream. We all fight. But at night, we watch TV.

Thursday and Friday…. Same thing…. I work. I slave. I kill myself for my pack of morons.

Then I spend the day Saturday tripping over the kids and we all fight. But at night, we watch TV. Sunday we go out, the whole family, we get on the bus and go for supper with the mother-in-law. I have to watch the kids like a hawk, laugh at the old man's jokes, eat the old lady's food, which everyone says is better than mine…. At night, we watch TV. I'm fed up with this stupid, rotten life! This stupid, rotten life! This stupid, rotten life! This stup…

They sit down suddenly.

LISETTE On my last trip to Europe…

ROSE There she goes with her Europe again. We're in for it now. Once she gets started, there's no shutting her up!

DES-NEIGES Verrette comes in. Discreet little greetings are heard.

LISETTE I only wished to say that in Europe they don't have stamps. I mean, they have stamps, but not like these ones. Only letter stamping stamps.

DES-NEIGES That's no fun! So they don't get presents like us? Sounds pretty dull to me, Europe.

LISETTE Oh no, it's very nice despite that…

MARIE-ANGE Mind you, I've got nothing against stamps, they're useful. If it weren't for the stamps, I'd still be waiting for that thing to grind my meat with. What I don't like is the contests.

LISETTE But why? They can make families happy.

MARIE-ANGE Maybe, but they're a pain in the ass for the people next door.

LISETTE Mme. Brouillette, your language! I speak properly, and I'm none the worse for it.

MARIE-ANGE I talk the way I talk, and I say what I got to say. I never went to Europe, so I can't afford to talk like you.

ROSE Hey, you two, cut it out! We didn't come here to fight. You keep it up, I'm crossing the alley and going home.

GABRIELLE What's taking Germaine so long? Germaine!

GERMAINE *(from the bedroom)* Be there in a minute. I'm having a hard time getting into my… well, I'm having a hard time…. Is Linda there?

GABRIELLE Linda! Linda! No, she's not here.

MARIE-ANGE I think I saw her go out a while ago.

GERMAINE Don't tell me she's snuck out, the little bugger.

GABRIELLE Can we start pasting stamps in the meantime?

GERMAINE No wait! I'm going to tell you what to do. Don't start yet, wait 'til I get there. Chat for a bit.

GABRIELLE "Chat for a bit?" What are we going to chat about…

The telephone rings.

— • —

Director's Notes: *Les Belles-soeurs*

It is very difficult to select one small excerpt from a multi-layered play such as *Les Belles-soeurs* that, like a hologram, would best reflect the whole.

With any good musical, the overture serves this function and the opening pages of *Les Belles-soeurs* perform this same task. Tremblay moves the audience beyond the local setting—beyond Germaine's small kitchen and the petty arguments and jealousies of the characters—by layering the realism of the opening dialogue between Germaine and her daughter, Linda, with two monologues and a chorus.

The argument between mother and daughter establishes the opening notes of a conflict between generations and the larger theme of the destructiveness of the family that emerges with the arrival of the "black sheep" sister, Pierrette, and later during the pregnancy crisis of young Lise, but is repeated throughout the play in the complaints of the older women about their children, and their own aged parents. This last is cleverly represented by the comic antics of Mme. Dubuc, who is alternately bemoaned and ignored by the sisters, as she drools, yelps and bites from her wheelchair. The ultimate failure of the family is repeated by passages such as the following, as the women remark on Lise's pregnancy:

> MARIE-ANGE Have you noticed Mme. Bergeron's daughter lately? Wouldn't you say she's been putting on weight?
> LISETTE Yes, I've noticed that…
> THERESE *(insinuating)* Strange, isn't it? It's all in her middle.
> ROSE I guess the sap's running a bit early this year.
> MARIE-ANGE She tries to hide it too. It's beginning to show, though.
> THERESE And how! I wonder who could have done it?
> LISETTE It's probably her step-father…[33]

Following the argument between Germaine and Linda, Tremblay introduces the second major motif of the play: the envy and hypocrisy of Germaine's "sisters." This theme is established in Germaine's telephone monologue, and immediately counterpointed by the "Luck" solo spoken by the first one to arrive for the evening, Marie-Ange Brouillette. The crescendo is reached when four other "sisters" enter inconspicuously, but just in time to join Marie-Ange in the chorus that explicitly introduces the major theme: "I'm fed up with this stupid, rotten life!" (*Chus tannée de mener une maudite vie plate!*) The chorus finishes as abruptly as it begins: Lisette and Rose "suddenly" return the audience (and the lighting) to the here and now, with a realistic beat of dialogue, reiterating the theme of envy on a new level. Actors, and lighting techs, will find the right transition between the realism and the theatrics of the chorus when they are able to delight and surprise an audience with both the start and the finish of this dramatic moment.

— • —

SCENE EIGHTEEN

The Coronation Voyage, Michel Marc Bouchard

Quebec playwright Michel Marc Bouchard began his professional theatre career in 1983. Since then he has written more than twenty-five plays, many of which have received both regional and national honours, including a Dora Mavor Moore Award and a Chalmers Award. His works have been translated into nine languages and are frequently staged at festivals around the world.

Whereas Tremblay's theatricality elevates naturalism using the structures of the classical theatre, temporarily removing his audiences from direct involvement in the stage action in a Brechtian fashion, Bouchard goes one step further. In his most complex dramas, such as *Lilies or The Revival of Romantic Drama* [*Les feluettes ou La répétition d'un drame romantique*] (1987), *The Orphan Muses* [*Les muses orphelines*] (1989), and *The Coronation Voyage* [*Le Voyage du Couronnement*] (1995), he consciously attempts to sustain audience awareness of the theatrical event they are watching: "Bouchard continuously reminds the outer audience of the ambiguity that exists when one tries to present so-called truth or reality on stage."[34] (In this respect Bouchard's plays share a style most familiar to English Canadian audiences through the plays of George F. Walker.) In *The Coronation Voyage*, the devices he uses to achieve this effect are quickly paced, ironic dialogue; a highly ironic narrator, "The Biographer," who both comments on and contributes to the action; and a non-linear, musical structure that repeats and reinforces his images and themes.

Bouchard's work resembles Tremblay's drama in another significant way. He, too, portrays the destructive and repressive forces of family, church, and society on sexuality. *Lilies*, for example, is an attempt to create "new insights and an alternative representation of homosexuality on the contemporary stage."[35] Unlike Tremblay however, Bouchard often uses the past to explore these issues: his dramas *Lilies*, *The Coronation Voyage*, and to some extent *Pelopia's Doll* [*La poupée de Pélopia*] (1985) and *The Orphan Muses*, all make use of past events to see the present more clearly. In doing so, Bouchard removes his audience another step away from the naturalistic kitchen of Germaine Lauzon, and several steps from the East End streets found in the plays of Dubé and Gélinas.

The Coronation Voyage is set in 1953 aboard the Canadian Pacific ocean liner the *Empress of France*. Many of the passengers are bound for England for the coronation of the new Queen, Elizabeth II. To this end, a Liberal Minister, Joseph Gendron, and his outspoken wife, Alice, travel with their talented daughter, Marguerite, who has been chosen to play piano at the Coronation. A second, contrasting family of three is also on the voyage for an entirely different reason. "The Chief" is a *mafioso* who is escaping Montreal's underworld with his two sons, Sandro and Etienne. A Canadian trade commissioner to London, known only in the play as "The Diplomat" is presumably on board to attend the ceremony, but is really there to provide illegal passports and new identities to The Chief and his two sons.

It is the Diplomat's unexpected demand that he be permitted to seduce Sandro before he hands over the new passports to The Chief that is the inciting incident of the plot. It also initiates a mock Abraham-Isaac sacrifice scenario in which The Chief finds himself. The audience soon learns that the old mafioso has already sacrificed his elder son's promising career as a pianist to save his own skin by allowing Étienne's hands to be smashed by the Montreal police. The hypocrisy of The Chief in his ironic effort to "save" his family from his past with new identities, paralleled by the hollow sacrifice Minister Gendron has made of his three sons at Dieppe, creates a major theme of the play – the destructiveness of the family. This is a major theme for Tremblay as well.

The relationships between the Diplomat and Sandro, Étienne and Marguerite, and to a lesser extent, The Chief and Minister Gendron connect the two worlds. Mlle. Lavallee, a protocol officer, is a minor character offering an officious foil for the Minister's wife. Some comic relief is provided by a final group of three, indistinguishable young females—all named Elizabeth—chosen in a contest to attend the Coronation of their royal namesake.

The play is divided into two acts, Part 1 and Part 2, each of which contains four scenes, or "episodes." Episodes in both Parts alternate between two sets: the First Class deck of the ship and the Empress Room and its adjoining lounge. The first two scenes of each Part (Episodes 1 and 5, 2 and 6) use the Deck and the Empress Room for their settings; the last two scenes of each Part invert this arrangement.

Bouchard extends this structural symmetry to the level of plot and theme. The first scene of each Part has a pair of lovers dominant: Episode 1, the Diplomat falls in love with Sandro and in Episode 5, Étienne falls for Marguerite, thus linking the two trios. The second scene of each Part offers a similar parallel: in Episode 2, Étienne expresses his hate for his father and the Diplomat demands The Chief give him "permission to seduce"[36] Sandro, his second son. In its opposing number, Episode 6, Étienne (after falling in love with Marguerite) forgives his father, and The Chief accepts the Diplomat's demand. The third scenes of each Part are the longest and most complex. Each develops the theme of the play beyond the major theme of relationship between fathers and sons already established. This is the theme of historical truth and lies. It plays on two levels: in the political world it is seen in the hypocrisy of the politician's world represented by Minister Gendron, and in its inverse, the underworld past that The Chief is trying to erase with a new passport. In the personal world, it concerns the search for new—or true—identities by The Chief and his sons, and each character inevitably finds his own answer.

Character foils deepen these themes. For Gendron, it's his wife, Alice, who in Episode 3 exposes the historical lie that the Dieppe landing was a success. (It killed her three sons, yet was ordered by her husband's government.) In Episode 7 she similarly exposes the imperialist hypocrisy of Mlle. Lavallee's Coronation rehearsal. For The Chief it is The Diplomat who acts as a foil.

In the concluding Episodes to each Part, Bouchard again establishes a parallel. Major themes are reiterated in both episodes, and an important plot question raised (The Chief asks The Biographer to find a solution to the passport/Sandro crisis) in Episode 4; and in Episode 8 an unexpected answer to the passport crisis (and to a certain extent, the theme of historical truth and identity) is given when Sandro and Étienne admit they have murdered the Diplomat. This means the loss of The Chief's new identity (and his future) and indicates that his sons have taken charge of their own lives.

This elaborate and intriguing structure has the effect of subordinating the traditional linear plot to a repeated series of images and emotions. It creates an effect of musicality that again reminds one of *Les Belles-soeurs*. In fact, all these musical elements: the four "episodes," or movements, the repetition of three triads in the cast list, the use of inverse movements, the tonic and dominant themes are reminiscent of the structure of the sonata. In sum, Bouchard's play, like Tremblay's work, is innovative, metatheatrical, and complex in its form, yet remains vital and compelling in its content.

— • —

THE CORONATION VOYAGE

Episode 4

Smoking lounge.

One of the main doors to the ballroom is ajar, illuminating the silhouette of THE CHIEF who is smoking a cigar. He is listening to the music coming from the ballroom. THE BIOGRAPHER is nearby. Someone is rehearsing Chopin. There is a deep sadness in the air.

THE BIOGRAPHER The passengers had quickly unpacked their trunks, eager to check, once again, their outfits for the London festivities. The ship forged ahead calmly, with no apparent crises, no untimely incidents. The Chief of Chiefs had punctuated the passage down the St. Lawrence with memories of his exploits in each port. Shawinigan, a clever transaction. Rivière-du-Loup, a settling of accounts. Quebec City, the dance halls and the conquest of so many lovely legs.

THE CHIEF You can still manage to make up a good story?

THE BIOGRAPHER It is the historian's task to interpret the hero's silences.

THE CHIEF Look at me. How do you interpret tonight's silence?

THE BIOGRAPHER I have children myself, sir, and…

THE CHIEF And?

THE BIOGRAPHER I try to be as close to them as possible. We try to tell each other the truth, and we look for solutions together.

THE CHIEF Sometimes I envy you ordinary people.

THE BIOGRAPHER Sandro entered with the horned larks. Before speaking to his father, he was careful to take off his glasses.

> *SANDRO enters. He takes off his glasses and slips them into his pocket.*

THE CHIEF I don't want to see him.

SANDRO I'm already here, Papa.

THE BIOGRAPHER The Gulf of the St. Lawrence. Day two of the crossing. Evening. *(to THE CHIEF)* Shall I order you a whiskey, sir?

> *He exits.*

SANDRO I waited for you in the dining room.

THE CHIEF You waited for me?

SANDRO Weren't you hungry?

THE CHIEF I wasn't hungry.

SANDRO You missed the Minister's wife making a scene.

THE CHIEF She made a scene?

SANDRO She wanted to be seated at the Captain's table. *(beat)* The Captain gave her his place.

THE CHIEF I missed all that.

SANDRO Is that the substitute who's playing?

THE CHIEF Who?

SANDRO That's what Étienne calls her.

THE CHIEF I don't know who's playing.

SANDRO The fog has lifted. We've left the lights on the North Shore behind.

THE CHIEF Already?

SANDRO It's very dark.

THE CHIEF Really?

SANDRO Étienne is still on the deck.

THE CHIEF Still in the same place?

SANDRO He spent the whole night there.

THE CHIEF It's because of his hands.

SANDRO You should tell him to come inside. *(speaking of the birds)* They're horned larks. The big one is called Pacific. The other one is Atlantic.

THE CHIEF People take dogs for walks, not birds.

SANDRO He's known a lot of women.

THE CHIEF Who has?

SANDRO The diplomat. He showed me some pictures. They're very good-looking. But the prettiest one is his wife.

THE CHIEF There are lots of young people your age on the boat, you could have a good time with them, instead of hanging out in some diplomat's cabin.

SANDRO 259 first-class cabins, 441 tourist-class.

THE CHIEF Sandro!

SANDRO *Quattro saloni, tre sale da pranzo, due sale da ballo–*

THE CHIEF Stop!

SANDRO It's the first time someone important has been interested in me.

THE CHIEF Put your glasses back on!

SANDRO You say I look ugly with my glasses.

THE CHIEF You can see him again, if you wear your glasses.

SANDRO I'm allowed to see him? *Grazie! (quickly correcting himself)* Thanks!

THE CHIEF Have you and I ever had a real talk?

SANDRO Isn't that what we're doing now?

THE CHIEF A man-to-man talk.

SANDRO Sure, we talk about all sorts of unimportant things, but that's how men talk to each other, isn't it?

THE CHIEF You know, sometimes in life, you have to make big sacrifices for other people.

SANDRO And I'm making a big one for you.

> *Beat.*

THE CHIEF *(worried)* What do you mean?

SANDRO I know everything. The diplomat explained everything to me.

THE CHIEF What do you know?

SANDRO I know that forgetting Louise is a big sacrifice I'm making so I can follow you. *(beat)* Are you crying?

THE CHIEF It's the music.

SANDRO One day, God appeared to a man whose faith was unshakable. He said: "Sharpen your knife, prepare the wood for a burnt offering, lay it on your son's back and lead him to the highest mountain. When you have reached the summit, immolate your son, your beloved son, as a sacrifice to me." The man sharpened his knife, chopped the wood, and led his son to the mountain. That is when the son asked the father what animal he was going to sacrifice. Which sheep? Which lamb? Which ram? He replied that God would decide. When they reached the designated spot, the father prepared the fire and tied the hands and feet of his son who'd fallen asleep. His heart and his soul were heavy, but he knew it was to ensure his prosperity. Strange. Sacrificing his descendant to ensure his future. That's the way legends are. The father placed the son on the altar. He took the knife and raised his hand to slay his son, and then, one second, two seconds–

THE CHIEF That's enough!

SANDRO I haven't finished.

THE CHIEF You've been getting on my nerves ever since we boarded the ship.

SANDRO I haven't finished.

THE CHIEF When you're not babbling about suits and tailors, you're babbling about sheep and God. God's travelling with the rabble, two decks down, in tourist class. Leave him where he is.

SANDRO I haven't finished.

THE CHIEF Who told you that story?

SANDRO Somebody.

THE CHIEF Who?

THE DIPLOMAT enters.

THE DIPLOMAT I did. To console him.

— • —

Director's Notes: *The Coronation Voyage*

In the previous excerpt, the opening beat of Part 1, Episode 4, The Chief makes a feeble and ultimately unnecessary attempt to explain to his son, Sandro, why he must let The Diplomat seduce him.

In character with the structure of the play, the scene has a tragic-ironic soundtrack, the sad strains of Chopin being rehearsed in the next room, presumably by Marguerite in rehearsal for her recital for the Queen. Thus, just as The Chief wrestles with the idea of "sacrificing" his son Sandro, the audience is subtly reminded of the mafioso's early sacrifice of Étienne's career as "Chopin's Great Disciple."[37]

The Chief is perplexed and saddened by the dilemma that The Diplomat has presented him. The Biographer can offer no solace. Finally it is Sandro himself who surprises the audience in two respects: first, he says to his father, "I know everything," meaning he knows of The Diplomat's demand to seduce Sandro in exchange for the passports. This fact surprises the audience who, at this point at least, thinks he is innocent of the proposal. The line is also doubly ironic, since The Chief himself first says it to Étienne, revealing the father's complicity in the breaking of Étienne's hands. Secondly, Sandro gives a perfect recitation of the Biblical story of Abraham and Isaac, leaving out only the original names. It is an allusion whose irony is lost neither on his father nor on the audience.

— • —

ENDNOTES to Chapter Four: A Revolution in Quebec

[1]   Anton Wagner, ed., *A Vision of Canada: Herman Voaden's Dramatic Works 1928–1945* (Toronto: Simon and Pierre, 1993), 10.
[2]   Elaine F. Nardocchio, *Theatre and Politics in Modern Quebec* (Edmonton: Univ. of Alberta Press, 1986) 115.
[3]   Ibid., 8, 9.
[4]   Ibid., 10.
[5]   Ibid., 16.
[6]   Ibid., 22.
[7]   Ibid., 22.
[8]   L. E. Doucette, "Drama in French" in Eugene Benson and L.W. Conolly, *The Oxford Companion to Canadian Theatre* (Toronto, Oxford, New York: Oxford Univ. Press, 1989), 178.
[9]   John Ripley, "Gratien Gélinas" in *The Oxford Companion to Canadian Theatre*, 228.
[10] Doucette, *The Oxford Companion to Canadian Theatre*, 176.
[11] Anton Wagner, ed., *Canada's Lost Plays, Vol. 4, Colonial Quebec: French-Canadian Drama, 1606–1966* (Toronto: Canadian Theatre Review Publications, 1982), 28.
[12] John Ripley, "Tit-Coq" in *The Oxford Companion to Canadian Theatre*, 555.
[13] Ben-Z. Shek, "Marcel Dubé" in *The Oxford Companion to Canadian Theatre*, 183.
[14] Renate Usmiani, *Studies in Canadian Literature: Michel Tremblay* (Vancouver: Douglas and McIntyre, 1982), 31.
[15] Nardocchio, *Theatre and Politics in Modern Quebec*, 66.
[16] Usmiani, *Studies in Canadian Literature: Michel Tremblay*, 30.
[17] Nardocchio, *Theatre and Politics in Modern Quebec*, 73.
[18] Usmiani, *Studies in Canadian Literature: Michel Tremblay*, 8.
[19] Nardocchio, *Theatre and Politics in Modern Quebec*, 35.
[20] Usmiani, *Studies in Canadian Literature: Michel Tremblay*, 10.
[21] Gratien Gélinas, *Tit-Coq*, trans. by Kenneth Johnstone (Toronto: Clarke, Irwin, 1967), 81–83.
[22] Nardocchio, *Theatre and Politics in Modern Quebec*, 45.
[23] Ibid., 42.
[24] Usmiani, *Studies in Canadian Literature: Michel Tremblay*, 10.
[25] Marcel Dubé, *Zone*, trans. by Aviva Ravel (Toronto: Playwrights Canada Press, 1982), 5.
[26] Nardocchio, *Theatre and Politics in Modern Quebec*, 42.
[27] Renate Usmiani, "Michel Tremblay" in *The Oxford Companion to Canadian Theatre*, 568–69.
[28] Usmiani, *Studies in Canadian Literature: Michel Tremblay*, 35.
[29] Ibid., 79–108.
[30] Ibid., 36.

31   Renate Usmiani, "Michel Tremblay" in *The Oxford Companion to Canadian Theatre*, 568. For an explanation of "the range, complexity, and colour of Quebecois swearing" see Usmiani, *Studies in Canadian Literature: Michel Tremblay*, 44 45.

32   Usmiani, *Studies in Canadian Literature: Michel Tremblay,* 35.

33   Michel Tremblay, *Les Belles-soeurs*, trans. by John Van Burek and Bill Glassco (Vancouver: Talonbooks, 1991) 98.

34   Sara Graefe, "Reviving and Revising the Past: The Search for Present Meaning, Michel Marc Bouchard's *Lilies, or The Revival of a Romantic Drama*" in *Theatre Research In Canada / Recherches Théâtrales au Canada,* Vol 14; No.2 (Fall/Automne 1993) 165.

35   Ibid., 165.

36   Michel Marc Bouchard, *The Coronation Voyage*, trans. by Linda Gaboriau (Burnaby: Talonbooks, 1999) 33.

37   Ibid., 54.

A Revolution
in English Canada

Although writers such as Voaden and Davies, Gélinas and Dubé wrote successful Canadian plays, theatre companies in the Fifties still complained it was difficult to find, at best, one Canadian drama per season for their audiences to enjoy.

Aside from the relative novelty of the Canadian play, theatre artistic directors were frequently hired from Europe, and often had little experience or interest in local dramas. One consequence of this dilemma was that it was almost impossible at this time to earn a living as a professional playwright (unless, like Dubé, one wrote for television as well). Theatre companies operated largely by private subscription and without government subsidy; they were dependent on a small, devoted public, and were unwilling to tamper with a repertoire that hadn't first proven successful in London or New York.

By the 1960s, the economics of theatre began to change. First, the Canada Council, a government cultural funding agency established following the all-important *Massey Report* of 1951, subsidized the construction of regional theatres across Canada. By the end of the decade, Canada had an established range of provincial cultural establishments. The Vancouver Playhouse, the Manitoba Theatre Centre, and Halifax's Neptune Theatre, to name a few, were joined later in the Sixties by others, such as Toronto's St. Lawrence Centre and Montreal's English-language Centaur Theatre. Yet, with the exception of one or two new venues such as the Centaur, each regional theatre still offered a season rich with the contemporary "hits" of British, Irish and U.S. stages, with typically, one additional Canadian drama, usually played in the smaller, "second" stage of the centre. Foreign directors, British traditions, and the eternally risky economies of the arts led to few innovations in programming, in spite of the new operating grants. Even the jewel in the crown, Ottawa's National Arts Centre, completed in 1969 and initially mandated to tour nationally and to support resident companies in both English and French, essentially became another regional theatre, importing its season from abroad.[1] Ontario's Shakespearean and Shaw Festivals complemented the regional repertoire with their classics of the British stage. In many cases, British artistic directors were named to head these Canadian theatres.

Fortunately, events in the Sixties changed these historical patterns of foreign domination. First, Canada had a remarkable centenary celebration in 1967. Together with the Montreal World's Fair, Expo 67, this gave rise to a broadly resurgent Canadian nationalism, probably not witnessed since the Canada First movement of the 1880s. The energy and enthusiasm of the centenary celebrations encouraged regional theatres to premiere Canadian plays on their main stages. The influential Dominion Drama Festival, for the first time in its 35-year history, required indigenous dramas be submitted for its Centennial Year competition. More significantly, Canadian directors such as George Luscombe and Paul Thompson returned to Canada from acting in populist, politically engaged theatre companies in Europe (Luscombe was trained in Britain's Theatre Workshop and Thompson with Roger Planchon in France) and, eager to bring these alternative ideas to Canadian audiences, discovered a public not only willing to listen, but thirsting for a new cultural direction.

Luscombe's company, Toronto Workshop Productions (TWP), produced plays that were "characterized by polished ensemble acting, spectacular but minimal theatricality, and a commitment to left-wing politics."[2] Luscombe brought to Toronto audiences a documentary style of theatre not seen since Oscar Ryan's *Eight Men Speak*. Although TWP was not agitprop, it did use the anti-illusionist, physical, and choral techniques of that style, as Luscombe did in TWP's most popular production, the 1974 documentary *Ten Lost Years*, based on Barry Broadfoot's history of the Depression in Canada. But innovative documentary, or docudrama, was only one half of the new formula for a new Canadian theatre. A method known as collective creation completed the equation.

Paul Thompson took over direction of Toronto's Theatre Passe Muraille (TPM) in 1972. The title came from France and signalled to the public that their new "theatre without walls" was a company that didn't need expensive theatres in which to perform but, like the agitprop of the 1930s, could perform on a street corner, if need be. The summer of 1972 proved to be a turning point for the young company. Thompson and a half dozen actors from TPM travelled east of Toronto to a small farming community to research and produce—collectively—a play about the area and its people. Six weeks later, in a barn in Clinton, Ontario, "the dominant form of Canadian documentary had its birth...." Paul Thompson's "collective creation," *The Farm Show*, caused a small revolution in Canadian theatre: "[*The Farm Show*] stands as one of the finest works of the Canadian theatre, and it became the model for a form of community documentary theatre based on the actors' personal responses to the source material."[3] In this case, the residents of Clinton provided the 'source material' for Thompson and his cast. And the initial venue for this seminal drama was not a comfortable, urban theatre, but a country barn, with the audience sitting either on their own lawn chairs or on fragrant bales of hay.

Theatre Passe Muraille's collective creations—performances born from actor improvisation and performed without a formal script—not only were a radical re-thinking of the shape of theatre text, but also rearranged the traditional hierarchy of the regional theatre, so much so that the roles of writer, actor, and director now belonged democratically to every member of the cast.

The two terms—documentary and collective—were really parallel theatrical ideas which culminated during the 1970s in many remarkable works: for example, *The Farm Show* (1972/76) and *1837, The Farmer's Revolt* (1975) from Theatre Passe Muraille; prairie docudramas such as *Paper Wheat* (1977) from Saskatoon's Twenty-Fifth Street Theatre; and *Buchans: A Mining Town* (1974) from Newfoundland's Mummers Troupe. In each case, the work was based on local, historical or topical sources, created from company improvisations, staged with rapidly changing, minimal sets, and presented using agitprop techniques by actors in multiple roles. Later, the success of these collectives inspired individual playwrights, such as Rex Deverell (*Medicare!*) and Carol Bolt (*Buffalo Jump*) to create more Canadian plays in the documentary style.

Indeed, Alan Filewod, whose book, *Collective Encounters*, offered an essential study of the docudrama, argued that there is a tradition of "didactic historical theatre" in Canada that extended as far back as Sarah Anne Curzon's *Laura Secord* (1887). Together with "international tradition of documentary theatre originating in Europe in the 1920s" (that, as we have seen, inspired agitprop plays such as *Eight Men Speak*) this tradition created "a direct line of descent" to modern collective dramas:

> Canadian drama has from its beginnings been partial towards what might be called the authority of factual evidence. This can be seen in a long line of plays that seek to revise Canadian history, a list that begins in the early 19th century and continues to the present day.[4]

It can also be argued, I believe, that the Canadian taste for political satire, first noted in Chapter 2 (Victorian drama), possessed a similar national lineage.

Although not at first committed necessarily to the production of distinctly Canadian dramas, by the early 1970s the alternate theatre movement was moving clearly in a nationalist direction. Many, if not all, of the collective dramas mentioned above were created by companies "defining their identity and cultural base in local history."[5] Where once theatre companies struggled to find one "suitable" Canadian play per season, now entire companies played nothing else; venues such as Toronto's Factory Theatre Lab posted banners over the entrance declaring its theatre "the home of the Canadian playwright." Close by, the Tarragon Theatre promised in its manifesto in 1971 that its goals were "to nurture Canadian playwrights," and to "make a contribution to this country's culture."[6] Tarragon followed through on its commitments, developing the careers of playwrights Carol Bolt, David French, Sharon Pollock, James Reaney, Michel Tremblay and George F. Walker, among others. As a result of such encouragement, more than fifty *new* Canadian plays premiered in Toronto alternate theatres in one remarkable season – 1971–72. To critic Urjo Kareda, this was a time "during which, creatively, all hell had broken loose. A common subconscious barrier had somehow been lifted, releasing forces which transformed our theatrical character."[7]

The success of the documentary and the collective traditions influenced many Canadian playwrights during the 1970s and 1980s. Gradually the collaborative processes of TPM were absorbed and evolved by the mainstream of Canadian playwrighting. This new direction not only produced "collective" collaborations like Rex Deverell's docudrama, *Medicare!*, developed at Regina's Globe Theatre, but broadened historical drama into new genres. Alternative theatres and regional ones (such as Theatre Calgary under John Neville) mandated the development of local playwrights and nurtured powerful new talents like David French and Sharon Pollock. Encouraged by their environments (Tarragon and Theatre Calgary respectively), these new playwrights quite naturally broadened the Canadian canon with each new premiere. Some writers, like David French, wrote in a naturalistic style, as in *Leaving Home,* the first of the Mercer family trilogy of dramas; others, like Pollock, began writing historical docudramas, but evolved the genre in psychological directions with complex structures with plays such as *Blood Relations*. Still other influential writers of this era, like George F. Walker and James Reaney, pushed the boundaries of Canadian drama in entirely different directions.

One lesson of this era is that any national drama is limited only by the extent to which the country encourages and financially supports its native talent. If writers can make a living in the theatre, or at least be assured of a venue for their work, then the way each writer chooses to interpret the Canadian reality—his or her choice of dramatic style and structure—has no limits.

An often overlooked style of Canadian theatre is immigrant drama, yet it has influenced Canadian culture since the first French or British soldier stepped on stage to deliver a prologue. The immigrant experience has shaped Canadian literature and, of course, influenced Canadian drama: from the British colonial preferences of the DDF to the contribution of European worker's theatre to Canadian agitprop and docudrama, to the ethnic companies who kept theatre tradition and art alive in the smallest community halls. On many occasions in the last century, a preference for British and other cultural models has been made consciously by Canadians to counter the overwhelming influence of the U.S. mass entertainment. Recent immigrant dramatists in this modern era, such as those from the Black community, may provide similar cultural armour in this century.

Plays such as Andrew Moodie's *Riot* (1995), George Elliott Clarke's *Whylah Falls: The Play* (1997) and h. jay bunyan's *Prodigals In A Promised Land* (1981) all explore variously the perspectives of the new Canadians of African descent. These are modern expressions of an old tradition, in part begun by slaves escaping the U.S. As Black playwright and anthologist Djanet Sears points out, "There is a remarkable legacy of Black theatre in this country."[8] (Indeed, the first Black in Canada was Mathieu d'Acosta, who "accompanied Champlain on his expedition to eastern Canada in 1604,"[9] perhaps making him a participant in Marc Lescarbot's *Theatre de Neptune*.) In *Prodigals*, the audience experiences Canada through the individual struggles of an immigrant family who try to reshape their identities within a new society. It is both a recent, and an abiding, Canadian immigrant experience.

SCENE NINETEEN

The Farm Show, Paul Thompson and Theatre Passe Muraille

Ted Johns, an actor who worked with Paul Thompson on *The Farm Show* recalled a favourite audition technique used by Thompson:

> ...Thompson asked each actor to do five Canadian accents. Well, that floored 'em. So Thompson would say, "You're taking all your models from the movies or TV. I ask for a tough guy and I get Marlon Brando. I ask for sincerity and I get Robert Redford." [10]

Thompson was more interested than his contemporaries to create theatrical moments in which Canadian audiences could actually see themselves. When he took his actors west of Toronto in the summer of 1972 to improvise a collective about a small Canadian rural community, his purpose was "to do something in a place where nothing had been done." [11] *The Farm Show* was successful with Clinton audiences because it held a mirror to their lives; it was successful across Canada because the actors reflected characteristics that were recognizable to all Canadians. It never played New York.

Aside from "transforming localism into art," Thompson's creation developed a new way to structure a drama. Although *The Farm Show* was not a complex play, it was more than a series of scenes and monologues strung together. The apparent arbitrariness of the collective process—including days of rehearsal where "nothing" seemed to be progressing—evolved, selected and refined improvisations, balanced monologues with dialogues, found humour in some scenes, poetry in others, and created and solved dramatic problems as they arose.

Thompson and his actors were careful not to parody the Clinton farmers they portrayed in *The Farm Show*: "...any suggestion of patronizing self-parody is offset by... sincere representation of the characters... the actors perform the characters just as they themselves have met them." [12]

During the scant six weeks it took to create *The Farm Show*, Thompson insisted that his actors perform daily exercises to familiarize them with the innovative style of the play. (In addition, each actor had to volunteer to work as a farm hand for part of the research period. One actor quit over this issue, but Thompson stuck to his plan.) In Thompson's rehearsals actors were asked to:

1. create portraits of local characters – from these grew the monologues;

2. physicalize landscape – out of which grew the actor portrayals of farms, snowstorms, farm buildings;

3. mythologize – by this means, the actors evolved common objects, such as the John Deere tractor, into memorable symbols of farm life;

4. create transformations – using objects, such as a shopping cart as a car, and using an object as anything but what it was intended for originally. [13]

For student actors attempting the following scene, or challenged to develop their own collective creation, a good first step is to rehearse these techniques until they become second nature. These four skills are the "memorized lines" of *The Farm Show.*

— • —

"The Winter Scene" from *The Farm Show,* featuring a raked stage with map of township, bedsheet snowstorm, and crates to represent buildings.

THE FARM SHOW

ACT I, Scene IV. Winter Scene.

Actress playing winter enters and covers both crates with a large white sheet. She stands quiet a second and begins "Winter Poem" before the audience is aware that "Round the Bend" is finished.

Verse one
The middle of winter.
Inside, everything is cozy and warm and small.

WINDOW *(mime window)*

FROST *(blows on the frosted window three times to make a hole to look outside)*

ICICLES *(mime shape of icicles dripping, with icicle sound)*

SNOW *(wind and snow created from blowing sound and by flapping the sheet around like snow)*

VOICE CODE FOR FEMALE SPEAKER	VOICE CODE FOR MALE SPEAKER
1. *Wife/Mother/Jane*	1. *Husband/Father/John*
2. *First Boy (Youngest)*	2. *Michael (Older son)*
3. *Second Boy (Older, perhaps Michael)*	3. *Radio*
4. *Neighbour Woman*	4. *First Boy (Perhaps Michael's Younger Brother)*
5. *Susan (Oldest Child)*	5. *Jim, the Bartender*
6. *Joan, another neighbour woman*	6. *Herb, the Neighbour*
	7. *Dance Caller*

Each actor creates voices and sounds appropriate to the different speakers and situations. Frequent overlap is not dictated by the content of the speeches so much as by the movement of the actors as they tunnel through their separate days and by the feel the two actors develop for each other's presence and rhythms.

FEMALE SPEAKER

1 Rrrring! *(alarm clock)* Up you get! Oh, John, just look at that blizzard.

2 Mummy? Can I get up now?
1 All right, come on downstairs.
You can help me with the orange juice.

Top drawer!

1 Here's the opener.
2 I can... I can do it.

MALE SPEAKER

1 Uhh? Didn't *think* it was going to let up... using the car today?

Michael, get up. You've got to plow out the drive.
2 Right now? Aw Dad...
1 Jane? Have you seen my *underwear?*

1 Be sure to call that oil man... check the furnace.

1 Do you want some coffee
before you go, John?

3 Hey Mom! Where are my
hockey skates?
1 Under the bed. You can't
sleep with them you know.
2 Mom, can I open the new
Muffets?
3 Aw, *he* got that last time,
Yeah, but you've got *eight*
Mahovaliches and I got
only three.

1 Here's your eggs. Now, eat
up. You're supposed to trade
those cards aren't you?
3 Aw... I can't eat those.
1 Well you'll need your strength
for the game. Come on, boys.
Put on an extra sweater.
2 Mummy? Can I come with you?
1 No, dear. Susan will be up
soon and she'll play with you.
Come on boys.
When we leave, hold on to
my hands. You can't see a foot in
front of your face.
*Leaves crate 'house' and climbs into
shopping cart 'car'.*

1 Mike! Get up now.

1 No I'll be back for breakfast
in an hour or so.

*Leaves crate 'house', struggles across
stage to 'barn'. Sound of cattle,
waking farm animals.*

1 Get *over*, Elizabeth!
Move over now.

*Milking machine, mooing, little pigs,
radio, etc.*

3 "And now for the weather:
A cold front moving in a
northeasterly direction over
Moosonee..." etc.
Leaves 'barn', returns to 'house'.

1 Going to have to do that drive
again before the day's out.
Coffee...

1 Susan? The bacon ready?

Wife sitting in shopping cart 'car', husband under crate 'house'.

Verse two
Mountains of snow
Block the driveways, ridge the roads.
Map the landscape.
Arms stretched to the sides, steady stare ahead.

FEMALE SPEAKER

*Starts 'car' and pushes it along
to bean dryer 'arena' with
appropriate noises.*

3 Aren't you going to watch?
1 Not to-day. If the storm lets
  up, come over to Mrs Tindles'.
  It's just a block away
  you know. Good luck.
  Bye.

*'Car' goes to Mrs. Tindles'.
Wife gets out and climbs under
Mrs. Tindles' crate 'house'.*

1 Hi Gloria.
4 Good heavens, you
  made it out.
1 Better take ten dozen.
  You never know when
  I might not be able
  to make it out again.
4 Did you hear about
  the Gelling's baby...
  blue.
1 Heavens, yes. Got
  a card from them
  asking for a prayer.
4 Well, I don't know
  what good my
  prayers will do.
1 Well they've got a
  good family anyway.
  A girl and two boys.
1 Uh huh. Oh here's
  the boys, better be off.

2 Can we stay inside
  for a minute?
1 No, come on now;
  get into the car. See you
  later Gloria. Thanks for
  the coffee.

MALE SPEAKER

1 Don't take Judy out in this
  weather... bundled up or not...
  remember the guy who got
  lost between his house
  and the barn?

4 Daddy? Can I go with you?
1 No, I'm going over to the
  other barn...
1 I'll take the snowmobile...
  be back around five.

*Leaves 'house', drives old mailbox
'snowmobile' to other 'barn'
making sounds for snowmobile
and then little pigs,
feeding noises, etc.*

*Leaves another 'barn', snowmobiles
to 'bar' in town.*

5 Close that *door*!
1 Let me *in* first... have two
  beers Jim.
5 Hear McFarlane's workin for
  Taylor now...
6 Show him what a day's work
  is, heh, heh.
5 Used to be preem-yeer of the
  country...
6 I'm a city man myself...

4 Take it easy now.
3 Mom. You know
what he did?
He let in eight goals.
2 You didn't *see* that...
1 No fighting. Now get
into the back seat.

*'Car' returns home, wife climbs
under crate 'house'.*

2 Boy, I'm going to build a
snow fort!
1 No you're not. In you get. Oh
Susan, did you get the coffee
urn up from the basement?
5 Yeah... it's on the table.
5 I put the roast in the oven.
1 Oh, good, honey. Thanks.
1 You'll see that the dinner gets
on will you? I've got to go early to
the square dancing
to-night with refreshments.
5 Yeah.
2 Mommie, see what I did?
1 Oh *that's* lovely. Why don't
you put it on your wall?
Now is that everything?
1 Bye now.
1 Oh, a new dress.
6 That's something, eh?
I picked the material up in
Goderich last summer and
finally got around to it.
6 Say, where's the men?
1 Well, I can tell you where
John was. Oh here he comes.

1 Now she's a *good woman*...
5 Ever been out of work before
(laughter of various kinds)
1 Wife's got plans for the dance
tonight... yah... not me,
I guess.
5 Close that *door*!

*Leaves the 'bar', snowmobiles to
bean dryer 'arena', parks, climbs
under. Or, if there's time, goes back
home first, talks to the kids, puts on
tie, etc. Obviously the two actors have
to work out their own timing so
they arrive at the 'arena' for
the appropriate mesh of dialogue just
before Freeze 3.
(for example:)*

1 Where's your mother? Oh.
Did you see my red tie
anywhere, Susan? No, you
can't go over to Billie's. You
saw him yesterday. Once
a week is enough. Never see
your mother from morning
to night some days. Going to
the dance. Be back by
midnight. Yah. O.K.
Don't touch the furnace.

1 Good to see you, Harold...
You know women, ...always
get the best of the bargain.
1 Where's Janie?

Both wife and husband huddle out of sight under the bean dryer 'arena'.

Verse three

STILL

QUIET *(pause)*

STARS *(make three stars with hand and sound)*

THE SNOW

CREAKS WHEN YOU WALK ON IT *(three squeaking sounds making footprints with hands)*

SQUARE DANCE CALL

Bean dryer bounces in time, sounds of dancing, applause, fatigue, etc., from the 'crowd' in the 'arena'.

Now, on to your partners!
Now, corners address.
Now all join hands, and circle left!
Circle left, go round the ring
Around the ring with a pretty wee thing,
Now break and swing!
Now, first couple! Up to the right!
And dip and dive across the floor,
Go in again out again in again
Once again!
All the way there,
And all the way back!

FEMALE SPEAKER	**MALE SPEAKER**
1 Ohhh! Hey.	
1 I must have lost ten	1 I'm gonna buy some
pounds on that one.	heifers from him.
6 Come over sometime.	1 Herb, get away from
1 I'll give you a call	that bar.
tomorrow. Okay.	1 Janie, are you coming?
	It's after midnight.

Both leave the 'arena', pause, look at the stars

1 Stopped.

1 That's a blessing.

1 Watch that corner,
it's treacherous.

Into their respective vehicles and drive home with appropriate noises.

1 I'll hold that door for you.

1 Susan? Are you still up?

5 Yeah… watching the late movie.

1 Well, get to bed as soon
as the show's over.

1 Well there was no
stopping *you* tonight, you
must have danced every
dance.

1 Well, I should *say*!

1 Move *over*, you lug!

1 I was just trying to get
warm.

Both actors back in their original crates.

Verse four

THE MOON *(mime moon with hands)*

Bright.

THE SNOW *(look straight ahead, stretch both arms straight in
front, and slowly spread them to the sides)*

Stretches, for miles.

— • —

Director's Notes: "Winter Scene" from *The Farm Show*

Although the lines and scenes appear arbitrary, there is an order that balances
the chaos and creates a fine, dramatic tension of form. There is a rhythm of noise
and silence, of many and few, of dialogue and monologue. The Winter Scene,
a gem which occurs almost midway through the first act of the two-act play,
achieves this tension through the busy activities required of a farm family on
a snowy winter day, contrasted with the stillness and beauty of the rural winter.

The Winter Scene also reveals that *The Farm Show* is, at heart, a work of
improvisation, produced by a fortuitous assembly of very talented actors, skilled
in techniques of improvisation, timing and physicalization. This script is what the
improvisation of life looks like on paper.

Thus, actors will find stage directions during this scene they haven't encountered
before in scripts. For example, after the "father" leaves the "bar" he *"snowmobiles
to bean dryer 'arena', parks, climbs under. Or, if there's time, goes back home*

first, talks to the kids, puts on tie, etc. " This direction means that the actor, using a mailbox as a snowmobile (and making appropriate sounds) crosses to the town's hockey arena—still the focal point of any rural, Canadian town in winter—and places himself as well as he is able "under" the bean dryer which represents the arena building. Each actor must time his or her movement to the rest of the cast, and be inventive enough to create new moments (including new dialogue) if required.

Secondly, the "script" is, of course, a soundscape of overlapping dialogues and sound effects which requires a great deal of concentration to achieve the effect of realistic imitation. In the Winter Scene, the voices of six female actors overlap with those of seven male actors. Each actor is responsible for voice as well as vocalizations, such as car engines, milking machines, little pigs, cows mooing, and so on, as required by their actions. A radio voice gives the family the weather forecast.

Props—a grocery cart, a bean dryer, an old mailbox—represent things they are not – a car, an arena, a snowmobile, respectively. Since there is no association with these objects and the actual props required (other than the fact that these props were all discovered by the cast in Clinton) any objects will do. Crates, just large enough for actors to crawl under, represent the 'house', 'bar' and 'barn'.

Finally, the "plot" of the scene describes the movements of a farm family from dawn to late evening on a winter day, after a particularly heavy snowfall. The busy lives of the family proceed, hardly taking notice of the snow, but its beautiful, humbling presence is felt throughout the scene. This contrast is initialized by the actions of the first actor on stage. She recites the four "verses" of the "Winter Poem" and performs an accompanying pantomime – a show and tell of how a heavy snowfall transforms the landscape, yet never slows the comings and goings of the family. The "poem" and the mime offer a quiet counterpoint to the noisy voices and the busy movements on the stage.

Rehearsals can begin with the physical actions (or the exercises used by Paul Thompson for the original production, listed before the excerpt) or with a read-through of the overlapping dialogue. Whatever the starting point, the layers of this original, complex, little scene seem to be a perfect reflection of the entire play.

— • —

SCENE TWENTY

Leaving Home, David French

In addition to inspiring collectives such as *The Farm Show*, alternative theatres in the 1970s nurtured new Canadian playwrights. The three most successful of these new voices were James Reaney, George F. Walker and David French. Each playwright produced a trilogy that became the cornerstone of his career and epitomized the creative, productive potential released when writer, theatre, and director work collaboratively over a number of years.

James Reaney's *Donnelly Trilogy* was directed by Keith Turnbull at Tarragon Theatre, including *Sticks and Stones* (1973), *The St. Nicholas Hotel* (1974), and *Handcuffs* (1975). George F. Walker, a Toronto cabbie until he submitted his first play to a new script competition held in 1972 by Factory Theatre Lab, wrote his *Power Play* trilogy (not about hockey, but the cases of political reporter, Tyrone Power) starting with *Gossip* (1977), then *Filthy Rich* (1979), and *The Art of War* (1983).

But it is Newfoundland-born David French with his *Mercer Trilogy* of plays (expanded later into a tetralogy) and a career that exceeds three decades, who has been called "the single playwright [who] can be said to epitomize the success of modern Canadian drama" [14] Working with director Bill Glassco of the Tarragon Theatre, French produced *Leaving Home* (1972) and *Of The Fields, Lately* (1973) and completed the cycle of naturalistic dramas some ten years later with two "pre-quels" to his first two plays, *Salt-Water Moon* (1984) and *1949* (1989).

As with many Canadian writers, the CBC provided this playwright with his first job – as a radio actor. *Leaving Home* began as a CBC Radio play titled *The Keeper Of The House*. [15] Once French submitted it to Bill Glassco at Tarragon Theatre, the play began its transformation into Canada's most successful naturalist drama, and cemented the career-long collaboration of French and Glassco. This play and its sequel, *Of The Fields, Lately*, "did much to convince audiences that seeing Canadian experience on stage could be exciting and moving." [16] The two plays also "consolidated the reputation of Tarragon Theatre in Toronto," [17] in the same way *The Farm Show* had built Theatre Passe Muraille a national reputation, proving that although the job of nurturing new talent was both an intensive and expensive process for a theatre company, it paid double dividends over a number of years.

Leaving Home is set in the 1950s in the working-class Toronto home of Jacob Mercer. Jacob is a crusty patriarch, raised in an "outport" fishing village in Newfoundland before it became the last province to join Confederation in 1949. Jacob's ways mean little to sons who have been raised in urban Toronto. Yet, he stubbornly tries, and fails, to force Ben and Billy to accept his view of the world and his understanding of manhood. Jacob's wife, Mary, acts as a mediator between the father's anger and the sons' rebellion – especially between Jacob and his oldest boy, Ben, – an act that Jacob views as treason and one which further emasculates Jacob in his eyes. The inciting incident of the drama is the imminent wedding of Billy to his pregnant girlfriend, Kathy. A comic element is added to the drama by means of Kathy's outspoken mother, Minnie, who shares many of Jacob's values (and, in fact, is an old girlfriend). Minnie's current partner is Harold, the undertaker who embalmed her former husband and who sits silently throughout the entire play, a comic presence, introduced in the following way:

> MINNIE
> He ain't got an ounce of humour in his body, Harold. *(looking at JACOB)*
> But he's got two or t'ree pounds of what counts. Don't you, Lazarus?

Harold's silent potency is an ever-present reminder for Jacob that he is losing his manhood as he loses control over his family. This contrast is one of many French uses in his exploration of "leaving home": both literally, as Jacob's two sons find reasons to leave their family, and figuratively, as Jacob, the immigrant, fails to find new roots in his adopted Toronto home.

Not the least of these contrasts is the modern, urban language of the young trio of the play, Billy, Ben, and Kathy, and the outport dialect of Jacob, Mary and Minnie. French's autobiographical play offers a wonderful lesson in the inflections, tones, nuances, and references of the Newfoundland dialect. The voices of the older speakers, their humour, pace, and prejudices, are given a memorable energy by French's remarkably dynamic vehicle of language.

It is the contradictions and nuances in Jacob's speeches, forced by Ben's intention to assert his independence, that drive the central conflict of the play. They're "two peas in a pod," remarks Minnie as Ben stubbornly confronts his father in the final act, after the news that Ben is leaving home with Billy and Kathy. Ben has had enough of his father's controls and contrivances and in spite of a last-minute attempt by Mary to barter a truce, the son, like the father, cannot resist the urge to have the last word. This prompts Jacob to lose his temper completely, and, taking off his belt, he beats Ben in a rage. Yet, the audience cannot hate Jacob. In spite of his stubbornness, his prejudices, and his anger, he is not a hateful man. Like Willy Loman, or Juliet's father, he is motivated less by self-interest, than by a desperate—tragic—urge to preserve his notion of the family. It is this universal theme, set to the rhythms of the Newfoundland dialect, which makes *Leaving Home* a Canadian classic.

— • —

Leaving Home

JACOB *(expansively)* I t'ink a drink's in order. What do you say, boys? To whet the appetite. *(He searches in the bottom of the cabinet. He speaks to MARY.)* Where's all the whiskey to? You didn't t'row it out, did you?

MARY You t'rowed it down your t'roat, that's where it was t'rowed.

JACOB Well, boys, looks like there's no whiskey. *(He holds up a bottle.)* How does a little "screech" sound?

BEN Not for me, Dad.

JACOB Why not?

BEN I just don't like it.

JACOB *(sarcastically)* No, you wouldn't. I suppose it's too strong for you. Well, Billy'll have some, won't you, my son? *(He turns down the music.)*

BILL *(surprised)* I will?

JACOB Get two glasses out, then, and let's have a quick drink. *(BILL does and hands a glass to his father.)* Don't suppose you'd have a little drop, Mary, my love? *(He winks at BILL.)*

MARY Go on with you. You ought to have better sense, teaching the boys all your bad habits. And after you promised your poor mother on her death-bed you'd warn them off alcohol…

JACOB Don't talk foolishness. A drop of this won't harm a soul. Might even do some good, all you know.

MARY Yes, some good it's done you.

JACOB At least I'd take a drink with my own father, if he was alive. I'd do that much, my lady.

MARY *(quickly)* Pay no attention, Ben. *(to JACOB)* And listen, I don't want you getting tight and making a disgrace of yourself at the rehearsal tonight. You hear?

JACOB Oh, I'll be just as sober as the priest, rest assured of that. And you just study his fingers, if they'm not as brown as a new potato from nicotine. I dare say if he didn't swallow Sen-Sen you'd know where all that communion wine goes to. *(to BILL)* How many drunks you suppose is wearing Roman collars? More than the Pope would dare admit. And all those t'ousands of babies they keep digging up in the basements of convents. It's shocking.

BEN That's a lot of bull, Dad.

JACOB It is, is it? Who told you that? Is that more of the stuff you learns at university? Your trouble is you've been brainwashed.

BEN You just want to believe all that.

MARY And you'd better not come out with that tonight, if you knows what's good for you.

JACOB *(to BILL)* Mind – I'm giving you fair warning. I won't sprinkle my face with holy water or make the sign of the cross. And nothing in this world or the next can persuade me.

BILL You don't have to, Dad. Relax.

JACOB Just so you knows.

BEN All you got to do, Dad, is sit there in the front row and look sweet.

JACOB All right, there's no need to get saucy. I wasn't talking to you! *(He pours a little "screech" in the two glasses. He speaks to BILL.)* Here's to you, boy. You got the makings of a man. That's more than I can say for your older brother.

> *JACOB downs his drink. BILL glances helplessly at BEN. He doesn't drink.*

Go on.

> *BILL hesitates, then downs it, grimacing and coughing.*

You see that, Mary? *(his anger rising)* It's your fault the other one's the way he is. It's high time, my lady, you let go and weaned him away from the tit!

MARY *(angrily)* You shut your mouth. There's no call for that kind of talk!

JACOB He needs more in his veins than mother's milk, goddamn it!

BEN *(shouting at JACOB)* What're you screaming at her for? She didn't do anything!

JACOB *(a semblance of sudden calm)* Well, listen to him, now. Look at the murder in his face. One harsh word to his mother and up comes his fists. I'll bet you wouldn't be half so quick to defend your father.

MARY Be still, Jacob. You don't know what you're saying.

JACOB He t'inks he's too good to drink with me!

BEN All right, I will, if it's that important. Only let's not fight.

MARY He's just taunting you into it, Ben. Don't let him.

JACOB *(sarcastically)* No, my son, your mother's right. I wouldn't wish for your downfall on my account. To hear her tell it I'm the devil tempting Saul on the road to Damascus.

MARY Well, the devil better learn his scripture, if he wants to quote it. The devil tempted our Lord in the wilderness, and Saul had a revelation on the road to Damascus.

JACOB A revelation! *(He turns off the record.)* I'll give you a revelation! I'm just a piece of shit around here! Who is it wears himself out year after year to give him a roof over his head and food in his mouth? Who buys his clothes and keeps him in university?

MARY He buys his own clothes, and he's got a scholarship.

JACOB *(furious)* Oh, butt out! You'd stick up for him if it meant your life, and never once put in a good word for me.

MARY I'm only giving credit where credit's due.

JACOB Liar.

MARY Ah, go on. You're a fine one to talk. You'd call the ace of spades white and not bat an eye.

JACOB *(enraged)* It never fails. I can't get my own son to do the simplest goddamn t'ing without a row. No matter what.

BEN It's never simple, Dad. You never let it be simple or I might. It's always a test.

JACOB Test!

MARY Ben, don't get drawn into it.

JACOB *(to BEN)* the sooner you learns to get along with others, the sooner you'll grow up. Test!

BEN Do you ever hear yourself? "Ben, get up that ladder. You want people to think you're a sissy?" "Have a drink, Ben. It'll make a man out of you!"

JACOB I said no such t'ing, now. Liar.

BEN It's what you meant. "Cut your hair, Ben. You look like a girl." The same shit over and over, and it never stops!

JACOB Now it all comes out. You listening to this, Mary?

BEN No, you listen, Dad. You don't really expect me to climb that ladder or take that drink. You want me to refuse, don't you?

JACOB Well, listen to him. The faster you gets out into the real world the better for you. *(He turns away.)*

BEN Dad, you don't want me to be a man, you just want to impress me with how much less of a man I am than you. *(He snatches the bottle from his father and takes a swig.)* All right. Look. *(He rips open his shirt.)* I still haven't got hair on my chest, and I'm still not a threat to you.

JACOB No, and you'm not likely ever to be, either, until you grows up and gets out from under your mother's skirts.

BEN No, Dad – until I get out from under yours.

The doorbell rings.

MARY That's Kathy. All right, that's more than enough for one night. Let's have no more bickering. Jake, get dressed. And not another word out of anyone. The poor girl will t'ink she's fallen in with a pack of wild savages.

JACOB *(getting in the last word)* And there's no bloody mistakin' who the wild savage is. *(With that he exits into his bedroom.)*

MARY Billy, answer the door. *(to BEN)* And you – change your shirt. You look a fright.

BEN exits. BILL opens the front door, and KATHY enters. She is sixteen, very pretty, but at the moment her face is pale and emotionless.

KATHY Hello, Mrs. Mercer.

MARY You're just in time, Kathy. *(MARY gives her a kiss.)* Take her coat, Billy. I'll be right out, dear. *(She exits.)*

KATHY Where is everyone?

BILL *(taking her coat)* Getting dressed. *(As he tries to kiss her, she pulls away her cheek.)*

BILL What's wrong? *(He hangs up her coat.)*

KATHY Nothing. I don't feel well.

BILL Why not? did you drink too much at the party?

KATHY What party?

BILL Didn't the girls at work throw a party for you this afternoon?

KATHY I didn't go to the office this afternoon.

BILL You didn't go? What do you mean?

KATHY Just what I said.

BILL What did you say?

KATHY Will you get off my back!

BILL What did I say? *(slight pause)* Are you mad at me?

KATHY *(looks at him)* Billy, do you love me? Do you? I need to know.

BILL What's happened, Kathy?

KATHY I'm asking you a simple question.

BILL And I want to know what's happened.

KATHY If I hadn't been pregnant, you'd never have wanted to get married, would you?

BILL So?

KATHY I hate you.

BILL For Chrissake, Kathy, what's happened?

KATHY *(sits on the chesterfield)* I lost the baby…

BILL What?

KATHY Isn't that good news?

BILL What the hell happened?

KATHY I started bleeding in the ladies' room this morning.

BILL Bleeding? What do you mean?

KATHY Haemorrhaging. I screamed, and one of the girls rushed me to the hospital. I think the people at work thought I'd done something to myself.

BILL Had you?

KATHY Of course not. You know I wouldn't.

BILL What did the doctor say?

KATHY I had a miscarriage. *(She looks up at him.)* You're not even sorry, are you?

BILL I am, really. What else did the doctor say?

KATHY I lost a lot of blood. I'm supposed to eat lots of liver and milk, to build it up. You should have seen me, Billy. I was white and shaky. I'm a little better now. I've been sleeping all afternoon.

BILL *(slight pause)* What was it?

KATHY What was what?

BILL The baby.

KATHY Do you really want to know?

> *BILL doesn't answer.*

BILL What'll we do?

KATHY Tell our folks, I guess. My mother doesn't know yet. She's been at the track all day with her boyfriend. *(slight pause)* I haven't told anyone else, Billy. Just you.

— • —

Director's Notes: *Leaving Home*

This scene has two parts. The first dialogue, between Jacob, Mary, Ben and Billy—the Mercer family—gives the strongest indication yet that the dispute between Ben and Jacob will explode into the central conflict before it resolves the drama in Act Two. It has been preceded by the warmest and liveliest beat of the play when Jacob, dressed in his tuxedo, ready to go to Billy's wedding rehearsal, dances a jig with Mary and then encourages his two sons to take a turn. This moment is a picture of what *could* have been, and contrasts to the gathering storm that begins the Jacob-Ben conflict.

The second beat of the selection occurs when Kathy arrives with the news that she has lost the baby in a miscarriage earlier that day. At this point, it is news only for our ears and Billy's – later it provides a dramatic plot reversal to end Act One, as everyone is made aware that Billy's wedding to Kathy may no longer be necessary. In this scene, however, Kathy's lines reveal both her insecurities about her marriage and that she may have inherited a few of her mother's powers of manipulation (developed later, as Kathy's conflict with her mother compares to Jacob's conflict with Ben). For Billy's character, though, this scene is his only extended dialogue in the play. It must be used to show the younger son's sense of innocence and confusion – events seem to be happening to him too fast.

The scene also shows that the religious prejudices of Jacob's outport upbringing have followed him to Toronto. His son is getting married in the Catholic Church, and Billy has converted in preparation for the marriage. Later in the play, Minnie will use this irony to her advantage, further developing this theme. It presents one more obstacle separating father and son, the older generation and the new, and shows that David French has rendered his Canadian portrait, warts and all.

— • —

SCENE TWENTY-ONE

Blood Relations, **Sharon Pollock**

Prairie playwright Sharon Pollock's career has had several parallels to the career of Toronto's David French. She too trained as an actor and, by 1970, had begun writing for radio and the stage. Her early dramas were in the documentary style—*Walsh* (1973), about the treatment of Sitting Bull by the RCMP, *The Komagata Maru Incident* (1978) describing racist attitudes toward Sikhs in Canada—influenced by the presentational styles of the 1970s and her own interest in "setting the record straight" with regard to the interpretation of Canadian history. [18]

In 1980, Pollock appeared to move in a different direction. *Blood Relations* premiered at Theatre 3 at Edmonton's Citadel Theatre in March 1980, and soon after received the first ever Governor General's Award for Drama. It concerned the story of Lizzie Borden who, in 1892 in New England, was accused and later acquitted of the axe murder of her own parents. This was a historical source to be sure, but Pollock's play was not in a documentary form. It was a psychological study of the possible motivations for murder and, more importantly, the thin border between history and psychology. Pollock was not abandoning history, only proving her versatility by changing dramatic styles to examine more deeply historical characters rather than events.

Pollock undertakes this journey in a novel way. *Blood Relations* is set in 1902, ten years after Lizzie's acquittal. The play has two main characters, Lizzie and The Actress. Over the course of two acts, the audience sees a re-enactment of the circumstances leading up to the murders, as Pollock develops a play-within-a-play, using The Actress to play the role of Lizzie Borden at the time of the crime, and the character of Lizzie to play the role of the Borden household maid, Bridget, the only other witness at the time of the event. In spite of its complexity this extended device never intrudes on the rhythms of the play. Indeed, the play-within-the-play device allows Pollock, in the first place, to delve beyond the question of who committed the murder to a psychological examination of the nature of murder itself. Although the audience experiences many of the motivations Lizzie had to commit the crime—mostly as a result of restrictions Victorian society placed on the role of women—Pollock never really answers the key question: did Lizzie do it? In the play's final scene, as Lizzie, carrying a hatchet, moves behind her sleeping father, the audience is unable to see whether or not she was carrying an axe behind her back, nor at this point does it matter. The dramatic tension is energized instead by Lizzie's motivations – compellingly portrayed by The Actress and then further commented on by Lizzie, as herself or in character as Bridget. Thus, the audience is diverted from the crime itself to the possible reasons for the murder. These are presented compellingly enough throughout the play to make every member of the audience a murderer, given Lizzie's society and circumstances. As a result, *Blood Relations* is less a departure from the docudrama for Pollock than it is a development; the audience witnesses the sociological causes of a psychological event. By extension, Pollock's play reveals, through the microcosm of Lizzie Borden, the cause and effect relationship between society and the individual. Sharon Pollock bridges the gap between Paul Thompson's *The Farm Show* and David French's *Leaving Home*, creatively unifying the success of both theatrical styles over the course of her own career.

— • —

BLOOD RELATIONS

MR. BORDEN enters. BRIDGET sees him. LIZZIE slowly turns to see what BRIDGET is looking at.

LIZZIE Papa?

MR. BORDEN What is it? Where's Mrs. Borden?

BRIDGET I... don't know... sir... I... just came in, sir.

MR. BORDEN Did she leave the house?

BRIDGET Well, sir...

LIZZIE She went out. Someone delivered a message and she left. *(LIZZIE takes off her hat and looks at her father.)* ...You're home early, Papa.

MR. BORDEN I wanted to see Abbie. She's gone out, has she? Which way did she go? *(LIZZIE shrugs, he continues, more thinking aloud.)* Well... I... I... best wait for her here. I don't want to miss her again.

LIZZIE Help Papa off with his coat, Bridget... I hear there's a sale of dress goods on downtown. Why don't you go buy yourself a yard?

BRIDGET Oh... I don't know, ma'am.

LIZZIE You don't want any?

BRIDGET I don't know.

LIZZIE Then... why don't you go upstairs and lie down. Have a rest before lunch.

BRIDGET I don't think I should.

LIZZIE Nonsense.

BRIDGET Lizzie, I–

LIZZIE   You go up and lie down. I'll look after things here.

LIZZIE smiles at BRIDGET. BRIDGET starts up the stairs, suddenly stops. She looks back at LIZZIE.

LIZZIE   It's alright… go on… it's alright. *(BRIDGET continues up the stairs. For the last bit of interchange, MR. BORDEN has lowered the paper he's reading. LIZZIE looks at him.)* Hello Papa. You look so tired…. I make you unhappy…. I don't like to make you unhappy. I love you.

MR. BORDEN   *(smiles and takes her hand)* I'm just getting old, Lizzie.

LIZZIE   You've got on my ring…. Do you remember when I gave you that?… When I left Miss Cornelia's – it was in a little blue velvet box, you hid it behind your back, and you said, "guess which hand, Lizzie!" And I guessed. And you gave it to me and you said, "it's real gold, Lizzie, it's for you because you are very precious to me." Do you remember, Papa? *(MR. BORDEN nods.)* And I took it out of the little blue velvet box, and I took your hand, and I put my ring on your finger and I said "thank you, Papa, I love you." …You've never taken it off… see how it bites into the flesh of your finger. *(She presses his hand to her face.)* I forgive you, Papa, I forgive you for killing my birds…. You look so tired, why don't you lie down and rest, put your feet up, I'll undo your shoes for you. *(She kneels and undoes his shoes.)*

MR. BORDEN   You're a good girl.

LIZZIE   I could never stand to have you hate me, Papa. Never. I would do anything rather than have you hate me.

MR. BORDEN   I don't hate you, Lizzie.

LIZZIE   I would not want you to find out anything that would make you hate me. Because I love you.

MR. BORDEN   And I love you, Lizzie, you'll always be precious to me.

LIZZIE   *(looks at him, and then smiles)* Was I – when I had scabs on my knees?

MR. BORDEN   *(laughs)* Oh yes. Even then.

LIZZIE   *(laughs)* Oh Papa!… Kiss me! *(He kisses her on the forehead.)* Thank you, Papa.

MR. BORDEN   Why are you crying?

LIZZIE   Because I'm so happy. Now… put your feet up and get to sleep… that's right… shut your eyes… go to sleep… go to sleep…

She starts to hum, continues humming as MR. BORDEN falls asleep. MISS LIZZIE/BRIDGET appears on the stairs unobtrusively. LIZZIE still humming, moves to the table, slips her hand under the clothes, withdraws the hatchet. She approaches her father with the hatchet behind her back.

She stops humming. A pause, then she slowly raises the hatchet very high to strike him. Just as the hatchet is about to start its descent, there is a blackout. Children's voices are heard singing:

"Lizzie Borden took an axe,
Gave her mother forty whacks,
When the job was nicely done,
She gave her father forty-one!
Forty-one!
Forty-one!!"

The singing increases in volume and in distortion as it nears the end of the verse 'til the last words are very loud but discernible, just. Silence. Then the sound of slow measured heavy breathing which is growing into a wordless sound of hysteria. Light returns to the stage, dim light from late in the day. THE ACTRESS stands with the hatchet raised in the same position in which we saw her before the blackout, but the couch is empty. Her eyes are shut. The sound comes from her. MISS LIZZIE is at the foot of the stairs. She moves to THE ACTRESS, reaches up to take the hatchet from her. When MISS LIZZIE's hand touches THE ACTRESS's, THE ACTRESS releases the hatchet and whirls around to face MISS LIZZIE who is left holding the hatchet. THE ACTRESS backs away from MISS LIZZIE. There is a flickering of light at the top of the stairs.

EMMA *(from upstairs)* Lizzie! Lizzie! You're making too much noise!

EMMA descends the stairs carrying an oil lamp. THE ACTRESS backs away from LIZZIE, turns and runs into the kitchen. MISS LIZZIE turns to see EMMA. The hand hatchet is behind MISS LIZZIE's back concealed from EMMA. EMMA pauses for a moment.

EMMA Where is she?

MISS LIZZIE Who?

EMMA *(A pause, then she moves to the window and glances out.)* It's raining.

MISS LIZZIE I know.

EMMA *(puts the lamp down, sits, lowers her voice)* Lizzie.

MISS LIZZIE Yes?

EMMA I want to speak to you, Lizzie.

MISS LIZZIE Yes Emma.

EMMA That… actress who's come up from Boston.

MISS LIZZIE What about her?

EMMA People talk.

MISS LIZZIE You needn't listen.

EMMA In your position you should do nothing to *inspire talk.*

MISS LIZZIE People need so little in the way of inspiration. And Miss Cornelia's classes didn't cover "Etiquette for Acquitted Persons."

EMMA Common sense should tell you what you ought or ought not do.

MISS LIZZIE Common sense is repugnant to me. I prefer uncommon sense.

EMMA I forbid her in this house, Lizzie!

> *Pause.*

MISS LIZZIE Do you?

EMMA *(backing down, softly)* It's... disgraceful.

MISS LIZZIE I see.

> *MISS LIZZIE turns away from EMMA a few steps.*

EMMA I simply cannot–

MISS LIZZIE You could always leave.

EMMA Leave?

MISS LIZZIE Move. Away. Why don't you?

EMMA I–

MISS LIZZIE You could never, could you?

EMMA If I only–

LIZZIE Knew.

EMMA Lizzie, did you?

MISS LIZZIE Oh Emma, do you intend asking me that question from now 'til death us do part?

EMMA It's just–

MISS LIZZIE For if you do, I may well take something sharp to you.

EMMA Why do you joke like that!

> *MISS LIZZIE is turning back to EMMA who sees the hatchet for the first time. EMMA's reaction is not any verbal or untoward movement. She freezes as MISS LIZZIE advances on her.*

MISS LIZZIE Did you never stop and think that if I did, then you were guilty too?

EMMA What?

THE ACTRESS enters unobtrusively on the periphery. We are virtually unaware of her entrance until she speaks and moves forward.

MISS LIZZIE   It was you who brought me up, like a mother to me. Almost like a mother. Did you ever stop and think that I was like a puppet, your puppet. My head your hand, yes, your hand working my mouth, me saying all the things you felt like saying, me doing all the things you felt like doing, me spewing forth, me hitting out, and you, you–!

THE ACTRESS   *(quietly)* Lizzie.

MISS LIZZIE is immediately in control of herself.

EMMA   *(whispers)* I wasn't even here that day.

MISS LIZZIE   I can swear to that.

EMMA   Do you want to drive me mad?

MISS LIZZIE   Oh yes.

EMMA   You didn't… did you?

MISS LIZZIE   Poor… Emma.

THE ACTRESS   Lizzie. *(She takes the hatchet from MISS LIZZIE.)* Lizzie, you did.

MISS LIZZIE   I didn't. (*THE ACTRESS looks to the hatchet – then to the audience.*) You did.

— • —

Director's Notes: *Blood Relations*

Blood Relations really has two settings, the two days surrounding the murders, in 1892, and ten years later in 1902, the year of the "dream thesis," as Pollock terms the play-within-the-play. Throughout the script the audience is taken from one time to the other and back, all without blackout. Pollock cleverly saves the blackout for the moment at the end of the play when, as The Actress playing Miss Lizzie raises a hatchet over Mr. Borden's head, the audience never gets the answer to the key question. It is at this crucial point that Pollock places the murder weapon tantalizingly in the real Lizzie's hand. The audience now expects the true story to be revealed.

A mere crime mystery ending is not Pollock's intention, of course. She wants the audience to recognize that they are just as capable of murder – indeed, are partly responsible for these murders – as Lizzie Borden.

Preceding the excerpt, The Actress/Miss Lizzie has taken Abigail Borden, Lizzie's stepmother, upstairs and murdered her with a hatchet. The audience never *sees* the crime, although they do see the weapon in "Lizzie's" hand; however, when the real Miss Lizzie returns as Bridget and looks up the stairs, she is suitably shocked, and The Actress/Miss Lizzie begs her to be her accomplice and help her cover up the crime.

Just before Bridget can agree, Mr. Borden returns in search of Abigail. The Actress/Miss Lizzie deftly covers her tracks and then dismisses Bridget/Miss Lizzie who withdraws slowly, reluctant to witness another murder. Alone with her father, Lizzie becomes very affectionate, partly to lull her father into a sense of security and partly to remind the audience of her motivations.

As the stage directions at this point indicate, after a children's skipping rhyme heightens the suspense, the hatchet is transferred from The Actress/Miss Lizzie's hand to the real Lizzie. Her older sister, Emma, then enters. This is the only character in the play, other than the two principals, who is not imaginary (that is, seen only in flashback, as part of the dream thesis). Emma is then drawn into the intrigue and is likely to become Lizzie's next victim without the intervention of The Actress, who returns (this time playing herself) to stay Lizzie's hand. Pollock then concludes the play by burying the hatchet, so to speak, in the audience's hand with Miss Lizzie's final line.

— • —

SCENE TWENTY-TWO

Prodigals in a Promised Land, h. jay bunyan

In *Hill-Land*, Herman Voaden's 1934 expressionist drama concerning the lives of three generations of settlers, the youngest member of the family offers the following words of hope for the "new land:"

> **PAUL**   Each year there is more hope, new life. Soon it will be spring again. I love the land. It's mine. And the frontier is passing.... There are hopes everywhere. It will be easier to lift above life. We shall win through, Mother, where my father and grandfather failed. We shall have a land fit to shape men like gods. [19]

Voaden's character both expresses the toll extracted by immigration—two generations of the family have "failed" to adapt to the new land—and exposes the immigrant's unrelenting idealism, the force that drives him to leave his own land in search of a better life.

This theme has run through Canadian literature from Susanna Moodie's *Roughing It In The Bush,* to Voaden's *Hill-Land*, to Mordecai Richler's *The Apprenticeship of Duddy Kravitz.* The romantic dreams of the immigrant collide with the harsh realities of the new land to produce questionable success or, more often, tragic disappointment. Playwright h. jay bunyan's *Prodigals in a Promised Land* explores this landscape in the context of the Black immigrant, who struggles not only with his new reality, but with racism.

Prodigals is an examination of the forces that drive the romantic ideals of the immigrant – expectations from within the family, from those left behind, and the demands of the new society. It is the story of how a young Caribbean Black couple, Theo and Gloria, and their Canadian-born daughter, Atiba, grapple with the unrealistic dreams of the immigrant, and begin to find in themselves, not in the expectations of others, the answers they have been seeking. Don Rubin expresses the play's dilemma in this way:

> The closer they [Theo, Gloria and Atiba] get to the reality of particular situations, however, the further they get from the dream. The Canada presented at the beginning of the play, for example, is not a real Canada but a dream Canada. A land of milk and honey covered by a thin layer of pristine snow. But once they are in Canada and they see the reality, the Caribbean becomes the land of dream. [20]

Gloria returns to her homeland. She finds little reward in Theo's dogged and ultimately bitter pursuit of a university education and returns, alone, to the Caribbean. Theo gradually revises his dream when he begins to understand that the relationships he has sacrificed to attain status in the white man's world have left him bitter, empty, and without family. Finally, like the children of most immigrants,

Atiba is torn between two worlds. Yet, because her dreams have been tempered by the disappointments of her parents, there is the hope that she will eventually forge a realistic, successful future.

In many respects, Hector Bunyan's *Prodigals* returns us to the essential Canadian theme of immigration first encountered in Marc Lescarbot's *Masque de Neptune*. Although Lescarbot himself returned to France after only a year in the new land, his little "entertainment," with its diverse ensemble of natives, fishermen, soldiers and aristocrats, sought the same integration of the old world with the new.

— • —

PRODIGALS IN A PROMISED LAND

Scene VI

THEO returns home from work, a lunch box in one hand and a coat over his shoulder.

GLORIA *(meets him at the door, her finger to her lips)* Shhh. Shih just fell asleep.

THEO *(seems apprehensive at her presence)* Hi… wuh happening?

GLORIA I okay. How everything with you?

THEO *(sheepishly)* Well. *(He shrugs.)* You can see for yuhself.

GLORIA Yeah… yuh know, yuh shouldn't leave her by herself.

THEO Sometimes we have to take chances… yuh want a drink?

GLORIA Naw.

THEO I need one.

GLORIA You still drink so much?

THEO Only when I need it.

GLORIA If you ruin your health yuh goin' to deprive Atiba of her father.

THEO I'm a big boy now.

GLORIA *(pause)* Shih tell me yuh having a party for her birthday.

THEO Yeah. Ah hope yuh coming.

GLORIA Do you want me to?

THEO You should. After all, you're her mother.

GLORIA And this is your home.

THEO So?

GLORIA I don't have any say in what goes on here.

THEO Ah! Don't be silly.

GLORIA Well. *(She shrugs, then a moment of silence.)* How things at school?

THEO Ah taking a year off.

GLORIA Why?

THEO Ah gotta reconsider certain things.

GLORIA Like what?

THEO That's what ah still trying to find out.

GLORIA *(smiles)* Good to see you can laugh now… you and Atiba laugh a lot?

THEO Sometimes. But ah thinking about getting a bigger place so we can have bigger laughs. *(They smile.)* She misses you. *(silence)*

GLORIA *(opens her purse and removes a letter)* We got a letter from home. Mih mother-in-law says she's coming for a visit.

   THEO reads the letter.

You haven't told her about us.

THEO No.

GLORIA Are you going to?

THEO That depends on… ahm…

GLORIA What?

THEO Yuh get a job yet?

GLORIA Not yet. But ah get a few good offers.

THEO *(reaches into his pocket and removes some money)* Look. Take this.

GLORIA Dat ain't necessary. Use it for Atiba.

THEO She's okay…

GLORIA And buy yourself some clothes.

THEO I ain' interested in clothes.

GLORIA Yuh neglecting your health and ignoring your appearance. Yuh have to take care of yourself y'know.

THEO I doin' okay. And nobody would be interested in looking at me, yuh know.

GLORIA Don't be too sure about dat.

THEO Well, you should know what yuh saying.

GLORIA That's right, Theo.

> *A moment of silence. GLORIA reaches for THEO's hand, holds it. He stiffens, withdraws his hand.*

THEO Now is not the time. We still have a lot to talk about.

GLORIA Words drove us apart, Theo.

THEO Not words, misunderstanding.

GLORIA And how will we ever understand each other if we don't start now?

THEO Look... I...

GLORIA *(almost a whisper)* You're still a cold man, Theo... maybe I've made you hate me too much... funny thing is that you're the only man I ever...

THEO *(enraged)* What only man?! Don't deceive yourself. You know you've had other men...

GLORIA *(in tears)* So what did you expect of me? You rejected me, Theo. You turned me against myself! And now you're rejecting me again!

THEO I'm not rejecting you.

GLORIA *(harsh tone)* Then why don't you talk to me? Tell me how you feel about me? I'm the mother of your child, Theo...

THEO Look, I've taken enough punishment for the day. Don't let's argue.

GLORIA But you're not giving me a chance to...

THEO Please...

GLORIA Okay. Suit yourself.

> *She leaves, slamming the door. THEO sits at the table, sipping a drink and staring vacantly. He lights a cigarette and starts flipping the pages of a book. ATIBA stirs in her bed.*

THEO *(glancing over his shoulder at ATIBA)* Not sleeping?

ATIBA What was all that noise? *(She looks around, blinking her eyes and rubbing them.)* Where's Mommy?

THEO She left.

ATIBA *(sulking)* You had a fight.

THEO An argument.

ATIBA *(sits up in the bed)* Why?

THEO That's the story of our life.

ATIBA *(serious)* But this time it should have been different.

THEO Maybe we try too hard to be consistent.

ATIBA Be serious.

THEO What's wrong with you now?

ATIBA How could you fight with her when she tells you she loves you?

THEO *(shocked)* What?

ATIBA You never listen to anybody!

THEO Try to understand, Atiba. *(tries touching her)*

ATIBA Don't touch me! I hate you!

— • —

Director's Notes: *Prodigals in a Promised Land*

In this scene, from the final act of the play, Theo returns home from work to find his estranged wife, Gloria, in his one-room apartment. Theo has recently assumed the parenting of their daughter, Atiba, because Gloria has had a violent falling out with her new lover, frightening Atiba out of her mother's apartment and into Theo's untidy flat.

In spite of the long, acrimonious separation of her parents, Atiba (and the audience, of course) hope for reconciliation. This scene is the closest the family comes to returning to face the new land together. Gloria's attempt at reconciliation fails, even though she has come at a most opportune time; Theo has just realized that his long cherished dream of success through a university education, a major cause of their separation in the first place, has not provided him with any answers. The audience expects that Theo's dramatic reversal of intention will be complemented with an equally dramatic and emotional reunion of the family.

The playwright opts for a more realistic ending. Theo refuses to forgive Gloria and rejects her tender gesture of reconciliation. He cannot accept her on her own terms—that she faces the same new realities that he does—with the added struggle of being a woman. Ironically, it is his mother's advice in the next and last scene of the play (Gloria informs Theo of her coming visit) that provides Theo with one answer: "Yuh have education but no common sense." It is this truth and a life of "moral strength,"[21] the skills the immigrant needs to survive and succeed in the new land, that resolve the play.

— • —

ENDNOTES to Chapter Five: *A Revolution in English Canada*

[1] Richard Plant, "Drama in English" in Eugene Benson and L.W. Conolly, eds. *The Oxford Companion to Canadian Theatre* (Toronto: Oxford University Press, 1989), 160–61. See also, entries for the theatres listed.

[2] Alan Filewod, "Toronto Workshop Productions" in *The Oxford Companion to Canadian Theatre*, 557.

[3] Alan Filewod, *Collective Encounters: Documentary Theatre in English Canada* (Toronto: University of Toronto Press, 1987), 24.

[4] Alan Filewod, *Collective Encounters*, 5.

[5] Alan Filewod, "Alternate Theatre" in *The Oxford Companion to Canadian Theatre*, 17.

[6] Robert C. Nunn, "Tarragon Theatre" in *The Oxford Companion to Canadian Theatre*, 517.

[7] Urjo Kareda, "Introduction" in David French, *Leaving Home* (Toronto: Anansi, 1972), v.

[8] Djanet Sears, ed., *Testifyin': Contemporary African Canadian Drama, Vol.1* (Toronto: Playwrights Canada Press, 2000), i.

[9] Ibid., vii.

[10] Alan Filewod, *Collective Encounters*, 27.

[11] Ibid., 49.

[12] Ibid., 39.

[13] Ibid., 39.

[14] Jerry Wasserman, ed. *Modern Canadian Plays, Vol. 1* (Vancouver: Talonbooks, 1993), 159.

[15] For this information and the following, see Chris Johnson, "David French" in *The Oxford Companion to Canadian Theatre*, 216–18.

[16] Ibid., 216.

[17] Chris Johnston, "The Mercer Plays" in *The Oxford Companion to Canadian Theatre*, 216–18.

[18] Diane Bessai, "Introduction" to Sharon Pollock, *Blood Relations and Other Plays* (Edmonton: NeWest Plays, 1981), 7–9.

[19] Herman Voaden, *Hill-Land* in Richard Perkyns, ed., *Major Plays of the Canadian Theatre 1934–1984* (Toronto: Irwin, 1984), 61.

[20] Quoted by Djanet Sears, 145.

[21] Ibid., 211.

— • —

chapter
6

The Web and Circle
of Native Drama

Well-known Canadian environmentalist, David Suzuki, in his book, *Wisdom of the Elders,* (co-authored by Peter Knudtson)[1] suggests that the Native ethos—the spirit and beliefs characteristic of the North American First Nation peoples—may provide solutions to the environmental problems created by those of us who came after Cartier and Columbus. Some understanding of this Native ethos is essential as well for interpreting Native drama.

Suzuki sees enormous differences between Native and non-Native views of the environment, and of life itself. "Traditional Native knowledge ...tends to view all—or at least vast regions—of nature, often including the earth itself, as inherently holy, rather than... wild, or wasteland."[2] Native societies feel a responsibility and reverence for the environment that evolves quite logically from the view that all the "things" in nature are a part of a web of the divine spirit. Moreover, many Native theologies do not imagine a supreme being responsible for the creation of mankind and the direction of the natural world, but "Nature's bounty is considered to be precious gifts that remain intimately and inextricably embedded in its *living web* rather than as "natural resources" passively awaiting human exploitation"[3]

Just as the Native "living web" may challenge the European notion of space, broadening a limited view of the physical world to include a powerful, spiritual dimension, so do Native views augment our idea of time. Native culture "...tends to view time as circular (or as a coil-like fusion of circle and line) as characterized by natural cycles that sustain all life, and as facing humankind with recurrent moral crises – rather than as an unwavering linear escalator of *human progress.*"[4] Prince Hamlet's "mortal coil" may be appropriate imagery, but we never, according to Native thought, "shuffle it off."

The U.S. philosopher Christopher Lasch has extensively and profoundly questioned this European notion of linear progress as well, dedicating a treatise in search of the answer to one question: "How does it happen that serious people continue to believe in progress, in the face of massive evidence that might have been expected to refute the idea of progress once and for all?."[5] Lasch reasons this notion is one legacy of Christianity to the Western world. In the 20th century, writes Lasch, the idea that history is a "process generally moving upwards by a series of majestic stages" has been refuted by many modern philosophers, from Christopher Dawson, who called it the "deadest of dead ideas," to Lewis Mumford, who wrote that linear progress was "the one notion that has been thoroughly blasted by the facts of 20th-century experience."[6] This chapter, however, is concerned with less philosophic answers. Suffice it to say that linear and circular notions of time and "progress" appear a major difference between European and Native thought.

How broadly do these cultural differences affect our reading of Native drama? Broadly enough – any performer of the scenes that follow must speak the lines with a reasonable understanding of Native space and time. If, in this Native ethos, co-exist two worlds, one "real," the other supernatural, then again, rather than sharing Hamlet's Western, Christian worldview that upon death we "shuffle off to the undiscover'd country from whose bourn no traveller returns," a student should be guided by an understanding of the web and circle of life. In other words, many characters in Native drama feel ultimately responsible for the natural world; moreover, their actions affect the quality of this life, the next one, and indeed, the infinite weave of all life.

Consequently, searching for a typical, Western, linear plot may simply lead to confusion. In many Native dramas, characters "progress" through experience that is not linear, but circular, by temporarily participating in, and learning from, the supernatural world. The circle is the obvious geometry of Nature. Seasons change and return to begin anew the cycle of life; seasons are in turn timed by the cycling of the moon, and of the daily return of the sun. "To Native eyes," writes Suzuki, "the... universe is temporarily unified by a vast continuity of personal glimpses— by vision quests, songs, and ceremonies, by dreams and creation stories—into the sacred whirlpool of timeless cosmic, mythic, time"[7]

The three scenes in this chapter offer three of these "personal glimpses" some 2500 years apart – from the *Hamatsa Ceremony* to *The Ecstasy of Rita Joe* and *Aria, A One-Woman Play in One Act.* Together they use ceremony, dream, song and dance to provide a unique, "temporarily unified" vision of the world of Native Canadian drama.

— • —

SCENE TWENTY-THREE

The Ritual Drama of *The Hamatsa*

During the 5ᵗʰ century B.C., as Aristophanes watched the masked chorus of his comedy, *The Birds*, satirize Greek society, oceans away other artists, among the Kwakiutl Indians of the northwest coast of Canada, created a similar dramatic flowering. The foremost of these dramas, the Hamatsa ritual, progressed far beyond the purely ceremonial and into the world of theatre. The Hamatsa demonstrated all the qualities of drama, including: "intense preplanning," a five-act play structure, and a "prodigious stagecraft" expressing character transformation, disappearances, stage doubles, trap doors, make-up, and "those magnificent Kwakiutl masks."[8] The Hamatsa served two purposes: efficacy—it initiated a young man into an adult society and reaffirmed social positions within the tribe—and entertainment—it filled the dreary days of a northwest winter with the magic tricks of *tsetsehka*, or legerdemain.

Significantly, a modern interpreter noted that the Hamatsa plot worked "in a circular motion that linked all of creation and went beyond the barriers of time and space... also, in its circularity, suggest[s] the cyclic and the infinite, and how much of creation [is] beyond man's control."[9] Echoing Suzuki's comparison then, in the Native world of the 5ᵗʰ century B.C., space was not two-dimensional, vast and empty, waiting to be discovered, conquered and "developed," and time was not linear nor progressive; rather both contained a powerful spiritual dimension which served in "the humanizing of a man."[10] The sketch of the double circle structure of the Hamatsa plot (see *The Hamatsa Circles*)[11], and a brief outline of the drama to follow, hopefully express these qualities.

— • —

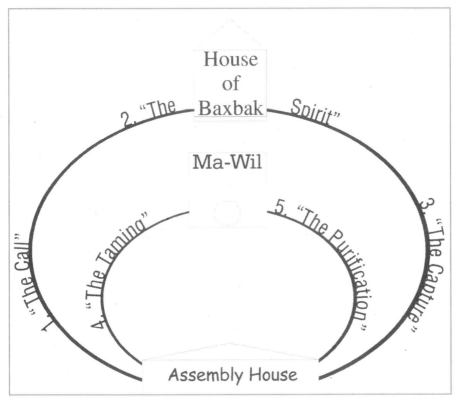

The Hamatsa Circles.

Director's Notes: The Ritual Drama of *The Hamatsa*

To provide a dramatic context for ritual drama in the classroom may be rather daunting, even to the experienced teacher; however, if the story of the Hamatsa is initially explained as a "coming of age" tale, even though it is much more than that, work can begin. By emphasizing the ceremony as a journey of self-awareness for the main character, and even for the student playing this role, the spiritual nature of the ritual can be respected as the structure is explored. The student actor must take a journey – re-enacting personal history, performing the "new secrets" learned from the supernatural part of the journey, and finally, defining a future role as a contributing member of the community. This exciting journey can be made as personal and as individual as the student performer will allow.

In the days leading up to performance, students should prepare an improvised "script" for the ritual to audition for roles and to rehearse their speeches, songs and dances, in order to respect and reflect the "intense preplanning" of the ceremony. A modern interpreter summarizes the ancient plot in general terms this way:

The dramatic content of the Hamatsa ceremony involved a highly coherent tale of loss, danger and gain. The novice Hamatsa left his people, wandered around the world in the company of the fierce Baxbak and, through the careful efforts of his earthly friends, returned bringing mighty supernatural powers with him for the benefit of all the community. It was a simple tale, tending toward the heroic and the picaresque, centred on one person's enormous cosmic adventure, and it was invariable from one Hamatsa ceremony to the next. But to this tale many stories could be appended: the meeting with the first ancestors, the incidents that led to the receiving of certain dance prerogatives, or the gaining of secrets from Baxbak, redolent with ancient, yet still vital reality. [12]

The primary setting is the Assembly House, the main stage for the action, at the centre of which stands the ceremonial "winter pole." Within this area resides a second separate "house," the Ma-Wil, to which the wild and untamed novice retreats after his supernatural journey. A third and final setting is the House of Baxbak, a supernatural land of the spirit and teacher, Baxbak, and his "demonic attendants" Raven, the trickster, and Hohhuq, a monster bird. "Magnificent Kwakiutl masks" are carved of cedar, painted and decorated to express fear and create respect among the participants for these supernatural creatures

The plot is structured in five acts. Act One, "The Call," begins with a stately processional entrance by the different participating societies (the Hamatsas being only one such society). After the procession, the novice's father establishes himself as the host of the ceremony, through words, dance, and a song. *His* father-in-law (the novice's maternal grandfather) begins the action with a gift giving (object, dance, song) which essentially repays the son-in-law—a kind of dowry in reverse— what he gave, years before, in exchange for the novice's mother. Thus, there is a settling of debts. This initiates the settling of debts among *all* participants. The winter pole is used as a touchstone to proclaim and affirm these commitments, and those to follow. The participants are then told, "the winter spirit would soon be called and that everyone must prepare to alter their names, their songs, their style of living, and indeed, their whole tone of living." [13] Student actors can explain, through prepared song and dance, the story of their new choices of name and tone of their lives (perhaps having made real, personal changes in their own lives days before in preparation).

The final "scene" of the first act is the "disappearance of the novice." Many participants give the novice gifts (their stories, songs, dances); by these entertainments, the origin and position of the novice within the society is made clear to all. In a student workshop, actors can make the ceremony more meaningful by using this occasion to relate real events and stories from the life of the "novice." Other participants, costumed and made-up to imitate the novice, appear to play roles in these stories, songs and dances.

Outside, the eerie and dangerous whistles of the supernatural Baxbak can be heard as the spirits of the winter ceremony are invoked by this dramatic and spiritual activity inside. All members participate in the experience of the novice: "All matter was shared: the novice's danger became their danger and his gains in supernatural powers theirs." Apparently, the spiritual journey of one man becomes, in effect, "a multi-directional trek with the incorporation of the action and questing of many." [14] Or, as Suzuki expresses it: "the universe is temporarily unified by a vast continuity of personal glimpses into the sacred whirlpool of mythic time." The novice's personal pool reflects quest for meaning in all our lives.

After the novice disappears, the second act, "The Spirit," begins. There are really two, strongly oppositional actions which energize this act: the precise, prepared *order* of the various "dancing societies," each with their processions, dances and regalia (tallow, cedar, drums, bark, eagle down), powerfully and physically opposed to the wildness and *chaos* of the world of the winter spirits. Many moments of intense drumming and frenetic dancing, measured by fewer and fewer contrasting moments of ordered procession and even silence, indicate the supernatural entering and overwhelming the world of the assembly, just as it had previously taken possession of the novice:

> Just as [the novice] was stolen away and made wild, so were they; just as he encountered strange spirits, they witnessed the antics of the Fool Dancers, the Grizzly Bears, and cannibalistic (like Baxbak) Hamatsas. Finally, they too were plunged into uncoordinated violence and the act ended in a rough dispersal. [15]

The next act shows the return of the novice from his supernatural journey. It is the first of the final three acts in which he is "Captured" (Act Three), "Tamed" (Act Four), and "Purified" (Act Five) to be returned to his community, a wiser and fully productive member. A friend who knows him best, a character called *Leaning Against*, is used to entice the novice back from the wild journey. Through songs and dances by this individual, by others experiencing the same return, and by the various societies, the wildness of the supernatural is driven away and the novice returns. Throughout Acts Three and Four, suspense is cleverly maintained by two means: first, the novice appears, only to disappear and second, the dances and songs performed to capture him may not be learned and executed well enough, with sufficient order and precision to overwhelm the forces of chaos and must be repeated until known. (Directors take note!)

"The Capture" then has two scenes: the enticing of the novice and, after repeated mistakes and repetitions, the capture of the novice, who himself dances (sings, demonstrates) what he has learned too imprecisely to be understood and flees to behind the Ma-Wil until his wildness can be tamed in Act Four. The commentator, Hoffman, "scripts" the final two acts in the following way: [16]

Act IV "THE TAMING"

Action A: *The long summoning*
Subaction 1: Messengers invite all to come and pacify the
supernatural one.

Subaction 2: Another group of messengers repeats the
    announcement to each house.
Action B: *Pacifying the Novice*
Subaction 1: Women dance.
Subaction 2: Shaman dances.
Subaction 3: Shaman demands more eagle down, the singing of
    sacred songs.
Action C: *Appearance of Supernatural Beings.*
Subaction 1: Raven performs.
Subaction 2: Baxbak performs.
Action D: *Taming is accomplished.*
Subaction 1: Taming with fire.
Subaction 2: Taming costume put on.

ACT V "THE PURIFICATION"

Action A: Construction of the "Man."
Action B: Novice is washed.
Action C: Novice is put through the "Man."
Action D: Critique of ceremony.

The action of the five acts has many circles. The boy who begins the ceremony hours (or days) before is now a "Man"; he will initiate his own son one day to complete the circle. "The plot, which at first glance might seem a rigid, lifeless edifice useful only for repetitive ritual but not for drama, worked in fact in a linear and a circular motion that linked all of creation and went beyond the barriers of time and space."[17]

The theme of the drama is the relationship between the gods and man: Baxbak is powerful, but can be outwitted by man: "Man could meet him, participate for a while in his unspeakable existence, and return unharmed bringing back the creature's powers."[18] What the novice learns, he will contribute to his society, "humanizing" him as he comes of age as a full participant in the affairs of his community. (The costume he assumes in Act Five symbolizes his unique contribution.) One can only admire the sense of custom, tradition, and social status such a ceremony must have created in the youth of the Kwakiutl Nation.

— • —

228 THE BARON BOLD AND THE BEAUTEOUS MAID

SCENE TWENTY-FOUR

The Ecstasy of Rita Joe, George Ryga

As a result of George Ryga's uncompromising moral vision and socialism he becomes, in the words of *The Oxford Companion to Canadian Theatre,* "both one of the best-established and least-performed Canadian dramatists."[19] This irony can be explained to some extent by the difficulty both audiences and some critics have had dealing with the structure and other innovative elements of Ryga's most enduring work, *The Ecstasy of Rita Joe.* In his introduction to the play, critic Jerry Wasserman notes that a central conflict of the drama is the clash between the worldviews of the white and aboriginal characters:

> Central to Rita's torment is the cultural and epistemological schism between whites and Indians, represented in its extreme form by the contrast between the mechanical, life-denying pseudo-rationalism of the Magistrate and the humane, intuitive impressionism of David Joe. These ways of seeing and understanding the world are so fundamentally different that the results of their clashes are sometimes comical.[20]

The awkwardness of Wasserman's description illustrates his frustration when he attempts to express the ideas of Native space and time without the understanding of writers such as Suzuki, Hoffman, critics such as Denis Johnston[21], and Native writers like Tomson Highway.[22] Wasserman's best choice of words is "intuitive;" coincidentally the same word R.B. Parker uses twenty years earlier in his introduction to the first publication of *The Ecstasy of Rita Joe.*

> The stage directions refer constantly to "memory," "reverie," "dream" and "mood" as keys to the sequence of events, and it is also several times emphasized that such thinking is typical of the intuitive Indian mind, which communicates by fragments of reminiscence not by abstract concepts.[23]

Parker then goes beyond "intuitive" to nail down, with remarkable insight, the dream-like, circular structure of *The Ecstasy of Rita Joe,* which was, at the time of first production in 1967, a radical and bewildering drama to many audiences:

> The several trials of Rita Joe are intermingled until they all seem the same trial, recurrent throughout Act I and recapitulated, with an almost musical effect, in the penultimate scene of Act II. Similarly, the climactic rape and deaths are heralded from the first, and this circularity is emphasized by the circular ramps of the playing area (and further by the blocking of the original production).[24]

As "circularity" is the key to understanding the *Hamatsa,* both in structure and theme, so too is this notion essential to any reading or performance of *The Ecstasy of Rita Joe.*

As Parker indicates, Ryga's use of the circle begins with his opening description of the circular ramp, for all practical purposes the spiral proscenium of the play. The fact that his description is unusually detailed indicates that, to Ryga, the director who alters the shape of the ramp ignores its obviously symbolic nature. Suzuki suggests that the spiral is a "common ground between Western and indigenous thought, …a fusion of time's circular and linear aspects." [25] Ryga's vision is similarly perceptive.

His stage is material representation of the "coil-like fusion of circle and line." What the ramp symbolizes is Ryga's attempt to make sense of his protagonist's fragmented, alienated world. Rita's universe is "temporarily unified by the vast continuity of [her] personal glimpses." These are her visions of her past and of her future, some presented as "flashbacks," others as tragic "flash-forwards." They assume a greater importance in the structure and meaning of the play than the "main" plot of the courtroom. By means of his deliberate deconstruction of linear, progressive time – through Rita's dreams, visions, songs and stories, Ryga truly and remarkably allows the audience to enter Rita's "timeless, mythic world," to identify with her tragic life.

— • —

THE ECSTASY OF RITA JOE

ACT I

A circular ramp – beginning at floor level stage left and continuing downward below floor level at stage front, then rising and sweeping along stage back at two-foot elevation to disappear in wings of stage left. This ramp dominates the stage by wrapping the central and forward playing area. A short approach ramp, meeting with the main ramp at stage right, expedites entrances from wings of stage right.

The MAGISTRATE's chair and representation of court desk are situated at stage right, enclosed within the sweep of the ramp. At the foot of the desk is a lip on stage right side. At the foot of the desk is a lip on stage right side. The SINGER sits here, turned away from the focus of the play. Her songs and accompaniment appear almost accidental. She has all the reactions of a white liberal folklorist with a limited concern and understanding of an ethnic dilemma which she touches in the course of her research and work in compiling and writing folk songs. She serves, too, as an alter ego to RITA.

No curtain is used during the play. At the opening, intermission, and conclusion of the play, the curtain remains up. Because of this, the onus for isolating scenes from the past and present in RITA Joe's life falls on highlight lighting.

Backstage, a mountain cyclorama is lowered into place. In front of the cyclorama, a darker maze curtain to suggest gloom and confusion, and a cityscape.

House lights and stage work lights remain on. Backstage, cyclorama, and maze curtain are up, revealing wall back of stage, exit doors, etc.

Cast, SINGER, enter offstage singly and in pairs from wings, exit doors back of theatre, from auditorium side doors. The entrances are workmanlike and untheatrical. When all the cast is on stage, they turn to face the audience momentarily. House lights dim.

Cyclorama lowers into place. Maze curtain follows. This creates a sense of compression of stage into the auditorium. Recorded voices are heard in a jumble of mutterings and throat clearings. The MAGISTRATE enters as the CLERK begins:

CLERK *(recorded)* The court is in session. All present will rise... *(shuffling and scraping of furniture)* ...Magistrate's Court reconvenes. The court calls Rita Joe to the stand. Rita Joe!

The cast repeat "Rita Joe, Rita Joe." A POLICEMAN brings on RITA Joe.

MAGISTRATE Who is she? Can she speak English?

POLICEMAN Yes.

MAGISTRATE Then let her speak for herself! *(speaks to the audience firmly and with reason)* To understand life in a given society, one must understand laws of that society. All relationships...

CLERK *(recorded)* ...Man to man... man to woman... man to property... man to the state...

MAGISTRATE ...are determined and enriched by laws that have grown out of social realities. The quality of the law under which you live and function determines the real quality of the freedom that was yours today.

The rest of the cast slowly move out.

Your home and your well-being were protected. The roads of the city are open to us. So are the galleries, libraries, the administrative and public buildings. There are buses, trains – going in and coming out. Nobody is a prisoner here.

RITA *(with humour, almost a sad sigh)* The first time I tried to go home I was picked up by some men who gave me five dollars. An' then they arrested me.

The POLICEMAN retreats into shadows. The SINGER crosses down.

MAGISTRATE Thousands leave and enter the city every day...

RITA It wasn't true what they said, but nobody'd believe me...

SINGER *(sings as a recitivo searching for a melody)*
Will the winds not blow
My words to her
Like the seeds
Of the dandelion?

MAGISTRATE *(smiles, as at a private joke)* Once... I saw a little girl in the Cariboo country. It was summer then and she wore only a blouse and skirt. I wonder what she wore in winter?

> *Murderers hover in background, on upper ramp. One whistles, and one lights a cigarette – an action which will be repeated at the end of the play.*

RITA *(moves to him, but hesitates)* You look like a good man. Tell them to let me go, please!

> *MAGISTRATE goes to his podium.*

MAGISTRATE Our nation is on an economic par with the state of Arkansas... we are a developing country, but a buoyant one. Still... the summer report of the Economic Council of Canada predicts a reduction in the gross national product unless we utilize our manpower for greater efficiency. Employed, happy people make for a prosperous, happy nation...

RITA *(exultantly)* I worked at some jobs, mister!

> *The MAGISTRATE turns to face RITA Joe. The murderers have gone.*

MAGISTRATE ...Gainful employment. Obedience to the law...

RITA *(to the MAGISTRATE)* Once I had a job... *(He does not relate to her. She is troubled. She talks to the audience.)* ...Once I had a job in a tire store... an' I'd worry about what time my boss would come... he was always late... and so was everybody. Sometimes I got thinkin' what would happen if he'd not come. And nobody else would come. And I'd be all day in this big room with no lights on an' the telephone ringing an' people asking for other people that weren't there.... What would happen?

> *As she relates her concern she laughs. Towards the end of her dialogue she is so amused by the absurdity of it all she can hardly contain herself.*
>
> *Lights fade down on MAGISTRATE who broods in his chair as he examines court papers.*
>
> *Lights up on JAIMIE Paul approaching on backstage ramp from stage left. He is jubilant, his laughter blending with her laughter. At the sound of his voice, RITA Joe runs to him, to the memory of him.*

JAIMIE I seen the city today and I seen things today I never knew was there, Rita Joe!

RITA *(happily)* I seen them, too, Jaimie Paul!

He pauses above her, his mood light and childlike.

JAIMIE I seen a guy on top of a bridge, talkin' to himself... an' lots of people on the beach watchin' harbour seals.... Kids feed popcorn to seagulls... an' I think to myself – boy! Pigeons eat pretty good here!

RITA In the morning, Jaimie Paul... very early in the morning... the air is cold like at home..

JAIMIE Pretty soon I seen a little woman walkin' a big black dog on a rope... dog is mad... dog wants a man!

JAIMIE Paul moves to RITA Joe. They embrace.

RITA Clouds are red over the city in the morning. Clara Hill says to me if you're real happy... the clouds make you forget you're not home...

They laugh together. JAIMIE breaks from her. He punctuates his story with wide, sweeping gestures.

JAIMIE I start singin' and some hotel windows open. I wave to them, but nobody waves back! They're watchin' me, like I was a harbour seal! *(laughs)* So I stopped singin'!

RITA I remember colours, but I've forgot faces already.

JAIMIE Paul looks at her as her mood changes. Faint light on MAGISTRATE brightens.

RITA ...A train whistle is white, with black lines... a sick man talkin' is brown like an overcoat with pockets torn an' string showin'... a sad woman is a room with the curtains shut...

MAGISTRATE Rita Joe?

She becomes sobered, but JAIMIE continues laughing. She nods to the MAGISTRATE, then turns to JAIMIE.

RITA Them bastards put me in jail. They're gonna do it again, they said... them bastards!

JAIMIE Guys who sell newspapers don't see nothin'...

RITA They drive by me, lookin'...

JAIMIE I'm gonna be a carpenter!

RITA I walk like a stick, tryin' to keep my ass from showin' because I know what they're thinkin'... them bastards!

JAIMIE I got myself boots an' a new shirt – see!

RITA *(worried now)* I thought their jail was on fire... I thought it was burning.

JAIMIE Room I got costs me seven bucks a week...

RITA I can't leave town. Every time I try, they put me in jail.

POLICEMAN enters with file folder

JAIMIE They say it's a pretty good room for seven bucks a week...

JAIMIE begins to retreat backwards from her, along ramp to wings of stage left. She is isolated in a pool of light away from the MAGISTRATE and the light isolation between her and JAIMIE deepens, as the scene turns into the courtroom again.

MAGISTRATE Vagrancy.... You are charged with vagrancy.

JAIMIE *(with enthusiasm, boyishly)* First hundred bucks I make, Rita Joe... I'm gonna buy a car so I can take you every place!

RITA *(moves after him)* Jaimie!

He retreats, dreamlike, into the wings. The spell of memory between them broken. Pools of light between her and the MAGISTRATE spread and fuse into single light area. She turns to the MAGISTRATE, worried and confused.

MAGISTRATE *(reading documents in his hand)* The charge against you this morning is vagrancy...

MAGISTRATE continues studying papers he holds. She looks up at him and shakes her head helplessly, then blurts out to him.

RITA I had to spend last night in jail... did you know?

MAGISTRATE Yes. You were arrested.

RITA I didn't know when morning came... there was no windows... the jail stinks! People in jail stink!

MAGISTRATE *(indulgently)* Are you surprised?

RITA I didn't know anybody there.... People in jail stink like paper that's been in the rain too long. But a jail stinks worse. It stinks of rust... an' old hair...

MAGISTRATE looks down at her for the first time.

MAGISTRATE You... are Rita Joe?

She nods quickly. A faint concern shows in his face. He watches her for a long moment.

I know your face... yet... it wasn't in this courtroom. Or was it?

RITA I don't know...

MAGISTRATE *(pondering)* Have you appeared before me in the past year?

RITA   *(turns away from him, shrugs)* I don't know. I can't remember...

> The MAGISTRATE throws his head back and laughs, the POLICEMAN joins in.

MAGISTRATE   You can't remember? Come now...

RITA   *(laughing with him and looking to POLICEMAN)* I can't remember...

MAGISTRATE   Then I take it you haven't appeared before me. Certainly you and I would remember if you had.

RITA   *(smiling)* I don't remember...

> The MAGISTRATE makes some hurried notes, but he is watching RITA Joe, formulating his next thought.

(naively) My sister hitch-hiked home an' she had no trouble like I...

MAGISTRATE   You'll need witnesses, Rita Joe. I'm only giving you eight hours to find witnesses for yourself...

RITA   Jaimie knows...

> She turns to where JAIMIE had been, but the back of stage is in darkness. The POLICEMAN exits suddenly.

Jaimie knew...

> Her voice trails off pathetically. The MAGISTRATE shrugs and returns to studying his notes. RITA Joe chafes during the silence which follows She craves communion with people – with the MAGISTRATE.

My sister was a dressmaker, mister! But she only worked two weeks in the city.... An' then she got sick and went back to the reserve to help my father catch fish an' cut pulpwood. *(smiles)* She's not comin' back... that's for sure!

MAGISTRATE   *(with interest)* Should I know your sister? What was her name?

RITA   Eileen Joe.

> EILEEN Joe appears spotlit behind, a memory crowding in.

MAGISTRATE   Eileen... that's a soft, undulating name.

RITA   Two weeks, and not one white woman came to her to leave an order or old clothes for her to fix. No work at all for two weeks, an' her money run out.... Isn't that funny?

> The MAGISTRATE again studies RITA Joe, his mind elsewhere.

MAGISTRATE   Hmmmmmm...

> EILEEN Joe disappears again.

RITA   So she went back to the reserve to catch fish an' cut pulpwood!

MAGISTRATE I do know your face – yes! And yet...

RITA Can I sit someplace?

MAGISTRATE *(excited)* I remember now – yes! I was on holidays three summers back in the Cariboo country... driving over this road with not a house or field in sight... just barren land – wild and windblown. And then I saw this child beside the road – dressed in a blouse and skirt, barefooted...

RITA *(looking around herself)* I don't feel so good, mister.

MAGISTRATE ...My God, she wasn't more than three or four years old... walking toward me beside the road. When I'd passed her, I stopped my car and then turned around and drove back to where I'd seen her, for I wondered what she could possibly be doing in such a lonely country at that age without her father or mother walking with her.... Yet when I got back to where I'd seen her, she had disappeared. She was nowhere to be seen. Yet the land was flat for over a mile in every direction – I had to see her. But I couldn't... *(stares down at RITA Joe for a long moment)* ...You see, what I was going to say was that this child had your face! Isn't that strange?

RITA *(with disinterest)* Sure, if you think so, mister...

MAGISTRATE Could she have been... your daughter?

RITA What difference does it make?

MAGISTRATE Children cannot be left like that.... It takes money to raise children in the woods as in the cities.... There are institutions and people with more money than you who could...

RITA Nobody would get my child, mister!

> She is distracted by EILEEN's voice in her memory. EILEEN's voice begins in darkness, but as she speaks, spotlight isolates her in front of ramp, stage left. EILEEN is on her hands and knees, two buckets beside her. She is picking berries in mime.

EILEEN First was the strawberries an' then the blueberries. After the frost... we picked the cranberries... *(laughs with delight)*

RITA *(pleading with the MAGISTRATE, but her attention on EILEEN)* Let me go, mister...

MAGISTRATE I can't let you go. I don't think that would be of any use in the circumstances. Would you like a lawyer?

> Even as he speaks, RITA has entered the scene with EILEEN picking berries. The MAGISTRATE's light fades out on his podium.

RITA You ate the strawberries an' blueberries because you were always a hungry kid!

EILEEN   But not cranberries! They made my stomach hurt.

RITA goes down on her knees with EILEEN.

RITA   Let me pick – you rest. *(holds out bucket to EILEEN)* Mine's full already – let's change. You rest…

> *During exchange of buckets, EILEEN notices her hands are larger than RITA Joe's. She is both delighted and surprised by this.*

EILEEN   My hands are bigger than yours, Rita – look! *(takes RITA Joe's hands in hers)* When did my hands grow so big?

RITA   *(wisely and sadly)* You've worked so hard… I'm older than you, Leenie… I will always be older.

> *The two sisters are thoughtful for a moment, each watching the other in silence. Then RITA Joe becomes animated and resumes her mime of picking berries in the woods.*

We picked lots of wild berries when we were kids, Leenie!

> *They turn away from their work and lie down alongside each other, facing front of stage. The light on them becomes summery, warm.*

In the summer, it was hot an' flies hummed so loud you'd go to sleep if you sat down an' just listened.

EILEEN   The leaves on the poplars used to turn black an' curl together with the heat.

RITA   One day you and I were pickin' blueberries and a big storm came…

> *A sudden crash of thunder and a lightning flash. The lights turn cold and blue. The three Murderers stand in silhouette on riser behind them. EILEEN cringes in fear, afraid of the storm, aware of the presence of the Murderers behind them. RITA Joe springs to her feet, her being attuned to the wildness of the atmosphere. Lightning continues to flash and flicker.*

EILEEN   Oh, no!

RITA   *(shouting)* It got cold and the rain an' hail came… the sky falling!

EILEEN   *(crying in fear)* Rita!

RITA   *(laughing, shouting)* Stay there!

> *A high flash of lightning, silhouetting the Murderers harshly. They take a step forward on lightning flash. EILEEN dashes into arms of RITA Joe. She screams and drags RITA Joe down with her.*

(struggling against EILEEN) Let me go! What in hell's wrong with you? Let me go!

MAGISTRATE I can't let you go.

The lightning dies, but the thunder rumbles off into the distance. EILEEN subsides and pressing herself into the arms of RITA Joe as a small child to her mother, she sobs quietly.

RITA There, there… *(with infinite tenderness)* You said to me what would happen if the storm hurt us an' we can't find our way home, but are lost together so far away in the bush?

EILEEN looks up, brushing away her tears and smiling at RITA.

RITA & EILEEN *(in unison)* Would you be my mother then?

RITA Would I be your mother?

RITA Joe releases EILEEN who looks back fearfully to where the Murderers had stood. But they are gone. She rises and collecting buckets moves hesitantly to where they had been. Confident now, she laughs softly and nervously to herself and leaves stage.

(rising and talking to EILEEN as EILEEN departs) We walked home through the mud an' icy puddles among the trees. At first you cried, Leenie… and then you wanted to sleep. But I held you up an' when we got home you said you were sure you would've died in the bush if it hadn't been for us being together like that.

EILEEN disappears from stage. The MAGISTRATE's light comes up, RITA shakes her head sadly at the memory, then comes forward to the apron of front stage. She is proud of her sister, and her next speech reveals this pride.

RITA She made a blouse for me that I wore every day for one year, an' it never ripped at the armpits like the blouse I buy in the store does the first time I stretch… *(stretching languidly)* …I like to stretch when I'm happy! It makes all the happiness go through me like warm water…

— • —

Director's Notes: The Ecstasy of Rita Joe

A production of the preceding scene (from the opening pages of *The Ecstasy of Rita Joe*) should establish in some way the four essential components of Ryga's setting, which create the atmosphere for Rita's dreams. Foremost is the ramp, encircling the central acting area, lowering itself two feet below the downstage lip at front, and "sweeping along stage back at two-foot elevation," then rising to support ominously the Murderers above the heads of Rita and Jamie Paul, who themselves are "wrapped" within the acting area below. (The ramp should be circular, even though the temptation is to make it an oval to more easily reflect the dimensions of the proscenium stage. A circle serves the director both symbolically and practically, allowing more room than an oval for the actors on entering and providing larger acting areas downstage of the ramp, on left and right.)

Secondly, the high desk of the Magistrate, right of centre, within the ramp's enclosure, must also be higher than the actors at centre. Ryga intends the Magistrate to "look down upon" Rita in every sense and reflect the reality of Western Canadian courtrooms, where "the bench" is often placed halfway up the end wall to dominate the room and to impress (or intimidate) those standing trial.

Thirdly, two contrasting "cycloramas" exist: one of mountains and light, seen dimly through a superimposed, second "darker maze curtain to suggest gloom and confusion" of a cityscape. And finally, the technical effects specified by Ryga are key components, no matter how primitive. Pools of light, recorded sounds, voices and incidental music are necessary to create effective, dreamlike transitions, as are the actors' circular movements, which are, we are reminded by Parker, a vital part of the "blocking of the original production."

This opening scene clearly creates the central conflicts, the key characters, and the two settings (city and reserve). Additionally, we see Rita's alienation and isolation in the threatening claustrophobia of the courtroom, momentarily suspended and contrasted to her wellspring of happy memories, all under the dark shadows, and her prescient awareness of her Murderers. All of these ideas place great demands on the actor playing Rita, who must, like her Hamatsa novice ancestor, convince the audience in a few moments on stage that her present, past, and future are one.

— • —

SCENE TWENTY-FIVE

Aria, A One-Woman Play in One Act, Tomson Highway

The first years of Tomson Highway's life were spent in the remote northwestern forests of Manitoba. Born on his father's trap-line, he left this entirely Cree ethos at the age of six to spend the next ten years immersed in the English-speaking world of Christian residential school, high school, and foster homes. Studying classical piano at university, his talents led him to London, England and London, Ontario where he was an assistant to well-known playwright, James Reaney.

Highway draws from these two, divergent spheres to create his best-known plays, *The Rez Sisters* (1986) and its sequel, *Dry Lips Oughta Move To Kapuskasing* (1989). *Aria, A One-Woman Play in One Act*, is written between these two masterpieces, in 1987, and expresses a distillation of the characters, imagery, and themes of Highway's longer works.

Literary critic Denis Johnston imagines both of Tomson's "Rez" (reservation) plays as defined by the image of the circle. He writes:

> In *The Rez Sisters* and *Dry Lips Oughta Move to Kapuskasing*, linear elements generally show characters becoming lost by stubbornly following a straight line, where circular elements signal regeneration. [26]

Johnston further suggests, "the strength of the play depends on cyclical character journeys rather than on the plot line." [27] He reaches these conclusions after quoting Highway himself on Cree culture:

> This is the way the Cree look at life. A continuous cycle. A self-rejuvenating force. By comparison, Christian theology is a straight line, birth, suffering, and then the apocalypse.... Human existence isn't a struggle for redemption to the Trickster. It's fun, a joyous celebration. [28]

Highway carefully reiterates this last point in his own "Note on Nanabush" which precedes the text of *Dry Lips Oughta Move to Kapuskasing*:

> The dream world of North American Indian mythology is inhabited by the most fantastic creatures, beings and events. Foremost among these beings is the "Trickster," as pivotal and important a figure in our world as Christ is in the realm of Christian mythology. "Weesageechak" in Cree, "Nanabush" in Ojibway, "Raven" in other, "Coyote" in still others, this Trickster goes by many names and many guises. In fact, he can assume any guise he chooses. Essentially a comic, clownish sort of character, his role is to teach us about the nature and the meaning of existence on the planet Earth; he straddles the consciousness of man and that of God, the Great Spirit. [29]

Highway explains that two other defining notions separate the Native ethos from the English, Christian worldview:

> And secondly, [Cree language] is very visceral. You talk quite openly about the functions of the body, which in English are taboo. The Trickster was a very sensual character—making love, eating—all those bodily functions, he celebrated them, he lived for them. The Trickster's most frequent conversational partner was his anus. In English the immediate impulse is to censor that, but in Cree it makes perfect sense.
>
> The third distinction is that there is no gender given to the world. By that system of thought the mythological Trickster is neither exclusively male nor exclusively female; or is both simultaneously. [30]

All three ideas, the web of real and dream worlds, the polymorphous Trickster, and his/her love of visceral language, and in addition, Highway's aim to "expose the poison" of years of racism, abuse, and violence makes some non-native audiences more upset than entertained by his plays in performance. Of course, meaningful, innovative art often makes viewers (not to mention reviewers) uncomfortable, and thus Tomson Highway's theatrical world is the type of art which offers confrontation rather than comfort, invention rather than reassurance.

Aria is a compelling refinement of these three essentials. First, each monologue contains a "personal glimpse" of a supernatural reality; what an early character, The Mother, calls, "webs of wonder." Secondly, although its single actor is female, the roles call for polymorphous, Trickster-like changes of wardrobe. And, Hera Keechigeesik's monologue contains the visceral element.

Any confrontation is as much within the Native speakers as without. Through its myriad of monologues, the difference between the two, opposing views of the world, one white and one Indian, so well described by Suzuki and others, is in clear evidence. Moreover, audiences also experience the tension this unresolved dialectic creates within each speaker who, in the modern world, must make sense of the white man's urban, technological, material landscape, one which stands in stark contrast to the natural, cyclical, spiritual world of the Indian. Tomson's own life is testimony to this struggle, beginning in one world and achieving first success in one art form and then another. The title and staging of *Aria* are drawn from Highway's background in classical music and opera, as Ric Knowles and Monique Mojica point out in their excellent introduction to the play. They also note that the aria is never sung.

> At the very end, when the diva is finally ready to sing, the piano music releases itself into this gorgeous, romantic "bel canto" introductory passage and, as the diva—back once more, inside the body of her gown—opens her mouth to form the first vowel of her song, the lights fade into blackout. It remains for the audience members themselves to sing, in their minds, the aria, the "song of woman." [31]

But, perhaps Highway also intends this unresolved musical tension to mirror his continuing struggle to resolve these two, apparently irreconcilable worlds.

Fortunately, audiences recognize Highway's characters as spiritual guides—our own brief journey with Baxbak, to harken back to a much earlier quest—to learn and understand the nature of this new song. *Aria* sets the stage and introduces our diva-like guide who surprises us with her appearance, much like the Trickster.

— • —

ARIA, A ONE-WOMAN PLAY IN ONE ACT

THE WIFE stands on the porch landing of her house on the reserve. A rickety old washing machine is before her; she is doing laundry. She "talks" a lot with her hands.

THE WIFE My husband's socks, my husband's pants, my husband's shirt, my husband's underwear. My shirt, my socks, my pants, my underpants. Hey, the way this life of mine has gone, loving him and him loving me and me and him go fishing in the lake. You throw the net. And the water sticks in the *(hand motions making the shape of the webbing in the net)* catching the sun. Handfuls of light come "phht-phht" in your face. "*Hera Keechigeesik*, don't rock the boat too much. Scare the fish away," he say to me. Me and him. Hey, *ta-p'wee-sa pee-sim* [1]...

The years me and Zachary were fishing and trapping up north, summertime we live in tents. The lake is there, the island, the island hanging from the sky. Our men were all gone hunting. So it was just us women. And the children. Alone.

All of a sudden "haw-woomp." This "phhhrrroommm." Very black. First I thought it was a moose. But no. "Haw-woomp, haw-woomp," the water went, "haw-woomp, haw-woomp, haw-woomp." It was terrible. There was this... *pee-s'tew* [2]... this... foam... foaming in the water. It reached the shore. It was huge. Bigger than any man. Covered with hair. No lips. Eyes flames of ice. It was. The Weetigo! Ohhh, the breath of the Weetigo can freeze you 'til you're stiff as a statue. Then the Weetigo enters you. Right into your soul. And you become. The Weetigo! And you eat people. Brrrr.

So anyway. There. The Weetigo. On the shore. Right before our very eyes. So us women. We grab our children and take to the hills. And we waited. And I watched.

The Weetigo went into my tent! Rowwwowwwooorrrr! *(roars and bangs the sides of the washing machine)* It roared and raged. The tents were in shreds. The dogs? All dead. He was so big he tripped on the stove and burned our camp to the ground. Everything was in flames.

---

[1] This phrase is used at various times in this monologue, in various permutations. Its approximate meaning, in Cree, is "Hey this sunshine sure feels good...."
[2] "Pee-s'tew" means "foam" in Cree.

Then. And only then. "Haw-woomp, haw-woomp, haw-woomp, haw-woomp, haw-woomp," it swam back to the island. Brrrr! The Weetigo is a terrible, terrible thing to see.

(Abruptly, she begins to sing, happy as a lark.) La-la-la-la-la-la-la the mouth of high July, hey! *(speaks)* The life of wives sings in the summer the furniture needs dusting, hey! *Ta-p'wee-sa pee-sim nee-ta-cha-ga-soo.* "*Hera Keechigeesik*, that yellow sunshine sure looking good on that brown belly of yours," he say to me. Zachary. My Zachary.

My husband's socks, my husband's pants, my husband's shirt, my husband's under.... The time that Nataways woman brought his underwear home to me. In a box, all nice washed and folded.

She stands there. Curlers. Blouse wrinkled and dirty tits stink of ashtrays and men. One step down on my rickety porch, paint is gone long ago, wood rotten sand blow through the cracks. Jacket, Zachary's pup, the ugly one, dropped his shit by the step again.

That Giselle Nataways. She took a shit on Liza Jane Manitowabi's lawn. She opened her legs to seventeen-year-old Dickie Bird Halked right in front of Black Lady Halked's face. She made two babies by Raggedy Annie Cook's husband without missing one single goddamn bingo game. But no woman come near Zachary Keechigeesik.

I, Zachary Keechigeesik's wife, never let her children go hungry, never missed a payment at Andy Manitowabi's store. I, Zachary Keechigeesik's wife, walked 40 miles to the Anchor Inn in January through that blizzard to sober up Rosie Kakapetum the medicine woman to save this woman's own mother from the blood from that accident, the gun in that drunken brawl this woman's own father was the one that pulled the trigger and just about shot her foot off. I walked that 40 miles.

She stands there. Her lips smile. But her eyes? *Ee-pa-pee-it a-wa k's'ka-na-goos. Ku-nu-wa-pa-ta oos-kee-si-g'wa.* [3] I freeze. I hear rushing water in my head. *(screams uncontrollably)* I kick with my knee. I kick and I kick and I kick and I kick and I kick. *(Pause. Calm again, she whimpers.)* Blood got all over my hands. Blood and clumps of sticky bloody hair. I kicked her in her pregnant belly. Her shitty brown bum spread naked in the dirt by my broken steps, squeaking like a sick mink.

I was ever alone. Three days. I sit in my living room. Curtains shut. Don't eat. Don't wash. Nothing. Three days. Stare straight ahead. Three days.

He come home, shy as a puppy dog, this... suitcase full of dream visions under his arm—the very first TV on the reserve. So. So now me and him and him and

---

[3] Cree: "She's laughing at me, this female dog. Look at her eyes."

me. We lie on this couch at midnight. *(pause)* Can't see the TV too good cuz his knobby old knee's in the way, hey. *Ta-p'wee-sa ma-na a-wa pee-sim.*

THE INDIAN WOMAN   *Oo-oo n'si see-tuk*
  Hey, ta-p'wee sa mi-thoo ki-noh-s'koo-si-wuk
  Oom-see-si ka-ga-noh-pi-ma-g'wow ma-na see-tuk
  Hey, tas-kootch ma-na oo-tee pee-cha-eek
  Ee-moo-see-thi-muk a-wi-nuk
  U-wi-nuk ee-nee-pa-wit
  U-wi-nuk ee-pa-gi-ta-ta-moot
  U-wi-nuk ee-p'mat-sit
  Oo-oo n'si see-tuk
  Hey, ta-p'wee sa mi-thoo us-ki-tu-goo-si-wuk
  I-thi-gook ma-na een-tay-thee-ta-man
  Ta-na-ta-g'wow; ta-na-ta-g'wow
  I-goo-see-si nee-s'ta tay-si-pa-gi-ta-ta-moo-yan
  Tay-si-moo-see-ta-an pee-cha-eek
  Oo-oo n'si see-tuk these trees… [4]

THE WHITE WOMAN   The taxis.
  The taxis are yellow this afternoon
  And seem to float just centimetres
  Above the grey cement, the two
  the taxis and cement—
  Are separate and apart.

  The traffic.
  The traffic is heavy, this afternoon
  And seems to float just centimetres
  Above the grey cement, the two
  The traffic and cement—
  Are separate and apart…
  makes horrible racket,
  This traffic.

  The stores.
  The stores are numerous this afternoon

---

[4] *(Translation for production personnel only, not for audiences.)*

These trees	These trees
So tall, straight	Green so rich
I look at trees like this	I want
Inside of me—here—	To talk to them
I feel someonew, a being	Walk in them
Someone standing there	Breathe in them
Someone breathing there	Live inside their breathing
Spirit alive and living	These trees

244 THE BARON BOLD AND THE BEAUTEOUS MAID

So are the windows in these stores
You can see your own reflection in them
As you pass. There are also many
Restaurants in which to have lunch
And talk business and sometimes
Of things that touch the heart.

The spirits.
I see no spirits whatsoever
On this cement, I don't know
What this other woman is talking about.
I walk on this cement, and the two
This cement and I—
Are distinctly separate and apart.

THE SECRETARY What the well-dressed girl will wear:

Wash'n'wear polyester chalk-stripe wrap-around in slimming come-again
navy blue. Sixteen ridiculous dollars. Designed to please the man who calls
her "secretary girl."

Cute little navy blue pumps with heels high enough to entice, low enough to
run. *Armé de Salvation.* $4. But only her best friend needs to know.

This snappy ensemble is completed by a fin-blue cotton T-shirt with slit-neck
and droopy loopy sleeves by Alfred Sung. $125. She was depressed and she…
simply had to go shopping.

Nevertheless.
She stands.
A veritable soldierette.
On the brink of pay equity.
Success will be hers before you can say:
"Phew-phew!"

THE EXECUTIVE SECRETARY *(in the rhythm of a slow samba)*
Today:
I live in closer proximity
To the man in the pin-striped suit
My vocabulary has increased
The first time I heard the word
"Proximity" I thought it was some new
Disease or at least some obscure Brazilian
Dance not unlike the bossa nova, the cha-cha
Or the samba. Hey!
Living in closer proximity
To the man in the pin-striped suit
I'm aware of the greater power

I've acquired over my own fate
My destiny, my life
My will and I appreciate
That power I embrace that power
And that power looks attractive
And beguiling on my sleeve
On the shank of the old left leg.
I'm no longer some lowly minion
A servant girl, a lackey
A gofer or an ornamental exercise
I'm Executive Secretary now and
I live in more intense proximity
To the man, the man in the pin-striped suit
More intense proximity to
The man in the pin-striped suit
Is a state of being I much
Appreciate I get to stand
Behind the man and place my
Hands upon his back so that
He doesn't fall when he finds
He doesn't have the time or
Finds he is incapable or
Finds he doesn't have the answer
Like right now, he'll ask me and
I'll go: "Yes, this is the way"
Or "No, that's not the way"
Or "Yes, I'd do it this way"
Or "No, the prices are extravagant"
          horses are an asset"
     begonias will not do"
Or "It's more than once I've
Climbed into your shoes and
Steered you through the darkness
Of your pin-striped mind, my man
That's my job"
Living in such intimate proximity
To the man in the pin-striped suit
I began to feel that the pin-striped
Suit is sticking to my skin.
In little bits and pieces this morning
I got up and there before me
In the glass two pins and a stripe
Were sunk into the
Outer layer of my forehead not an inch
From my brain at noon I'm

Eating lunch with my soup spoon
Raised with three pins and two stripes
Announce themselves on the palm
Of my right hand so it seems
That if I choose persistence
In this close proximity to the man
In the pin-striped suit! Oh... but...
Well, it's like a tool, a hammer
Or a sickle or a sword that I
Wield and I flash and I order
Secretaries hither and secretaries thither
Flocks, gangs, hordes of secretaries
At my bidding and they part
Like the deep Red Sea before
My gliding, whispering
Sleek and sinuous Executive
Secretary form young girls
Sprouting shards of fire-painted
Fingernails in love within electrified
By their IBM Selectrics and I
Glide past them like an elegant fish
To the side of the man
The man in the pin-striped suit.

My vocabulary has expanded
"Proximity" is a concept
That I appreciate
So
Much.

THE EXECUTIVE   Good morning, gentlemen.

Gentlemen, in October of 1986, the Executive Committee of the Ontario League of Native Brotherhood Centres hired me as Executive Director to operate and monitor the costs of programmes province-wide. It must have become evident to the Executive Committee and every member of the Board that the status of the organization is tenuous and unstable at best.

With reference to the Ontario Native Courtworker programme, first put into place in 1961 to reduce the percentage of Natives incarcerated in the Canadian penal system, the success quotient has stabilized at 40%. It was your goal to train and equitably distribute Native courtworkers to Brotherhood Centres across this fair province. It was to be incumbent upon the Courtworkers to interpret legalese to Native offenders, access lawyers and interpret to the courts the cultural perspective of Natives standing trial.

Time and money for the implementation of this essential service has been eaten away by the bickering, by the jockeying for position and by the ridiculous political posturings within the Executive Committee itself. It is my contention that in becoming abscessed with the might of its own power, this Executive Committee has forgotten what it was first put in place to do.

As a result of mismanagement, misdirection, and what amounts to near criminal negligence, our Courtworkers are facing impossible working conditions and are inadequately paid for responsibilities too numerous for them to negotiate.

I can walk into the Premier's office tomorrow and get that additional $200,000. You've tried. You've failed. I'm telling you, I can do it. I have the interest, the personality, the speaking ability, the power, the vision, the determination, and the drive.

We could put that $200,000 into a comprehensive training package and put at least eight more Courtworkers into the system. However, in the interest of maximum efficiency with respect to the delivery of programmes to our Native community, I can offer each member of the Executive Committee: $100 a week for in-town travel; a Tilden rent-a-car credit card; dental, medical, optical, family, and other benefits. And a darned good business lunch. In return for which, the Executive Committee will grant me tenure. And complete unlimited… control.

So this is what it's like. This is what I came to do. To change this fabulous masculine world. Succeed? Of course. I'm a success. I sit on top of the world, men scattered at my feet like roses at a shrine. And here I thought I would move these incredible motionless men, waken them to the voices of these many thousand women in their blood… make them understand this energy, my spirit… that clings to the pores of my skin like the mouths of a million frightened children. So…

Thank you, gentlemen.

THE DIVA Woman… alone… forest
Hunter
Marry… her lodge
Two sons… good wife
Grown careless… work
He spies on her
Naked
Hissing snakes
Penetrating… every orifice
Hunter kills… snakes
Soup… blood…
Feeding… wife.
"You have eaten blood of your lovers."

She runs... see... dead lovers
Sons... flee
Hunter gives... medicine... for protection.
"If sky red tonight," he tells sons, "I have died."
Wife returns
Hunter axes... her head
Slashes her body
Throws it to the sky
Woman's skull attacks... devours
Fleeing sons see red sky... know...
Coldness...
Mother's rolling skull cries
"Come to mother."
Sons throw medicine...
Thorn patch... entangles skull
Boys escape
Beaver helps her
Chase
Mother's skull again cries
"Come to mother."
Sons throw second medicine
Huge cliff stops skull
Boys escape
May-may-quay-sik helps her
Chase
Skull cries
"Come to mother."
Sons throw third medicine
Flames surround skull.
But still... skull chases
Boys throw fourth medicine
Poplar stumps entangle skull
Skull frees itself
Chase...
"Come to mother."
Boys throw last medicine.
Water gushes
Water bird helps skull
But falls in water
"My sons. Save me."
Boys throw rocks.
Split skull
Skull sinks
Boys free...

THE DIVA/THE WOMAN OF THE ROLLING HEAD
I loved my husband once.

Then in my soul one night
Crept the dark spirit silently
And in the forest I made love
To ten thousand snakes
Night after night.

Crying, writhing,
Singing at the moon,
One night he saw me there
My husband saw me then
And cut my head off with an axe.

My body falls
But I refuse.
I will not die.
I will not die.

My head leaps.
My mouth leaps.
I tear his throat.
Feast on his flesh.

My sons
I tear their throats.
Feast on their flesh.
And my sons, sons
And on and on and on

> "Babies. My babies. Come to your loving mother."
> I am the Woman of the Rolling Head
> I loved ten thousand snakes
> I loved ten thousand snakes
> I loved ten thousand snakes
> "Children. Come. Come to me. Your mother…"

(speaks) I can't. I can't. This is wrong. This is all wrong. The wrong way.
Wrong way. Wrong way to tell the stories. We've forgotten how to tell the old
stories. They're fading. Fading. No. No. They can't. Can't. What am
I doing here. What am I doing here.

MARILYN Ooooh!
How long
Are you going to
Love me
For?

THE PROSTITUTE Hey, mister. Gotta cigarette?

Hey, mister. Got the time?

Hey, mister…

Hey…

Starlight, starry night, bright light and I'm alright…

Hey, mister. Wanna buy me a drink?

Hey, mister…

He sits there in his brand-new sky-blue/chrome Chevrolet Impala. Drives by in the starry night and doesn't even see the goddamn stars…

Chevrolet Impala, eh? Hey, where's that guy in the great big BMW who came to me last week, whimpering between my legs like a puppy dog in need of a home?

Hey, mister. Wanna give me a ride?

Street life gets to one sometimes and after a while… what the hell and damn it all anyway, a girl's gotta make a living and a girl's gotta be able to buy a drink.

Starlight, moonlight, I'm alright…

Car lights glide past me. Glide past. These men, these anonymous men, these lonely men, they cast their hungry eyes at me and peer real deep into this little old red heart of mine. What the fuck do they wanna see? The reflection of themselves and their lolling tongues?

Hey, mister. Wanna see me? The real me?

Wanna see the me beneath all this lipstick, rouge, eye-liner shit I've slapped on my face to make myself look just a little more white?

Hey, mister. I promise you, mister, it'll make you feel so good you'll come for days. And it'll cost you only sixty bucks. Sixty bucks. That's all…. What do you expect, pork chops at the IGA down the street is going for $3.95 a kilo this week and they don't even come anywhere near…

Hey, mister. Hey, wait a minute. I was just…. Oh shit.

Gettin, a little chilly. Gotta buy me more pantyhose tomorrow. My ass is gettin, a little loose around the edges gotta do something about it, maybe take up judo or Tae-kwon-do or something… that way maybe I can protect myself against any man who may come along and abuse me with his… his fists, like beat me up, like pulverize me, like beat the shit out of me. This way I could just give him a judo chop right across the neck like this, "ha!" and he'd fall dead right on top of my two tits…

Yes, pantyhose…

Well, now, there's starlight and car light and there's nightlight and city light, neon light and street light and starlight and I'm alright and starlight and shit car light's glaring at me like they've never seen a woman before, what's a matter, your wife won't give ya…

Hey.

THE EARTH And the songbird paused.
My spirit… like a mist.
There was a gift came down to me.
(sings) Kees-pin ki-sa-gee-hin.
(speaks) Strange and mysterious goings-on.
And pain becomes power.
Here is the aisle.
Me and him and him and me.
U-wi-nuk ee-pa-gi-ta-ta-moot.
Are separate and apart.
Like ahmmm… so, anyway.
I touch you and you speak.
Closer proximity to.
I can offer each member.
Ten thousand snakes.
Oooh, how long?
Starlight, moonlight and I'm alright! Hey!

I knew she was alive.
I know Earth is alive.
I can feel through the soles of
My moving feet…
Earth.
Nuna.
Us-ki!

Blackout.

The end.

— • —

Director's Notes: *Aria, A One-Woman Play in One Act*

This excerpt includes 11 of the 17 roles of the play. Highway describes the staging as an opera diva's gown that drapes the entire stage, including the proscenium. It is fitted on a frame, centre, from which the actor can emerge to play various roles as required, with props scattered about the stage. Upstage, silent and still at a grand piano is seated an Indian, male pianist costumed in both tails and native dancing regalia.

For a deeper understanding of *Aria*, the actor must return to the thread of contrasting worlds introduced before the excerpt. Tomson Highway himself notes, in a very useful essay on his own work, that Native mythology has to be "re-worked... if it is to be relevant to us Indians living in today's world." Furthermore, Highway states he is, "urban by choice," and as such must "apply these myths... to the realities of city living." To drive this point home at the time of this article, Highway uses his typical humour.

> So, "Weesageechak" the trickster figure who stands at the very centre of Cree mythology... still hangs round and about the lakes and forests of northern Manitoba, yes, but he also takes strolls down Yonge Street [Toronto], drinks beer, sometimes passes out at the Silver Dollar and goes shopping at the Eaton Centre. You should have seen him when he first encountered a telephone, an electric typewriter, a toaster, an automobile. I was there. [32]

It is during the same year those words are written, 1987, that he writes and stages *Aria*, as Artistic Director of Native Earth Performing Arts in Toronto. The first monologuist in *Aria* reflects on this "re-working of the mythology": "This thing they call a telephone is a living thing."

In the preceding excerpt, from the last pages of the play, a perceptive actor or director can help this reworking—this tension—between the natural and urban landscapes emerge. The Indian Woman speaks poetically in Cree of the trees, feeling them breathe, wanting to "live inside their breathing." She mirrors an earlier monologue of the Mother who sees in her newborn, "webs of wonder." And, this spiritual dimension of the natural world (the "living web") is contrasted vividly in the next monologue, The White Woman, who views the world as "separate and apart":

> The spirits.
> I see no spirits whatsoever
> On this cement, I don't know
> What this other woman is talking about.

The three roles that follow echo this theme, with the longer monologues of the Executive Secretary and the Executive re-creating the material and bureaucratic obstacles of the white, urban landscape. (One can hear Ryga's Magistrate resonating in the lines of Highway's Executive.) The final lines of the Executive's monologue, however, ironically re-introduce the "webs of wonder" theme, in the voice of this bureaucrat. With the Diva's monologue the musical accompaniment begins and "we enter the fabulous dream world of Cree mythology" to the "atonal... increasingly cacophonous and frenzied" sounds of the keyboardist who has, until this point sat motionless upstage at his grand piano. [33]

The Prostitute returns the audience to the urban reality, and the distorting dichotomy of urban and natural: "Well, now, there's starlight and car light and there's nightlight and city light..." Appropriately, the last monologue belongs to the Earth, and her last lines issue a call to the spiritual world.

— • —

ENDNOTES to Chapter Six: *The Web and Circle of Native Drama*

1. Peter Knudtson and David Suzuki, *Wisdom of the Elders* (Toronto: Stoddart Publishing, 1992).
2. Ibid., 13.
3. Ibid., 14 (emphasis added).
4. Ibid., 14 (emphasis in original).
5. Christopher Lasch, *The True and Only Heaven* (New York: Norton, 1991), 13.
6. Ibid., 40–41. Ernest Lee Tuvson, Christopher Dawson, and Lewis Mumford as quoted by Lasch.
7. Knudtson, Suzuki, 145.
8. James Hoffman, "Towards an Early British Columbia Theatre: The Hamatsa Ceremony as Drama." *Canadian Drama / L'Art dramatique Canadien* 11.1 (1985), 235.
9. Ibid., 240.
10. Ibid., 242.
11. Ibid., 240.
12. Ibid., 241.
13. Ibid., 241.
14. Ibid., 241 for this, and the previous quotation.
15. Ibid., 241.
16. Ibid., 239.
17. Ibid., 241.
18. Ibid., 240.
19. Christopher Innes "George Ryga" in Eugene Benson and L.W. Conolly, eds. *The Oxford Companion to Canadian Theatre* (Toronto: Oxford University Press, 1989), 479.
20. Jerry Wasserman, *Modern Canadian Plays, Vol. 1* (Vancouver: Talonbooks, 1989), 26.
21. Denis W. Johnston, Lines and Circles: The Rez Plays of Tomson Highway" in W.H. New, ed. *Native Writers and Canadian Writing* (Vancouver: UBC Press, 1990).
22. Nancy Wigston, "Nanabush in the City" in *Books in Canada* (March, 1989)
23. R.B. Parker, "The Ballad Plays of Ryga" in George Ryga, *The Ecstasy of Rita Joe and other Plays* (Toronto: General Publishing, 1971).
24. Ibid., xvi.
25. Suzuki, Knudtson, 145.
26. Johnston, 255.
27. Ibid., 257.
28. Ibid., Johnston quoting Wigston, 255.
29. Tomson Highway, *Dry Lips Oughta Move To Kapuskasing* (Calgary: Fifth House, 1989), 12.
30. Wigston, 8–9.

31   Monique Mojica and Ric Knowles, *Staging Coyote's Dream* (Playwrights Canada Press, Toronto, 2003), p. 78.

32   Tomson Highway, "On Native Mythology," in Rubin, Don, ed. *Canadian Theatre History, Selected Readings* (Playwrights Canada Press, Toronto, 2004), 404–07.

33   Mojica and Knowles, p. 78.

SELECTED RESOURCE / WEBSITE BIBLIOGRAPHY

Benson, Eugene, and L.W. Conolly. *The Oxford Companion to Canadian Theatre.* Toronto: Oxford University, 1989.

Bert, Norman A. *Theatre Alive! An Introductory Anthology of World Theatre.* Colorado Springs: Meriwether, 1994.

Derkson, Celeste. "Out of the Closet: Dramatic Works by Sarah Anne Curzon." *Theatre Research in Canada / Recherches Théâtrales au Canada* 15:2 (Spring 1994), 3–20.

Cameron, Ron. *Acting Skills For Life.* Toronto: Simon and Pierre, 1991.

Creighton, Donald. *John A. Macdonald, The Old Chieftain.* Toronto: Macmillan, 1955.

The Drury Lane Prologue by Samuel Johnson and The Epilogue by David Garrick, 1747. Humphrey Milford, ed. London: Oxford University Press, 1924.

Hoffman, James. "Towards an Early British Columbia Theatre: The Hamatsa Ceremony as Drama." *Canadian Drama / L'Art dramatique Canadien* 11.1 (1985), 231–44.

Filewod, Alan. *Collective Encounters: Documentary Theatre in English Canada.* Toronto: University of Toronto Press, 1987.

Fulks, Wayne. "Albert Tavernier and the Guelph Royal Opera House." *Theatre History in Canada,* 4;1 (Spring, 1983), 41–56.

Graefe, Sara. "Reviving and Revising the Past: The Search for Present Meaning, Michel Marc Bouchard's *Lilies,* or *The Revival of a Romantic Drama.*" *Theatre Research In Canada / Recherches Theatrale au Canada* 14;2 (Fall/Automne 1993) 165.

Highway, Tomson. "On Native Mythology," in Rubin, Don, ed. *Canadian Theatre History, Selected Readings.* Toronto: Playwrights Canada Press, 2004, 404–07.

Knudtson, Peter and David Suzuki. *Wisdom of the Elders.* Toronto: Stoddart Publishing, 1992.

Lasch, Christopher. *The True and Only Heaven.* New York: Norton, 1991.

Lee, Betty. *Love and Whiskey: the Story of the Dominion Drama Festival and the Early Years of Theatre In Canada 1606–1972.* Toronto: Simon and Pierre, 1982.

Lord, Barry. *The History of Painting in Canada.* Toronto: NC Press, 1972.

Mojica, M. and Ric Knowles. "Introduction to *Aria*." Staging Coyote's Dream. Toronto: Playwrights Canada Press, 2003, 77–79.

Nardocchio, Elaine F. *Theatre and Politics in Modern Quebec*. Edmonton: U of Alberta Press, 1986.

New, W.H. ed. *Native Writers and Canadian Writing*. Vancouver: UBC Press, 1990.

Plant, Richard and Anton Wagner. "Introduction: Reclaiming the Past" in Anton Wagner and Richard Plant, ed. *Canada's Lost Plays, Volume One: The Nineteenth Century*. Toronto: CTR Publications, 1978, 4–15.

Perkyns, Richard ed., *Major Plays of the Canadian Theatre 1934–1984*. Toronto: Irwin, 1984.

Ryan, Toby Gordon. *Stage Left: Canadian Theatre in the Thirties*. Toronto: CTR Publications, 1981.

Saddlemyer, Anne ed. *Early Stages: Theatre in Ontario 1800–1914*. Toronto: Ontario Historical Studies Series, 1990.

Saddlemyer, Anne and Richard Plant, ed. *Later Stages: Essays in Ontario Theatre from the First World War to the 1970s*. Toronto: U of T Press, 1997.

Smith, A.J.M. "A Rejected Preface" in Michael Gnarowski, ed. *New Provinces: Poems Of Several Authors*. Toronto: U of T Press, 1976, xxvii–xxxii.

Smith, Mary Elizabeth and Suzanne Alexander, eds. "Occasional Pieces, Theatre Documents, Plays and Sketches From New Brunswick Newspapers 1789–1900" *Scripts and Documents in Electronic Form at the ACTS (Atlantic Canada Theatre Scripts)*. The Electronic Text Centre of the University of New Brunswick Libraries, http://www.lib.unb.ca/Texts/Theatre/Texts

Usmiani, Renate. *Studies in Canadian Literature: Michel Tremblay*. Vancouver: Douglas and McIntyre, 1982.

Van Cortland, Ida. "Address to the University Women's Club of Ottawa," *The Taverner Collection*, Performing Arts Centre, Toronto Reference Library, (c. 1918).

Wagner, Anton. ed. *A Vision of Canada: Herman Voaden's Dramatic Works 1928–1945*. Toronto: Simon and Pierre, 1993.

———— *Canada's Lost Plays, Vol. 4, Colonial Quebec: French-Canadian Drama, 1606–1966*. Toronto: CTR Publications, 1982.

———— "Introduction" in Anton Wagner, ed. *The Brock Bibliography of Published Canadian Plays in English 1766–1978*. Toronto: Playwrights Canada Press, 1980, i–xi.

Wasserman, Jerry. *Modern Canadian Plays, Vol. 1.*Vancouver: Talonbooks, 1989.

Wigston, Nancy. "Nanabush In The City." *Books in Canada* (March, 1989), 7–9.

SCENE BIBLIOGRAPHY

Bouchard, Michel Marc. *The Coronation Voyage* Burnaby: Talonbooks, 1999.

bunyan, h. jay. *Prodigals in a Promised Land* in Djanet Sears, ed., *Testifyin':* *Contemporary African Canadian Drama, Vol. 1.* Toronto: Playwrights Canada Press, 2000, 145–214.

Cameron, George Frederic and Oscar F. Telgmann, *Leo, The Royal Cadet.* Kingston: Henderson and Co., 1889.

Curzon, Sarah Anne. *The Sweet Girl Graduate* in *Grip-Sack*, 1 (1882), 122–37.

Davies, Robertson. *At My Heart's Core* in Richard Perkyns, ed. *Major Plays of the Canadian Theatre 1934–1984.* Toronto: Irwin, 1984, 70–124.

—— *A Voice From The Attic.* New York: Viking Press, 1960.

Denison, Merrill. *Brothers in Arms* in *The Unheroic North: Four Canadian plays.* Toronto: McClelland and Stewart, 1923.

Dubé, Marcel. *Zone.* Toronto: Playwrights Canada Press, 1982.

Dumas, Alexandre, 1824–1895. *Camille, A Play In Five Acts.* New York: French, 1889.

French, David. *Leaving Home.* Toronto: Anansi, 1972.

Fuller, William Henry *H.M.S. Parliament, or The Lady Who Loved A Government Clerk* in Anton Wagner and Richard Plant, ed. *Canada's Lost Plays, Volume One: The Nineteenth Century,* Toronto: CTR Publications, 1978, 158–93.

Gélinas, Gratien. *Tit-Coq,* Toronto: Clarke, Irwin, 1967.

Grip. The Baron Bold and The Beauteous Maid. 23; 1 (July 5, 1884).

—— *Society Idyls* 17; 11 (July 30, 1881).

Highway, Tomson. *Aria, A One-Woman Play in One Act.* Mojica, M. and Ric Knowles. *Staging Coyote's Dream.* Toronto: Playwrights Canada Press, 2003, 80–96.

Hoffman, James. "Towards an Early British Columbia Theatre: The Hamatsa Ceremony as Drama." *Canadian Drama / L'Art dramatique Canadien.* 11.1 (1985), 231–44.

Joudry, Patricia. *Teach Me How To Cry: a drama in three acts.* New York: Dramatists Play Service, (c. 1955).

Lescarbot, Marc. *Le Théâtre de Neptune* in *Queen's Quarterly,* 34; 2 (October, 1926), 217–23.

Mojica, M. and Ric Knowles. "Introduction to *Aria*." *Staging Coyote's Dream*. Toronto: Playwrights Canada Press, 2003, 77–79.

O'Neill, Patrick. "Prologues and Epilogues as Performed on English Canadian Stages" in *Scripts and Documents in Electronic Form at the ACTS (Atlantic Canada Theatre Scripts)*. The Electronic Text Centre of the University of New Brunswick Libraries, http://www.lib.unb.ca/Texts/Theatre/

Pollock, Sharon. *Blood Relations and Other Plays*. Edmonton: NeWest Plays, 1981, 11–70.

Ryan, Oscar, et al. *Eight Men Speak* in Richard Wright and Robin Endres, ed. *Eight Men Speak and Other Plays from the Canadian Workers' Theatre*. Toronto: New Hogtown Press, 1976, 20–89.

Ryga, George. *The Ecstasy of Rita Joe and other plays*. Toronto: General, 1971, 33–132.

Sheridan, Richard Brinsley. *The School for Scandal and Other Plays*, Michael Cordner, ed. Oxford: Oxford University Press, 1998, 262–93.

Telgmann, Oscar F. *Leo, The Royal Cadet, Vocal Score*. Kingston: Henderson and Co., 1899.

Theatre Passe Muraille and Paul Thompson. *The Farm Show*. Toronto: Coach House Press, 1976.

Tremblay, Michel. *Les Belles-soeurs*. Vancouver: Talonbooks, 1991.

Voaden, Herman. *Hill-Land* in Richard Perkyns, ed. *Major Plays of the Canadian Theatre 1934–1984*. Toronto: Irwin, 1984, 25–63.

ILLUSTRATION CREDITS

(in order of appearance)

Taverner Collection, Performing Arts Centre, Toronto Public Library: Ida Van Cortland (*Cover Photo*).

Dene Barnett, *The Art of Gesture: The Practices and Principles of 18th century Acting* (Heidelberg: C. Winter, 1987), 95–98: Gesture illustrations (*Ch.1*).

Taverner Collection, Performing Arts Centre, Toronto Public Library: from Taverner Company advertising card, actress unknown.

H-Net, Humanities and Social Sciences On-Line, http://www2.net-msu.edu/~canada/reviews/igartua.html Photo of Sarah Anne Curzon (*Ch. 2*).

New Brunswick Museum Archives and Research Library, http://www.lib.unb.ca/Texts/TRIC Poster for *Camille*, St. John Dramatic Lyceum, 1867 (*Ch.2*).

Taverner Collection, Performing Arts Centre, Toronto Public Library, The Van C. Company card, front and back (*Ch.2*).

The Herman Arthur Voaden Fonds, Archival Collection, York University, Toronto, http://info.library.yorku.ca/depts/asc/Finding_aids/Voaden_webpage/hvindex.htm Stylized altar from *Hill-Land*, 1934 (*Ch. 3*).

Paul Henri / National Archives of Canada: http://www.nlc-bnc.ca/index-e.html *Tit-Coq*, 1948 (*Ch. 4*).

http://www.canadiantheatre.com/b/bellessoeurs.html *Les Belles-soeurs*, original cast, 1968 (*Ch.4*).

Theatre Passe Muraille and Paul Thompson, *The Farm Show* (Toronto: Coach House Press, 1976), 37: Winter Scene (*Ch.5*).

James Hoffman, "Towards an Early British Columbia Theatre: The Hamatsa Ceremony as Drama" in *Canadian Drama/L'Art dramatique canadien*, (Vol. 11, No.1, 1985), 240: The Hamatsa Circles Diagram (*Ch.6*).

APPENDIX A

From Oscar F. Telgmann, *Leo, The Royal Cadet, Vocal Score*
(Kingston: Henderson and Co., 1899).

Leo, The Royal Cadet – The Music

Crook The Elbow (cont.)

Chorus.

Crook the el_bow lift the cho-rus! What care we for crown or pall? All is ours that lies be-fore us

Lib - er - ty   for   one and all!

The Life Of A Rover Is Mine

1. I've
2. To-

written some Psalms and some songs . . . , I've dab-bled in most of the arts . . . ; Qui-
day, as you see, I am here . . . , En-joy-ing my pipe and my bowl . . . : To-

xu - te like right-ed some wrongs . . . In fact, I have played ma-ny parts . . . I've
mor-row, and I may ap-pear. . . . In-scrib-ing my name on the Pole . . . The

seen both the bright and the dark . . . Of the world and the things that are its . . . Like the
next day may see me once more. . . Con-tent as a hog up-on ice . . . Far

The Life Of A Rover Is Mine (cont.)

dove that flew forth from the ark, _____ In a word I am giv_en to flits, _____ For the
down on the Flor_i_da shore, _____ Ex - ist_ing on bac_on and rice, _____

life of a rov_er is mine,   A rov_er by land and by sea,   With a

la_dy to love and a flag_on of wine, Oh, the world is the vil_lage for me. _____

Glory and Victory

Glory and Victory (cont.)

Glory and Victory (cont.)

swal-low fol-lows the   spring: . . .   Glo — ry   and   Vic — to — ry!

This is the sol_dier's aim   With   sword and   shield   In   o - pen   field   To

win   a   wreath   of   Fame! . . .   The

Glory and Victory (Chorus)

He Sleeps The Sleep

He sleeps the sleep that knows no wak-ing 'Up on some far and dis-tant shore. Not know-ing that my heart is break-ing Un-heed-ing of the love I bore.

He Sleeps The Sleep (cont.)

True Love Can Never Alter

True Love Can Never Alter (cont.)

Brian Kennedy has an MA in Canadian Studies and has previously authored *Two For the Show*, an anthology for theatre students. Currently, he teaches Drama and English, a career which he has enjoyed for close to thirty years. His students led him to learn more about the history of Canadian theatre. They surprised him (as they usually do) by immediately identifying with the remarkable, yet unknown, lives of the writers within these covers, and eagerly absorbing their words. When he's not teaching, Brian tries to improve his hockey skills. This task may take another lifetime.